THE GOLDEN PEARL

THE GOLDEN PEARL

CASSANDRA BECK

ARCHWAY PUBLISHING

Archway Publishing books may be ordered through booksellers or by contacting:

Archway Publishing
1663 Liberty Drive
Bloomington, IN 47403
www.archwaypublishing.com
1 (888) 242-5904

ISBN: 978-1-4808-4248-9 (sc)
ISBN: 978-1-4808-4249-6 (hc)
ISBN: 978-1-4808-4250-2 (e)

Library of Congress Control Number: 2017901458

Print information available on the last page.

Archway Publishing rev. date: 2/21/2017

For all those incredible people who believed in me, I love you!

"No!"

My eyes burn hot with tears, and my sweat-soaked dress clings to my chest. My muscles ache, and all I want to do is to rip the arms—those of the man holding me back—out of their sockets.

"Please, Dad, no!" I sob.

He stands between my boyfriend and me.

The anger growing within him increases from a slow rolling simmer to a full raging boil. His eyebrows are tightly knitted, his face is red and stern, and his stance is as rigid as the tower on the east end of the palace.

"I've given you more freedom than most princesses will ever have! Why is it you've tried to dishonor our family!" he yells, spit flying from his mouth.

"We haven't done anything," I plead, pulling against the arms restraining me.

"Now, that's where you're entirely wrong," my father says. He glares dangerously at the boy kneeling across from me. "I've warned this young man to keep his distance, and he deliberately disobeyed me. What do you have to say for yourself!"

The boy's dark hair falls slightly over his piercing blue eyes as he looks up at my father. "Your Majesty, I'm in love with your daughter. Is that such a crime?"

"Is that such a crime?" my father mocks. "It is when you've killed hundreds because of a tantrum based on not getting your way."

The boy looks down, ashamed.

"It was an accident!" I sob. The portal wall spins rhythmically, kind of like a heartbeat, but not in any way beating as fast as my own.

"It doesn't matter," my father snaps. "I should have trusted my first instinct. I should not have allowed a mixed blood to obtain a munera. It's too much power for someone who doesn't know what to do with it." He looks down at my boyfriend in disgust.

We were planning to run away together, but somehow it didn't work out.

"And you, my dear." He turns toward me with hurt and rage in his eyes. "I have been too easy on you. You will both be punished, but because you are my daughter, I will allow you another chance. As for you, my boy, you will spend the rest of your life with only a memory of this love. You will never see my daughter's face again."

"No! No! Please, no!" I sob.

"Dear, you won't remember a thing. You will have a fresh start," my dad insists almost sympathetically.

I yank harder and harder. All I want is to be in the arms of the man I love. The idea of not knowing him shatters my heart, and I just want to scream and end this all.

My best friend, a look of disgust on his face, steps in next to my father.

"You know what needs to be done," says my father.

He nods, and I feel the betrayal sink in. He's a distorter, and though he promised he'd never use his gift on me, like Judas, he stands before me.

I watch as several more soldiers come in behind my love, trying to restrain him. I scream his name over and over again, my throat turning raw. Sweat and tears fall down my face. My head and chest hurt so badly it's as if someone pushed me off a cliff and I landed on the rocks below.

I feel the memories leave my head, and my mouth falls silent. Why was I screaming? My body aches, and I watch blankly ahead as my friend moves away from me. What just happened? The boy kneeling in front of me is still screaming, echoing my last fading scream. He is very handsome... Why is he screaming the name Lilyryn? Is that my name? All of a sudden, it looks as though he doesn't recognize me. He is hoisted up by two of the men who steer him around me toward the oddly moving wall... Why is it moving? I watch as he looks back at me once more. He has beautiful eyes. I gasp as they push him through.

"Come along, dear," says my father.

CHAPTER 1

THE PRESENT...

I CAN'T DO THIS! SOME NIGHTS I THINK THAT I CAN ACTUALLY fall asleep, but tonight I can't. I toss and turn in my sheets; I am restless. Tomorrow's my seventeenth birthday, and I am too anxious to sleep. I wipe my forehead. A cold sweat drenches my brow and the back of my neck even though heat pours into my room. I want to cry. There is a throbbing in my heart, and I know something *is* missing. I've seen several healers about this, but all of them had different responses, so I'm starting to believe I'm either depressed or going crazy. I feel that there was something or *some-one* in my life who has just vanished, but I can't recall the details. It's been like this for as long as I can remember: the phantom voice; the short, sudden glimpses of a man's face that disappear pretty much as soon as they come; and the absolute longing in my heart. None of it ever seems to go away. I've never told people about any of this because I know that they'll tell me it's ridiculous.

I live on Margaritan, meaning "pearl" in Latin. It is a small planet in a system of ten planets. Tomorrow I no longer will be considered a child. When we hit the age of seventeen, we are respected as young adults. Each is blessed with his or her munera on the last day of his or her birth month. There is such a large variety of munera that none of us really know what to expect. Some are given powers like speed, strength, or the ability to control the elements. When both my sisters turned seventeen, they were given enviable gifts. Coral, my eldest sister, was given the ability to move things with her mind; Flora was given the power to heal.

I take several deep breaths and, awaiting sleep, chug a glass of water.

"Arianna… wake up… you're going to be late if you don't get up now," says my nurse, Maybell, shaking my shoulders. Unfortunately, we barely get to see our parents—only at mealtimes or on special occasions.

"Good morning," I say midyawn, stretching out my stiff limbs.

"You must hurry. We only have one hour to get you ready and to arrive in the ballroom," Maybell says, her short arms frantically helping me out of bed and gently pushing me into the bathroom to bathe. Thankfully, she never says anything about my blotchy red cheeks in the mornings.

After I'm clean, I put on a silk robe. Maybell immediately starts to dry my hair with a towel but then switches to the dryer, which goes a lot faster. When my hair is dry, she pins some up and allows some strands to fall down my back in golden ringlets. I watch her as she dabs her stubby fingers in golden glitter and deposits some on my face and sprinkles some in my hair. She is shorter than I am, and plump, and she has the slight start of wrinkles in the corners of her eyes.

When both my hair and makeup are done, she hands me a white silk dress that I slip into. It reaches down to the floor, even with the matching white heels. The bodice is slightly ruffled, and there are glistening jewels at the top. Over the silk is a thin layer of delicate fabric. It is see-through, but there are different swirling patterns in the white on the fabric. The dress is tighter around the waist, but it flows at my hips down to the floor. I have been looking at this dress for weeks, and now I can finally wear it!

Although I haven't done anything, I'm exhausted. I look into the full-length mirror. I am amazed to see how professional, mature, and different I look. Despite my size, narrow shoulders, and thin face, I look older somehow, perhaps from wearing these high shoes. My heart throbs against my chest. I am really excited. Every kid dreams of the day of his or her ceremony. Who each one becomes is determined by the munera ceremony. It is finally my turn.

"Wow! This is amazing! Thank you!" I cry out eagerly and twirl as the dress flows around my legs. I give Maybell a huge hug. I try to push the throbbing in my heart aside, but it lingers greatly and without mercy.

She lets me go, reaches up, and places a shiny golden crown encrusted with pearls on the top of my head, revealing that she is finished.

"There. Now it's perfect," she says, stepping back to admire her work. Her eyes are sad but excited.

I love my caretaker; she is just like a mother to me. She treats me like I am actually her daughter and not just a job. Though she hasn't ever told me, I know she is many years older than my mother. She loves me for who I am and not for my rank, status, or family name. Many people are just nice to me because they are afraid to get in trouble for "picking on the princess." Few people actually spend time to get to know me; my nurse is one of the few.

A soldier knocks on the door, walks into the room, and says, "It's time." He is wearing a golden uniform with a black belt and white pants, the uniform that every soldier wears for special occasions. He is one of the younger soldiers in training, maybe a few years older than I. When he sees me, his jaw drops, and his cheeks flush a shade of pink. "You look absolutely beautiful, Miss," he says, giving me a kind smile.

"Thank you," I reply, feeling my own face get warm. I just hope my face isn't as red as it feels. I feel bad that I don't remember the soldier's name. I think he is one of the transfers who recently came for a position to work in the palace. There are several new transfers whom I haven't yet met.

QUICKLY WE ARE ESCORTED TO THE BALLROOM. WE TURN DOWN several hallways that almost all look the same. There are so many hallways in the palace, but each is as beautiful as the last, with marble tiles, golden walls, and exquisite paintings. One of the reasons you don't get lost in the palace is because at the beginning and at the end of every hall there are pictures hanging off the walls. You just need to remember which one is where. The roof is a high arch, and there are paintings covering the ceilings, and there are golden beams that run down to the floor. Several chairs line the hallway leading to the ballroom; they have red fabric and fancy patterns engraved in the metal feet. Every time I walk by them, I think they look exquisite.

When we finally get into the throne room, I am steered to the back of the room for a grand entrance. The high-rise ceilings continue into the throne room, with more paintings. In the very front of the room where the thrones are is high crystal-looking stained glass. Rows upon rows of benches are decorated for the event, and so many people are dressed elegantly with their hair done up fancy. A good portion of these people I do not even recognize.

A few other girls, also in white gowns, and boys, in white

suits, stand at the back. They are all groomed nicely. Some of them are from school; two of the boys that I recognize are identical twins, Adrian and Chet.

"Hey," they whisper at the same time. They are both brown haired, with thin faces and goofy grins. They are the only ones born in the same month as me from our kingdom. Not many people choose to have children in this month, because it is the month of harvest time. People usually want to have children when it is not the hottest month of the year.

"Hey," I whisper back. "You excited?"

"Yeah," they say at the same time again.

"It's going to be awesome," says Chet.

"Hey, hey, hey, shhhh," says one of the men in charge of the ceremony. "Line up," he says, pushing me closer to the front of the line. Both Adrian and Chet roll their eyes at the same time and punch each other jokingly.

They wait for me to get into position. These people all share the same birthday month as me, even though mine is the last day of the month, so we all celebrate in a birthday banquet. Everyone in the province gathers to celebrate. At age seventeen we are considered adults, so we celebrate together. We are each given a flower, one that represents our homes. The twins and I receive a lotus flower; it is a lovely pale pink and is delicately light to hold in my hands.

CHAPTER 2

It's hard walking in high heels, but it's mandatory for a person receiving the munera to dress elegantly. I try very hard not to trip, but it is actually hard not to, considering the heels of my shoes are maybe five inches high. After smiling and the occasional nod while walking down the aisle, we finally reach the end. At the end is an empty vase with water in it. I drop my flower into it, and the others do the same. The flowers together in the vase are a symbol of unity throughout the province.

My father sits on the middle throne wearing a golden crown and a red cloak. On his left sits my mother, wearing a golden tiara and an elegant green gown. Coral and Flora both have thrones to his right. Coral also wears a gold tiara just like mine, only it has diamonds instead of pearls; she is dressed in a pale blue strapless gown. Flora also has a gold tiara, but unlike Coral's or mine, hers has sapphires imbedded in the metal. Her gown matches the radiant sapphires in her tiara. Both of my sisters have their hair done up exquisitely, shaped neatly in some kind of bun with ringlets falling down their backs. Their hair gives them a delicate, gentle look, the curls shaping their faces beautifully.

I stop in front of them and give a small curtsy. Everyone lines up on either side of me and does the same, except the boys; they bow. My father gets off his throne and strides in front of me. He grabs my hand and turns me around to face the crowd.

"Today we are celebrating the seventeenth birthday of Princess Arianna Garcia." The crowd cheers blissfully. The rest of the group walks closer to the edge to wait for their turns.

We turn and walk, his hands on my back guiding me toward a grand stand called *piscinæ fati, the pool of destiny*. It looks like a huge bird bath, only it is too elegant to be a bath for birds. A thin but strong force field protects the magic waters inside. I can see the milky layer protecting the waters. It moves around rhythmically with a look of almost ice on it, a sparkle, a glimmer that is beautiful and stronger than it looks. Only a person whose seventeenth birthday is that month can reach into the waters. If it isn't your birthday month and you try to put your hand in, you will get extremely sick, and a black mark will imbed itself into your wrist. Anyone who has a black mark on their wrist would get thrown into prison and would never see the light of day again. They would disappear. The black mark is impossible to hide, and it is a symbol of dishonor. Even with a metal cuff around your wrist, the mark would be visible through the metal.

The king says some blessings in Latin and tells me to reach my hand into the center of the pool. I am kind of afraid of the force field. It looks like it could be dangerous. I overcome that fear quickly, and my chest clears. The fear is replaced with excitement instead. I am really doing this; my munera is coming to me. I take a deep breath and slip my hand through.

My hand tingles as it goes through the force field. It stops when my hand is entirely in. Inside the force field there is a crisp breeze. I feel energy build up in the palm of my hand. I can't see past my wrist anymore. I can just feel energy. With this energy surging through and around my hand, I feel exhilarated, in an indescribable way. I feel like the planet is mine just by the energy I possess. I feel it seeping through my veins and covering every inch of my body. It's a feeling I have never felt before.

I slip my hand from the pool, but the aura of the energy remains, both in my hand and surging through my veins. I open my eyes to see all of the power I am enduring is in the form of a golden pearl. Never has anyone actually received an item from these waters. It is absolutely beautiful. *How did I get one? What is so special about me?*

Usually when people pull their hands from the waters they get a glow in their skin for a moment and then go back to normal again. The name of the gift they have received is written in milky lettering in the force fields surface. The name of their gift is revealed, one after another. The only way you can tell someone possesses a gift is he or she will have a small silver star tattooed on the side of his or her neck below his or her left ear.

I stand still and wait. I stare at the pearl in my hands. What do I do?

Tension dances around the room. Everyone waits for something to happen, but nothing does until a man near the back whistles an extraordinary tune. A short moment later the pearl is engulfed in a radiant beam of light. The beam plunges into my skin and disperses till it covers my entire body. I am lifted off the ground by the light, floating higher and higher until I am high above the ground. I am unusually calm. I just hold my breath.

What used to be my beautiful white dress is now a shimmering golden strapless gown with golden slippers instead of those wretched heels. I feel like a brilliant golden star shining brightly and eminently in the air. I am so bright. Many people try to cover their eyes, and others just stand there trying to capture the history in the making. The group of the other seventeen-year-olds all look away, even the twins.

Finally the brightness dims, and I am planted back on the floor. I feel numb all over. Everyone waits in silence for the word to appear in the force field. I look all over the room, into some people's eyes; they seem scared.

Sorceria finally appears in golden lettering rather than in the usual murky white.

Shrieks come out from every direction. Clearly "sorceress" is not the most wanted gift in the kingdom. The last time a sorcerer was called, he ended up getting eradicated to another planet because he killed a bunch of people. I don't think it was on purpose. I think he just didn't know how to harness his powers properly. He wasn't even given a second chance; there were no previous sorcerers to explain his powers to him. I hope that doesn't happen to me.

For every munera there is a ceremonial cloak. For example, the girl from last time was given the capability to command water. She was given a sparkly blue cloak. Or the boy—fire. He was given a cloak with patterns of flames red, orange, yellow, and some black. It was beautiful. Every time he moved it glinted and appeared as if it were a real flickering fire. I'm curious as to what kind I will get. No one has *ever* been given a pearl before. I wonder if they even have a cloak for me. It just feels so strange to be this different. I feel like I have always been different, but now I feel like I really don't belong here; my differences are just getting bolder every day.

Although my curiosity will soon come to an end, I stand rolling the pearl back and forth between the palms of my hands, feeling the softness of its surface. A young boy dressed in white walks slowly toward me and my father, holding a bag that consists of my cloak. He hands the bag to my father, bows, and heads back in the direction in which he came, swiftly but calmly.

My father begins to open the bag, and inside is a white cloak. The trim and the hem are both golden. On the back are three symbols, also in gold. They are the symbols of the planet. The first consists of four diamond shapes connected together with a triangle in the center. The second is a triangle with two loops connected with a small dot in between. The last is the most recognizable—a perfect sphere, a *golden pearl*.

He slides the cloak over my shoulders. "I never thought I would ever have to hand this cloak to anyone during my time," he murmurs silently, looking disheartened, "especially to my own daughter." He looks away but grabs onto my hand.

"Our *Sorceria*," announces my father, gripping my hand tightly and raising it high so everyone can see.

People clap grievously, with looks of worry on their faces.

The rest of the group takes their turn. I barely notice the time going by as I sit on the bench in the front and stare down at the pearl in my hands. I feel people's eyes on me, drilling into me. I wish I didn't have to go first. I almost wish I didn't have to be the one who stands out among everyone else. Couldn't I be normal like everyone else?

Everyone else gets the usual murky lettering and the regular beam of light—everyone except me.

After the last name is called and the second twin receives his gift, Tracker, we all stand up together. Both twins got the same gift. What are the chances of that? Then again, what's the chance of getting what I got? Everyone is congratulated, except me. I understand why; the past frightens people.

The rest of the evening drudges on by. We have a feast and cake, which both are delicious. But everyone seems to be relatively avoiding me; it's actually quite awkward, *being at your own banquet and being neglected*. Everyone dances around the room. I even see the twins dancing with several of the girls who were at the ceremony as well. I weave through the people and head toward the door.

I get so bored I have to leave the ballroom to wander around the halls. Although I've been in every room and found every nook and hiding place, I don't know exactly what I want to do.

I hear the music fading as I wander further down the hall. I pass my dad's study but then stop two steps away. I glance behind me and see that the light is on. My father often spends most of his time in his study but usually not when there is a celebration going on. The door is slightly open, so I back up and peer inside, my heart pounding against the inside of my chest. My father stands, talking to another man in the corner of the room, and my mother sits in a rocking chair sobbing into an already *soaked* handkerchief.

"I don't care if she's a princess, she's a Sorceria," yells the man in a harsh voice. "Remember what happened last time we had a sorcerer."

"I remember!" bellows my father. "But I can't just send my daughter away."

My heart drops, and I release the breath I never knew I was holding in. The man grabs my father by the shoulders, looks him in the eyes, and asks, "Would you rather lose one person or thousands? Sorcerers don't know how to control their emotions. We all know what can happen if they get infuriated. Remember when Lilyryn fell in love with one? Do what's better for the people, Trenton. You can't just let one live here and not expect problems."

Who's Lilyryn?

Then there is silence. I wait impatiently for his response, standing on the tips of my toes, searching his face for any kind of sign that he might share the answer I hope for.

"Well, I guess we know what we need to do," my father says, sighing. "We have to send her away... for... the good of the people."

Suddenly feeling lightheaded, I gasp and start to turn to run and get away as fast as I can, but I trip over the skirts of my gown and fall with a loud thump. My mother, whose eyes spill over with fresh tears, looks up, along with my father and the other man. My father walks over to the door and pushes it open. When he sees me sitting on the floor huddled in a ball with tears flooding in my eyes, he looks away—ashamed. The other man stands behind him with his arms crossed over his chest. He wears a straight face with next to no emotion. He just stares at me.

CHAPTER 3

I DON'T REMEMBER HOW I GOT UPSTAIRS AND INTO BED, BUT somehow I did. When I open my eyes, it is rather early; light streams in through the window. I dress in a black blouse and white khaki pants. I fasten my long blond hair in an even braid down my back. I want to go barefoot, but I guess my feet might hurt less if I wear shoes. Sitting on my dresser are the luxurious golden flats that used to be my white high heels from last night. I snatch them off the dresser and slide my feet into them. I've never worn more comfortable shoes in my life. After all the pinchy heels I've worn, once you put these on, it is instant relief. I usually tend to lose my shoes, but I don't think I'll lose these ones.

I glance around my room; it doesn't feel as cozy as it once did. Now it feels distant, as though it's not even mine, a room—a haunting room of old memories, which creeps me, now, into a fit of sadness, waiting for the right moment to tear me open and spill. The photos on the walls have my sisters and me, my friend and Maybell, even a family photo; all the eyes of those happy people in the photos now watch me with their haunting eyes as well.

Not really being in the mood to talk to anyone, I look away

from the eerie walls and crawl out of my window to avoid all the people I would meet if I went out the front door. Then I remember the pearl. I slide back into my room and snatch it off my nightstand. When I get back on the ledge outside of my window, a wave of warm air blows in my face. I inch closer to the edge and prepare for a hard landing as my window is about six feet high.

Thump!

It's definitely not a graceful landing, but at least I was somewhat expecting that, so it isn't too much of a shock.

I stand up and stretch my newly afflicted limbs; I think I have a bruised tailbone now.

The sun peeks into view. I glance at the beautiful courtyard; it is extremely difficult to imagine living anywhere but here. The courtyard is covered with freshly trimmed grass, and trees border it. There is a walking path with stones. Several are cracked, but they are still pretty. When was I young, I used to always run up and down them with Maybell.

Margaritan is my home, and now it is being taken away from me. Just at the thought of leaving my heart throbs in agony. I know it's coming; I'm going to be forced to leave. I wonder how the other sorcerer must have felt. Was he as hurt as I am now?

I wrap my hands around the pearl and close my eyes, trying to capture the beauty with my mind so I never forget it. The pearl glistens even in the minimal sunlight.

Besides the courtyard, one of the other places I will miss most is Ribbon Beach. It's kind of a strange name. The reason it's called Ribbon Beach is because there are several colors of sand. There's purple, white, and green. The colors stretch alongside the ocean like a ribbon. The purple has always been my favorite. I would rather go say good-bye there now before people arrive for swimming and surfing, so they won't see me breakdown.

After a few minutes of running down the stone walkway, I

reach the beach. I take off my shoes and dangle them on the tips of my fingers. I've always loved to scrunch my toes in the sand of this spacious beach. Savoring every moment of the salty ocean air, I breathe all of it in.

"Hey Arianna," calls a familiar voice.

He jogs to meet me; his light wavy brown hair bounces in his face, covering his blue eyes. Jeremy has been my best friend since, well, *forever,* I guess. We met on the first day at King Trenton's First School when we were assigned to sit beside each other. After that we pretty well hit it off, and we were instantly friends, completely inseparable.

When he catches up to me, I notice my cheeks are damp from crying. I wipe my eyes on the sleeve of my blouse and tuck the pearl in my pocket. I manage a weak smile. He wraps his muscular arms around me, knowing the smile I gave was really forced and not legitimate. It feels good being comforted, especially by one of my best friends I know I may never see again.

"How are you?" he asks.

"I'm great," I lie as I choke back tears. I never, ever want to cry in front of him. But he gives me a look that says, "I don't believe you." Finally I can't hold the tears pooling in the back of my eyes any longer.

He pulls me into his arms again with no effort. The tip of my head is barely level with his shoulders. All I want to do is stay here, in his arms forever, where I know I'm safe and he can protect me.

We stand like this for a few minutes. When we let go, I feel awful that I soaked his T-shirt, but I think—hope—he understands. He grabs my hand, and we walk in silence further down the beach as the waves lap the colorful shore. Even though neither of us is talking, it's comforting to know he's here for me. He has never really spoken to me about his munera. He got it several months ago, and he hasn't even told me the work position he does now. He is very quiet about it. I wasn't able to attend his ceremony. I can't really remember why, but I'm pretty sure I had another commitment that day, because I'm sure I would have gone to it if I didn't have anything else.

I hardly notice that we've reached the end of the beach; it is a very long stretch of beach. Then I see the village up ahead. It is probably around noon. My stomach grumbles loudly. I haven't eaten since the banquet yesterday, and I barely ate anything then because I felt like puking as I was so nervous.

Jeremy smiles and asks, "Are you hungry?"

I'm just about to say no because I don't want him spending any money on me, when my stomach grumbles again for a reply. We both laugh. It's the first time in a while; everything has just been so tense lately. I haven't had anything to laugh about since I've been preparing for the ceremony.

"Do you still like Sandy's Subs?" he asks, leading me toward the white steps leading to the village.

"Of course!" I say kind of shocked. 'Sandy's Subs' is my favorite place to eat! They have the best food there. Jeremy and I have always gone there; he knows it's my favorite place. "Do you?" I ask with a smile.

"Absolutely, Sandy's is the one and only in the universe," he says and makes a goofy grin.

In the center of the village stands a huge water fountain made of marble, with gold-engraved patterns on the sides. The water spills out over a tower of pearls, and at the top is a perfect golden pearl. It's absolutely magnificent. There are buildings everywhere, and the ground is similar to the stone walkways by the courtyard, only these are slightly more cracked then the other one.

I pause and realize I'm just standing here staring at the water fountain I've seen hundreds of times. I must look ridiculous. Jeremy stands patiently by Sandy's Subs, holding the door open for me with a gentle smile. I hurry over to the door and step inside. Instantly the smell of food makes my stomach grumble again. Jeremy looks at me and chuckles. "I'll go order."

It smells heavenly, completely fresh.

It's a small building with a long counter and high stools. The walls are sea blue with white and gold patterns of flowers. Sandy is a young woman, maybe in her twenties; she has sandy blond hair, which is where I think she got her name from. She has beautiful gray eyes and a naturally friendly smile. When she turned seventeen, she was given the gift of extraordinary senses, like sight, hearing, taste, and smell. That's why she is such a good cook.

I pat the pearl in my pocket, to make sure it's still where I put it, walk over to the counter, and sit down on the stool next to Jeremy. He and Sandy are talking about business and how well her restaurant is doing.

"Congratulations, Your Highness. I heard you were given quite the extraordinary gift. Hope it'll be fun. Do you know where you're planning to work?" she says enthusiastically, obviously trying to cheer me up. I nod and force a pleasant smile.

"I'm not too sure yet. I might just request to be placed somewhere." I don't know what's going to happen. Clearly she doesn't know what's really going to happen either. They are probably going to send me away and tell everyone I died, just to hide the truth.

Usually after you receive your munera, you can request to be placed somewhere for your job, or you can choose where you want to work. Usually your job depends on your munera.

She hands us each a shake and a voluminous sub gaping with lettuce and cheese and just plain *yum*!

I take a great big bite, already satisfying my hollow stomach.

"This is delicious, thank you." I acknowledge Sandy with a smile, and she heads back into the kitchen with a satisfied glow.

After the meal, I am so full I probably couldn't take another bite... if I tried. I give the rest of my food to Jeremy, which he finishes easily. We bid our good-byes to Sandy and thank her again.

"Thank you," I say to Jeremy faintly as he holds the door open for me. When I step out into the village, I feel that something is wrong. It is quiet, and the hair on the back of my neck rises. There is basically no one in the streets; they are empty, and usually around this time the streets are crowded.

"I just held the door open for you," he replies questioningly, with a flirty smile.

"Oh yeah, that too. I meant for the dinner and for everything else you've done for me," I say.

"You're very welcome," he says contently. "But what else have I done for you?" he asks, hinting for a compliment.

"Just for being my friend when no one else wanted to be," I reply.

We stand by the water fountain for a few minutes when he starts to say, "It's because, I—" but he is interrupted by several soldiers running straight toward us holding swords.

"Get her!" orders the captain as he points a finger at me.

Four men dressed in white uniforms with dark belts and weapons tied to their belts run toward us.

Jeremy steps between me and the charging men. Just as one is a short distance away and raising his sword, some kind of energy flows to my hands, and I raise one to push Jeremy out of the way. I don't even touch him, and he gets tossed in the direction I was going to push him, only a lot further. Luckily he lands in a bale of hay and then falls to the ground, which is really quite ironic because he should have landed on the ground and not the hay, but at least it softened his landing, I hope. In the building beside Jeremy, several scared faces gaze through the window in horror of this scene.

The man who tried slicing Jeremy is now really close to me,

so I decide to try whatever it was that I did, *again*. I point my hand at him and tip it toward the left, opposite to where Jeremy landed. To my surprise it works again, and the man goes flying and crashes into the other two men running. They all land with a huge thud beside the water fountain—I wish they had landed in the fountain. I smirk, feeling a thrill in what I just did.

I take a few running steps toward Jeremy, hoping to find out if he is okay, but two immense hands snatch me up off the ground effortlessly. I struggle, kicking and hitting the man; it still doesn't make him loosen his tight, breathtaking grip. The captain steps around and into my view; he is tall, with dark hair, brown eyes, and a smug grin, which makes me angry. He holds a little white pouch up to my mouth and nose. I try pulling away, but the fumes somehow make their way into my system; my muscles fall weak, I stop squirming, and my vision goes fuzzy. The last thing I see is the captain grinning and Jeremy in the background talking to one of the soldiers. *Why is he talking to them? I thought he was hurt.* And then I'm out.

My head throbs. It feels like have I just been punched in the head with an iron glove. I try to make sense of things, but my mind keeps spinning and my vision blurs in and out. Silver is the only thing that I can make out. Even closing my eyes does not help; it just continues to ache painfully.

The only thing that could cause this much pain and cause me to lose consciousness would be Kopolo herbs. If these herbs are consumed or breathed in, they cause searing pain like this. It aches, but it doesn't hold me back from wondering if Jeremy was actually hurt. His eyes were closed when I glanced at him—before they knocked me unconscious. But then he was talking to them like nothing had happened. What's up with that? Did I really throw those men against the water fountain? Everything just happened so fast.

I attempt to stand but the pain advances, and I drop back to the floor and prop myself up against the wall. I close my eyes and try to coax myself to fall asleep, but the pain will not allow it, so I just sit and take my now-knotted braid—from the wind and action—out. I run my fingers through my hair, trying to comb out the knots, but some remain.

I look around the room; it is small and dimly lit. There are metallic walls and a door, but what catches my attention is one of the walls appears to be moving. But then again it could also just be my mind making it appear to be spinning.

I lay my hands on my lap, bumping the pearl in my pocket. I reach in and pull the precious pearl out. I roll it back and forth in my fatigued hands. What could possibly be so important about me to receive a gift such as this?

I hold the precious golden pearl level with my face. I see my reflection in it, my hair newly weaved, and my green eyes. My eyes have golden specks in them, which are rare—three golden spots near my retina. Unfortunately around my eyes, my cheeks are blotchy and swollen from crying. I take the hem of my blouse and try to absorb the water from my cheeks, but it just soaks my blouse and makes no difference. I give up and lay my head against the wall; it's not the most comfortable position. I just don't feel like moving more than I have to. My head is still throbbing.

I close my eyes but am soon interrupted from the sound of heavy footsteps coming toward the door. Quickly I slide the pearl back in my pocket, close my eyes, and tuck my legs close up to my chest, in a small ball pressed up against the wall.

Light floods the room as the door swings open. I open my eyes to see my father walking into the room carrying a small bag that is dark gold, with beautiful black designs and patterns all over it.

His face looks distraught, and he looks older somehow. On Margaritan most people grow at an average rate till age twenty and then their speed in growth slows dramatically, but more influential people look older. Also stress can make any person age faster. People on Margaritan can live up to 150 years old and look young. My father is already a very influential person because he is the king, so he looks about thirty-five, normally. Now with these new heavy bags under his eyes and his few gray hairs growing out of his brown hair, he was starting to look about forty-five.

"Arianna?" he asks as he settles down on the floor across from me.

I give him a questioning look as if to say, *"What's with the bag?"*

"This is your travel bag, for your... *trip*," he says, his voice lingering on the word *trip*, handing the bag to me. I grab it and start to open it, curious as to what's in it. "That's the one you liked, right?" he asks, his face curious. A few weeks ago Maybell, my nurse, and I went to the village to do some shopping, and I saw this one and absolutely loved it. I suspect Maybell told my father. I suppose it's a kind last gesture.

"Yes, thank you," I say and force a weak smile. He lets out a sigh of relief and starts twiddling his fingers.

I unfasten the small, button-like clasps and open the bag. Inside it contains only a few items. There is my gold hairbrush from my room and a small velvet pouch. I snatch it up and pull the two strings that restrain the contents from falling out, but there's nothing. I look at my father with confusion, about to ask, "What's the point of this?"

"Oh... that is a peram. It fills up with any type of currency you need," he explains.

On Margaritan, our money is gold and silver coins. However we don't usually use the word *coins;* we call them *nummos.* It means the same thing, just in Latin. A single nummos could purchase a lot of things. We learn a lot about other planets, the life on them, and their societies, in school. On every planet money means the same thing, only it has a different name.

I close the drawstrings and put the pouch back in the bag. I pull out another pouch. Inside it has a glimmering gold locket with a photo of my mom and dad on the left and my two sisters and myself on the right. I feel tears pooling up behind my eyes again.

I lean over and wrap my arms around him; he squeezes me in a hug. I forget how angry I was a second ago—about Jeremy—about being knocked out by the palace guards, whom I've known all my life. I see now that he loves me dearly and actually doesn't want me to go, just by giving me the locket.

When we let go, my father ties the locket around my neck, and I close up the handbag. There is more stuff inside, but I'd rather look at it later.

"So where am I going?"

"Earth," my father says. "It's the only place where people actually look like us and you'll fit in well."

Margaritan is one out of ten planets in the *Pretiosas Galaxia*. It means *Precious Galaxy* in Latin; it is called that because every one of those planets mines a precious jewel. Margaritan is pearls, because we are mainly ocean and jungle. Some of the other planets have diamonds, sapphires, rubies, emeralds, amethysts, and others that are extremely rare and are not even named. I would like to go to one of those planets someday, although some of the people there have a skin color that is tinted a lighter version of the planet's gem. On *Smaragdus,* the planet of the emeralds, their pale skin is tinted a light green. It's barely noticeable, but another way you can tell is they all have bright green eyes. On *Adamas,* the planet of diamonds, they have a very unique appearance. Since diamonds are clear, the people of that planet have almost translucent skin, and *they are extremely pale.* You can see through them, but you can't see their insides. If they are standing in front of you, you can see what's behind them. *Onychinus* mines an onyx gem. It is the only planet that doesn't exactly take on the appearance of their gem, only their eyes and hair. They have ghastly white skin, with hair as dark as the night sky, with matching eyes. I wonder if they even have pupils, and if they do, *what do they look like?*

Onychinus is a very depressing planet; they have mostly shades. There are very few colors there. The sky is usually either gray or black. Even the plants that grow there are not colored, although they are very exquisite; they generally have a silver sparkle to them. There is *no* sun, only moonlight. They are the tenth planet, the furthest away from the sun. Three moons revolve around *Onychinus,* so they get light from the moon every day for the entire day. Personally I would not want to live there. I like colors and it wouldn't be the same without them, but if you grew up without them, I guess you would get used to it.

It's very fascinating learning about all these races; in my classes I think I was the most intrigued, compared to everyone else. In history class we learn about a lot of the planets and we get to see pictures of what they look like and the inhabitants that live there. Only five planets in *Pretiosas Galaxia* abide life. Five of the planets were killed, *not* destroyed. All life has been taken from them.

"How long will I be there?" I ask, already knowing the answer. *Probably forever, you're a danger to society, so you can go be a danger to life elsewhere.*

"I'm not sure," he says with a sigh, looking over at the swirling wall.

My head has finally stopped spinning, and all that's left of pain is the occasional pulse. All but the one wall stands still. It is moving in a strange rhythmic pattern.

"Is that a portal?" I ask. I've heard about portals, but I've never actually seen one. A lot of people told me that there was one on every planet; it can take you anyplace within the universe's reach. I've been in every room in the palace, so I don't understand how I missed this room, if I am still even in the palace.

"Are we still in the palace or—"

"Yes. This room is hidden very well. We try to keep people out, so they don't get lost and end up in some strange forbidden place—which has happened before—so we have concealed the doorway. No one will ever discover that it is right under their nose," he explains with a chuckle, like he's laughing at a private joke.

When his face becomes firmer, my father looks as if he's going to burst into tears at any second. Instead he leans over and gives me a huge, breathtaking hug. You know when a little kid finds their most favorite toy in the world, and they just hug it like it's the most valuable thing, because they are afraid they will lose it again. Yeah, that's the kind of hug he gives me. I lean my head against his burly chest and wrap my arms around him tightly, knowing this might be the last hug I ever get from him. I cherish every moment of it.

"Why did you send soldiers to attack me?" I ask as we pull out of the long hug, remembering what happened in the square.

He could have at least told them to ask me nicely to go back to the palace, rather than the soldiers knocking me out with those toxic Kopolo herbs. It was embarrassing and humiliating in front of everyone. I lost some respect for my father having treated me this way.

"I did it because I love you," he says in a careful tone. It sounds somewhat believable, but that must be a harsh way of loving someone. I don't understand. If he loved me, he wouldn't have done that.

"If you loved me, why would you embarrass me in front of the entire village and *Jeremy?*" It sounds harsh saying it the way I do, but it was harsh what he did to me. You don't just send out soldiers to attack someone in front of everyone they've known all their life and say that you did it because you love them.

I expect him to start yelling and telling me not to backtalk, but he just nods and sighs "You're right." He grasps my hand tightly, and says "It was wrong of me. I'm *truly* sorry." A tear trickles its way down his cheek and drips onto his white dress shirt.

Then he gets to his feet, still holding my hand, and pulls me up. I pick up the handbag sitting on the floor by my feet and hang it from my shoulder. I give him one last look, nod my head, and turn toward the spinning portal. I take a few steps toward it, suddenly feeling dizzy again. Before I'm about to take the last step inside, my mother and Maybell come running into the room. My mom gives me a hug and plants a huge kiss on my cheek, and then she opens my purse and slides in a small white box.

"I love you," she says, a fresh stream of tears running down her cheeks.

My mother and I look a lot alike; we both have the same blonde hair and green eyes, only mine have gold specks in them. She also looks older, with silver streaks through her golden hair.

Maybell taps my mom on the shoulder, and my mom steps away. Maybell places a black and gold leather-bounded book in my purse and closes it up. "I love you and always will, no matter how far away you are," she says reassuringly, and hugs me tightly and kisses me on the cheek. I'm truly going to miss Maybell. She is as caring and loving as ever.

I step back and give them all one last look and say, "Goodbye." Then I turn toward the portal, shuddering. Afraid of what I might find, I step inside.

CHAPTER 4

I DON'T KNOW EXACTLY WHAT I WAS EXPECTING, BUT INSIDE THE portal it's warm and peaceful. Then I realize I am in a light ray. Ever heard that *there's nothing faster than the speed of light?* Well, now I can say I've traveled as fast as light, but I don't think anyone would ever believe it. Everything seems to be in slow motion. Maybe it is magic or something, but you wouldn't believe that traveling this fast you could see everything as clearly as what I'm seeing now.

The planets are so beautiful. My heart leaps. I can vaguely recognize them; they're more extravagant seeing them in person rather than in photos from the *Astronomy Book of Knowledge*. The *Smaragdus* is green, just like the emeralds they harvest. *Adamas* is way more spectacular because it's almost see-through, but you can still tell it is solid and not just a big ball of shining dust. It glimmers in the sunlight just like diamonds, shimmering off the colors of the rainbow. *Topazius* is the planet of topaz stones; it looks like the color of water with the reflection of a bright blue sky. *Smaragdus, Adamas,* and *Topazius* all appear to have some kind of luminous appearance, which make them look healthy and radiant.

The next few look *dead*. These are the planets whose life was taken from them. There was *Sapphirus, Citrino, Spinel, Amethystus,* and *Rhodolite*. That's a lot of planets whose life had just died. I feel my eyes fill up again. Being in the presence of five planets that *used* to be plentiful and abide an abundance of life and now are inanimate—it's horrifying.

Onychinus almost blends in with the darkness of the sky, though it too has a luminous glow that makes it stand out rather than appearing like a shadow of darkness. It looks cold, evil, and miserable yet beautiful at the same time. How can darkness look beautiful? As I pass it, I feel tension and despair in the air. A murky-looking gas floods around me. It is chilling and thick. Moments later I emerge through. I glance behind me to catch a final glimpse of *Pretiosas Galaxia*. Even with how far away I am, I still know which one is my home. Stars scatter across the endless sky, and rainbows of gas decorate it.

I pass two more galaxies in almost a blink of an eye. Up ahead is a milky bundle of lights. I recognize it from a book I read—this must be *the Milky Way*. The place definitely fits the name; it is murky and bright. I get the same feeling I did when I went through the last murky gas, chilled. On the other side of the gas, everything goes in slow motion again. The beauty of this galaxy fills my heart with excitement.

The sun blazes brightly with hues of orange and yellow. The flames dance. I'm probably about fifty meters away from the hot ball of fire. Normally if someone was this close to the sun, they would have been burnt to nothing. When I get closer, it gets a little warmer, but nothing, so far, serious. A musky brownish planet appears; it doesn't have life on it because there is no luminous glow. It is followed by another, only a little bigger and redder, again *no* life. For a second I am afraid Earth isn't in this galaxy, but just for *a* single second.

Then I see it. "Earth!" I cry out joyously in my head and sigh with relief. There is no possible way this isn't it. It floats in a big, bright blue, green, and white sphere and has every means to hold life. It also has a beautiful luminous glow to it. *Absolutely amazing,* is all I can think. I am about to turn to Jeremy and ask him if he was seeing what I am seeing, *the magnificence of this place,* but he isn't here. I am alone. *Alone.* Just the thought of that makes my heart want to burst. The moment of joy ends as it had come, instantly. *Alone,* why am I alone? Then I remember why! Now the Earth doesn't seem so bright or exciting anymore. Why does *every* sorcerer get banished because of one person's mistake? I'm sure it was an accident. They should have given him a second chance, and they should have given me a chance, at least one… but they didn't.

Every planet has a barrier; some are hard to get through, and others are simple. Hopefully this will be a simple one. I am a light ray—it should be simple. How else would this planet have life if light couldn't get through its barriers?

Below me I see everything—colors and some plants I've never seen before. There are hundreds of thousands of lights; it is all so amazing. I promise myself I will try and let myself like it here and give it a chance. Maybe things will be okay after all. Although it isn't *Margaritan,* it is still beautiful. It just isn't *Margaritan.*

Earth looks so different from the way it did in the photos we saw in school. Earth has what is called a *Hubble Telescope* floating around in space taking pictures of a few of the other galaxies and the development of stars and planets. We have what's called *MM eximius imaginum inventore.* In English it means "super image explorer 2000." I got to see some of the images taken a few times, and they were crystal clear, even from a million light years away. Earth's aren't as clear as ours, but they still get some good images. Knowledge wise, Earth has the least information about the universe they live in; they believe they are the only life out there.

They are *so* wrong! Every planet has a portal that can lead them anywhere within the universes reach, but they don't even know that. From our planet we use our portal to send out explorers to go into new galaxies. Here people think too much about ways they can go through their barrier with shuttles.

From the distance I can see a storm arise. I've seen storms forming before, but not at this level. Its appearance is spectacular. The clouds roll swiftly and noisily across the sky, casting a dark shadow over a small town. It becomes gloomy. About half the feeling in my heart is excited; the other half is unsure.

As the sky darkens quickly, my light ray begins to fade and I start to see the outline of my arms and hands. My beam of light is now only a small crevice peeking through the fierce storm clouds. They roll powerfully around me. My light fades so quickly now I can see my actual arms and hands. I'm no longer a beam of light; I am me, and I am falling.

I can hear a bloodcurdling scream—mine. A searing pain runs up and down my throat every second. I let out another scream. It is suddenly overpowered with the sound of crackling thunder. Rain pours down in tremendously large sheets, soaking my clothes and hair, sending a chill through my entire body. Every time I shriek or make a noise, it is instantly drowned out with the sound of thunder. I am sure I'm going to die. There is no way I could survive a fall from this height.

At about one hundred feet I close my eyes, spreading my arms and legs out like a starfish so it will slow me down before I land. I tense up and clench my teeth, preparing for impact. It doesn't come. I open my eyes and realize I linger in the air, cushioned by an invisible force. It drops; I fall into a low puddle of mud. *How did that just happen?* Usually there is impact whenever something or someone falls—in this case a huge impact—but nope, not even a little thud.

Mud is splattered all over me, some even tangled in my hair. As much as I've always hated being dirty, I've never been happier in *all* of my life to be in a mud puddle. I can easily stay in the mud for a while longer and splash. I feel so relieved. But still I feel somewhat confused.

Lightning slices through the sky, and a second later thunder crackles loudly. The storm—now directly above me—wails. I figure it will be best if I move, so I get to my feet slowly and look around. There is a road that leads far into darkness.

Rain falls from the sky so hard it's like having someone constantly dumping pails of water one after another on you from a high distance. In a way it is good because it will rinse some of the mud off me, but it makes it extremely hard to see even a short distance in front of me. I pull my braid loose, hoping the dirt chunks will wash out soon.

Where is my purse! A sudden flash of panic erupts through me. I look around, frantically trying to spot it. Another flash of lightning tears through the sky. At the same moment thunder howls loudly, casting a bright light onto the trees along the roadside. Dangling on one of the highest branches is my purse. Not even a speck of dirt materializes on its soft surface. It makes me so relieved. It would have made me angry if it happened to be ruined. It is one of the few things I have from my planet, and for it to have been wrecked from a *tree* would have not been good.

"Now how do I get it down?" I mumble grumpily to myself. It dangles really high up. "Climb it? No that would be too dangerous. I could throw something and try to knock it down? No, that could wreck it."

Then I figure it out. I remember what happened in the square when I threw around all those men without physically touching them. I will just try that again. I look up at the branch where my purse is attached. I close my eyes and try focusing my mind only on moving it off the branch. It doesn't work.

I thought it took *willpower* to move it, but it's not working. Forget what I did earlier—maybe I just reacted out of panic. I reached out to push Jeremy out of the way, but he moved without me touching him. The movement of my hands had created a force that moved him for me.

I look up at the high branch, then down at my hands. "This is crazy," I murmur and shrug. I point my hand at the tree, aiming it at my purse. I jerk my hands straight down, creating a huge snapping noise. Terrified of where it came from, I crouch down in the shrubs. There is no one around. It is still only me. There is nothing where the branch once was when I look up. Lying on the ground ahead of me sits my purse, still spotless and dry. Relieved, I retrieve it and sling it over my shoulder.

The storm still doesn't let up. It continues to pour with the pounding thunder and lightning that slices through the darkness of the clouds. I am further in the bush of trees, but the road remains still slightly visible. Two cars drive by, one after another, splashing and bumping through puddles. I'm slightly surprised anyone would be out in this weather. Margaritan doesn't have cars. We travel through underground tunnels. When you step inside, you can be wherever you want within a few minutes. All the tunnels are charmed. I know about cars because in school we have explorers who come and speak to us about where they've gone. The explorers also bring back books from every planet, and they are all very fascinating. I've read almost all of them.

Rain spills from the sky endlessly, making the mud thicker, seeping into my shoes and between my toes. As I start toward the road, I suddenly wish I wasn't wearing those gold flats anymore. When I look down at my feet, they are filthy. You can't even tell they were gold anymore. My khaki pants aren't their natural color anymore either; they are stained, and my blouse clings to me. I just hope someone will give me a ride. I don't know where, just somewhere clean and dry and warm. That is if they want to give someone this dirty *a ride*.

Finally I stumble onto the edge of the road. Up ahead I can see another set of headlights coming toward me. At first it appears like it is going to stop. Nope, it drives right into a huge pothole filled with muddy water, resoaking me from head to toe with filth. Maybe they didn't see me. Maybe they did and they just didn't want to pick up a filthy person who would get their interior muddy. I'm just going to stick with the theory that they didn't see me.

Instead of waiting on the side of the road to get splashed again, I start walking. Maybe somebody will see me if I am moving.

It starts raining even harder. It is so cold I can see my own breath—barely—before it is dissipated by the rain. Hopefully someone will come soon. My arms have little bumps, and I can't stop shaking. I wrap my arms around myself trying to warm up, but it makes no difference.

Two more headlights blur into view. If it weren't for the angry-sounding engine, I would not have even noticed the lights. I turn around slightly just in time to see it pull over. A tired, younger-looking man hops out of his truck and slams the door behind him, running toward me, peeling off his jacket.

"What on earth are you doing out here in this weather? And at this time?" he asks, hurrying to wrap his jacket around me and over my shoulders.

I feel extremely tiny in his jacket, but it is warm.

"I… I… got lost," I say, my teeth chattering loudly, making my head ache, and my body shivers from the cold.

"Come with me," he says, putting his arm around my shoulders, helping me to the passenger door and helping me climb in.

Slamming the door, he runs around the hood of the truck and climbs into the other seat.

"What's your name?" he asks, scanning my face. His slick brown hair drips water drops down onto his forehead, and his light eyes stare deeply into mine.

"Arianna." I sneeze, pulling his jacket around me tightly, trying to prevent myself from trembling.

"Oh! I know you," he says with a sudden look of recognition. "You're Trenton's kid." I don't quite remember actually ever meeting this man but yet he knows me? Weird.

"Yes. How do you know me, and what is your name?" I ask, actually quite curious as to *how* he *knows* me.

"I'm Clay and your father informed me you'd be coming but I just didn't know when or where, until the storm," he says, shrugging his shoulders.

"But how did you know it was me?" I ask.

"You're the only one roaming around the night, in the middle of a storm, all muddy and wet," he says, chuckling.

He turns the key, and the engine roars back to life. Then he leans over and grabs my seat-belt and clicks it in its place.

"Are you a Margaritan or...?"

"Both," he says as we bump along the road.

"How can you be both?" I ask.

"My father was Margaritan, and my mother was from earth." He shrugs. "My father was one of those explorers, and when he and his group came to earth, he fell in love," he explains.

"What happened?"

"It wasn't allowed. No two planets can have children together." He sighs, tightening his jaw and gripping his hands tighter on the steering wheel.

"Why?" I ask, very curiously, as we bump farther along the road.

After a long pause, he continues. "Their children could be very vigorous. Having two different heirlooms could bring down a planet if the child had a single tantrum." He chuckles again.

"Does Earth have any powers?" I ask.

"Few do, and it's because they have two parents from different planets. Usually they never find out about their other parent. They usually learn how to harvest their powers on their own."

"So what kind of heirlooms do you have?" I ask, feeling like a burden, peppering him with so many questions.

"Well, my father could control the elements. I never got to choose for myself in the pool of destiny on my seventeenth birthday, so I inherited the same gift as him," he explains.

"You should show me sometime," I say in the middle of a yawn. My eyes are drooping so heavily. I try to stay awake, but sleep gets the better of me. My eyes fall, the weight of my eyelids too heavy to lift again.

"HEY, ARIANNA?" CLAY ASKS. "YOU AWAKE?" HE NUDGES MY shoulder. In response I squint my eyes. "We're here."

He parks in front of a large, beautiful house. It's very hard to make out the details in the dark, but I can see the grand front porch with rustic flowerpots hanging from the covered part of the deck. Everything else gets blurred out by the rain. The thunder and lightning have calmed down a lot, but the rain remains thick and the wind picks up.

He unbuckles his seat belt and gets out of the truck, pulling the hood of his sweatshirt over his head, and runs to my side. I unbuckle mine the second he opens my door.

Together we run to the side door. As lightheaded as I am, I don't want to be out in the rain any longer. The wind casts a chill that runs up and down my spine. *Cold again!* Clay fumbles with the keys for a few moments, and finally he finds the right one. He opens the door wide, letting out precious heat, and I step in quickly, soaking up all the heat around me.

"Here, let me show you around." He gestures toward the hallway, leading into what I think is the main room.

"Can I clean up first?" I ask, remembering how muddy I am.

"Oh, right, yes, you'll be a lot warmer."

"Thank you," I say, feeling relieved. I'd hate myself if I got his beautiful home dirty, leaving a trail of mud everywhere. "Do you happen to have some spare clothes I could possibly acquire temporarily?" I ask, gesturing to my no longer white khaki pants and blouse. His jacket, which I was wearing, is now soaking wet and clinging to me.

"Leave your shoes and that coat here, and follow me. I'm sure I can find something," he says as he heads down the hall.

The main room is extremely beautiful and spacious. The kitchen is amazing, with a green granite island in the center of it and beautiful oak cupboards. The island has five tall stools. In the dining area sits a great table with eight chairs. Beyond that is another hallway with several doors and a staircase to the right.

Clay's disappeared! I must not have been paying much attention to just lose him when I think I was supposed to follow him.

"These will do for now," he says, emerging from one of the doors from down the hall. Wow, he's fast.

"The bathroom is the second door to the left," he says, handing me a small stack of clothes.

"Thank you," I say quietly as I stumble past him and make my way down the hall.

I've never felt more relieved to shower in all my life. The clothes he gave me are several sizes too large, but they are going to do. The hoodie reaches down to my knees, and the sweatpants have to be tied tightly with the drawstrings in order for them to stay up. Suddenly remembering, I hurriedly remove the pearl from my ruined pants and slip it in the hoodie pocket. It beats wearing my clothes, dirty as they are. I have had enough mud to last a lifetime. I stare into the mirror at my reflection. I am tiny for my age, with long wet hair descending its way down my back. My eyes are swollen and my cheeks red from crying. I am a mess.

Clay takes me on a tour of the whole house. I'm just too tired to remember any of the rooms. But the ones I remember for sure are my room, the bathroom, and the main room. I fall asleep as soon as my head hits the pillow.

CHAPTER 5

"You get to keep your name, but you need a new story," says Clay the next morning. "You're my niece from South Africa, your parents died in a car accident, and I am the only relative you have left."

"Okay and what's the name of this place?" I ask, biting into a piece of toast.

"Chyraville, in Alberta, Canada," he explains, chowing down on a bowl of cereal. "I enrolled you in CVHS for this semester," he says with a mouthful.

I haven't even thought about school until now. It will be quite strange learning everything new.

"How long till then?" I ask.

"Only a few days, so you won't have to wait too long," he says, finishing off his bowl. "We'll have plenty of time to go buy you new clothes before then. Your father said he gave you a peram?"

I nod. I still hadn't even looked at everything that was packed in the bag for me yet.

"Great, I can take you this afternoon if you like," he says. "I don't care for shopping, but I can help show you around. And show you what kids wear these days."

"Okay," I say with a smile. "Um, do I have to wear this into town?" I ask, gesturing to the oversized hoodie and sweats. It would look very strange wearing this into town, someone totally new who dresses like a slob.

"No." A sudden wave of relief floods through me. "I managed to clean most of the stains out of your pants. They are slightly visible. You can only see them if you look at them really close," he says reassuringly, standing up from his seat.

"How?" I ask, almost doubtful. I thought it would be impossible to get something *that* dirty clean.

"Elements, remember?" he says, pouring himself a cup of coffee.

"You have to show me sometime," I remind him.

He slides back into his chair with his cup and a plastic bag. He hands the bag to me and places his cup in front of him on the table. I take the bag willingly.

Where I'm from, next to nothing is impossible. I guess it shouldn't have surprised me how he managed to get them nearly unblemished.

At the top of the pile are my golden flats. They look nothing like they did earlier—grungy slippers. They look just like new.

"Well, go on upstairs, and after you're dressed, I'll show you the farm."

"This is a farm?"

"Yep, this house isn't exactly in town. It's a few miles away."

"Cool," I say, standing up from the table and walking toward the staircase with the bag in my hand.

THE FARM IS ACTUALLY QUITE LARGE, NOT AS BIG AS SOME OF the farms on Margaritan, but it is still big. Clay's farm is absolutely beautiful. Very understandable, considering he can control the elements. He could command the land to do whatever he wants it to do. On Margaritan most of the people who receive that gift usually enjoy working on farms. I still don't understand what a sorceress does or the powers I will get. So far, I have telekinesis. Hopefully that won't be the only gift I will get.

His farm only has a few horses and a small beagle named Hydra. It has a large crop of wheat and another of canola. He also has a huge orchard with an array of fruit trees.

He talks endlessly about—I have no idea what. But when he asks me a question, I snap back into the real world.

"Huh?"

"I said, 'What do you think?'" he says.

"I love it! It feels and smells like home," I say, sucking in a deep breath of fresh air. The truth is it does. It is a distinct smell in the warm summer breeze, though it feels cooler than on Margaritan. There is no way I even noticed it last night. The wind was too harsh, and everything just smelled musky.

"That's what I was trying for." He sighs. "I lived on Margaritan for eight years with my dad, till I was sent here." The way he says it, it sounds like a punishment. Which it is! "I tried to make it feel like home," he says, fiddling with a small red ball.

I nod. "It does."

"Hydra, come here, girl!" he cries out to the little dog bounding after a butterfly.

"Why'd you name her Hydra?"

"Because she is an animal from Margaritan. She cannot die. Hydra is a Greek monster that cannot die. Every time you cut off one head, two more grow back. You see, animals from Margaritan can only choose to die if their master dies. But of course, Margaritan animals don't grow back double the heads if one is cut off." He chuckles. "I named her Hydra because she cannot die."

The little dog pounces happily at Clay's feet, tongue dangling, ears flapping, and her tail wagging profusely. She jumps up playfully, landing with most of her weight on her front paws, her whole body wiggling from the movement of her tail.

"Will she be this playful forever?" I ask, giggling, as the little dog continues growling, her little body jiggling.

"Always this playful," he replies.

Clay reaches down, showing the small red ball he was fiddling with earlier to Hydra. Instantly Hydra sits up attentively, her tail wagging anxiously, awaiting for her command to fetch.

"Go!" he yells. The little dog takes off running. Clay then throws the ball really hard, letting the wind carry it wildly across the yard.

Then something unexpected happens; Hydra jumps higher than I've seen any dog ever jump before. She catches the ball in her mouth, barreling toward the ground. Just before she's about to crash into the ground at full impact, she stops in midair about a foot above the ground. Landing gracefully, she prances to where Clay and I stand.

"How did she do that?" I ask in awe.

"Magic isn't only in stories. Where we come from, magic is in everyone and everything. It's reality," he says, grinning. To be honest even on Margaritan I haven't seen a dog jump that high before. "Here magic is a thing to be hidden."

He is quiet again. "Wow! Noon already," he gasps, glancing down at his watch. "Well, time sure does fly by fast. Are you ready? We can leave for town right away."

I FEEL KIND OF BAD. I DIDN'T EVEN LOOK AT MY ENDOWMENTS from home yet that were packed in that bag for me. I would have liked to have had more time, but I was rushed. At least they gave me the morning. I was able to spend it with Jeremy until they ripped me away from him and knocked me unconscious.

Although I would love to sneak a peek at the endowments Maybell and my mother both tucked into my bag, Clay is waiting for me downstairs. It'll have to wait. I snatch it off the little black desk in the corner of my new room and gently place the pearl inside it. Not wanting to take too long, I boot it down the stairs.

Clay is still waiting for me by the front door, ready to lock it once I'm out. I slip by him and start walking down the path leading to the truck. Considering how muddy it was last night, his truck is shining, not even a single speck of dirt visible. It is actually quite strange. Then it occurs to me—control over the elements. I can't believe I have to continually remind myself.

Clay runs up behind me, his keys jingling in his coat pocket.

On the way to town, he chatters on and on endlessly about the town and the people in it and pretty well everything. My mind is more focused on the mountains, their snowy peaks reaching high into the sky, reaching to home.

As we pass a small lake, I notice six kids. Five have hair so dark it looks like each strand is half purple and half black. They all have the same perfect ivory skin tone. All are around my age except for one. He looks maybe a few years younger. The sixth is tall and muscular, with pitch-black hair and a golden tan, which makes him stand out from the rest of the group. He leans against a jeep chatting and laughing with the group.

His posture, his goofy grin, and his handsome jawline seem so familiar to me. I think I actually *have* seen him before. How could I have seen him before? And why does he look so familiar?

The second he looks up at our truck... at *me*... a huge tug rips its way into my stomach. I cringe the same moment he winces, wrapping his arms tightly around his stomach. We make eye contact a split second just before our truck disappears behind more trees, making our way to town.

"Huh?" asks Clay.

"What?"

"I asked if you want to get lunch before we go shopping," he says, gesturing to my stomach. I haven't even noticed how tightly my arms were wrapped around my waist. My ribs feel like they are going to crumble under the pressure. The pain slightly lingers, but I no longer want to eat. I would much rather puke. Maybe it would make me feel better.

I don't want to make Clay worried, so I just say, "Oh! Lunch sounds great. I'm starving." It's a little white lie, but I don't really want to tell him. It'll just make me sound crazy. I release the pressure but it's almost comforting, having my arms around my waist, just in case the pain returns.

"About five minutes till we get to town," says Clay cheerfully.

All through lunch my mind is working on theories of where I'd seen that guy before. There is only one theory, but it's impossible. I tell myself, *There's no way you have seen him before, so stop worrying about it.* Part of me wants to believe it, but another part of me doesn't want to ignore it. My mind buzzes with so many things all at once. It feels like it's going to burst. It makes me feel weak. I really want to talk to him. I feel like I *have* to.

Clay continues talking. I feel rather awful that I haven't been paying attention to him. As we eat, he asks me questions, so I nod periodically or sometimes ask him to repeat his question.

We go through the racks in a retail store, and he still talks. I wonder if he ever gets tired of talking.

It is overly crowded. Luckily we beat rush hour, barely.

"All right. It's usually pretty chilly around here," he says, pulling several hoodies off a rack and wool sweaters. He dumps them into my arms and tells me to go try them on.

By the end of the afternoon, I am exhausted. I have never done *this* much shopping before. Then again I have never moved to another galaxy before and had to refill a closet so I could blend in at a new school. My head aches from all the different light fixtures, and my arms are numb from trying on so many clothes. We try not to buy too much. Supposedly I'm going again later. It still feels like we did a lot of shopping. I think it's because this is the most stuff I got in one day.

"Are we almost done?" I ask, shrugging on a thin windproof, black jacket.

"Yes! We'll bring all these bags to the truck and then go home. I want you to meet somebody," he says with a grin.

It feels like an eternity just to walk to the truck, but finally, when we get there and finish unloading, it is an instant relief.

"So who is it that you want me to meet?" I ask as we begin to drive through the parking lot.

"Haley."

"Who's that?"

"She's my wife." He grins. "She's also your English teacher this semester."

"Does she know about... Margaritan?" I ask. "About me?"

"Of course. She just got back from a teachers convention, this afternoon," he adds cheerfully. "I phoned her earlier and told her you'd be coming. She is so excited to meet you!"

"I'm excited to meet her too!" I reply a little too enthusiastically.

It sounds almost sarcastic, but it doesn't faze him whatsoever, which is great. I think he is just too anxious to see his wife to notice. The truth is I really am excited to meet her.

Back home I didn't get to meet very many new people. Being a princess you don't get much freedom. On second thought, I got a lot freedom; I spent a lot of time outside of the castle hanging out with Jeremy and Maybell whenever she brought me into the village. Both my sisters followed the rules. I didn't as much. I like my freedom; I get more freedom here than I ever would get back home.

My steady heartbeat quickens with the pain of anxiety as we near the lake. It is deserted. There are only a few fishermen sitting on the dock with a stereo and their fishing poles. I try to calm myself. The teenagers probably all went home. No matter how hard I try, I cannot forget the tugging sensation when I made eye contact with *him*. I've searched and searched all of my memories all afternoon, but I just can't remember.

As we pull up into the driveway, I see a woman smiling in the window. Just as Clay parks the truck, the woman comes running out of the front door to meet us. She has light wavy brown hair flowing down her back and dark brown eyes. She is very beautiful, with delicately pale skin and a huge welcoming smile with deep dimples on either side. Her yellow sundress flutters behind with each stride she takes.

"Hey, I missed you so much," she cries, jumping into Clay's open arms. It's really sweet seeing how perfect they are for each other. They are beautiful together. My parents look sweet together too, although the last time I saw them they were both crying. I barely know much about my parents. They never really told me about how they met, how they fell in love, nothing. Even at dinnertime, if either of my sisters or I asked about them, we were given a look as if to say, "Don't ask again." I never really understood why. It was a harmless question.

"I missed you too," Clay says, embracing her in another tight hug. "This is my niece, Arianna," he says, gesturing to me as I step in front of the truck. I still don't know if he actually is my uncle, or if he just told her that.

"Oh yes! Clay phoned and told me you'd be coming," she says gingerly. "You are quite the beautiful young lady."

"Thank you," I blush. I don't understand why, but every time I am complimented I blush nervously.

She lets go of Clay and grips me in an immense hug. She smells of sweet perfume, and when she backs up into Clay's arms, she grins. She and Clay make an amazing couple; they are both sweet and genuinely nice.

"I can't believe you guys went shopping without me," she says, putting on a fake frown. "How much did you buy?" she asks, curiously standing up on the balls of her feet, peeking into the window of the truck to see how many bags are on the backseat. But there are none. We put them all in the box with the lid rolled down, so nothing would fly out.

"Don't worry, I didn't buy too much. You can take her out again if you want," he jokes.

It takes only one trip for us to bring everything in and up-stairs. We all slump down in the cushy chairs in the living room, and I let out a huge sigh of relief.

"Well, that was… fun," says Haley with a comical grin. Even when we are all exhausted, she still gets us to smile. Her cheeri-ness is entertaining. "You guys hungry?"

To be honest, I didn't realize I was hungry till she asked just now. Who knew that shopping could be quite the workout? Clay raises his hand high, waving it in the air as if he were a child who knows an answer to a teacher's question and wants badly to be picked.

She nods in response with a chuckle. "How 'bout you?" she asks, nodding toward me.

"Yeah."

"Great, because the pizza delivery guy *should* be here shortly," she says with a satisfied grin.

So far she has not stopped smiling since we met. She seems very nice.

I've never tried pizza before, but it certainly looks tasty, sitting on my plate. It tastes even better than it looks! I wish I learned about pizza earlier. I sure have been missing out on a lot of stuff; getting to ride in a truck, eating pizza, and being able to spend time with people who are just so nice.

"Thank you. This was amazing!" I thank Haley, dabbing the corners of my mouth with a napkin.

"I can't believe you've never tried pizza before," she exclaims.

"Most of the food back home is grown in crops. Nothing is processed," I say.

"Yeah, it sucks out there. Okay, I'm going to watch the game," announces Clay, switching on the huge flat screen mounted on the wall.

"Sure," Haley says, picking up the waste scattered all over the coffee table. I quickly get to my feet, reaching down to pick up the empty box. She smiles at me gratefully as we walk to the kitchen to throw out the waste.

"Do you need help organizing all that stuff you guys bought?" she asks kindly.

My mother would have never asked me that. Most of the time she was really busy, but she had spent a lot of time with my sisters when they were young. She never spent that much time with me. I only remember once, when I was seven, my mother came into my room just to play dolls with me. She was really upset about something; her cheeks were blotchy with red and her eyes blurring. She tried to keep up a small smile for me and mask her pain. She asked me how I was doing. At the time everyone was very depressed and all kept up gentle smiles for me and continually asked how I was holding up. I don't remember why. I was really young at the time, so I never did understand what happened. I still don't.

That was really the only time my mother had actually spent quality time with me. Not anymore, but most of the time I was with Maybell. I really enjoy company and don't really care for being alone. Sometimes it's nice, but other times, like now, it's nice to have company.

"Sure, thanks," I reply.

Her face lights up with joy. I wish my mother would have been that excited to help me with something. Although my mother hasn't always been there for me, I still miss her dearly.

Most of the clothing we bought was sweaters and jeans. There were a few pairs of shorts for phys ed, pajamas, and some other stuff. Most of the styles here are very similar to Margaritan, but some of it looks a bit different to me. There is no need for pullovers back home; it is always warm, and it is never cold enough to need to wear one.

"So, how do you like it here?" Haley asks, hanging a black sweater up in the closet.

My heart aches thinking about all the differences. There are so many.

"It's very different from back home." I shudder at saying the word *home* because really *how* can it be home if I'm not wanted there.

"Clay had the same answer, when I asked him the very first time." She sighs, struggling to open another package of hangers. The way she says it, it sounds like she's asked a few times.

"Has Clay told you much about our planet?"

"No, not much. He described it faintly and told me about his gift. I think he tries to forget, so he won't always feel like a chunk of his life is missing." She sighs again. "I don't blame him," she says, setting down the unopened package of hangers she was struggling with earlier.

For a moment it is dead silent. You could hear a pin drop. Finally I decide to break the silence. "I have two sisters," I say. Maybe if I talk a little bit about home, I'll feel a little better.

Haley looks up as the words leave my mouth.

"A nurse named Maybell, who treated me like I really was her daughter," I sigh fighting tears from surfacing my eyes. "And my best friend's name was Jeremy." I pause. "He was my *only* best friend."

At the thought of Jeremy, I stop fighting the tears and just let them flow down my face. She crosses the room and sits beside me on the quilt covering my bed and wraps her arms around me as I cry, comforting me.

CHAPTER 6

OVER THE NEXT FEW DAYS, BEFORE SCHOOL STARTS, HALEY brings me to the mall and helps me with the few extra things Clay forgot. We pick out a few more pieces of clothing. I absolutely fall in love with a wool purple sweater. She helps me pick out a few scarves and a colorful beanie, pretty girly stuff. Clay just picked out basic stuff.

She teaches me how to apply eyeliner, which I actually really like. It looks kind of cool. Back home we didn't wear eyeliner, just powder that gave our faces a little more color. I usually wore just gold glitter, but I like the look of the eyeliner way better.

I also entertain Haley, Clay, and myself by practicing my telekinesis. I tease Hydra by pretending to throw the ball, but instead of actually throwing it, I let it hover in the air behind me. Hydra gives me a dirty look and sniffs at my feet, whining and whimpering. She is adorable.

"DON'T WORRY IT WILL BE FINE," SAYS HALEY WITH AN ENCOURaging smile as we drive to school.

I am so nervous my hands are trembling, and I can't sit still. We pass the small lake. I glance out the window to see if the boy and his friends are there. Nope.

I stuff my hands in the pockets of my jacket, so they are no longer visible to Haley, and me.

It takes a little while before we finally pull into the parking lot in front of the school. It is jam packed with vehicles. Hundreds of kids sit on their cars, in the front of the school, and well, everywhere. I am glad we went shopping so now I can blend in, almost.

"Ready?" asks Haley, snatching her purse from the backseat. She pulls it onto her lap, waiting for me to respond.

"I guess?" I pull my backpack onto my lap and comb my fingers through the gentle blonde curls surrounding my head.

"You have me first block English, so I'll show you to your locker; it's only a little ways away from the classroom," she says, passing me my schedule with a reassuring smile.

Locker 591. How big is this school? I glance out the window again. The school is huge with a gray front, black roof and lots of windows.

1	-	English 30-1	room	305
2	-	Phys Ed 30		gym
3	-	Astronomy	room	325
4	-	Calculus	room	213

I chuckle when I read astronomy on my schedule. I know all about space already. Back on Margaritan it has always been mandatory to have astronomy on your schedule. "We believe that it is important to know where it is you live in the universe. That was the first quote the teachers always said before the new school year. It is actually quite a relief to be in a class I am familiar with and that I have Haley for English.

THE HALLWAYS ARE CROWDED WITH TEENAGERS. IT'S A LONG while before we get to my locker. Gray and black lockers line both sides of the hallway. She shows me how to unlock the lock and writes the combination on my schedule, and disappears into the sea of swarming people.

It takes me few tries before I finally get it open. A tall boy with a football jacket walks up behind me and slams me into my open locker. A searing pain runs through my arm from the spot of impact. I push myself out of the locker and straighten my back so I stand tall, almost. I turn around to see him and three other guys in matching jackets, smirking down at me.

"Oh, she's gonna cry," says the boy to his friends, grinning, eyes piercing.

I just smile at him pleasantly and hang on to my backpack and my jacket. Leaving on my wool purple sweater, I grab my binder and lock my locker. If I pretend that their ignorance doesn't faze me then maybe they will leave me alone, I hope. Without making eye contact with them, I start making my way down the hallway toward room 305. I swerve around a mess of people. I can tell that those guys are following me, by the shrieks and the curses people make, as they get thrown aside, shoved to the floor or into lockers. I pick up my pace.

1. English 30-1

302. 303. 304. Finally 305. I veer into the classroom, relieved to see Haley sitting at the desk in the back. She wears her usual pleasant smile, welcoming everyone who walks into the class. She waves me over to her desk. There are about fifteen kids already scattered around the classroom, talking in small groups. It is a large classroom that can easily fit thirty students, with lots of room to spare if there were more desks.

"I found it," I say, giving a joking grin as I stop beside her desk. She smiles again.

"If you want, you can sit in one of these desks," she says, pointing to the desks in the back row. "Or do you want to sit near the front, or by the windows. I usually ask people near the front or the middle to answer questions, so if you don't want me to ask, you can sit near the back."

I would much rather not be noticed and not have people staring at the back of my head all through the class, so I decide to sit in the back.

"Back here is great," I say, sliding into a seat a few desks away from hers.

She shuffles through some papers on her desk and rearranges a few things. I glance through the doorway. Behind a group of kids filing into the classroom are the four football guys, staring at me with a savage look in their eyes, like when a predator looks at his prey, ready to pounce and sink its teeth into. The hair on the back of my neck stands on end. I look down at my binder, away from their icy gaze. Their stare is cut off by more kids coming into the room. When they finish coming in, the boys have disappeared.

I lace my fingers together, dropping them to my lap, to keep from trembling.

By the end of class we are given a handout and a novel to answer questions about. I'm about to leave the classroom, when Haley stops me and hands me a dark blue T-shirt that says "CVHS" in bold lettering, for phys ed.

2. Phys Ed 30

I SLIP INTO A PAIR OF SHORTS AND THE CVHS T-SHIRT HALEY gave me, and walk out of the girls' locker room.

Another girl maybe a head taller than me runs out behind me and stops when she catches up to me.

"Hey," she says with a smile. "You're new here, huh?"

"Yes, I am," I say, returning a smile.

"I'm Kelly," she says, holding out her hand.

I shake it and respond, "Arianna."

She brushes a strand of light brown hair out of her eyes. "I want to warn you. Some of the guys who are in our class are extremely rough," she says, pointing at the football boys as we walk into the gym.

I am just about to turn and hide my face when I make eye contact with the tall one. He nudges his buddy's arm, wearing a sadistic grin. I look away.

"Okay, everyone, gather in," yells a middle-aged man, wearing a navy blue track suit, a whistle hanging around his neck. He looks kind of bored, like he doesn't really care to be here today.

We all form a circle in the center of the gym around him. I stand beside Kelly with a boy on my other side.

"So this semester we will be doing a lot of stuff," he says, inspecting all of us from head to toe. "Since today is the first day, I will allow you to pick the game. I will be watching to see how well you participate and what shape you are in." He looks at me, the smallest one in the class, with distaste.

"Murder ball!" blurts out the tall football guy, grinning at me.

"All right, and since you picked, you're helping set it up. You, you, and you," he says, randomly picking people.

As they walk to the storage room, everyone breaks into conversation. Kelly links her arm in mine and drags me toward two other girls.

One has pale skin, dark hair, and huge chestnut eyes.

"Nish, Bre," calls Kelly, steering me toward them. "I want you to meet somebody." She pulls me in front of her.

"Hey," I say with a shy smile.

"This is Arianna," says Kelly to the two girls. "Arianna, this is Nisha," she says gesturing to the girl with the dark hair and large chestnut eyes. "And this is Breanne," to the other girl, with her light auburn hair pulled into a ponytail, and hazel eyes. They are both slim and seem cool.

They are both taller than me, along with everyone else in the class.

"We're going to die," says Bre, pointing to the boys. With their muscle protruding on their arms and legs, they look intimidating. There are a lot more boys in our class than there are girls.

"So we need two captains. Any volunteers?" interrupts the coach, walking back to the center with a large bag of balls, the football guy beside him. Two people raise their hands, but the coach doesn't acknowledge them. "Okay, too slow, I'll pick," he says glancing around. "Kelly and Brad."

Kelly and the tall guy walk to the front, to face everyone. So that's what the football guy's name is—the one who slammed me into my locker this morning—the one who has continuously given me evil looks since we first encountered each other. Brad.

Before they start calling names, I know I am going to be called dead last. But no—there are three guys and one girl left after I am called to be on Kelly's team. All the names are called, and Brad grins at me with a look in his eyes saying—you're dead. What is his problem? I don't think I ever did anything to him. Actually I *know* I never did anything to him.

Since everyone knows the game, besides me, Coach doesn't explain the game. Kelly looks at me funny when I tell her I've never played before, so she tells me how to play. It seems easy enough; try not to get hit and get everyone on the opposite team out by hitting them.

The whistle blows, and adrenaline surges through my veins. I sprint to the center and kick all the balls to my teammates before anyone else is halfway there. Coach stands on the sidelines, and he looks impressed. It feels nice to be able to move at full speed. It feels like forever since I have been able to do this. So far, I love it! I am actually quite good at it too. Every time Brad throws a ball at me, I easily sidestep it or dive to the floor.

There are four of us left on my side and six left on their side—Brad, a girl, and four more boys—when it begins to get difficult. On my side it is Kelly and a boy named Josh with curly brown hair that bounces in his eyes as he swerves around three oncoming balls. There is also Michael with spiky ash blond hair, who jumps in front of me, deflecting a ball from planting itself in my stomach.

"Thanks," I gasp.

"No problem," he says. He picks up another ball and tosses it to me.

I leap out of the way as another ball inches its way closer to impacting my knees.

"Ball! Ball! Ball! Ball! Ball!" cries out Kelly. I toss her my ball. She throws it hard. A boy grunts as her ball makes impact into his stomach. He walks to the side of the gym, cursing.

Four, Five.

I learn that if we keep a rhythm going, we can get their whole team out in a matter of minutes.

My heart is pumping deeply with adrenaline as I swerve around another one of Brad's failed attempts to hit me, which makes him angrier by the second. He gives me the most ferocious look I have ever seen someone give—a look of anger and pure hatred. How can someone hate someone they don't even know?

Brad runs over to one of his teammates and whispers something to him—his icy gaze running over me as he speaks. My heart pounds, and the hairs on the back of my neck stand on end.

I stand ready on the tips of my toes waiting for the right moment to throw my ball. I glance at the girl, her hair tied up in a messy ponytail, with eyes so sharp, you might cut yourself just looking at them. I close my eyes and whip the ball in her direction, as hard as I can.

I open my eyes just in time to watch the ball smack into her calves as she tries to leap out of the way, but she's too heavy to move in time. She gives me a dirty look and storms to the side, muttering to herself with her fists clenched.

Tied four, four.

Michael hurls his ball, breathing through his mouth, his ash blond hair staying in its spikes, sweat beading on his forehead. The corners of his lips curve into a devious grin; the ball plants itself in one of the boys' chests. The boy is caught off guard and stumbles backward—gasping for air, he walks to the side.

Four, three.

I am amazed as to how well my team is doing. From losing to winning by one man, I'd say we're doing pretty well.

Kelly and I glance at each other. We hurl our volleyballs at the exact same time, both hitting a boy with glistening black hair, one in the chest, the other smacking his stomach. For some odd reason, he chuckles to himself, shaking his head.

Four, two.

Two boys left on their team, Brad and another boy about the same height, but maybe a smaller, narrower build. His brown hair waves over his focused eyes as he releases his ball.

Kelly gasps as the ball slams into her stomach. She slumps to the side, her arms wrapped tightly around her waist.

Three, two.

Josh turns, an icy glare in his narrow, anger-stricken eyes. He picks up a ball rolling toward his feet, anger rippling through him. He lets loose the ball. It tears through the air. Just in case it misses, I lob mine in the same direction as the boy hits the floor. Josh's ball sails just over his head, causing a breeze that tousles his hair; mine pegs him in his left shoulder. He gets to his feet snarling.

I never knew there was a game this rough and competitive before—until I came here. Josh runs to my side, giving me a fist punch, trying to hold back hysterical laughter.

"That was awesome," yells Michael, coming to give me a fist punch too.

Just when we are about to turn to face Brad, a ball bounces from Josh's shoulder, hitting Michael, before it falls to the floor. Double hit.

One, one.

They both give me a pleading look as they walk toward the side. All of my teammates wear the same look. They want me to win the game for them.

Brad sneers at me with an evil, wild look in his eyes.

"Not going to take it easy on you," he says, the corner of his mouth turning upward, "sweetie."

Did he just call me *Sweetie!* Now he's pushing it, provoking me. I suck in a deep breath, not really wanting to exhale. He sure seems to be trying to irritate me—well it's working! But he won't get an outrage from me if *that's* what he is trying for. I try to stay calm but anger is building up in my chest, radiating through my veins.

"Nor will I," I say, staring deep into his eyes. I can see a brief flash of uncertainty and panic run through his.

"Good luck with that," he says, whipping his ball at me, thinking it is the last throw of the game. He stands loosely waiting for it to hit me.

I sidestep easily, hurling mine as hard as I ever thought I possibly could. It's completely off in its midair but curves at the last minute, planting itself right in his face.

My team runs off the bench, yelling and whooping. I feel guilty for hitting him in the nose, but everyone on my team just tells me, "He deserves it."

I glance over at him to see if he's all right.

His hands are cupped over his nose, with blood seeping through his fingers. The skin under his eyes already beginning to darken, he looks up with a furious glare and knitted eyebrows.

Coach stands by him chuckling, while writing a slip of paper to go see the nurse.

"You got a good arm," says Coach, walking past me to his office.

3. Astronomy, room 325

ASTRONOMY IS ABSOLUTELY ATROCIOUS. WE WATCH A SHORT film about some guy who goes to the moon. Not a very big accomplishment after where I've come from. I went from one galaxy to another in a matter of minutes. I thought this class would be as fascinating as it was back on Margaritan. Nope. It seems to drag on forever. I could teach this class. Of course no one would believe me.

4. Calculus, room 213

NISH AND KELLY WAVE AT ME TO SIT BY THEM AT THE BACK OF the classroom. Since it is the first day of school we only write a few notes. As it turns out, I already know this stuff. We never called it calculus. I learned this stuff a few years ago. After a while we switch to a movie, while the teacher sleeps at his desk.

"So how was your first day?" Haley asks on the way home.

"It felt like it was never going to end," I huff, rubbing my eyes. Besides phys ed, everything else was bitter. Everything they believe is difficult I learned at a young age, so it's all pretty well a basic review of first school for me.

"Well, I had a pretty entertaining block 3 English class." She chuckles. "A boy came into my class late. He had two black eyes, and his nose was really swollen. The funny thing was, when I asked him what happened, he said it was an evil little blonde girl. Apparently she was pretty wicked at murder ball," she says, winking at me.

Heat makes its way into my cheeks. All I can say is, "Oops."

She bursts out laughing. I can't help but laugh too. It is funny; an evil little blonde girl, maybe half his size, gives him a broken nose—with a volleyball.

"Don't worry, he deserves it. He's an ass," she says. Her laugh fades, but a smile is still painted across her lips.

I still don't understand how someone can deserve a broken nose. But I guess if everyone says he does—then maybe he does.

I glance out of the window just in time to watch the lake fly past us. A pain so sharp pierces my abdomen, just as I glance at—*him*. I shrink deeper into my seat, trying to hide from the pain but it lingers in a constant pulse pattern.

From the corner of my eye, I watch him crouch, his arms wrapped tightly around his stomach. His face contorts in agony—just like mine.

The five people around him look at him funny as he crumples to his knees.

The pain slowly fades away when we are no longer near the lake.

"What's wrong?" asks Haley, glancing at me with eyes wide with curiosity and concern.

I turn my focus on the mountains fleeting by, but my eyes blur and all I see is a fuzzy combination of liquid white, blue, green and gray.

Finally we get home. I swing my backpack over my shoulder, trying not to make eye contact. I don't want to be crying all of the time, especially here—on Earth. At last I feel heat rise up into my cheeks, and my face turns red. "I don't know," I say, trying to fight the stream of tears threatening to spill over my lashes. I don't want to be *caught* crying. I hate crying. It makes me feel weak and pathetic.

I speed walk to the house. I plan on sprinting up the stairs, until… Clay stands in the dining room, blocking my path to the stairs. I could swerve around him, but that would be rude.

He stands smiling with his hands in his jeans pockets. He lifts an eyebrow, and his smile slowly fades when his eyes find mine.

"What's up?" he asks Haley, who stands just behind me. She shrugs, shaking her head.

To be honest I don't know what to say to them. They deserve to know. They are going out of their way just to help me. I just don't know how to tell them without sounding *ridiculous*.

"Um…" I begin, my voice breaking. How could I say, *I'm in excruciating pain every time I am near this one guy. I thought I've seen him before I came here, but that is impossible.*

I'm going to tell them no matter how stupid it sounds. I slump down into one of the chairs by the long table, dropping my backpack to the floor. It echoes around the open room.

Haley maneuvers to Clay's side, crossing her arms. I look from one to the other. They both wear the same concerned expression: lifted eyebrows and lips pursed.

"It's gonna sound really strange," I admit, looking for a change in their faces. The next part all comes out in a rush. "Um… there's this guy. I've only seen him twice so far, and both times I got a stabbing pain in my stomach. I feel like I've seen him before. I just can't remember where, or when." I shrug, waiting for them to respond.

Both their faces look confused, rather than concerned. It makes me feel awkward.

"Well, maybe you have seen him before," says Clay. "The portal from every planet leads to another opening."

"Huh?"

I'm not exactly sure how that is relevant to the subject, but I guess it will be good to know *some* day.

"Why would we both be in pain when we are near each other?" I say, clarifying my first initial question.

"How do you know he's in pain too?" asks Clay raising both eyebrows.

"He cringed the same moment I did," I snap back.

I don't know if he actually believes me or if he thinks I'm as crazy as I thought what I said sounded.

"I don't... know." He shrugs, looking at the floor. It seems like he really doesn't know, but there is something about how he looks to the floor when he says it. It makes it a little hard to believe, so I question him some more.

"Clay, who is he?" I ask stubbornly.

He tenses. "I don't know his name. I will tell you though; all portals are linked, so many individuals end up here. If you look close enough, you can easily identify those who are of a different race. Arianna, there is a chance that you do know that boy. There are several others from Margaritan who live in this area... and some from other *places*. You see, Earth is kind of a fall-off place because many planets send"—he pauses—"*delinquents* here. Earth is a weaker planet in other race's eyes, so it is believed that this is the best place to send criminals or troublemakers." He tells me the truth, but he tries to be careful with his choice of words.

"That's cruel," I whisper.

"It is, but it won't be stopped," says Clay bluntly. I don't argue because I know that it is true. It's probably been occurring since the beginning of time, and there's no way of stopping a habit that's been going on for that long.

CHAPTER 7

"THANK GOODNESS IT'S FRIDAY," GASPS KELLY. AS IT TURNS OUT her locker is only a few down from mine. On either side of hers are Nish and Bre. How lucky is that, to have friends whose lockers are near to yours?

"Yeah, I agree." I swing my backpack over my shoulder and walk down the hall toward theirs.

A ball rolls out across the floor in front of me.

I jump to the side so I don't have to kick it or stumble over it, but a large, muscular arm slams me in midair. The pressure takes my breath away. I stumble into a garbage can, trying to regain my balance. I don't even get to stand up fully before I am thrown against a classroom door. The handle jabs into my back. I let out a cry of pain and crumple to the floor. On top of that, I feel the sharp stabbing pain in my stomach again.

Kelly slams her locker shut and runs to my side to help me up. I look up through teary eyes to see Brad and his buddies tromping down the hallway, giving each other high fives.

Brad has been trying to get back at me for breaking his nose—all week. None of the times have actually worked, until now. My back throbs. Nish comes to my other side. She and Kelly help me up from my crumpled position.

Everybody stares at me as I regain my balance. I clench my teeth when I straighten to my usual height. I'm afraid I may have punctured something. I probably didn't, but the pain is just terrible.

"What did you do to make those jerks want to hurt you so bad?" asks Kelly.

"I don't know," I say through my clenched teeth, fighting a war against tears. I would like to confront Brad and his buddies, but they are just so strong, and I am afraid to be hurt—again. They seem to think they are in control of everyone and everything around here. It's disturbing.

"Well, I guess you kind of broke his nose in gym class," says Bre, coming up from behind us. "But I think he should have gotten over that by now."

"It's Brad," replies Nish sarcastically.

"So what are you doing tonight?" Kelly asks me, trying to change the subject.

"I'm not sure, why?"

"Well, I was invited to go to a bonfire tonight, and I was told I could bring a few friends. Nish and Bre are both already coming. Do you want to come also?"

"I'll have to ask." I sigh. "But if they say yes, I would love to come." Deep down I feel like it's not a very good idea, remembering the pain in my back. But my friends are going, so I guess I should be fine.

"Okay, call me before seven so I can know to give you a ride or not," she says, swinging her backpack over her shoulder.

The three of them start making their way down the hallway. I turn in the opposite direction, to meet Haley in her classroom.

My back throbs with every step I take, causing me to wince every so often.

Hopefully I'm allowed to go; this is the first time I have actually been invited to something by a group of people. I used to only get invited to stuff because I was a princess, not really because I was wanted there.

I stumble into the classroom, just as Haley gets up from her chair holding her bag and her laptop.

"Hey," she says with a smile.

"Hey." I wince; she doesn't seem to notice—good.

She turns to lock the door when I finally decide to ask. "So I was wondering, my friends invited me to go to a bonfire tonight. Can I go?" The worst she could say is *no*.

"It's okay with me." I sigh with relief, but then she adds, "But you'd have to ask Clay." I guess there is something worse than *no*. If Clay is anything like my dad, I am definitely *not* going.

"WHY... WOULD YOU WANT TO GO TO THAT?" ASKS CLAY, RELAtively shocked.

This would have been the exact reaction my dad *would* have had. Only his automatic answer after that would be *no*. With his eyebrows raised, crinkling his forehead, he actually could pass for my dad. He has the *exact* same facial expressions, despite the smirk. My dad didn't have that—and if he did, he wasn't around me when he did it. I barely remember him even being happy or even joking a little.

I shrug. I've been to a bonfire before, but it was a celebration, and there was actually meaning behind it. This bonfire is for fun.

"I'm not sure if it's a very good idea," he says.

"Clay—why not? She just got here and made some friends

who invited her to go to a bonfire with them. You're just going to say *no*?" asks Haley, winking at me.

Inside my heart, I'm grinning. On the outside I just look up at him with a tiny faint smile, meeting Clay's eyes.

Clay gives up—his shoulders drop—and he lets out a sigh of defeat.

He can say *no* to me, but when Haley is on my side he can't.

"Fine, you can go," he says, clearly annoyed.

A smile spreads across my face as I wrap my arms around him, *almost* forgetting the pain in my back—a*lmost*. I am quickly reminded; I flinch when I feel the pull.

"Thank you," I gasp, trying to ignore the pain and enjoy the fact that I can go tonight! A thought pops into my head—what if Brad is there? Oh no… I hope I don't encounter him tonight, *if* he is there.

"I need to make some rules," he states, letting go. "Be back before midnight."

"Clay…?" complains Haley. "She's a responsible girl. Maybe she can be out a little longer than *that*?"

She winks at me again—Clay rolls his eyes when his back is turned from her. I giggle. Haley trying to let me have more time and Clay saying less. Their goofy, playful arguments are amusing.

"Fine." He pauses. "You can have until one."

"That's better," whispers Haley, with the sound of success in her voice.

"Thanks."

HALEY TAGS BEHIND ME ON THE WAY TO MY ROOM.

"So what time is it at?" she asks, bouncing on my bed like

a child, looking at me curiously, like I'm going to tell her a big secret.

"Kelly wanted me to call before seven, so she could know whether or not to pick me up."

She tosses me the phone just as I slide into the chair by my desk.

I can hear the excitement in her voice when I tell her I can go. She says she already knows where Clay lives.

Haley grins after I hang up. She seems more excited than I am—and I am really *excited*.

"So what are you wearing tonight?" she asks, a tone in her voice hinting that she wants to pick.

I take the hint. "I don't know. What do you think is suitable?"

A smile spreads across her face. She leaps off the bed and runs to my closet. She pulls out a Black Bench pullover.

She hands it to me and steps out of the room so I can slip into the sweater. I feel the pull in my back when I barely raise my arms, and it hurts.

I stride to the full-length mirror. I gently lift the corner of my sweater up to examine where the pain is coming from. It is a dark purple and black bruise, the size of a door handle, which *caused* it.

I open the door. "Tah-dah."

Clay brings us both food, while Haley fiddles with my hair. As it turns out Haley is an only child, who has never been able to do a little sister's hair. She's never had a sister, and I have two older sisters who barely ever did anything with me. It's kind of like having none—but not. In the end she decides that just a tiny braid—made up of hair from my long, grown-out bangs—looks pretty, leaving the rest, in its natural loose curls, fall down my back.

THE SUN SLOWLY DISAPPEARS. TRAILING BEHIND IT ARE STREAM-
ers of pinks, oranges, and yellows. Shadows dance evilly around
us, making our surroundings darker.

I already trust Nish and Kelly because of their kindness toward me, but I'm not so sure about Bre.

I guess I should be used to getting looks, like the ones she
gives me... but I'm not.

"You know, this is going to be fun," declares Nish.

"Yeah! Hey, I wouldn't have gone if you guys didn't come with
me," Kelly replies. "I'm glad you were able to come, Arianna."

"I agree—me too. Thank you for the invitation."

Kelly, Nish, and I go together, whereas Bre caught a ride with
someone else, when she heard I was going too. It kind of hurts to
be disliked that much by so many people.

Mostly everyone sits by the cozy heat of the fire. That or some
are making their way to the group.

An icy gust rips through my sweater, chilling me, the hairs
on the back of my neck and arms rise. I feel as though I'm being
watched. I whirl around and glance into the dim light, but no one
seems to be there—just the shadows.

Nish grabs the sleeve of my sweater, dragging me along with
her and Kelly, toward the fire.

The yelling and singing flourishes as we near the group.
Several people playing guitars whoop, while all the others scream
their heads off, *way* out of tune. Some others pass around dark
glass bottles filled with darker liquid inside.

We slide onto a fallen tree next to a few people. They hardly
even notice us. They are too distracted yelling their heads off. But
one stops when one of the dark bottles is passed into their hands.
He takes a huge gulp and then passes it on to me. I take it from
him. Whatever it is it must not be that great. His face twitches
as he swallows, as if the liquid were bitter. The foul smell fills my

nose. I don't want to drink it, so I pretend to take a sip and then just pass it on to Nish, who takes a quick sip and passes it on. Her face also twitches into the same expression. Why would someone drink something that tastes foul?

The quick transfers of the heat and the cool breeze mixed with the horrific noise, causes my head to spin. I suddenly feel like I'm going to pass out. I shake my head, trying to clear it, but it is only making things worse. The heat causes my hair to stick to the back of my neck, but the next gust of wind chills me worse than before.

I look over to Nish and Kelly, who have both already begun singing along to a tune I've never heard before.

They probably wouldn't mind if I disappeared for a few short minutes on a walk.

THE COOL BREEZE WHISPERS IN MY EARS AND RUSTLES THROUGH my hair. The music and the singing fade the further I walk away. It feels nice to be alone. It has been so long since I have actually gotten the chance. Despite the dying light, approaching darkness, and ever-growing amounts of shadows, I feel utterly free.

I pull my hood over my head, trying to block the icy air from eating away at my ears, and stuff my hands in my pullover's pocket, continuing through the trees, not quite sure where I'm going.

Snap!

I whirl around in the direction of the noise, only to find… nothing. Another crisp blast tears through me, this time chilling me to the bone. The wind begins to pick up, and the trees seem to shudder.

I see it from the corner of my eye; a shadow advances quickly behind a tree just as I look up. The shadow maneuvers closer, moving just as swiftly and silently as before.

I cringe, my stomach aching painfully; I turn and run further in the woods. My foot catches in a tangle of vines. I nearly lose my footing but catch myself against a tree.

The barely audible footsteps near as I dash around another tree. Despite my heart heaving and stomach aching, I push myself forward and duck behind a small bush, waiting to see what will happen. I set my feet so I'm ready to leap out of my crouched position, if I need to get away.

Through the darkness I see a dark, built figure, lingering near a large-based tree. I hold my breath, thankful for my dark sweater and hood helping me blend into the shadows. I wait for the figure to continue, but it stands still as a statue.

Snap!

The dark figure glances in my direction and stares at the bush I'm hiding behind.

My heart races, and I fight the urge not to fall to the cold earth floor and cry, my stomach throbbing badly.

Snap!

The dark figure instinctively looks behind him and runs again, not toward me but past me, leaving behind in the breeze the smell of cologne and sweat.

I slump against the tree behind me, glad for the support, and close my eyes. The slight seconds of peace are over when I hear a group of booming voices and more branches snapping, coming straight toward where the dark figure had gone.

I sink closer to the ground, hiding behind the wide base of the trunk. Quietly I shift my body closer to the opposite side. Anxiety takes over, and my hands begin to tremble as I hear their noisy stomping and voices pass by.

I take a deep, shaky breath when they are out of hearing range and slump back against the tree.

My stomach feels like it is being stabbed over and over.

I hear a gasp from somewhere behind me. I jump. Then the dark figure drops to his knees beside me and plants a hand on my shoulder.

The pain vanishes.

I am about to cry out in surprise, but he plants his other hand over my mouth, catching the scream before it has a chance to be heard.

"Shhh!" he says, pausing. "I'm going to let go—okay—just promise me you won't scream?" he asks in a low, urgent voice.

I roll my eyes slightly and nod my head, my whole body now trembling. His long, narrow fingers uncover my mouth.

He stares at my face a moment, making sure he won't need to clamp a hand over my mouth again. I won't scream.

"They're gonna be back," he says. I sit still, like a frightened child, up against my tree, not sure what to respond. "As in—we should probably go," he says, somewhat annoyed.

He leaps to his feet, reaching down for my hand. I give it to him, letting him help me up, still not sure whether I should trust him or not.

Like everyone else, he is a lot taller than me, the top of my head barely level with his shoulders. He wraps his long, narrow fingers through mine, and together we run. My smaller legs hold me back a little; it is hard to keep a steady pace with his long strides. He slows down a bit, so he isn't dragging me behind him. Several branches scratch at my face while we run.

He looks behind him—at me—the corners of his mouth lifting into a grin. He shakes his head.

His dark hair bouncing in spiky strands across his forehead—the boy from the lake.

"Shorty, you should pick up the pace. They're after you, not me," he says almost jokingly, although I know he's right.

"What?" I almost yell, nearly tripping over a fallen tree. I never realized we were actually this far from the party.

"Brad," he says, pausing his sentence for a short breath. My lungs are beginning to burn and hurt, the cold air slicing down my throat. "And his buddies were planning to get back at you, ever since you broke his nose."

"Wait," I gasp, as we continue down the messy trail leading down the ravine. I nearly trip again but he reaches his arm around me and catches me before I fall. "How do you know I broke his nose?"

"Wow!"

"What?"

"That's what you want to know?" He shakes his head, "Not why he's so cruel by wanting to beat up someone of your"—he pauses—"size?" He chuckles.

"Then why?"

"Because you showed him up, put his dignity at a lower level. He wants to regain it."

"This is not the way I came," I state, changing the subject. We seem to be going in a different direction. I come to a halt, pulling him down by our linked hands. "Where are we going?" I demand.

His face now serious, he says, "My truck is parked along the highway just a ways away from the bonfire, and we're close." Impatiently searching for the right words, he says, "We can't go straight to the bonfire. They would be waiting there if they didn't find you out here already." He looks past me; I follow his eyes, just as four large guys appear at the top of the ravine. Standing among them is a monster full of hate and fury—Brad.

The boy with the dark hair jerks my hand as he sprints further down the trail, me stumbling slightly behind him. I double my strides just to keep up with him; my hood flies off my head, letting the cold air blow through my hair.

Just when I am nearly out of breath, but still running, I am struck in the back of the head with something hard. How did they get so close so fast? Oh wait; they had the inclination of the ravine. The edges of my vision blur. I try to shake the fuzzy feeling out of my head, but it just increases. I touch the tender spot gently; I clench my teeth to prevent myself from crying out. When I pull my hand away, it comes back covered in a dark liquid, almost black. I nearly fall over, but I somehow manage to keep my balance and continue on. I try to push myself harder. I *have* to get away from them.

Then I am struck again. This time gravity pulls me to the ground, yanking my hand from the boy's.

Brad stands above me, grinning at my crumpled form, with a large baseball bat in his hands, or maybe it's a stick—who knows? My head spins, and I feel like my skull is going to shatter, throbbing so intensely. I close my eyes. If he's going to kill me, I don't want to watch him do it.

I hear a yelp, then some fists being thrown, making contact with other bodies. I can barely open my eyes, even a narrow slit, to see what's going on; my lids pull down heavily, not wanting to open again. Sleep tries its hardest to yank me under. I refuse to surrender; I squint them, just to see the boy leaning over me, a tiny flashlight shining over my eyes. Where did he get a flashlight?

His face is full of concern. I see his mouth move, but I don't hear anything—just feel him pull me up into his arms almost effortlessly. He slips his arm under my knees.

He runs through the trees, me bumping along in his arms. My cheek is pressed into his chest and my hands in my lap. He holds onto me tightly. I feel a warm liquid run down my neck, streaming down my back, its warmth turning to icy cold fingers slicing everywhere it touches while the breeze bites at my nose and face.

As I am about to close my eyes again, he taps my face quickly. "Don't close your eyes—please—just don't close them," he says, sounding desperate. I wish I could see his face, but I can't. Everything hurts. "Finally," he gasps as we near a dark truck alongside the road, exactly where he said it'd be. I guess I can trust him.

He gently puts me into the passenger seat and runs around to the driver's side. My head feels heavy like lead, and my eyes droop, refusing to stay open. All I want is sleep. I am about to be pulled under again, but the boy reaches over the steering wheel and shakes my shoulder violently.

After what feels like forever, we finally stop. He gets out again and picks me up like a rag doll and runs toward a large opening. I am placed carefully on a bed. My eyes are forced open, and more lights are shone in them, causing my head to pound in resentment. My head hurts. My eyes want to close, but I'm not allowed sleep. Why am I not allowed?

CHAPTER 8

My mouth tastes bitter, and my tongue feels like sandpaper. I am barely able to open my eyes, them still being heavy with sleep. I manage to open them partly.

The room is small, with a few chairs and white walls. On one of the walls is a single picture—a kitty hanging from a tree branch saying, "Hang in there." On another wall is a window, with dark green curtains.

Something weird tingles in my hand. I look down. A single plastic tube runs into my hand and is taped there, to hold it in place. On my other hand is a small thing on my index finger attached to a beeping machine, with squiggly lines running in a continuum. I take a deep breath only to feel it catch in my throat, more tubes running into my nose. I try to sit up straight, but the wires and tubes pull, making it uncomfortable for me to move. I gasp, trying not to cry, but the tears run, burning down the sides of my face. I shouldn't move. It'll make everything hurt worse.

"It's okay," says a kind voice. I look up and see a slim woman in a pair of scrubs. She has long, dark hair tied back in a ponytail, standing close to the machine. She smiles graciously and gently touches my arm. She steps away from a liquid bag attached to the tube running into my hand. "I'm so glad you finally woke up. I'll go get the doctor."

What does she mean "finally woke up"? *How long was I out? It couldn't possibly have been that long? Could it?*

I expect the lady and the doctor to walk in when the door opens, but no. The boy with the dark hair walks in, closing the door behind him. He holds a steaming mug. His hair is tousled, and minor shadows form under his eyes. My heart leaps at the sight of him.

He trudges toward one of the chairs at my side, but then he looks up at me—and our eyes meet. A smirk of relief washes over his face.

"Finally you decide to wake up!" he says, picking up his pace; he drops down into the chair. "I was almost worried." His face beams.

I open my mouth to say something, but it comes out dry and scratchy, impossible to understand.

"Oh," is all he says. He gets up and walks to a shelf in the corner of the room that I hadn't noticed earlier. On the shelf, there sits a pitcher and several paper cups. He fills one and walks back over, handing it to me. I wince as I try to pull the cup to my mouth. Snatching the cup from my hands, he grins, shaking his head. He sets it on the side table and fumbles with the wrapper of a straw. When he finally gets it open, he pulls the cup and straw close to my mouth. The water feels heavenly running down my throat, cleansing it on the way down. After I empty the cup, he sets it back on the table.

"Better?"

"Thanks," I whisper, still unsure if my voice is back or if it's still hoarse.

He grins in response, looking down at his clasped hands

sitting on his lap. He looks relieved, more awake then he did when he first walked into the room.

"Random question," I begin.

"And what's that?" he asks, looking up.

"What's your name?"

"That's not exactly a random question." He laughs. "I would want to know that too." He pauses studying my face. "Max."

Max. It's a nice name. Now that there is actual light, I can see the fine details in his face. Black hair with dark brown strands, golden skin, and a lean but muscular build. His eyes—his eyes are beautiful, so completely extraordinary, a crystalline look to their magnificent blue. He wears a black jacket that has a zipper that goes up to his neck, outlining a sharp jawline. He still remains strangely familiar to me.

"How about you?" he asks.

"Me what?"

"What exactly is your name? I've heard about you. I've seen you around, but I never actually got to meet you. Everyone refers to you as 'Tough Girl' or 'Little Blond Girl' or even just 'The Girl Who Broke Brad's Nose.'" He laughs, a tinge of curiosity in his laugh. "I was a maintenance worker for the school this year. You can learn a lot from the students' gossip."

"Arianna," I reply.

"That's a pretty name," he says. "But can I give you a nickname? Your name is quite a mouthful."

"It depends," I say.

"On what?" he asks.

"What you choose, nothing too... cheesy," I reply, grinning.

"Okay." He taps his chin with his index finger, studying me, one eye squinting. "How about Reena?"

I like it. Having a nickname could mean that I could have a fresh start, a *real* fresh start.

I instantly regret it when I try to nod my head. It begins to throb. "I like it," I respond, wincing.

"Good." He laughs, clearly not noticing me wince. "Cause I was gonna call you that anyway."

I smile in response. He's definitely somewhat familiar to me, the brightness in his eyes and the cheeriness in his smile, I feel like I've seen him before. Not just when I came here, but before. That's impossible. Or is it?

"How did you know where I was? And why did you help me, if you didn't know who I was?" I ask.

"I feel like I've met you before," he says, "and after I heard of their plan, to snatch you up and drag you into the woods at the bonfire, I figured you'd need help." He pauses. "So I followed you."

"Thank you." I pause. "Both you and the nurse had the same reaction when I woke up. How long was I out, and um, what exactly happened?" I ask, almost dreading an answer. I twiddle my fingers out of nervous habit and wait for him to answer.

His face straightens. "Almost a week—six days actually. They hit you in the back of the head with a heavy piece of wood and gave you a very bad concussion."

I breathe out heavily, remembering Clay and Haley. I was supposed to come home. My heart fills with dread, and I have a difficult time trying to remain calm. I can hear the beeping on the monitor speed up.

"Does Clay know where I am?" I blurt out, not thinking that he might not know who I'm talking about.

"Clay...? Oh, Mr. Brown," he says. "He came a few times, actually even this morning; he sat with you for a while."

"Okay," I say, feeling somewhat relieved. I'm glad he at least knows where I am. "What about Brad and—?" I begin, but he cuts me off.

"Let's just say they probably won't be bothering you anymore." He grins and shrugs.

I feel myself smile. "Thank you," I say and reach out for his hand, barely lifting my arm off the bed. I can only imagine what he did.

He cups both his hands around my outstretched one, his long, narrow fingers gently sliding over my wrist.

The door squeaks open, and in walks the nurse and doctor. The doctor, with graying hair and square glasses, smiles as he sets down a folder at the foot of my bed.

Max sits up straight in his chair, releasing my hand from both of his, just leaving one, with his fingers entwined with mine.

"How are you feeling, Ms. Garcia? Clay will definitely be overwhelmed to know you're awake." He smiles kindly. "You got quite the nasty concussion." He flips back and forth through the nearly empty folder. I wonder how there is even anything in it. "If this young fellow hadn't brought you in when he did, you probably would've died," he continues, gesturing to Max.

I look over at Max gratefully. His face turns almost a pale pink but is immediately back to its original color. The nurse adjusts the clear bag full of liquid, attached to the tubes in my hand, adding something.

"You had a nasty gash on the back of your head when you came in. We stitched you up, but you lost quite a bit of blood. You were barely conscious. Then"—he hesitates—"you slipped into a coma. We were afraid you would have brain damage when you'd wake up… that is if you'd wake up. Luckily you didn't crack your skull. You may suffer from memory loss and you will have to reteach your muscles to work. Even after a little while of being in a coma, your muscles tend to weaken."

I nod, looking down into my lap, at my hand in Max's. What

is there for me to say? Nothing, but that I am in great debt to Max—he saved my life.

"You're quite the miracle. I'll have someone notify Clay. He'll want to know the good news," says the doctor, leaving the room, followed by the nurse. As the door closes, a brisk gust of air runs across my skin, allowing for goose bumps to appear. I rub my arm, trying to warm myself, but my icy fingers chill me more.

Noticing, Max releases my hand and bends over me, reaching for the other end of the blanket. He smells like cologne and fresh air. He places a fleecy blanket on my lap all the way up to my shoulders.

"Did you feel it too?" he bursts out randomly, leaning over me, his hands on my shoulders where he holds the blanket up.

"What?"

"The pain, every time we were near," he asks desperately, looking into my eyes.

"Yes," I squeak, nausea overtaking my head. I have a sudden need to puke, but there is nothing in my stomach for me to let out. I can barely hear him or even notice him still leaning over me. My vision goes fuzzy, and his words sound distant, my eyes close and I feel heavy. I barely notice Max grasp my hand, his face flourished with a new look of concern.

The room transforms.

I—we—Max and I are both back at the palace. I recognize the gold and white walls and the fancy architecture, the high-rise domes. It changes to the scenery of my father's study. Max, still grasping onto my hand, looks at me wide-eyed. Inside the study my family are all kneeling with their hands behind their heads. Dozens of men are all wearing entirely black from head to toe.

Except one—

He is tall and also wearing black, but his head is uncovered. His skin is ghastly white, even more pale with the mass of dark hair covering his head. Eyes like I have never seen before—like pits, almost entirely black, just a thin line of silver for the iris—only one race.

Onychinus.

"Where is it?" yells the man with the pale skin, glaring down at a badly bruised man, barely recognizable, my father.

"Where is what?" asks my father calmly.

"Oh, don't play stupid with me. You know exactly what I came for," yells the man again. "And what a lovely family you have here," he says in an agitated yet eerily calm voice. "I'm sure you wouldn't want their deaths to be on you, just because you were too stupid not to give me what I ask for."

He walks over to Flora; he grabs her hand from behind her head and yanks her to her feet.

Shadows have formed under her eyes so deep blue that they appear almost as if they're bruises. Maybe they are?

"You know, I hadn't exactly planned on killing anyone today, but I'm sure I can make time, under the given circumstances you are not willing to do as I ask." He pulls a shiny dagger with an ancient-looking pattern on the handle out of his waistband.

My father glares at the man. Flora's face is nearly the color of snow, but still she stands calmly. That's one of the things I admire about her; no matter what happens, she always stays calm. I wish I were more like her, to hold all that bravery that she carries.

I'm about to run to her, but I'm not exactly sure what I will do when I get to her. Max stands still, his hand clamped around mine so tightly I fear he's snapping my bones. I wince, but he barely loosens his grip, not enough to let me slip out of.

"No!" yells my father. "It is not here! Don't hurt her or I swear I'll—"

"You'll what?" He mocks, playing with the blade. "Banish me, like you did my son. You know I always find my way, wherever you would send me; I would come back and I would kill you."

What is he talking about? If he's from another planet then how could he have a son here?

Max and I both exchange a questioning look.

"You know I'm kind of bored of your stalling. Tell me where it is if it's not here."

"Never!"

"Okay, have it your way," he says plainly. He raises the knife high, bringing it down with great force.

"Wait!"

The blade lingers maybe millimeters away from Flora's heart. Now I see the fear in her eyes. Coral gazes at the dagger, trying to move it with her mind, but the dagger remains unmoving in the man's hand.

The man glances down at her. "You know magic doesn't work on this blade, love, so I would quit staring at it if I were you." She doesn't move her gaze. She remains still, trying to rip it from his grasp. It doesn't move. He pushes Flora out of his way and steps in front of Coral, kneeling down in front of her. "Will you tell me where it is, since you're so keen on getting my attention?"

"No."

"You are all useless!" he spurts angrily, and plunges the dagger deep into her chest.

My heart races and tears flood my eyes—again.

He turns and yanks Flora over beside him and drags her so she kneels in front of our father. Now fear is written entirely over her face.

Why doesn't anyone move—can't they fight back?

Little silver cubes sit in every corner of the room. How come I don't ever remember seeing them there before? I couldn't save Coral—it happened too fast, but maybe I can save Flora. I try to run again, but Max holds me back.

"Let me go!" I demand, trying to wrench my arm from his grasp.

Max holds his grip and leans close to my ear. "We can't do anything. This is a directive."

A directive? So I can't let go of his hand or I will be alone during this… I can't be alone. Not now. The only thing keeping him with me now is our connecting hands. I've heard of directives but I don't understand how they work.

"It's on Earth," whispers my father, holding his breath.

"Of all places, you send it there?" asks the man, almost laughing. How can someone laugh after murdering someone? "Oh well, you never were the smartest man now were you? Hey, maybe I'll be reunited with my son."

"Well, you know where it is now. Let my family go," says my father.

"No," the man says bluntly, picking at his cuticles with the blade. "I'll need your cooperation further on. For all I know you could be lying and the source could still be here." He pushes Flora to the tiled floor.

"No!" I scream, afraid he's going to kill her too. No one hears me, only Max. I drop to my knees, sobbing; he drops down to my side and wraps his other arm around me.

The man doesn't kill Flora. Perhaps he's being merciful. I see Coral's body on the floor motionless, her face silenced with death, but her empty eyes are on me. Did she see me? Was she the one who sent the directive? I try to fight the burning liquid flowing behind my eyes, but it doesn't go away.

My heart breaks, and emptiness overcomes me.

Maybell, Father, and my mother all have the same horrified faces. Flora stays down.

"If you do not cooperate with me, I will kill this young lady, as well as everyone on your planet one by one. But I will leave you, so you can watch it all. Every death, all that blood on your hands. Then when everyone is dead, I will kill you and preserve you in a star for all of eternity where you will be immortal and suffer with the memories of these deaths all alone," he says, wiping Coral's blood onto a handkerchief taken from the table beside him. "This was just an example, so that you know I am not bluffing."

From the place where my sister was pierced glows a dull golden light, lifting up into tiny particles, kind of like a star. It dissolves, just before the man turns around.

"Some of my men will stay here to keep things in... order," he says, "and you, sir, will stay on my planet until I find it and am finished with you."

"You're a monster," shouts my father.

The man laughs.

Then the vision blurs. The last thing I see is my sister laying on the floor lifeless.

CHAPTER 9

WE ARE BOTH BACK IN THE HOSPITAL ROOM. MY SKIN FEELS warm and damp, and my eyes burn. Don't cry, I tell myself. I blink, trying to push dampness back, but every time I close them I see death painted on the insides of my eyelids.

Someone has sent me a directive. My family, my planet, and even me—we are all in danger.

I glance over at Max with glassy eyes. "You saw that—right?" Of course he did. How could he not have?

"Yeah." He pauses. His face is darkly stricken. He tugs the collar of his jacket higher up his neck. "So you're the princess?" he says.

"Yeah, why?" I flush with anger. The *only* thing he caught out of this display was that! My sister just got murdered in front of us, and he *only* caught one small, unimportant detail!

"Never mind," he says, shaking his head. "Oh my God," he says, his face horrified.

Seriously, he should just get over it, I think, and then I decide to say it out loud. "You know if you can't deal with—"

"Do you think that directive was sent just now or awhile ago?" he interrupts.

Okay, great, he's not still upset about the whole royalty thing. But then the question really sinks in. When was that message sent? They could be on their way now. Oh no.

"We have to go," he says, almost in a daze, staring at the wall across from us.

"Not just yet."

"Why? Whatever it is that they want, they won't bargain for it—they will kill and take," Max says, his blue eyes strikingly serious.

"I need to speak to Clay," I tell him. I was unconscious for a week. I can't just randomly get up and leave as soon as I wake up, without telling him.

"Fine, you stay here and wait for him to come. I'm going to my place to pick up a few things; I'll be back in a little while." He gently squeezes my hand and leaves the room.

I slide my hand to my neck. It catches on my locket. I start fiddling with it around my neck. I had completely forgotten about it. I am a little surprised that it is still with me, considering everything I had before I got here is now gone, except my shoes, which sit under the corner of my bed. My clothes are gone; I wear just a hospital gown, which is extremely thin.

I snap open the locket and peek inside. The photo of my whole family; my father and mother on one side and my sisters and I on the other, all of us smiling, a sight I will never see again. The worst part about Coral's death is I *couldn't* do anything to stop it; I just stood there and watched. It feels as though I've betrayed my entire family. As much pain as I feel, only a single tear runs down my cheek, nothing more. I run my fingers over all of their faces in the picture. "I love you, and I will avenge you," I whisper.

I slide my fingers over the photo once more, and that's when I feel it—a rather large bulge protrudes from under it. How did I not notice it before? I peel back the photo of my sisters and me, and behind it is a small, folded piece of paper.

I take it out. My shaky hands barely manage to unfold it.

A tiny baby, maybe a few months old. She looks a lot like me, but I know it can't be. This little girl already has a star under her ear. My heart sinks. In the background stands my father, Flora and Coral. I stand beside my mother, smiling down at the infant, holding her hands. I was always told that the baby had died. I remember being very little and never understanding why my mother never spoke to me as often as my older sisters.

But now I know. She had lost a child all those years ago, who looked quite a bit like me. Why would my father give me this?

On the back are words that make my heart stand still.

Dearest Arianna,

This is Mira. She was born when you were about six years old. You probably don't remember her. She had her mark when she was born. She is very powerful, and also has a very bold destiny... like yours. She is still alive and on earth also. She was sent away so she could learn her powers at a safe distance. Anyways, I want you to find her.

PS: Read the letter in your bag.

—KT

My brain swarms; with so much newfound knowledge my head aches.

I just saw one of my sisters murdered. My parents and friends are all in danger. My home is at a high risk of being destroyed. And I just found out I have a sister whom I believed was dead all those years ago, who is alive, and my father wants me to find her.

I fold the photo back up and place it the way it was before and snap the locket shut.

I don't know what I feel. Happy I have a little sister, that's still alive? Angry, that my father never told me this before, and has been lying all these years? Disgusted that they sent an infant away, just because she was powerful... like me, although they didn't send me away as a little baby? Or sad and torn up because my oldest sister was murdered right in front of me and I wasn't able to do anything about it? And horrified, that corrupt men are going to destroy my planet and everyone on it, and possibly even myself, and make my father immortal so he'll have to suffer from the memories?

I thought Brad was the worst of my problems, but now every-thing is way more complicated than high school drama. Brad is no longer even a problem now.

Clay comes into the room with a huge grin painted on his face, "Nice to see you awake sleepyhead—" He stops when I look up at him. "What's wrong?"

"I need to leave," I say.

"What? Why?"

"My oldest sister was murdered, corrupt and cruel people are coming after me, and staying in this bed is an easy place for them to find me," I say bluntly. His face is stunned, and he looks like I spoke to him in a different language, dumbfounded.

"Well, how do you know?" he asks with pain in his eyes.

"I was sent a directive. Max saw it too."

"What? Who sent it? How? What?" He doesn't even really know what he's asking, but I see the pain growing in his eyes.

"Did you know that I have a little sister?" I ask. The question has been eating me up ever since I found out.

His face turns instantly red, and he looks down at the floor.

"You did? Why didn't you tell me?"

"It wasn't my place to tell you," he whispers. "It was your father's."

THE GOLDEN PEARL | 89

Seeing his discouraged face, I try to push my jumbled emotions back and try and focus on what I'm going to do.

"Do you know where she is? I am supposed to find her."

"Yes."

"Clay, I'm going to need your help," I say, calming my voice.

I ask him to bring me clothes, but luckily he has already brought some, because he knew I was awake and would ask sooner or later.

The beeping increases dramatically when I pull the wires off me. The nurse runs into the room. "What on earth are you doing?"

"I need to leave, and this beeping is giving me a headache. Will you turn it off?" I stare into her eyes, she does exactly as I say. She flicks off the machine, and the lines disappear. And my head clears, slightly.

The second gift I have learned since my birthday—coercion, meaning I am able to compel people to do what I want them to do. I plunk a black beanie onto my head. I leave the bandage on, suddenly very self-conscious. Max and Clay and everyone else who visited me saw me sleep. How creepy is that?

I ask Clay to leave the room, and when he finally closes the door, I slip into a pair of jeans and sweater and stuff the shoes onto my feet. I lean against the shelf that holds the pitcher of water, to maintain my balance; I nearly forget how my muscles work. The doctor did say that it would take some time. The problem though is that I don't have time. I look up into the mirror above the shelf. My eyes have dark shadows underneath them, making the rest of my face look really pale. A few scabbing cuts are fixed into the right side of my face, probably from running through the trees, and a fading bruise colors a section of my forehead. My face looks horrible. I've also lost some weight, which I really didn't need to lose.

I pretty much compel most of the staff to allow me to leave.

Clay drives me home. What's home? Down the road I see just the rooftop of Clay and Haley's farmhouse. Everything that had begun to feel like home again is now a loss about to happen. Again I try to remember, what's home?

Haley runs to meet me when we step in through the front door. She wraps her arms around me. "I thought you weren't going to be home for a while. I'm so glad you're okay," she says, loosening her grip. "What's wrong?" she asks, backing up.

"Long story," says Clay. "She needs a few things, but then she needs to leave. I'll tell you later."

I can barely focus as I walk down the hallway and drag myself up the stairs.

My room is gloomy. Only overcast light seeps in through the window. Instantly I grab my bag from my desk and throw it onto the bed. I find a duffel bag in the very back of my closet. I empty some of my clothes from the room into the bag, mainly all the stuff I think I'll need. But I don't know what I need.

I find the golden pearl and stuff it into my pocket. This is what they are after. In my heart I know it.

It feels beyond unreal to be leaving this place. I thought it was going to be my new home. I thought that I would be able to keep my new friends, Kelly, Bre, and Nish, but I guess my future doesn't involve any of this. Again the same question that's been haunting fills my head. What's *home*?

I manage to get to the bottom of the stairs, without me passing out. I drop my duffel bag near the door but sling my other dark gold bag over my shoulder.

Clay and Haley are arguing, but I only catch one statement made. "She has a concussion and just woke up from a coma; she can't just go off to wherever." Clay must have told her.

Two dark vehicles, a jeep and a truck that I recognize to be Max's, pull up in the driveway.

"Well, I better get going."

"Take care of yourself," says Haley, stepping around the corner of the kitchen island. "I wish this never happened. I better see you again," she says, giving me another hug and kissing my forehead.

Clay stands beside her and gives me an envelope. After she lets me go, he gives me a hug as well. "I love you and I'm sorry."

Outside one of the vehicles honks their horn.

Max jumps out of the driver's side and takes my duffel bag from Clay and throws it into the box of the truck, then folds the cover over it. Then he runs around to meet me. He carefully takes my hand and helps me into the backseat of the truck. A boy, maybe a year or two younger than me, sits in the front seat. Max closes the door behind me, and I hear him and Clay talk in low voices together, but the only thing that isn't muffled is, "Take care of her."

It sounds almost like what a father says to his daughter when she sends her on a date for the first time, although this is *way* different.

Max hops back into the truck and follows the other vehicle out of the yard.

"So who's this?" I ask when we're on the highway. I'm heavy on pain meds, so I don't really understand everything I'm saying. The storm clouds hang low over the sky.

"Miles," says the boy. He turns around in his seat; he has black hair with tips that are dark purple. "So this is the girl Max saved?" he asks to no one in particular.

"Yes," I respond.

"He's been talking about you nonstop since you were in the hospital. I can understand why. You're so pretty," he says, looking back from me to Max. "Besides the few marks," he says again, gesturing to my cuts; he doesn't see the bruise on my forehead, because it's covered by my beanie.

"Shut up," Max replies.

"Okay, okay, I was just being friendly," he complains. "How old are you?"

I wait a moment before answering. "Seventeen, why?"

"Oh…" He drags on for a moment. "She's too young for you bro," Miles says, laughing.

Max turns his head and faces Miles and just glares at him, a glare that says, "I'll kill you if you don't shut up." How old is Max?

He opens his mouth to say something else, but Max punches him in the shoulder, and turns his attention back on the road. Miles cries out and then sits back properly in his seat.

"Best quit talking, or you'll ride in the trunk or in the jeep beside Ruban," Max says. Who's Ruban?

"Who's that?"

"Ruban—oh, that's this little shit's older brother," says Max punching the younger boy's shoulder. "You'll get to meet the others soon enough. They are much like us… but not in the same way. They are alike in the way that they are not from here."

I feel suddenly and completely nauseous, like throwing up. I guess that's a side effect of having a concussion. After I compelled the doctors, they ended up putting me on a medication that's supposed to relieve pain and dizziness, but I think it just made it worse.

The letter from Clay sits in my bag, as well as the one from my father. Clay's is closer, not by much, but it still is, so I decide to open it. It is fairly short.

Arianna,

The first thing I want you to know is that I really am your uncle. Your father is my older half-brother. I feel like it is all

my fault, that you got a concussion. I was supposed to take
care of you, but I didn't do my job. You got hurt. Mira is in a
private school, sent there by your father.

Tanako City,
Fall Avenue 961, ST. 28

All you have to do is look for a younger version of you. She is
much like you; I have met her once. She is kind, brave, and
powerful, though she doesn't quite know the extent of her
abilities yet. You'll need to be there for her.

I love you and wish you the best.

Clay

I'm kind of curious as to why Mira had been sent to a private
school, yet I was sent to live with Clay and Haley. Why couldn't
we have both ended up in the same place?

"Max, we need to go to Tanako City," I say.

"Why do we need to go there?"

"Because I have to find my sister," I reply, looking at the reflection of his eyes in the mirror.

I can see the confusion in them. He has witnessed one of my
sisters' deaths. And now, I'm telling him I have to find another. I
can understand his confusion. I'm confused myself.

"I know," I say, answering the question I know he is about to
ask. "I thought my little sister was dead for the past eleven years
of my life."

"All right." He nods, looking at me through the mirror. "It's
about a two-hour drive; you should probably get some rest."

Miles flicks on the radio station. It blasts loudly, making my head throb. I put a hand to my head. Max immediately turns it down lower, smacking Miles again.

I keep myself buckled in the middle seat and lay across the backseat, using my bag as a pillow.

CHAPTER 10

"Wakey! Wakey, sleepyhead," Miles says, leaning close to my face. I nearly bash my head when I back away from him. "You know you look really peaceful when you sleep," he says, now that my eyes are fully open.

We are parked beside a gas pump. A checkered blanket lies across my lap.

"We stopped once more before here," he says. "Max told me not to wake you at the last stop, but he never said I couldn't wake you this time." He laughs.

I sit completely upright and push all my hair over my shoulder.

"Why don't ya talk much?"

"Because she isn't feeling too great," answers Max, climbing back into the truck, holding a few plastic bags. "And she probably doesn't want to talk to idiots." He laughs. Miles makes a face at him.

He hands a water bottle to me and one to Miles. He hands me a straw, so I don't have to tilt the water bottle back when I drink from it. "Drink—you're probably dehydrated," he says. He mutters to himself, "I wish you still had that IV."

"I totally am," jokes Miles and begins chugging down his water.

I pop the straw into the bottle and take a small sip. "Thanks," I say.

"Whoa, whoa, whoa, dude. Why didn't you get me a straw? That's not fair," complains Miles, his bottle already nearly empty.

"You don't need one."

"What if I wanted one?"

"Well, next time I'll get you a straw, you big baby!" remarks Max.

"There better be a next time," says Miles.

"How much further?" I ask.

"About twenty minutes. What is the address?" Max asks.

Miles talks everyone's heads off. I basically only half listen to him. I mainly look out the window, at the moving landscapes, which kind of make my head spin. I learn within the twenty minutes that Ruban is Miles's older brother, and that Miles loves fries dipped in milkshakes. He talks about food continually. I'm surprised as to how skinny and gangly he is. He's actually quite entertaining, with the randomness he pops up with.

We finally get into the city; it takes us awhile to find the address. We pull up in front of a building. On a huge metal sign it reads:

Mavel Arts Academy for Girls

What am I going to say? I have never met her before. Last I saw her she was an infant. I don't even really know what to expect. My heart is both excited and nervous to finally meet her. I wonder where she would be safer, with me or here. The Onychinus men could come here easily and kill her, looking for me. I can't afford to take a chance, not with someone else's life. Not with my family's life. I wasn't able to prevent Coral's death, but I'll try to stop the chance of Mira's. I *want* her to come with me.

The building is tall and made of sharp-cornered bricks. Around it is a tall, dark metal picket fence. It doesn't look like the most welcoming place. It looks strict and shadowy. The grass surrounding it is all a dead brown, and all the leaves have already fallen from the trees, making it look messy around the yard.

Why would my father send her to a place like this?

"Do you want me to come in with you?" asks Max, seeing the concern on my face.

"Please."

This shouldn't be a problem. I can persuade people to do what I want, and I can get the teachers to let her go, if they are unwilling.

"I'll wait in here," murmurs Miles. That's got to be the first logical thing I have heard him say so far, after his hours of endless chatting.

Max helps me out of the truck. The breeze bites my cheeks, until we get into the school.

The school looks very professional. It is super clean, with not even a speck of dust to be seen. There are marble floors and dark bluish-gray walls. All of the furniture is black, even the staircase. A few girls in uniform walk into an office. Besides them, the hallway is basically empty.

"Can I help you?" asks a tall, thin, strict looking lady. She wears a dark suit jacket with a matching skirt. Her hair is pulled back tightly from her face, revealing some wrinkles around her eyes and some creases in her forehead.

"Ah, yes," I say, glancing at Max. "We are looking for a little girl, about eleven or twelve years old. Her name is Mira."

The lady's strict expression flickers into a look of shock, and her eyebrows raise for a short moment. "Come with me," she says and walks farther down the hall to our right.

Max and I follow her down the long corridor and turn a

corner, before she stops at a door. On the door it says on a silver plaque, "Detention."

I can't help but smile. My little sister got detention. I wonder what she did. Did she turn out to be a troublemaker, or are they just really strict here?

The lady takes the ring of keys off the chain dangling around her neck and unlocks the door. The lady opens the door for us to enter. It is very dark in the room

We step inside, and the lady follows us in. She flicks on a light switch.

In one of the far desks from the door sits a little girl. Her head is on her desk, and her hair like liquid gold falls all around her. The lady walks up to the desk and knocks on it loudly.

The little girl lifts her head slowly. Her eyes are watery when she looks up to see Max and me, standing at the door.

Her expression immediately changes to a huge grin. She pushes all her hair away from her face, with one stroke of her hand. "I knew it!" she shrieks. She jumps up from her chair and runs over to me, wrapping her arms around me. I almost lose my balance, but Max puts a hand against my back stabilizing me. "I told you so!" she shouts at the lady. "I wasn't lying."

"What?" Max asks, shocked, his hand still on my back. His eyebrows are raised, and he looks as confused as I feel.

"I drew a picture. Most of them come true! But *sshhheeee* didn't believe me." She drags the *she*, to add exaggeration.

"That's why you got detention?" I ask.

"Yep, it doesn't matter. I was right! I knew you'd come." She wraps her arms around me again.

"Okay. So we're in kind of a hurry," I say. "Do you want to come, I guess?"

"Yeah!"

"Miss, you can't just take her. We have strict policies here," interrupts the woman, her arms crossed against her chest. "It's kidnapping, and you will be charged."

"Go get your things," I tell Mira. "Max, can you help her, please?"

"You sure?" he asks, making sure I'll be all right on my own, his blue eyes full of concern.

"I'll be along in a minute."

He takes his hand off my back and grabs onto Mira's hand. She bounces excitedly out the door.

I step toward the lady, but she takes a step back. I look into her eyes and tell her, "You'll tell everyone Mira's relative is transferring her to another school. That she has left already and says good-bye to everyone." The lady looks back at me with blank eyes and nods. "Now go about your usual daily business," I finish. She walks out of the room.

I lean against one of the desks, exhausted. It doesn't seem to take much to tire me. My muscles are still failing me for trying to hold myself upright.

How did Mira know we'd be coming for her? I wonder if she even knows who I am. Does she know the situation? It's going to be heartbreaking to tell her, if she doesn't already know.

I wish she could have met Coral before she was murdered.

I'm going to take care of her. I'm going to make sure she's safe.

I step into the long, dark corridor and slowly make my way into the main room. Mira hops down the very last step, just as I turn the final corner into the main room. She wears her school uniform, which consists of a navy blue sweater, white shirt, and plaid navy blue and black skirt. She wears a matching hat with a ribbon bow. She carries her jacket, her small leather bag swung over her shoulder across her body. Max follows slightly behind carrying a small trunk. He raises his eyebrows at me when he sees me coming.

Mira runs to me and grabs my hand. She looks up at me, her face gleaming. I smile down at her.

She has heavy black eyelashes and curly blonde hair. She looks a lot like me, just like Clay had said. We both have the same facial features: round chin, fair complexion, and similar-shaped eyes. Her eyes are green too, but she has a single gold speck in one of her eyes, whereas I have three in my right eye.

Once we get into the truck, I ask Mira. "So, may I ask how you knew we were coming?"

"Oh, easy. I have this weird thing. I can see an image. It comes to me kinda like a snapshot, and the image is only there for about a second." She says, "I have to put it down on paper before I forget it. Later on I find out, it's true."

"How long have you had it?" asks Max, focusing on the road.

"Forever, I guess." She pauses. "The teachers at that school believed I was a danger to be around."

"So, I know you drew a picture of us, but how did you know we were safe to go with?" I ask.

She pulls a crumpled paper out of her bag and passes it to me. It is a drawing of me and Max together standing in the doorway of the detention room, smiling at her.

"I knew," she says proudly, "and also because of this." Reaching into her bag again she pulls out an identical photo to the one I have in my locket, and hands it to me.

"Do you know who I am?"

"Not exactly, but I know I have to be with you," she says. "You're this girl," and points at the little me, in the photo.

"Oh, my name is Arianna, but I go by Reena. This is Max and Miles." I gesture to the boys in the front seats.

Miles spins around in his seat, clearly happy I introduced him. "You know you two look a lot alike." He grins. "How old did you say you were?" he asks Mira.

"I didn't." She grins at him.

"She's too young for you, bro," Max says, laughing, repeating what Miles had said to him in the conversation we had earlier this afternoon.

"I wasn't asking that," growls Miles. "The point that I was getting at, before I was rudely interrupted was, you guys could be twins from different times."

"Oh, okay, sure, buddy, whatever you say," Max says chuckling.

"Hey I have a question," says Mira. She pulls her sketch pad out of her bag. "Do you recognize this man?" She flips through the pages, finally coming to the right one. She hands it to me.

On the paper is a photo of a man, with dark clothing and dark hair. His skin is left white on the page. His eyes appear to be like pits. He is the man who murdered Coral. At the bottom of the page are ten small glass cases. Five are full. Inside are the jewels of the lost planets; Citrino, Spinel, Amethystus, Rhodolite, and Sapphirus. The next one is open and empty, waiting for its jewel, my jewel. Surrounding the entire drawing are masses of swirls.

I gasp. I know exactly what this picture means.

"When did you draw this?"

"About an hour after I drew the picture of you and Max. What does it mean?" she asks.

"It means they found the portal," I whisper. My heart pounds in my chest, and my head throbs.

CHAPTER 11

THE TRUCK IS SILENT AGAIN. THE DAY IS SWALLOWED UP BY THE night. The clouds cover the moon, revealing only a dimly lit sky. On the dash the clock reads 2:25 a.m.

Miles snores, and Mira lies across the backseat and sleeps. I feel drowsy too. I would sleep too, but it wouldn't be fair to Max, who has to stay awake because he's the one driving.

"Hey, Max," I whisper.

"Yeah."

"I think we should pull over for the night and stop somewhere," I tell him.

"Good idea. There's about twenty more minutes before we reach the next town. We can rent a room then," he agrees, rubbing his eyes. He hands me his phone from his coat pocket. "Here, call Isla. It's on speed dial. She's in the jeep. Tell her we're stopping in the first motel we see."

The call gets picked up almost immediately. It doesn't even completely ring once.

"Hey, what's up?" asks the girl on the phone. She has a nice voice—strong, sweet, and slightly accented.

"Max says we're stopping in the first motel we see. There's about fifteen minutes till we get to town." I respond.

"Great, 'cause Ace can barely stay in between the lines."

"That's not good. Okay, bye."

The phone clicks off, ending the call. I hand the phone to Max. He stuffs it into his pocket.

It's an uncanny motel. Even if there was light outside, it would still have the same eerie effect. Paint from the siding peels in large quantities, leaving behind chips in the dirt beside the wall. Some of the windows are camouflaged behind thick spider webs, silvery in the minimal light. There are two floors, an upstairs and a downstairs. The stairs appear old. I will be afraid if I have to walk on them. The brittle steps look like they could crack even under the weight of a mouse.

Max and I go in through the front door; it creaks as he opens it for me. Inside is not as freakishly breakable as the outside appears to be. On the front desk sits a bell, beside it a note saying "Ring for Service." I pound my fist on it. It dings loudly, echoing in the nearly empty room, making me jump.

The loud abrupt noise definitely would have gotten me out of bed, but not the owner.

The walls are old, gross yellow, and a caving in vinyl flooring sheets the room. A large crack begins in the floor, from the corner all the way to the side table under a rug.

"This is ridiculous," hisses Max, pressing the bell over and over again.

We see lights flicker on in the back. Max quits pounding on the bell and grins at me. I shake my head and grin back at him.

A grumpy-looking old man walks out from behind the door.

His thinning gray hair is tousled, and he wears a frown that looks like it could be permanent.

"It's unmistakably ignorant to wake a man," says the man. His eyebrows crease in his forehead. He's a lot shorter now that he's closer. I choke down a hysterical laugh. He stands behind the desk; his cheeks are turned down into an angry frown. A stained bath robe and striped pajamas encase his round belly.

"What you laughing at, girl?" spurts the man.

I feel myself wanting to laugh again. Instead I choke it down, putting on a straight face. I know it won't last long. "Nothing, long day."

Max steps forward, closer to the desk.

"We need two rooms with two queen-size beds in each." Thank goodness he's doing the talking. Otherwise I'd have burst out hysterically by now.

"Sure you don't want one room?" he asks, yawning. He rubs his balding head.

"Yes. I'm sure. Do you have it or not?" asks Max, clearly getting frustrated with the man.

"Yeah," he replies in a grumpy voice. "Teenagers," he mutters to himself. He takes out two keys from a drawer. "It'd be five hundred, for both the rooms."

"What! Five hundred?"

"Yeah, is that an echo I hear?" mocks the man. "Take it or get."

"Fine, we'll take them." Max slides out his wallet from his back pocket. He has only a little bit of cash. "Do you take credit?" he asks.

"Buck only," the man says, grinning, with yellow teeth to match the walls, probably from years of tobacco use and not brushing his teeth.

I put my hand on Max's arm. I pull out my own wallet. When

I open it, there immediately is $500, in twenties. I count it in front of the crooked old man.

"Just make the girlfriend pay," he taunts. "And where does a young pretty girl like you get so many bucks?"

I don't answer. I'm afraid that if I do it'll cause trouble. Then he'd keep the money and not let us have the rooms.

Max stuffs his wallet in his back pocket. "Just give us the keys."

The man frowns, dropping the keys into Max's hand, and saying, "Room one-ten and one-fifteen."

Max grabs my hand and basically drags me out the door.

"You're welcome. Whatever, I'm going to bed," grumbles the man. He turns and walks back through the doors he came through moments earlier.

"I'm sorry," Max says, once we're outside.

"It's fine," I tell him. To be honest I have no idea why he's apologizing. "Let's just go to bed."

Room 110 and 115 turn out to be right across from each other. They are not overly big, but the bonus is they have beds, bathrooms, and hot water.

Max tells the others that the boys share one room and girls share the other. Isla, the one I spoke to earlier on the phone, immediately trudges toward one of the beds and kicks off her shoes. I learn the other girl's name is Elle; she dumps a backpack on the bed beside Isla and starts to take off her shoes.

Max follows me into the room with Mira in his arms; she looks so small and fragile. I would have carried her in myself, but I'm not exactly strong enough to carry my own weight right now, let alone someone else's body.

I slip her shoes off her feet, and Max slides her into the empty bed.

"Thanks," I whisper.

He nods toward the door. I follow him. It's a chilly crisp breeze outside. I can barely make out half his face in the darkness.

"You know they're right, the two of you definitely do look quite a bit alike."

I sigh. Because we look alike, my mother never spoke to me. I reminded her of her lost daughter, even though she still had me.

"There's something different though," he says.

"What?" I ask suddenly, very curious.

"I'll tell you when I'm one hundred percent certain."

I know he won't tell me the difference tonight, so I change the subject. Instead. I look down at my hands and intertwine them together. "I feel like a terrible person," I say.

"You're not," he says bluntly.

I shake my head slowly. "I never thought... Had I known she was still alive..." I feel my eyes burn.

"It's okay," he says. "It's not your fault."

I still feel like it's my fault, for not knowing. But there was no way I could have known. Margaritan has secrets. If they do not want you to know, then you won't.

I remember the sadness, the darkness of everything during that time.

"I should have showed you this before," he says. He unzips his jacket and pulls the collar down, just enough for me to see. It's silver, but it is rimmed with gold and another thin line of black beside it, his star.

I've never seen anything like it before. I've only seen solid silver ones, and mine, a solid gold one. I reach out and touch the skin under his ear. It is warm under my touch, despite the coldness of the air.

"It's amazing," I whisper.

"I feel like we've met before," he says. "You seem so familiar to me. I just can't seem to remember."

I feel the exact same way. Ever since I saw him by the lake, I've just wanted to be near him the whole time. We both had that pulling sensation, to get closer. When we made contact in the woods that night Brad came after me, when Max put his hand on my shoulder, the pain stopped. Kind of like a spell linking us together, or maybe causing pain to keep us apart. I don't know if I will ever find out.

His eyes study my face in the dimness. My hand is still on his neck. I pull it back. He catches it before it falls to my side and holds it.

I pull my hair to the side with my other hand and reveal my star, a solid gold one.

He looks at it, and seems to want to ask something. His eyes wear a questioning look. He shakes his head.

"We should go to bed," he says, releasing my hand.

"I guess." I really don't want to go to bed, but my mind is exhausted.

He starts toward his door. A dim light flickers above our heads.

"Hey Max?" I blurt out before he reaches it. He turns. "Thanks."

He nods his head and steps into his room.

It doesn't take me very long to crawl under the covers. I fall deep in sleep's grasp. But then the nightmares come.

I WAKE UP, TO MIRA SHAKING MY SHOULDERS. "WE'RE LEAVING," says Mira, holding up a drawing of earth, black clouds blur around it.

They are here.

"Max and the others are already in the vehicles," she whispers urgently.

"Why didn't anyone call me earlier?" I ask, bolting upright, instantly regretting it. My head goes fuzzy, and I almost fall back down, but I catch myself by propping an arm up.

"While you were talking to Max last night, Isla told me not to wake you unless it was an emergency," she says.

"Why?"

"Max said you were injured and needed rest." She pauses, "Sorry."

For a moment I hate that Max would get her to do that. I need to be notified just as much as the rest of them. I'm strong enough. I refuse to let my cut head prevent me from doing the same thing as everyone else.

"That's fine," I say, shaking out from under the covers.

I jam my feet into my sneakers and pull on my jacket. I readjust the beanie on my head and slip my curls out of my jacket and over my shoulder.

"Please ignore them next time and just tell me."

Mira hands me my bag from the table top. I double-check I have the pearl. I take one last glance into the room and walk out.

Miles sits in the front seat, again. "Blondes in the back." He grins, with the window rolled down.

Mira looks at me and rolls her eyes. It's a quiet little town, with a silence to it, kind of dingy, with old roads and falling apart buildings.

We make a quick trip to the grocery store and hit the road again.

Yellow and red leaves fall from the trees bordering the road. Back on Margaritan, there were trees that were naturally red and yellowed leaved. Here when the leaves die they turn blood red and burnt yellow.

As the days go by, the longer I'm here, the more my memories begin to blur.

"So what do you know?" asks Max, turning the radio lower.

"What! Come on, this is my jam!" complains Miles. The music had tuned into a really strange song, a mix between tempos, sounding almost electrified.

"About what?" Mira asks.

"Everything," says Max.

Mira giggles. "Oh, I'm gifted," she says. "I draw pictures that actually happen. Most of it usually happens within that day. But you already know that one." She searches for the right words. "Also, it's like I can transfer energy."

"How so?" Miles asks, turning around in his seat. He actually seems almost interested. That's a first. I never knew that was even possible. Throughout the entire drive he's been joking around.

"If I focus I can take the energy out of something, and put it back in if I wanted to," she shrugs. "A few weeks ago we did a science project, growing flowers. Anyways you know how if you talk to plants they grow faster? So I was sitting by mine talking to it, and I touched one of the leaves... *all* of the leaves shriveled up and turned brown. It died. I ran my fingers across the small pieces. You wouldn't believe it, but the pieces came back together. Like a puzzle," she concludes.

"Awesome!" shouts Miles. "You got anything else?"

"Yeah, actually, I can entice light."

"Huh?" He stares at her dumbfounded. "What? You lost me."

"I can't really explain it, but I'll show you guys sometime," she says.

The truck gets quiet again.

"Besides the academy, have you been anywhere else?" asks Miles.

"Yes, once I went on a field trip to see a play, in a huge theatre. It was amazing. I hope that one day I'll get to see another."

EVENTUALLY WE SWITCH PLACES. I GET TO SIT IN THE FRONT. Miles takes my seat in the back, beside Mira. We drive on for a few more hours.

"I can't feel my ass!" Miles cries out.

It's around middle afternoon. We drive by huge fields and trees. It's beautiful here.

"My ass fell asleep!" He cries out again, "I never knew an ass could fall asleep!" He shifts around uncomfortably in his seat. Mira giggles. "Max?"

Max stares down the road, trying to hold a straight face, but I can see the corners of his mouth fighting to stay down.

"Hey Max. Buddy. Can we pull over?"

He waits a moment.

"Max?" whines Miles, again.

"Fine, only for a little while," he says plainly. He pulls the truck over to the side of the road. The jeep stops behind us.

My legs are also sore.

I wander just a little ways down the gravel road. I still have difficulty holding myself up. I hear Max say something to the group. The gravel crunches under his shoes as he catches up to me.

"How are you doing?" he asks, coming to my side.

"Fine," I lie. To be honest, I don't even know if it is a lie. I don't know how I'm doing. My mind is racing with everything. It hurts. I hurt.

"No. Tell me the truth," he says. "How are you feeling?"

There are so many words that can describe what I'm feeling now; heartbroken, tired, upset, and rather anxious.

"Broken," I say.

"But you're not," he says. "You're still you. The only thing that can break you is yourself." We stop walking for a moment. I stare down at the ground. "You're still young; your life is just beginning."

"It's not a very good start." I choke back a sob. "I don't know how to tell Mira."

"I know. But soon you'll have to tell her, but I think she might already know. She has that family photo with you in it," Max says. He looks down at me. I meet his warm, icy blue eyes. I nod.

The cool autumn breeze swirls around us, swiping red and golden leaves from the trees, sending a chill through me. The sky is gray and patient.

"Be strong," he says. "Like the girl that broke the biggest guy's nose from her school, with a volleyball. Like the girl who found a way to wake from a coma not many people thought she'd wake up from, with her memory intact. Be strong like the amazing and beautiful girl that you are, that you always will be." He tucks a loose strand of my hair under my toque. I catch his hand before it falls down from my face. It's strong and warm. I give him a grateful smile.

No one has ever thought of me as *strong*.

Even Jeremy never thought of me as strong. He always did stuff for me, because he thought I never could do it. He believed I was weak and fragile, that I needed to be taken care of, that I was defenseless. When we were in our fourth year of school, he would refuse to let me do the parallel bars on my own. He had to be there, holding me up so I wouldn't fall.

Now, I have someone who believes in me. I've never had that before.

He looks down at me. His eyes study my face, from my forehead, to my eyes, to my nose, to my lips, down to my chin. "I will be there for you."

"Thank you," I whisper. I wrap my arms around his waist. The muscles in his back are tense. His muscles loosen up, and he embraces me back, his warm breath on my neck, and his hands on my back. The warmth he radiates is full of mystery and comfort. It feels *natural*.

We walk back toward the vehicle. I long for his warmth. He slips his arm around my waist.

"So where exactly are we going now?" I ask.

"Far away," he says. "So they won't find us."

"Eventually they will," I say. "We can't run forever."

"I know. That's what Miles, Ruban, Ace, Elle, and Isla have been doing most of their lives. But we won't."

I don't exactly understand what he means. But I trust him.

We hop back into the truck and start off again. This time, Max promises we'll pull over earlier than last night.

I look into my bag again. My father's letter sits, still untouched. I don't know if I want to read it, if I really want to know what else he has to say. But I have to.

I rip into it and slip the piece of parchment out.

Arianna,

You probably didn't want to open this. I don't blame you. And I don't expect you to forgive me either. I hope that you can start a new life, meet new people, and make new friends, which I'm sure you will. I know that you most likely found the note on the back of that photo before you opened this one. I wish for the two of you to be reunited. Many things have been going wrong here on Margaritan, after the first confrontation with Onychinus. They have been trying to get at our life source since the beginning. It is with you. You are the bearer of the golden pearl.

My eyes linger on that sentence. How can I be the *bearer of the golden pearl?* I never asked to be.

> *If anything bad happens, there is a safe house between the border of Canada and United States. I do hope that nothing bad does happen, but just in case, it's there.*

> *I love you.*

> KT

Underneath is a small map, with squiggly lines and colors.

"Hey, Max?"

"Yeah?"

"I know where we need to go," I say.

"Where?" he asks. "How?" He glances at me.

"He left us a safe house," I say, holding up the letter in my hands.

I read him the part where it says that Onychinus has been trying to get to us since the *beginning*, whatever that means. The beginning of what?

He nods once I'm finished speaking. "It's our best chance, and then we can figure out what to do from there."

"Reena!" Miles gasps.

Instantly I turn around in my seat. Miles stares down at her. She sits there in a daze and sketches ferociously in her open sketchbook. I watch her. An urgency to see what she sees, rushes through me. *What is she drawing now? Could it be another warning? Or another death? Please let it not be another death.*

Lines come together into shapes. Shades turn into darkness. Her picture shapes together in webs.

Her eyes clear and focus. She drops them onto the page, and the pencil slides from her fingers onto the seat between her and Miles.

A farmhouse.

Clay's farmhouse, even the tiny details of the front porch are almost exact. Around the house is darkly shaded with graphite.

She hands me the sketch. With shaky hands, I take it.

I know.

I just don't want to believe it.

They found Clay and Haley already. They might still be alive I hope. My eyes begin to burn again, and I feel my face get warm.

Max slips the paper from my fingers and looks at it, with one hand on the wheel. "Are you sure you want to stop for the night?" he asks, passing the sketch back to me. "They're moving fast. We could keep driving. Get farther away, then rest."

"No." I pause. "You can't drive the entire time. It's not good."

He doesn't even fight back. "Fine."

Max stares on at the road. I can almost feel his mind wander off. His jaw is sharp and his eyes are focused. He looks tired. Yet even in his tired state, he is handsome.

My heart always seems to beat faster when I'm around him. I feel more alive.

I thought I loved Jeremy, but he always made me feel locked in a box. Whenever that box opened, I was tied to a chain, unable to move freely.

Now I'm free.

But yet I'm not. I am on a chain against time.

WE PULL OVER INTO A GAS STATION IN THE EARLY EVENING. THE sun hangs low, but it is not setting yet. Max and another tall boy from the jeep fuel up the vehicles. I learn his name is Ace. Ruban, Isla, and Elle stand with them; they talk in low voices, occasionally glancing at the road.

I bring Mira and Miles inside to help me pick up a few things. We pick out a few sandwiches and a case of water.

"You both can pick out a treat or two. Get something for everyone else, okay," I say to Mira. I place everything onto the counter and look out the window. They seem to be arguing about something.

"Going on a trip?" asks the clerk. He's young, with hair falling a little below his eyebrows.

"Yeah, something like that," I say.

Mira and Miles dump their stuff on the counter. It consists mainly of candy bars and chips. I look at them with wide eyes. "Please tell me, some of this is for the others too."

"Aww, I have to share?" pouts Miles, jokingly.

The clerk chuckles and begins ringing the stuff through.

"I'm kidding, I'm not that big of a jerk," he says. "Okay, that's a lie. I am a jerk, but I was going to share. Okay, that's a lie too. I wasn't going to, but Mira convinced me otherwise."

I shake my head and grin. "Um, this and the gas for pump two and three." I say, pulling out my peram. He nods.

Max and Ruban turn around when we approach them.

The highway is fairly busy. The clouds hang low, and it feels like it's going to snow. I've never really felt snow before. Back home the snow never came. It was sunny half of the time, and the other half of the time it was pouring rain. I remember the thick, luxurious forests full of color, life, and mystery, dripping with sparkling water droplets. Everything seems different here!

When we walk by, Isla and Elle are already in the jeep.

"What's up?" I ask. I wish that I could have heard what they were arguing about, but I have a feeling they won't even tell me.

Ruban stands tall. He has broad shoulders, and you can basically see his muscles through his thin jacket. He has a similar build to Brad, which scares me a little, because I don't know what he's capable of. He has spiky hair, almost the same as Miles, but he wears a straight face and a hard expression. His face also has sharper angles and more pronounced cheekbones. I notice again how their hair shines slightly purple.

Ace has a more narrow build. You can still see his muscles through his jacket, like Ruban. His face also is a little narrower. He's growing a little bit of stubble, and he wears his hair flipped out in the front.

"We're gonna switch up the seating plan, for a bit, just till we get to the motel or safe house, whichever," says Max.

"Miles, you're riding with me, little bro," says Ruban.

"Ace is coming with us for now," Max says to me.

Ace steps closer to me. He drops his arm over my shoulders and says in my ear, "Dibs shotgun."

I grin when I see Max hold up the keys. "Of course, because you're driving, bud."

Ace makes a grumbling noise and snatches the keys from Max.

It's a little bit quieter now that Miles is riding in the other vehicle. Max and Ace speak in low, hushed voices.

CHAPTER 12

The sun is finally setting when Ace pulls into the parking lot of another motel. It is definitely cleaner than the last one.

We all take our turns showering. I slip into a hoodie and a pair of clean jeans. I brought a pair of pajamas too, but I feel like jeans are the better option.

I sit on my bed and attempt to brush the knots from my hair. The back of my head is very tender. I'm afraid the gash might open up again.

We decided that the youngest gets first shower, so Mira lays on her stomach switching the channels on the TV. Isla braided Mira's hair when I went for my turn. Most of the clothing Mira brought with her was clothing from her academy, uniforms. Since she is close to my size, I lend her a hoodie and a pair of sweats.

"Do you need help?" she asks, watching me struggle.

I hand the brush over to her. She takes it and crawls behind me. "I think you may have reopened the gash," she says, inspecting it—exactly what I didn't want—for it to reopen. "Just a little."

"Oh well," I say. There really isn't anything I *can* do about it. Someone knocks on the door. I jump.

"Is everyone decent?" asks Ace from the other side. Elle steps out of the bathroom drying her hair with a towel. She wears a thin black shirt, almost see-through, and a pair of leggings.

"Yeah," Elle says, dropping onto the other bed.

Isla runs over to the door and opens it for the boys. They all file in.

Miles takes a seat by the small table across from my bed. Ace and Ruban both lean against the TV stand. Max is the last to come into the room; he closes the door and sits at the end of my bed. He wears just a long-sleeved shirt and a pair of dark jeans. His hands are folded in his lap.

My hands itch to be clasped between his.

"So your dad, he left us a safe house?" asks Ace, looking down at me. "Max was telling us earlier."

"Yeah, it appears so."

"Makes you kind of wonder if your dad knew they'd come after us." Elle snorts from the far side of the room. She combs her thick, dark hair out with her fingers. Her dark eyes are serious.

"Yeah, this could all be a load of crap for all we know," retorts Ruban. "Could be all a setup to get us caught."

"Lucky for us, we got Mira. She's a Sibyl," says Miles. I never really thought that's what she is, until Miles says it.

"That could be a load of crap too," remarks Ruban, crossing his arms over his chest.

I suddenly feel very angry. I feel the heat rise up in my face, and I barely realize I'm biting the inside of my cheek so hard; I can taste the bitterness of my own blood.

"Maybe he knew, maybe he didn't," I hiss through clenched teeth. "My father was never a joker as far as I know. So no I don't think he set us up. Why would he?" I pause. "And if you ever dare to say my little sister's gift is a load of crap, *ever* again, I will punch you in the face."

I've never said anything that violent before in all of my life. It feels good to say it out loud. Mira stares at me stunned, her mouth turned up, almost in a smile.

Everyone else wears slightly stunned faces too. Except Ruban—he grins. They all knew she's my sister, but I haven't said it out loud to *her* before. I think this news isn't a surprise to her because she just looks relieved to finally know the truth.

"I'd like to see you try," he taunts. I clench my fists at my sides. I could hit him. But what I don't know is, how hard could he hit me?

"Look, we have to take into account even the smallest possibilities," interrupts Max. He looks from me to Ruban. I am the first to break apart from Ruban's glare. But I still feel his eyes burning holes into my face. "The best thing right now is not to fight each other Ruban!" Ruban quits trying to kill me with his eyes and turns to Max, giving him a cold look.

Of course it takes Max to get Ruban off his high horse. He seems to have control over all of them. He has a note in his voice that makes people want to listen to him, a true born leader. The room feels tense. Everyone seems to be on edge, ready to break into an argument. The anxiety of this trip eats away at everyone, I can tell.

"Don't you both agree?" asks Max. His eyes immediately find mine. I take a deep breath and try to slow my heart rate.

"Fine." I surrender, holding up my hands. I glance over at Ruban. Arms crossed, he leans stubbornly against the TV stand. He still looks at me with disgust.

"Ruban?" asks Ace. "If you happen to be right, and this is a setup, then you can say, 'I told you so.' How's that sound?"

He shakes his head. His face still as he drops his eyes to the floor. A crease deepens between his eyebrows. I can see the muscles in his arms flex. His jaw is tensed.

"She's our only chance," whispers Isla, who's been silent this whole time.

At this he finally backs down. "Fine," he grunts. "But this still doesn't mean I like you." He points a finger at me then lets his hand fall to his side.

"Great. Now then that's settled, what's the plan?" asks Elle, her dark wet hair thrown over her shoulder in a thick braid.

"We're going to find it," says Max. His face straightens. "It's probably the best option we have. I don't want to risk running into *them*."

After witnessing *them* murder my sister, I don't want to run into *them* either. They are strong, vicious, and deadly. Somehow they managed to eliminate all the power in the room. No one could even move. It's like they were frozen in place.

IT HAS BEEN A FEW HOURS SINCE THE BOYS LEFT THE ROOM. Everyone sleeps around me. I feel an urge to stay awake. Sleep will not come to me.

I reach under the bed and grab hold of my bag; I slip it up onto my lap. I shuffle the things around and pull out the book. It is made of smooth, dark leather and bound with a thin strap. Even in the dim light I can tell the book is old.

I move my fingers under the band. How many secrets are in here? I can't stop myself from wondering if I really want to know the words on these pages. My family, too, had—has many secrets. I really don't know how well I actually knew them. But deaths, eradications, and unexplained dilemmas are all the result of these secrets. Whatever they are, they are dark and deadly, and I need to know the past if I want to survive in the future.

There's only one way to find out.

I undo the band and flip it open to the first page. It is old. The paper is delicate and inked heavily with dark black cursive writing. It appears to be some kind of journal entry.

I strain my eyes to make out what the words say. It explains about a munera. In full depth and great detail, it describes how the alchemy from the pool is transferred into the receiver and how the munera is chosen for that being. It reads you, your past, your present, and how you will live your future.

I flip through the pages. They are documents and research about each kind of munera ever received. Sibyl. Healer. Telekinetic. Tracker. Distorter. Charmist: a compeller. And the one I am under: Sorcerer.

Mine is the only one where there are no words under the title.

I flip through the rest of the pages. They are inked all over. There are some sketched drawings and dashes with more knowledge, nothing on sorcery though. The book may be useful. My family wouldn't have left it with me if they didn't think it was. There are stories or some kind of poetry.

Something in my heart skips. I see it in one of the drawings. I recognize it. Two types of ink are used for this drawing—the people of Amethystus. They have black and purple hair, and the page is left blank for their skin color. There are fine lines and thicker ones. Together they build faces and bodies. They are beautiful.

Is that why Ruban was so angry earlier? Because he thought my father knew that they were still alive and sent people after them. In Amethystus, supposedly, everyone was killed. I guess not everyone. Somehow Ruban, Ace, Elle, Isla, and Miles all found a way to survive. Now I understand. This is why Max brought them with us. They are on the run for their lives too. If the Onychinus soldiers realize they are still alive, they are as good as dead. Like us. Like me. *I* have the pearl. I have what they are after. I have a piece that will eventually complete their compilation.

I see a movement outside the window, through the corner of my eye.

I slowly shut the book and wrap the band back around it and shove it into my bag. I sit up straighter, not daring to make a noise. Even the sound of my own heart beating seems too loud.

I see another quick movement.

I jump. Outside something breaks the night's silence. A window shatters and something else, like the sound of splintering wood.

The night is dreary and dim.

I slip out from under the covers. My feet through my socks are cold as they hit the floor. My chest is so tight. The breath I'm holding can't be released. I fear that anything I do will draw attention, despite the closed curtains.

I inch closer to the window. The floor creaks under my feet. I feel my face get warm, and I bite the inside of my cheek.

Halfway there.

On light feet, I sprint the rest of the way there.

I hear another window shatter. I take a deep, shaky breath and draw the curtains a little ways away from the window. Through the small opening, I peek outside.

The trees nearby are still, but the leaves below them rustle on the ground. A couple doors down, the windows of two rooms are completely destroyed. The doors are cracked into shards pointing everywhere; they barely hang on their hinges.

I wonder if Max is awake. That thought only increases when I see several dark figures step through one of the doorways of the dismantled rooms. I need to know if he's up.

Everything but their faces are dark. Two of them move onto the next room. One of them breaks through the window with a metal rod. It makes a clattering noise as the shards of glass crumple to the floor. They look like silver puddles, reflecting the night sky.

The other figure kicks the door. It dents. He kicks it again. This time the door gives way.

I look away from them. My heart pounds. My gaze falls onto one. He looks off to the distance, but then his eyes flicker. They are on me. I see darkness in them, a hunger, and hatred. Hatred, for what though? I'm not sure.

Another window breaks in the opposite direction.

The man's eyes stay on me. I instinctively let go of the curtain and let the small opening disappear.

They found us.

I feel a cold gust shoot out from the furnace. I shudder.

More windows break. And then it's silent.

I slip between the two beds and shake Mira's shoulder.

"What is it?" She stirs, her eyes blinking into focus. I immediately turn and wake Isla and Elle. I yank their blanket off them. They are not very pleased.

"What is wrong with you?" Elle glares at me.

"They're here."

Her face pales whiter than snow, and she bolts upright. Another glass breaks. This one is very close. I can almost feel their presence outside of our door.

I don't exactly remember when, but somewhere in the last few seconds I managed to toss my bag across my shoulders and slip into a pair of shoes.

I push Mira behind me. She already wears her jacket, her jaw is clenched, and I can see she is fighting to stay calm.

Outside, the floor creaks. A shadow takes its place in front of our window.

I hold my breath. Seeing the shadow reminds me of when I

was in the forest, the night of the bonfire. I saw Max. He was just a silhouette. All I can think about is him. I hope he's okay.

Both Isla and Elle stand beside me. They both hold daggers. The handles are black and silver, and just below the blade is a tiny jewel, and it glints purple. Where did they get the daggers from?

Another crash. This one is louder than the others. This one is ours. Shards of glass fly into the room. And I hear banging on our door. I lift a few of the shards from the ground without touching them. They float, reflecting a little light. They look like stars.

An arm reaches through the gaping hole, and with a shiny black glove it tears the curtains down. His face is ghastly white and very out of place among the darkness. His eyes are bottomless pits, and his mouth turns up into a crooked grin when he sees the four of us standing there.

I launch all but one of the shards at him. They strike his face. One of the bigger ones slices open his forehead, letting thick, dark blood seep into his eyes. He yelps and backs away from the window. I snatch the shard left over and hold it tightly in my hand. I feel it dig and cut into my own hand. But I ignore the stinging pain.

The man who kicked open the door runs for us. He lets loose a tiny silver cube. It falls onto the bed.

I hear shouts coming from outside, and more figures come into the room.

The man leaps for me. His weight lands on top of me, knocking me to the floor. I bang my shoulder into the wall on the way down. He snaps the shard out of my bloody hand. I thrash under his heavy weight. Something hard strikes my face. I feel my vision go fuzzy. I swing at him, but I miss. A fist drives into my ribs, shaking my insides. I gasp and claw for his face, but my arms are too short. Instead I shove my hand downward in the crease of his arm; he falls on top of me. He grunts. I slip my leg out from under him and kick him wherever I can. I yank one of my hands free and try to push him away, but the man pins my leg back underneath him and rights himself on top of me. He kneels on my stomach; his legs holding mine down, I can barely breathe. The pearl digs into my side. Holding my hands tight at my sides he glares down at me. I can tell that he knows where it is. His knees dig under my rib cage. I feel like all of the bones in my body are going to crumble under his weight. He yanks one of my hands across my stomach and holds both of my hands down with one. I struggle under his weight and try to protect the pearl by twisting my body away from his searching hand. He rams his fist into my ribs; I can feel some of my bones crack. I continue to twist away from him. His hand finds the pearl.

I try to throw him off me with my mind, but that doesn't work.

Someone runs at us. The man is torn away from me. I feel the heaviness remain on my chest though, making it hard to breathe. I choke down some air, feeling a very minimal relief with each breath. A hand reaches down for me. I take it, and it hauls me to my feet. Max. My head spins. I shift my eyes over to Elle. Her braid swings behind her as she fights against her own attacker with her blade. She gets shoved into the TV stand. The TV rocks and falls to the ground, breaking. Isla fights off another, slashing her blade through the air. Ruban just enters the room when he sees Elle fall. He lands a fist into the man's side.

Beyond the door are more noises.

Several of the men lie on the floor with gaping wounds. Blood is puddling around them. I think they are *dead*. Did Elle and Isla kill all of them while I struggled with just the one? Even Max killed him for me. His body lies on the floor, motionless, his head twisted in an awkward angle. I gag. The sickeningly bitter, sweet scent of blood lingers in the room. I snatch the pearl out of the dead man's hand and stuff it back into my pocket. I have a hard time standing up straight. My ribs hurt, but my head hurts a million times worse. I can feel it spinning, and I feel like passing out.

Elle pushes the crumpled TV away from her. That same attacker stumbles toward her, grasping his side. She backs away from him, holding her shoulder. Her lip is cut, and her face is bruised.

Ruban lunges for him, taking him off guard. He falls into the wall, breaking through the drywall.

Ripping the blade from his back pocket, Ruban brings it down, but the man shoves him in the chest, knocking him to the side. The blade clatters from his hand.

The man struggles with something from inside his jacket pocket, it is dark and slick, a gun. He gets to his knees and aims it at Ruban, who dives for the man's stomach, taking him down again. The man drives the butt of the gun into Ruban's forehead. Max dives in to help Ruban. He pins the man down. As the gun goes off, the noise rings in my ears and echo's in the room.

I gasp. My heart throbs. Who was shot?

I look up and grasp Mira's tiny hand. "Stay here," I whisper in Mira's ear. I let go. I find the shard with my blood on it and run toward Isla's attacker. He catches her arm as she swings the blade at him again. Her eyes flicker to mine. The man notices and turns toward me. I drive the shard deep into his chest. I feel his hot, dark blood run down my hands. I watch his dark bottomless eyes roll back. A tear rolls down his cheek, and I rip the shard out of his chest. He releases Isla's arm as he drops to the floor.

My heart jumps and fills with grief. Did I just kill a man? *Me?* I killed a man. I'm a murderer now. I never wanted to be, ever. *I killed* a man. I feel a burning tear roll down from my eyes as I register this. *I killed a man.*

I stand there, stunned into silence. Isla says something to

me, but I don't know what. She runs toward the boys struggling to hold the man down. Ruban reaches for his blade, while Max wobbles on top of him. He barely misses it, and the tips of his fingers slide the knife farther away. He grunts and reaches for it again. Dropping down to her knees, Isla drives her blade into the man's chest.

We are finished. I don't think there is anyone else.

Sirens wail in the distance. Through the door Ace and Miles run in.

"Are there any left in here?" Ace asks. Isla shakes her head. "Good. We have to get out of here." His voice is low and urgent and breathless. His jaw is bruised, and dark blood is smeared across his face and hands.

Isla steps around the bodies lying on the floor and heads toward the door. She slips her bloody hand in Ace's warm hand and walks out with him. Ruban and Max are both now on their feet, but Elle sits beside the body. She has a look of pain written across her face as she holds her shoulder. Ruban helps her to her feet and walks toward me, but he turns to Mira and takes her hand. Her face is completely horrified. Tears and blood streak her face. Was she hurt too? Please, I hope she isn't hurt. Ruban takes both her and Elle out of the room. She turns her head as she walks. Her eyes are on me. I don't know what to do or even what I'm supposed to say.

Max and I are the last in the room. His face is solid, and he doesn't really wear an expression. I tell *myself, You are not going to break; you are not going to* … I break. "I … I …" I sob. He comes toward me, stepping over dead bodies, one of which I am responsible for killing. He puts his arms around my shoulders.

"It's okay," he says.

"No, no it's not. I *killed* a man." I sob again. Crying is such a messy waste of time. My hands shake as I hold onto his T-shirt. I know we have to get out of here and I really want to, but my body is weak and it hurts me to move.

"Oh," he says. He releases me and leads me around the dead bodies. Around one of the necks I see a strange necklace, with a black onyx entwined between threads of silver that lead into a single chain. I take it before we near the door, and Max sees me do it. He takes the tiny silver cube from off the bed, where the man who attacked me first, dropped it earlier. I double check I have the pearl in my pocket and realign the bag across my body. With my hand in Max's we leave the room. "You want to avenge your sister's death?" he asks. I nod. "This is how. Learn to fight, and the ones you love won't get hurt."

The tears on my face dry. I will learn to fight. And I will never let anyone I love get hurt again, as long as I can stop it.

This is just the beginning. I know it will get worse before it's going to get better. It is going to get harder before it's going to get easier. Hatred before love. War before peace. Pain before happiness. We are still alive, and that's all that counts right now.

At even the darkest age, hope is there.

Thee is not entwined in cage, but free with peaceful air.

CHAPTER 13

"You know, Ace, I think you misread the map, buddy," says Max. Ace has the map propped up against the steering wheel, reading it while he drives. Max takes it from him.

We have been driving for two days straight since the attack. As it turns out, Ruban was shot. But whatever it was that was used for ammo had almost no effect. All it did was leave a small, dark, metallic-looking spot under the skin of his shoulder. He figures it's just a bruise, but I'm not sure. Onychinus have always been the strongest at three things; being among the darkness, technology, and strategy. Once upon a time, Margaritan used to trade with them, but that ended when they realized what Onychinus really was after: our gem.

We had to trade our vehicles in for different ones. Although Max was devastated when Isla came up with the idea, he agreed that we shouldn't take a chance of them following us in our old ones. I can tell he hates the idea because like every guy on earth he loves his truck. Now we have two black cars. There are too many of us to all fit in the same one, so we had to get two. Ruban and Max basically called dibs on driving most of the time. Mira has been silent. She just stares out her window and doesn't make a noise. I'm worried about her. This is way too much for such a young kid to go through. Same with Miles. Neither of them should have any part of this. They're just kids. I keep thinking of a way for them to both be safe, but right now that doesn't seem possible.

"No way, man, we're going the right way. See, the turn is right up ahead." Ace nods, gesturing to the upcoming tight corner.

I fumble with the tiny silver cube in my hands that was dropped in the room during the attack. Somehow it eliminated any chance for our magic to be used within a certain perimeter. I can't even lift it from the palm of my hand with my mind. It just won't budge. I give up after a short while and just stuff it into the pocket of my jacket.

"Actually, yeah, I think you might be right. Turn up ahead," says Max, tilting the map at an angle.

The gravel road is very long. Spruce trees with thick trunks are everywhere. Some thinner trees with bare branches are scattered here and there, but the spruce trees are more dominant in this area. Dead yellow and brown leaves clutter the ground in layers, quilting the frozen earth.

"I think that's it," says Max.

Ace leads the car down a narrow road. I think this is the driveway because I can see a building up ahead.

It is white and has blue shutters and is thickly surrounded by trees. It has a simplistic beauty to it.

All of the windows are dark, and it looks like it hasn't been lived in for a long time.

"Ruban and I will go check it out first. You guys wait in the car until one of us comes back for you, okay?" He looks directly at me. I don't know why because I wasn't planning on getting out of the car. He gets out of the car, and through the mirrors I can see Ruban doing the same. They make eye contact, and Ruban nods his head and tosses a blade to Max. He catches it with one hand while they walk toward the patio.

I feel my heart leap as the vehicle jerks into action. "What are you doing?"

"It saves time, to just naturally have the car parked so the front end is facing the road, so we can drive away whenever need be," Ace says in an annoyed and bored tone. He shakes his head. "Do you honestly think I would just drive away?"

I don't answer. Honestly, I think he could have, but I don't know if he actually would have.

"No," I whisper. "Where did you guys get the daggers?" I ask. It's been bothering me for a little while now, how I have no idea who these people are and how I know I can trust them. The only things I'm certain if is that they are friends with Max and they are from Amethystus.

"From home," he says. I want to ask more, but in the mirror I see a tinge of pain in his face. This is the most emotion I have seen any of them reveal. I decide otherwise and keep my mouth closed and bite the inside of my cheek. It has become a bad habit that I have been doing a lot lately, and the inside of my cheek has become rather raw.

I don't expect him to say more, but I'm grateful that he does. Even Mira looks up when he begins to speak. "I often wonder how we all would have turned out if we were still there."

"What is home?" I whisper, mainly to myself.

He shrugs his shoulders. "Home is the place where you belong," he says. "My home is Amethystus." He pauses. "But right now, Isla, Miles, Ruban and Elle are my home, and Max too."

"So it's the people who make home a home?"

He is silent again. "A home is different for everyone."

It must have taken him a lot to even tell us this. But I am greedy to know more, not only about them, but also about Max.

"Okay, let's go," he says in a low voice. I can hear it, the hidden, deep sadness that lingers in him. I know it's there because a similar feeling weighs me down.

On the deck stands Max. He waves for us to come inside, and then he disappears inside again.

We enter into the foyer. It is a nice size. There is a small coat closet just to the left. I walk further in. There is a living room to the immediate right. Thick dust-coated plastic covers lie on top of all of the furniture, making it difficult to distinguish what lies beneath them.

Light streams in through the window, revealing more dust lingering in the air. I run my fingers across a plastic covering what I assume is the dining table, and thick dark gray dust comes off onto my fingers.

Ruban comes running down the stairs. "There are three bedrooms upstairs and two downstairs."

"All right, there are eight of us. Who sleeps where?" asks Elle, searching a broom closet alongside the hallway. She finds a broom and dustpan and pulls it out. "Max?"

Max, leaning against the counter, looks up. "We'll decide after we clean this place up a bit."

I can almost see my breath in here. The combination of the dust and the cold air makes it difficult to breathe. I shiver. With my arms crossed over my chest, I rub them to help warm myself up.

"Mira and Miles, you two can look and see if there's any food here. I doubt it, but there might be cans. You never know," says Max. "Ruban, you can bring in the supplies and bags." Then he turns to face me. "Reena, Elle, and Isla, you can start cleaning. And Ace, you're gonna help me find the power box so we can get the heat and electricity going before it gets dark out."

We all spread out. I wonder how Max became their leader.

I would have thought it'd be Ruban, but they all seem to look to Max and Ace.

Elle yanks a plastic cover from one of the sofas, dumping a load of dust onto the hardwood floor; it billows up into the air, just as Miles turns the corner from the hallway. He opens his mouth to talk but gets a mouthful of dust. He sneezes. "Wow, be careful with that. It tastes nasty, and pretty soon it'll take up all the oxygen from the room," he says, choking. He turns into the kitchen. Mira, right behind him, is silent even though Miles is talking. They start searching the cupboards.

The dust burns my lungs, and my fingers are almost completely numb from the cold. They tremble in their tight grasp of the broom. Isla bunches up the plastic covers and carries them toward the door that leads to the garage. Everyone is silent. The glorious hum of power flickering on interrupts the silence. Through the vents air comes out, blowing more dust everywhere.

Max comes running into the room and flicks on a light switch, and the kitchen lights begin to beam.

"Great! Hey, Ace, it worked," he calls to Ace, who's in one of the rooms down the hall. "Okay, it'll take a while for it to heat up in here, but a little wait is better than nothing."

Ruban dumps several of the bags on the floor in the entrance and kicks the door shut behind him, but not before letting another chilly gust into the room.

It doesn't take us very long to clean up, now that everyone is helping. Almost all of the plastic covers are in the garage. There's not very much in there, basically just tools and boxes of stuff.

The couches are a navy blue fabric and the walls in the main room are light beige, and only a little bit of dust remains in the air.

We all sit in the living room. I know they are all talking, but I'm barely paying attention. I can't seem to wrap my head around anything; I blame the concussion, but I don't think that's it.

"Did you find any food?" asks Isla. Mira sits beside me in the armchair, the checkered blanket Max bought lying across our laps.

"Yes," she says, "but it was all expired."

"That sucks," says Elle. "We only have enough for a day, maybe two, at the most. Then what?" she says, leaning against Ruban, sitting on the far couch across from us.

"Obviously tomorrow some of us are going to make a trip to town. There's no time to head out there tonight. Everything would be closed by the time we'd get there," says Ace. "We should rest, then head out tomorrow for supplies and start training."

"Yeah," says Max. "Let's all go to bed."

"I'll share with Mira," I say.

"Okay. Miles, I guess that means we're sharing. We'll leave one room empty, and you four can decide who shares with whom," Max says, gesturing to everyone else.

Slowly everyone migrates out of the room, at their own pace. Only Mira, Max, Miles, and I are left in the living room.

"So basically everyone knows how to fight," says Max. "Except you two," he says to me and Mira.

"See, I'm the best. I already know how," brags Miles. He wears a grin and is spread out across the couch where Elle and Ruban were before.

"You all know how to use a blade, but that's about it. You have not fully developed your munera yet," says Max. "We will try and increase its growth rate within you, but how well it develops is all on you."

I didn't know Amethystus had a munera. "You have a munera? What is it?" I ask.

"Fire," states Miles proudly. "But it's not working right now. Max gave them to us. Amethystus doesn't actually get muneras. Max has the power to give out muneras." He flicks his fingers angrily, glaring at them. I didn't know that could be a gift, to provide muneras to others. Then I remember the tiny silver cube. It limits power usage.

I slip it from my jacket pocket and look at it. "I think that is their greatest form of defense they have against us," says Max, seeing what I have in my hands. "If we can learn to force our powers through it, I think that we could have the advantage,"

"Do you think it's possible?" asks Mira. This is the first time I've heard her speak in a while. She sits still, staring down at her tightly clasped hands.

"Yes," he says. "I do."

She stands up, and the blanket falls from our laps to the floor. "I would like to try," she says confidently.

I hand her the cube, and as she walks into the dining room, I pick up the fallen blanket. She sets the cube on the counter and positions herself beside where the light beams in through the windows. We all face her.

She dips her hands into the river of light and begins whispering something I believe is Latin, but it sounds older than Latin, more ancient. Her words are confident and strong. Both the light particles and the dust combine and pour into the palms of her hands like water. They take a shape. I don't recognize it. She glides toward us. The light gently glows in her hands. She smiles down at it as she drops down to the center of the floor carefully.

Miles gawks at her.

"What is that?" asks Max. He leans his elbows on his knees. His face is both curious and puzzled as he strains his neck to see.

She unclasps her hands a little more, revealing a tiny golden butterfly.

"Amazing," I whisper. I can see Max look up from the corner of my eye. His eyes drink me up, and his mouth curves into a grin.

How can she work through the energy released by the cube whereas the rest of us can't?

"Can it fly?" asks Miles. He slips off the couch and sits beside her on the floor.

She grins at him and raises her hands, straightening them, so the butterfly is fully visible. Pressing her lips close to it, she blows a breath of air onto it.

At that moment, the wings begin to flap gently.

I hold my breath as the butterfly takes flight, leaving her hands delicately. It gracefully glides through the air toward me, leaving behind minimal quantities of light to dissolve into nothingness. It lands on my knee and leaves almost as quickly. It circles around Max's head; his face is astonished. Miles tries to poke the tiny butterfly as it nears his face, but the butterfly flutters quickly away from him, back into the dining room, where it dissolves into the rest of the lessening beam.

"May I ask how you can use your munera, whereas the rest of us can't?" asks Miles.

She shakes her head, but then answers, "I was never one of you. Sure I was born there, but I never had a place to rely on to give me my magic." She pauses, and looks as if she's going to say something but thinks better of it. "I just have it," she whispers.

I don't understand how she can though. I have to know and find a way so I can get mine to work too. I wonder what Max's is; I don't believe I've seen him use it before. I really don't know enough about him, yet I feel drawn to him. I'm still so confused about it. How can someone love another if they do not know them? But I do. I love Mira and yet I barely know her. She's my little sister. I'm not sure what I feel for Max though, but I do know it's something strong.

He nods his head once in agreement, his lips pursed and his jaw tight. "All right," he says, though I know he is deep in thought. I wonder what he's thinking. "Okay. You all go to bed. I'll be on first watch."

As soon as Mira and Miles head up the stairs, I offer to stay up awhile with Max.

BY NOW THE SUN IS ALREADY BEGINNING TO FADE. IT IS EARLY evening. "I have a feeling it's going to snow pretty soon," states Max, watching through the window. It has been a while since he has spoken, and it surprises me a little bit. I have heard of snow once before, but I have never experienced it or even seen it for myself. The only thing I really know about snow is that it is cold. "I'm sorry," he says.

"What for?" I ask, sitting on the couch beside him, with the checkered blanket pulled up onto my lap.

"There's a lot about this place that you don't know yet, and I'm just bringing it up like you know everything."

"Umm, I really don't mind. I want to know more."

He looks down. His hands are clasped together. When I said "more" what I really meant was that I not only want to know more about Earth but also about him. There is so much to learn and so little time. It is unfair.

"Well, there are four different seasons; two are fairly warm, nothing like on Margaritan though. Right now we are beginning the coldest season; it is almost winter," he says.

"That's not what I meant," I say.

"Yeah, I know what you meant," he says and chuckles. "I was in love once." He lifts his head, and our eyes meet; his are honest. I feel my heart miss a beat. I don't remember or understand a lot about my past, and it is a tangled mess with some blank spots. I guess it could be from my coma. The doctor did say I could have some memory loss, although I didn't think that the memory loss could take away years. With a sad blankness in his voice he mutters, "I don't even remember what she looks like."

He reaches over and gently grabs one of my hands. I wince. I remember the cut on my hand as soon as his fingers brush my palm just over the rag. I haven't even looked at it since it happened. I've been avoiding it, though I know I shouldn't.

He slips his fingers under the bloodstained, dirty rag and slides it off my hand, revealing a thick, nasty gash. The skin around it is blue, purple, and the entire area is covered with crusty old blood. "What did you do?" he asks.

"That guy ripped the shard of glass out of my hand when he attacked me."

He looks like he is about to laugh, but then he covers it up with a fake cough. "You're one tough cookie, aren't ya? You don't complain about this or the concussion you had." He reaches his hand up to my face, his warm fingers brush my cheek. "Or this." I remember getting hit, but I didn't think it left a mark. He drops his hand, but the warmth remains.

"What is your munera?" I ask, changing the subject.

"I'm a sorcerer." He looks out through the window and smiles. "But it doesn't matter. I want you to see something." He gestures to the window.

Little white flurries fall from the sky, each so fragile and delicate, they look like tiny sprinkles of glass, dancing toward the ground. It is beautiful. "This is snow?" I ask. I kind of feel out of place, because I am the only one here who has never seen snow before whereas everyone else has. Luckily it's only Max who'll see my reaction to it. He won't judge me, I hope.

Max gets off the couch, fixing his black long-sleeved shirt as he stands up straight. I can see the muscles through the back of his shirt. He is strong.

"Are you coming?" he asks.

I quickly get to my feet and toss the blanket onto the couch. He turns to face me and chuckles as he looks down at me. "What?" I ask.

"You're just so trusting. That is your only fault, and love seems to be the only thing that keeps you going. You have to be careful who you put your trust in. They may deceive you."

By this statement I am slightly puzzled. I'm not that trusting, am I? I am. I put my trust into my people and they banished me. I also put my trust into my munera, and it failed me when I needed it. Now, I put my trust into these people and they have not yet deceived me. "Can I trust you?"

"Yes," he whispers. We stand very close, barely apart. He takes my hand again, then leads me to the door.

It is chilly outside, and the air bites my cheeks and chills me through my thin sweater. It has been cold for a while now. I wonder how long these seasons usually last.

Flurries fall from the sky, sparkling in reds and oranges in the setting sun. I reach out my good hand. Several snowflakes melt almost instantly when they make contact. Max stands behind me; I feel his eyes watching me and his radiating warmth.

"Now you have seen snow," he says. "Close your eyes, feel it, and listen."

I close my eyes. My heart is still heavy. I don't understand what I am supposed to be listening to. There is no sound. I don't know what I am supposed to feel, because I am blank.

"What do you hear?" he asks.

I hesitate before I answer. I don't know what kind of answer he is expecting, I don't want to make a fool of myself for giving a stupid wrong answer, so I tell him the truth. "It's quiet."

"That's just it—snow is peaceful, and it is quiet."

I hear him slowly take a few steps closer to me. I drop my

hand to my side and turn to face him. He now stands slightly away from me; I can see his breath and feel a chill run up my spine.

"Let me understand something," I say.

"Anything."

"Why are you continually protecting me?" I pause.

He creases his eyebrows and hesitates before he answers.

"Do I remind you of her?"

"I do not really remember her," he says, looking deep into my eyes. "If it weren't for her though, I would have never met you."

"What do you mean?" I ask. I know there is a pain behind his eyes, but I don't really understand it.

"I do remember how I got to earth though. We wanted to be together, but her father was against it. I didn't meet his expectations. He told me that if I ever spoke to his daughter again, he would kill me. I got angry, and I went on a rampage. I'm not proud of it. It was an accident. At the time I didn't realize all of my gifts. I still don't know that many of them. A lot of people died because of me, and I didn't mean to hurt anyone. Anyways I was banished, and I watched as they took away all of her memories of me as her punishment for going against her father's will, and they then wiped her appearance from my memory. I don't even remember what she looks like. I just remember her name, only her name. It was Lilyryn." His voice slightly cracks, and he coughs. He crosses his arms over his chest and looks down at the ground. "It was about two, possibly three years ago."

"They all made you sound like a monster," I whisper. He was the sorcerer my father and that man were speaking of, that night of my ceremony. I reach up and wrap my arms around him. "You are one of the farthest things from a monster." I feel a little bit jealous that I have never been in love with someone who would do that because of his love for me. He slips his arms over my shoulders, and I press my head against his chest and close my eyes.

Part of my mind wanders to Jeremy, but the other part of my mind just doesn't care about anything else. Jeremy is nothing more than a friend to me.

"Hey, Max?" calls out a familiar voice.

I look up. Miles stands in the back doorway. Instinctively Max and I break apart. He takes a step back, dropping his arms down to his sides. The coldness returns, even though I feel myself blushing. I look down at the ground; snow is already beginning to cover it. The cold wraps around me like a blanket and takes over the parts of me where his arms were. The parts that were warm are now cold.

"What?" replies Max.

"I'm hungry," says Miles, a little quieter this time.

Max lets out a low chuckle and grins at me. "I'll be right there." Miles's tall, scrawny figure returns to the house, closing the door behind him.

"Of course," says Max, the grin still on his face. His eyes are slightly glassy. A small smile makes its way onto my face. Of course Miles would come out now; he just has that nosy personality. "We better go in or he'll be back," he whispers close to my ear. He loops his arm around my waist and gently presses his lips to my forehead. Then he whispers, "The past is the past. Now is the present, and tomorrow is the future where anything can happen."

When we get to the back door, Miles is sitting by the table, his feet propped up on the seat beside him. He fiddles with the hem of his sleeve but looks up when we walk in.

"You know, I never thought it was possible."

"What is that?" I ask. A tightening creeps its way into my chest as I wait for him to finish. Max closes the door behind him.

"For me to be completely sick of sandwiches. If I have to eat another one, I will puke it all out on someone's head," he says and shakes his head in disgust, his tongue out of his mouth and his eyebrows creased.

Max walks past me and leans against the counter. "Well, don't you still have all that junk food left over that Reena bought for you?"

"No," he says matter-of-factly. "I ate it."

"Well, that sucks to be you then. You'll have to last until to-morrow," Max says. "We have nothing but gas station sandwiches and a few apples, and I think a few water bottles. Take your pick."

"Apple," Miles grumbles.

Max turns around and opens the fridge behind him. He was so happy when he found out that it actually still worked. Inside is a plastic bag. He slips an apple out and tosses it to Miles. "Now go to bed," he says to Miles, and then to me, "Reena, you should too. I'm on first watch. I don't think they'll find us for a while, but in the meantime you should get some rest."

"What about you?"

"I'll shift with Ruban," he says.

Miles takes a huge bite out of his apple and kicks his feet down from the chair, the legs making a squealing noise against the floor.

"Miles, do you know which room Mira went into?" asks Max.

"Yeah I do," he says and rolls his eyes.

"Great. Miles is going to show you to your room then," he assures me. Miles rolls his eyes again and walks right past me to the staircase. I nod my head at Max, and he just shrugs his shoulders. I don't argue that I should stay up too. I'm exhausted, and my head is still throbbing.

"Night," he whispers to me.

"Goodnight," I whisper back.

I feel a small smile creep its way onto my face as I climb the stairs after Miles. He walks quite fast. The steps squeak under my feet. The light downstairs turns off, and there is barely any light left.

"I saw it," he says when we get to the top steps, and then there is a blank silence.

"What?" I ask.

"You know what; Max is like another big brother to me. When I first met him he was devastated because of a girl. You are the first one he's met since her. What I mean is if you break his heart, I'll kick your ass. Poor guy's been through too much, we all have, and we don't need more drama."

"What makes you think I am anything like her?" I ask, feeling a quick flicker of anger, but I am too exhausted for it to flare up. Instead I let it dissolve. I rub my forehead with my thumb and my index finger. "By the way, have you ever even met her?" I ask lamely.

"No, but I hate drama, so you better not cause any. Ruban has a short temper so don't piss him off," says Miles. "It's better that I tell you than you figuring it out on your own. I like you and Mira, so don't act stupid." It sounds kind of strange coming from a fourteen-year-old.

"Miles," I say quietly, "I don't want to hurt him or any of you."

"That's just it," he says and shakes his head in dismay. "The ones you don't want to get hurt, get hurt the most. That's usually the way it goes. We learned that the hard way."

I don't know what to say to that, because it is true, and I don't really know anything I can respond to that with.

"That's your room." He sighs and gestures to the door on the right. "Just be careful. Night," he says and disappears behind one of the doors on the left side.

It is pitch black inside, but I feel around for the bed and crawl in under the covers. Mira sobs quietly lying on her side. I don't know what to do, so I wrap my arm over her and just lay beside her until she is silent and I fall asleep.

CHAPTER 14

I WAKE TO THE SOUND OF VOICES DOWNSTAIRS.

A yellowy-white color streams into the room. Now I can actually see around the room. It is small with pale blue walls. It has an old wooden dresser in the corner of the room, and close beside it is a closet with folding doors. My duffel bag is thrown on the floor beside the closet.

Mira isn't in the room anymore; she has already folded her side of the blanket back into place. I don't know if she will forgive me. I killed someone right in front of her. I know that the others did too, but that doesn't make it anymore right that I also did. None of us actually had a choice.

I slip out from under the cover, which is a beautiful quilt with yellow, blue, and green faded patches sewed together. I am still in the same jeans and shirt from yesterday, and now they are completely covered in wrinkles and half of the braid in my hair is falling out. I quickly get to my bag and exchange my clothes for black leggings and a long-sleeved shirt.

I undo the rest of my braid and comb my fingers through the curls. The voices continue as I leave the room. They grow louder as

I near the stairs. One of them definitely belongs to Ruban, and the other deep voice belongs to Max. It sounds like they are arguing, but I can't make out the words exactly.

I start down the stairs, but I feel them rattle under me as the front door closes. I finish going down the stairs, not really caring who hears me.

Max slouches, leaning his head in his hands on the edge of the couch, by the door. I don't see anyone else, just him. Did everyone leave?

"What's up?" I ask.

He looks up, his face worn out and upset. He has bags under his eyes, and his eyebrows are knitted deep in thought.

I slowly come to a stop beside him and lean my back against the couch facing the wall. "Are you all going to continue arguing and not let me in on anything?" I ask. "They are after what I currently am in possession of; I have a right to know."

"Yeah, you do," he agrees. He runs his hands through his tousled hair and straightens into the same position I'm in, facing the wall. "I really don't want to do it, there can be so many complications or in some cases none at all," he says, staring at the baseboard.

"Complications for doing what?" I ask. I have no idea what he is talking about, but he says it like I *did* hear their entire conversation.

"Healing your head so it doesn't slow you down," he says. "Unfortunately a concussion isn't like any regular wound. It is on the brain. We don't know how much damage there is. If I try and mend it, there are three possible outcomes."

"What do you mean?" I ask, relatively confused. What does he mean "three possible outcomes"?

He lets out a low hush of air. "All right, so the best case scenario is that nothing occurs. It just heals you."

"What's the worst case?"

"You can forget all of us, and lose some or even all of your memories and even how to do stuff. That or there's one more thing that could happen." He pauses and looks up again. "Have you ever heard of a distorter?"

"Yeah, on Margaritan that's one of the gifts, isn't it?" I ask.

"Yep, there is a wide range of gifts you can get within one title. One of the gifts within the distorter category is mind altering. It's usually very rare, but every now and then someone gets it. One of my friends got that when he turned seventeen. I don't know what happened to him. But I'm afraid that you may have possibly had your memories altered in the past, because you are a princess." He pauses again and straightens, staring back at the same baseboard. "If your mind was altered, one of the side effects could be getting all of what you lost back, entirely back, at once. You could possibly fall into a paroxysm and be completely *different* from what you are now."

"What's a paroxysm?" I ask.

"That is when you fall into a sudden violent outburst, and that would be caused by disappointment of the memories lost, whether you are upset or relieved about the information within them."

I don't know if I ever have had my mind altered. Then again how would I know? I stay silent for a moment. "I guess the first and the last aren't too bad. But I would hate to forget everything; I could be able to deal with a fit of rage. I think it would be better if you guys just locked me in a room for a while if that happened." I would really hate to forget him and my family and Mira. If I were to forget, I would be completely vulnerable. Onychinus could kill me all the easier. A fit of rage wouldn't seem too bad I think. "That's why you guys were arguing?"

"Yeah, oh and everyone left and Ruban told me it'd better be

done by the time they get back. I really don't want to be responsible for changing you," he says.

"Even Mira?" I ask, suddenly panicked.

"She went too, but she'll be fine. She's in the same vehicle as
Elle and Ruban. Ruban wouldn't let anyone hurt her," he says,
keeping his eyes on the wall.

I let my heart calm down a little before I start to talk again.
"Why does he ..."

"Care for her so much?" finishes Max. I nod. "Did you know
that Ruban had two siblings? You know Miles, but he had a little
sister too. She would have been eleven this past fall, about the
same age as Mira. He adored her and would have done anything
for her. When their home was attacked, there were eight of them
who were on their way to the portal; three of them didn't make it.
They were all close friends. I think this was about six years ago,
so they were all quite a bit younger. I'll sum up the story Ruban
told me, because I don't think he'll want to retell it:

Ruban's Story
He and his friends had heard about a war outbreak from their parents several times at the dinner table. Any time Ruban or any of
his friends even started to ask their parents about it, they just told
them that nothing was wrong and that no matter what happened
they would always love them. No reason to worry, although just
by saying that, it caused the kids to worry.

Every night he and his friends, who were mostly neighbors,
would head out to the pond, which they had discovered not much
earlier before, by accident. They would talk about everything their
parents would say, just to try and figure out what was going on
because no one would tell them.

One night Ruban's parents were much more restless than
usual. They just weren't able to hold still, even during dinner and

when they were doing the dishes. Ruban had decided he was going to ask them what was going on until he finally got a reasonable answer, because it just didn't seem right. He had never seen his parents more scared. While his parents were finishing up with the dishes, Ruban and Miles ran up behind them and grabbed onto the backs of their legs. Their mother jumped and gasped loudly. The kids backed away scared, while their father coaxed her into calming herself.

"Can you please tell us what's wrong?" Ruban asked.

"Nothing is wrong. Your mother is just not feeling well," replied his father. Although Ruban knew it was a lie, he did nothing. He just nodded his head because he knew they weren't going to tell them and that frustrated him. "I think that you kids should head on up to bed," his father said. His mother held onto the edge of the sink, her fingers gripping so tightly that her knuckles turned white. He couldn't see her face, but he knew it was really pale.

"All right," Ruban said.

Their little sister, Beebs, sat on a blanket on the floor playing with her dolly next to the table. Their dad scooped her up into his arms, and with his free arm he guided Miles toward the staircase, Ruban following closely behind. Then he heard his mother sob, and he turned around and ran back to her and hugged her. She seemed a lot smaller than she once was and quite a bit skinnier. He wondered how long she'd been like this.

"I love you," she sobbed. "Always."

"I love you too," he told her.

"Look, whatever happens, just remember both your father and I, we love you, Miles, and Beebs, forever."

"What's going to happen?"

"Bad people are coming, and they are dangerous," said his mother.

"When?"

"I don't know," sobbed his mother again, gripping him in a hug. "But you should head on up to bed. Goodnight," she said, giving a thin smile, and released him. "Remember that I love you. Now go on, while your father's there."

His father tucked him and his siblings into bed and said goodnight to them. It had taken quite a while for Ruban to fall asleep. All he could think about was what his mother had said about dangerous people coming. He woke to a tiny cold hand tapping at his arm that dangled over the bed.

Beebs stood on the floor beside him. She was too small to jump onto the bed, and usually when she wanted to wake him up she would just tap his arm until he woke up.

"What's wrong?" he asked her.

"Mama and Papa won't stop cryin'," she sobbed.

Ruban picked her up and set her beside him on his bed, and that's when they heard the bombs go off outside in the distance. A stream of bullets echoed downstairs, and they could hear two bodies crashing into the floorboards. Ruban knew exactly who they were. There were screams outside that haunted the air.

Miles came bolting into the room and closed the door behind him. "There's people in weird army clothes runnin' through the streets with guns," said Miles frantically.

"Okay, we've got to go," Ruban said. He got to his feet and ran to his dresser and pulled open a drawer. He ripped a lot of his clothes out and threw them on the floor until he found what he was looking for—blades. At school one of the things they were taught—because they lived on a military base—was how to handle blades and throw them. They lived near an army base, so it was mandatory that all of the children knew how to defend themselves. He took all of the blades he had and stuffed them into a bag that was lying in the corner on the floor. "Help Beebs down, please, Miles."

"Where are we going?" asked Miles, helping Beebs down from the bed. She clung onto her dolly, its face already wet from her tears.

"The pond," he said. They could hear loud feet pounding up the stairs. Ruban slung the bag over his shoulders and picked up Beebs. Miles ran to the window with Ruban, and they opened the window as quickly and quietly as they could. "I'll jump first," said Ruban.

He jumped with Beebs in his arms but ended up landing funny and broke his left arm, so he carried Beebs in his right arm. Miles jumped out just as some of the dangerous men came running into the room. It was amazing how all of the friends had had the same idea—to go to the pond.

At the bottom of the pond was actually a portal. They had discovered it when they were swimming there one day after a defense class. They saw that the bottom was spinning, and several fish swam into it and never reappeared. Together they had made a promise that if this war that their parents spoke of ever did occur, that they would all meet at the pond and they would experiment and go through the hole like the fish did. They thought that the worst thing that could happen would be they die.

The air was filled with smoke, and their neighbors' homes and many of the nearby trees were all on fire. There were screams, and everyone who was seen running in the streets were gunned down.

Ruban's house was just on the border line to the trees, so he and Miles ran immediately in that direction, which was also the direction to the meeting place. Several of their friends caught up with them and were running alongside them. They were all completely breathless when they finally reached the pond, all eight of them.

There were gunshots coming from straight behind them. One of the bullets was coming right for Miles, but Isla's older brother pushed him out of the way and yelled at them all to go ahead and jump into the pond. He got hit and fell to the ground. While everyone else got into the water Ace's older sister stayed behind. "Go in," she said. "As soon as all of you are gone in I will follow," she told Ace, and pulled out two of her blades and gave one to Ace. "This is now yours."

Ace jumped into the water at the same time as Miles, and Ruban and Beebs were the last to follow. Ace's sister fell into the water with a puff of blood around her. She had died.

Beebs had been shot. She was so quiet about it, Ruban didn't even notice until he saw the top of her nightdress soaked through with blood. When they dove into the pond she was shot in the back, but the bullet had made its way to her heart. She barely survived the journey and passed away moments after a beautiful sunset on Earth. Before she died Ruban had told her what their mom had said that last night. "Mama and Papa said that they loved us," he told her. "I will love you forever and always." She died with a tiny smile curved in her mouth. They buried her there on that hill where she died.

"THAT IS WHY RUBAN TAKES CARE OF MIRA," says MAX. "He feels like he hasn't done enough for his own little sister. Did you know that this year was the only year since then that he hasn't brought her flowers on her birthday? It was because of the Onychinus people. Also, he is the way he is because he hates when people lie to him. He likes news to be spit out bluntly whether it's good or bad. Usually if he doesn't like it, he gets aggressive and punches something or someone."

I feel an aching pain in my chest. That must have been really hard for all of them. They lost their parents and siblings all in the same day. And they lost their homes and traditions and everything they've ever known.

"All right, I think that it is best if you do heal me then, and whatever the consequences, it is probably for the best. I would really hate to be the one who slows us down."

He just nods his head once, looking at me, and replies, "All right."

I don't know if I really want this, but everyone is better at making decisions than me right now. If they think that it needs to be done then it will be done.

"Will it work, you know, with the cube just over there?" I ask.

"No, that's why we aren't doing it here," he says. "We're doing it outside." He opens the closet door, takes out our shoes, and then drops mine in front of me. "It's barely snowing right now, so it's a good time."

CHAPTER 15

THE CLOUDS ARE THICK WITH SNOW WAITING TO FALL, AND THE trees are broader here. Max leads the way through the trees. They are dark green and thick with pine needles. Others have thick trunks and stand very tall. The ground is already partly covered in crispy snow. We walk a while before Max stops to hold a low-hanging spruce branch out of the way. He nods his head, ushering for me to pass through. I smile at him. I feel his eyes follow me as I walk ahead of him, though he doesn't say anything.

I step into an opening in the trees, a fair-size gap. The grass is all crumpled and brown. If it were alive, it would all stand fairly high, but now it's all in clumps with snow on top. The trees surround the entire opening and some of the taller spruce lean near the top, shielding some of the opening from the sky.

"Why here?" I ask, and glance through the thick grove of trees.

Max comes up behind me; his shoes crunch the frozen grass and snow beneath his feet. "Because I don't think that there is anything here that could spark a memory attack during the process and also everything here is unfamiliar compared to Margaritan. Besides it's far away from the cube," he says.

"What am I supposed to do?" I ask.

He walks a little way past me, and then he quickly turns around and hands me the checkered blanket from the house. I didn't even notice he had brought it with us. I grab onto it. He begins clearing some of the snow and grass away before he speaks again. "You can bring that blanket here and lie it down now." I walk over to him while he pats down and brushes away a few more clumps of grass. "As a precaution, you'll be lying down. It's better than standing in case you suddenly drop."

I drop the blanket just as he says the word *drop*. "Drop?" I ask.

"No worries, that won't happen because you'll be lying down," he says.

I can feel a tightening return in my chest, and I feel myself holding my breath again. Why would I drop?

He looks up and sees the concern on my face. "Hey, it'll be fine." He grabs my hand from where I sit on the outstretched blanket.

"Have you actually done this before?" I ask.

He cocks his head at me and pretends to count on his fingers. "Twice."

"Seriously?" I ask, my voice a little shaky. "How did they turn out, and who did you do it on?"

"The first time was on a complete stranger. It worked out fine, and nothing went wrong. And the second time was on Isla. She had her memories altered when she was a kid. Her parents did it to her, so it was a little more difficult," he explains.

"So say if I did have my memories altered, it could go wrong?" I ask.

"Possibly, but if we don't try it, we'll never find out," he says. "Sit still. I don't know how long until they'll be back." He pats the blanket beside him and pulls out his phone to check the time.

I get to my knees on the blanket. The grass beneath it crunches under my weight, and I feel only a chill at the thought of what is about to happen.

Max slips his phone into his back pocket and kneels on the edge of the blanket. I lie down facing the sky. It is fairly dark, and I can't see the sun. "Will you see into my mind or anything like that? How will you know which outcome it is?"

"I can't see into your mind, and I will only know the outcome after it is finished," he says and leans over me.

"Okay," I say and close my eyes.

His hands gently brush the side of my cheek, and then he moves both hands to my forehead, his fingers close to my temples. They are warm.

I can feel a pulling sensation from my forehead into the nape of my neck, my skin pulling back together, closing the wound. For a moment I think he is finished. Maybe I am actually lucky and I won't have memory problems, I think to myself. But that's until I feel a pain shooting into the back of my head.

I can feel Max's energy surge through and around my head. I can almost visualize it flowing through my brain; a clean, pure energy flowing along with my blood. It hits a spot where I assume it's supposed to, and I can feel the swelling on my brain minimize into nothing. It's working.

A strange pressure, which I hadn't noticed was ever there before, slowly releases itself from my head, and it becomes clear. My head feels clearer than it has ever felt before. But that is until a sharp pain erupts and I feel myself wince.

The memories—they come like an explosion of fire.

A whole bunch of faces also; tears, laughter, and Max. My head is swarming with fear and a curiosity of Max. He is all over my memory. I see him everywhere. In one of the more clear memories, we are both hanging upside down on a branch high up in a tree. I remember the place. It is full of vines and thick leaves on trees with huge trunks. His face appears in so many places. Did I actually know him at one point? I feel my chest tighten again and a burning sensation behind my eyes.

The memories keep coming and coming. Some flicker in brief seconds; others last a bit longer. I don't know if Max's hands are still on my forehead anymore, but I want this to stop. They keep coming.

How many times has my mind been altered? I can't seem to open my eyes. The scenes won't go away. In another I am throwing blades at a target, and they are all striking the center area. I didn't know I could throw blades. I see myself later running through one of Margaritan's huge downpours with Jeremy and Max. In another I see my father screaming at me. Another, I am with Max and Jeremy again. They are both giving me a high five.

Who was I, before?

"Reena!" I hear, but it sounds almost like an echoing whisper. Is it real or fake too? My head is spinning and I feel my shoulders shake. "Reena!" This time it sounds a lot closer. "Reena!"

I open my eyes a little; it feels like they are on fire. My forehead burns like it is going to boil in on itself.

"Oh, thank God!" I hear. It is Max. He grips my shoulders and practically pulls me into a sitting position and hugs me, though my body is numb. I open my eyes completely. The sky is still clouded over, and the light hurts. I feel my heart racing in my chest, and my shirt feels hot and sticky, but besides that I feel extremely cold. Max's embrace warms me slightly. I hug him back and let out a sob. "Are you all right?" he asks.

"I don't know," I whisper in another sob. After what I just saw, I have no idea who I am now, let alone who I was then. But one thing I do know is that Max was in my past. By the looks of it, I think we were friends. Myself, Jeremy, and Max and a few others were good friends. Who would want me to forget that?

He pulls me back and examines my face. "I don't think I messed with your short-term memories," he states in a whisper. "Judging by the tears, it didn't go perfect. I think it's a little early to notice a paroxysm." I'm engulfed into the cold again. "You got your memories back, didn't you?"

I nod and let out another sob. "As it turns out, everything I know about myself is all a lie."

All of the images of me being with him confuse me. When I first saw him at the lake, I was going shopping with Clay; I thought that I did recognize him. I guess I actually did. But how did I recognize him even though my memories had been wiped? I thought that if your memories of someone had been wiped, you wouldn't even remember them.

"What did you see?" he asks.

I rub some heat into my arms. My clothes are still rather sweaty, and the cold air almost freezes them to me. Max leans past me and slides the corners of the blanket over my shoulders. "A lot," I say in almost a whisper. I don't feel exactly like crying, but I do wish I could understand everything I lost. "I didn't think my mind was altered. I thought maybe it was from the concussion, all my memory loss. How can someone be so cruel, to just take away another person's memories? Why would someone do that?"

Max looks at me and says, "They did it to me as punishment. My guess is that they wanted you to be and act in a certain way." Max gets to his feet and fixes the hem of his jacket. "More will come in time. Also the new ones you got back will only become clearer, and maybe you'll later recall conversations."

I nod. My head feels a lot better now. It doesn't throb when I nod.

"We should probably head back. Are you good to walk?" he asks.

"I think so," I reply, and get to my feet.

The clouds grow darker above our heads, and the wind picks up as he puts his arm around my waist. The wind blows over the checkered blanket over my shoulders, which deflects the chill a little.

He leads me through the opening where we first came through. "So did you see what you were like, before you forgot everything? Like were you mean, crazy, or disobeyed every rule in the book?" he asks with a grin at the corners of his mouth.

"Um, supposedly I was amazing at throwing blades," I say. I want to tell him that I also saw him from my past but I don't know how. "I think that I was probably pretty disobedient as well. I got into trouble a lot." We walk out of the way of a tree. "You were there too," I blurt out. My nose feels frozen, and my fingertips are numb. It's really cold out. The ground is already covered in about two inches of snow.

Max tilts his head at me and raises his eyebrows. "Is that so?"

"You were in a lot of them."

"What were we doing? I don't really remember any Ariannas back on Margaritan," he says, his arm still around my waist. The old leaves and grass and snow crunch under our feet. There is a silent pause, and another gust of wind blows through my hair.

"Well, in one, we were throwing blades together, you, me, and Jeremy. Neither of you boys could actually beat me."

"Huh," he says. "Interesting."

"What?" I ask. I can see the house slowly come into view. Two black cars pull up in front of the house. Everyone's back. I wonder what time it is.

He hesitates before he says what's on his mind. "Did you happen to go by another name, back on Margaritan?" he asks, stopping beside a tree. His arm around my waist pulls me to a stop too.

I don't ever remember having another name. Why would I have gone by another name? "I don't think so," I reply. "Why?"

He pauses, and his face drops in disappointment. His eyebrows furrow, and then he just shakes his head once and says, "No reason." Then he starts walking again, only this time he drops his arm from my waist, back to his side, leaving me chilled where his hand was.

Sometimes I wish he wasn't so secretive. But then again I have secrets too, which I don't exactly plan on sharing with him any time soon. I can understand why Ruban is the way he is. It really gets on a person's nerves, to not understand what is going on when it may be important. I do agree that honesty should be what everyone has … to an extent.

When we walk through the opening between the trees, Ace looks up from grabbing at a brown paper bag from the trunk. "We stocked up a lot," he says. "Lots of cans just in case the power goes out or something. Cold soup usually tastes fine."

"Great," says Max as we walk closer to the car. "Trip to town went fine I see."

"Yeah," says Ace holding the bag in his arms. "No weird signs."

Ruban comes through the front door. It squeaks before it slams shut, and the boards of the deck creak under his feet as he walks toward us. "Is it finished?" he asks.

"Yes," says Max and he reaches into the trunk and pulls out another one of the bags. Ruban grabs the last one and closes the trunk while Ace starts climbing the stairs. "Her mind had been altered multiple times by a distorter, so she ended up getting some of her memories back," he says, nodding his head as a gesture to me.

Ruban just sizes me up and down with his eyes and then follows Ace to the front door. "Doesn't surprise me all that much."

"Why do you say that?" I ask, a sliver of anger in my voice.

Max raises his eyebrows at me. Ruban turns on his heels,

stopping Max before the doorway. His face looks kind of intimidating. His eyebrows are furrowed, and his jaw is firm. His eyes, unyielding, hold contact with mine. I don't want to look away first; if I do it'll make me look like I'm scared of him.

"Darling, it's cause you're a princess. Most princesses are either rebels against their families or they are weaklings. Either way that gives them full power to easily alter your memories. That's just how it works," he says, wearing an annoyed look on his face. I look away. I know that's what I really didn't want to do, but it just happens.

What he says sounds a little bit like what Max told me. He shakes his head once and walks through the door. Max follows him in. I am the last to go in. One last gust of wind hits me, and it sinks in the unwanted truth.

It hits me like walking into a brick wall, the delicious smell of pizza. The first and the last time I had pizza was with Clay and Haley, which was months ago. I close the door behind me. Because of the picture Mira drew, I know that the Onychinus soldiers have found them, looking for me. I don't know exactly what happened to them. I don't know if they are prisoners now, if they're being tortured or worse, dead. I don't know, and that's what bothers me.

"Figured we'd get something already warm and that actually tastes good," says Isla. "You've had pizza before, right?" she asks me.

"Yeah, that was one of the first meals I ate on the first official day I got here," I say and slip my shoes off. I lean my back against the sofa. "Clay and Haley," I start. "I wish I knew what happened to them."

Ruban and Max drop their bags onto the counter, beside a bunch of matching brown bags. There is a silent pause, and then Max says, "We won't know till ... later. In the meantime let's just eat. Then we will see who is better at throwing blades, me or you. Your memories might be wrong cause there is only one person who is better at throwing them than me."

"Who?" I ask.

"Lilyryn."

"I guess there will be two of us that will be better than you. I know I can beat you." In one of my memories I could beat him. Surely I can now also.

Everyone stares at me. They all have a slice in their hands, except Max. His dark hair casts a shadow over his face. He slowly walks toward me, away from the counter. Even his dark eyebrows cast a shadow over his eyes. He looks handsomely dangerous. He stops maybe a few inches in front of me. "Do you want to bet?" he asks, looking down at me. He smells like cologne and the outdoors.

"Yeah, I do."

He chuckles, and I look past him. Ruban wears a smirk, and Miles starts shaking his head as if to say no. "All right we'll make a board. Each of us gets three blades. The person to hit the immediate center of all of the various lines drawn on the board wins. If either of us misses, we lose."

"What does the winner get?" I ask. I can feel his breath on me. He's trying to sound intimidating; he's good at it too. It almost scares me a little.

"Winner gets nothing, but loser gets the punishment of night duty," he says.

"Fair enough."

He takes a step back and goes toward the counter again. "Have fun on night duty," he says, snatching a piece out of the box, the smell of cologne and outdoors leaving along with him.

I shrug my shoulders and sneak over to get a slice too. It doesn't have the bland flavor of the sandwiches we've been eating;

it tastes rich and cheesy, although it sparks a memory of Clay and Haley. This one was not taken from me. Now that I think about it, I kind of abandoned them. I thought that if I left them, it would keep them safe and away from danger. Now I feel that if they get hurt it will be my fault. Just like I think that it is sort of my fault that Coral was killed, even though I know it really isn't. It just feels like it because I couldn't do anything to stop it.

CHAPTER 16

ACE EASILY FINDS A BOARD IN THE GARAGE AND ISLA FINDS A bottle of spray paint. Although it's not very full, it'll work. It's just enough to put a few markings on the board for a target.

"Go get your blade," says Max.

"I don't have one."

He hauls several boxes to the side wall. "Yeah you do. It's in your bag in a white box."

"How do you know what that is? I didn't even look at what was in there," I say. I knew that my mother had put a white box in my bag the day I left, but I didn't take time to look what was inside it. I really probably should have. I will.

"I asked Mira to get your peram so they could bring it to town with them. It was put back properly. I think she may have gotten sidetracked and looked in the box." He says it straightforwardly and goes to move another box. I can see the muscles through his shirt, and it makes me wonder—who was I before? Obviously I remember him, but why doesn't he remember me? Maybe he does but just doesn't want to say anything.

When I walk past the dining-room table, I look out the

window at Ruban, Elle, Miles, and Mira as they swing blades around. Mira swings hers during the instructions Ruban gives her. I don't know if I will be able to handle seeing her actually fight and kill someone. It really hurt me to kill someone, even though it was in self-defense, but with how fragile Mira is, it will really hurt me to see her feel the same pain I felt having to kill.

I want to run outside and rip the blade from her hands and hide her away from this madness, but I know I can't. It would leave her vulnerable if she couldn't fight and protect herself.

I race up the stairs and turn a sharp corner to my room. My bag remains in the same place as it was this morning. I pick it up off the floor and open the latch; the texture of the soft leather is smooth under my fingertips. I take a few steps and kneel on the edge of my bed and open the bag fairly wide. There are few contents, just the letters, my darkly bound book, my peram, my hairbrush, the white box, and several other small things. I snatch the white box out. It is actually fairly heavy. Inside the box is a blade about the same size as the Amethystus blades. There is a sheath over the blade, which is pearly white. The handle is gold and has a unique pattern engraved in it, and there are several tiny pearls embedded in the gold close to the blade. I slip the protective sheath off. The blade itself is silvery in color from the tip and darkens gradually to a dark grayish gold.

The handle feels familiar and almost comfortable in my hand. This definitely trumps a shard of glass for a weapon. I recognize it. This is one of the blades I actually used to practice with. I wonder why my dad took it away.

"Reena. Are you coming?" Max calls from the bottom of the stairs.

"Yeah, I'll be right there." I quickly slip the sheath back over the blade and toss the white box back into my bag. I slide my bag right next to my pillow and race toward the door.

As I run down the stairs, Max watches me and says, "Fancy blade. It's nice."

"Thanks," I say. "You've got a nice one too." In his hand is a metallic gold handled blade with an embroidered pattern. He just looks at it in his hand and shrugs his shoulders.

"Mira found a box full of them in the storage behind the stairs," he says. "I wish I had my old blades, but we may as well start using these ones. They're not the greatest, but they'll do." He pushes the door open for me and follows me as I pass by him.

The cold breeze hits me as soon as I step out the door. "I still don't think that you are going to win against me," says Max. "To be completely, honest I wouldn't be surprised if you could though."

"Well, I guess we'll see," I challenge. "You can throw first."

We walk toward the board that Ace and Isla are securing to a tree. Ace ties one last knot as we approach. With the black spray paint, Isla has created several fairly thin lines for targets. "So the person who gets their blades closest to or on the lines wins. Easy enough?" Ace asks, backing away from the target, over to the side.

I nod and so does Max, grinning at me.

I hold my blade, sheathed, in my hands. Ruban, Elle, Miles, and Mira all quit swinging their blades around and start walking toward where Ace stands. Isla brings out several other blades from a box near the tree. She hands two to Max and the other two to me, so we each have three. They feel cold in my hands, and I can see my breath in the air. It's colder than usual these past few weeks. This is the coldest place I have ever lived ...

Max rotates his shoulders and cracks his neck.

"Just letting you both know, this is not just a competition. It is also great practice," says Isla.

"Awesome, dual benefit," says Max. He squints his eyes and takes a breath in through his nose. His arm swings back with the blade in his hand. Just as quickly he releases the blade, after thrusting his arm forward. It hurls toward the board. The blade wedges itself into the wood about a millimeter beside the darkly painted line. He's good. He sends another one sailing through the air, and another. They both hit. One after the other, they both plant themselves closely to the center of their lines.

No one looks particularly surprised, not even Mira. I feel something drop into the pit of my stomach.

Max waves his hand, ushering me to come take my place. I walk over. The snow-covered grass crunches under my feet. I wonder if my confidence was too high earlier. Although if I could beat him before, I'm sure I can beat him now.

"Remember, watch duty … if you lose," Max reminds me. He turns on his heel, and we trade spots. "It's all yours."

I take a deep breath through my mouth and feel the cold air fill my lungs. I raise my arm, and the cold twists across and through my sweater, wrapping around me. I lurch my arm forward, releasing the blade at the last moment. It sails through the air, and I notice everyone watching as it goes head over handle, head over handle, and head over handle. Thump. It drills its way into the board.

"Whoa, I think she's actually gonna beat him," Miles whispers to Ruban.

Right in the center of the line sticks my blade. The gold handle glints along with delicately sparkling snow. Max's blade is so close, they are almost touching.

I don't even look over at Max, because I know he's already staring at me.

I aim the next and toss it. This time it too digs itself next to Max's.

"You can quit hitting the center anytime now," suggests Max. He almost wears a grin. He crosses his arms over his chest. It looks like he's both impressed and slightly annoyed.

"And why would I want to do that?" I smirk at him. He raises an eyebrow. "Isn't night duty the punishment for the loser?"

The last one of Max's blades is so close to the center of the line, I don't know if I can hit it.

I lift my hand. The handle of my blade feels smooth, but I know its tip is deadly. The movement of swinging and releasing the blade feels all so familiar, how the handle leaves my hand when my arm is fully extended. It slices through the air almost in slow motion. I can see exactly where it is going to embed itself.

My heart leaps as the blade slams into the board. It makes sort of an echo through the trees. I shudder slightly as I brush a hand through my windblown, wavy hair. At least now I don't have to worry about reopening the gash.

The last blade, again, sticks into the center of the spray painted line.

I glance over in Mira's direction. Ruban nods his head in approval. A thrill of excitement runs through me. I think I may have possibly won Ruban's approval. I never thought that was possible.

"Hmm," says Max and he starts walking toward the board. I thought he would be quite frustrated. But no. He actually looks kind of impressed. I guess now he really has been beaten by two people, both girls.

Everyone else gets back to what they were doing, and I start toward the board to gather up my blades. I can feel the snow and frozen grass crunch under my shoes. It is only a few more steps to the board, before Max asks me, "Where did you learn to throw like that?"

He yanks one of his blades from the board making a loud noise. The blade glints in the swift movement from shadow to light.

"My dad taught me," I say. It comes so fluently, the words. I feel like I've known that answer since forever, yet I only found out about an hour ago. "Supposedly I needed a little extra training in defense class. I think that's partially why I was training with you and Jeremy." The memory almost comes clear.

There are target boards much like this and others, in the shape of men, with circles in the centers of their chests. I am throwing blades with both Jeremy and Max. Both of them hit very near the center, but mine hits dead middle. I don't know what we're saying or even what we were talking about, but I recognize that we were having fun. My father was the first one to teach me to throw blades, the right way, when I was young. Then as I got older he managed to get me to take the higher up defense classes in school. That explains why Max was practicing with me and Jeremy. But how was Jeremy in the class too? Is he actually the same age as me, or is he older? I feel like I don't know everyone as well as I thought. Max has been a mystery to me ever since I saw him by the lake; I guess he's even more of a mystery than I knew.

"Interesting," he says. "Are you sure you didn't go by another name? Because I know I would remember an Arianna if she could beat me like that." He yanks another one of his blades from the board and slips the sheath over it.

"I really don't know. Not much has revealed itself as clear," I say. It takes some effort, but I manage to pluck my blade from the board. I take a few steps closer to him. I shiver even though I can feel the warmth in his presence; he is a familiar mystery to me. I used to know who he was, and now I'm barely remembering him.

He reaches for his last blade and slides the last sheath out of his back pocket. "It should become clear in time. I think that you should start focusing on remembering to fight. Looks like you have throwing blades down pat. Anything that can come in handy to fight these guys or even something that gives us an advantage against them." He covers the last blade and stuffs two of them in his back pockets.

I hold my blade up. It has a story behind it that belongs to me, a story that is linked with Jeremy and Max. "Do you recognize this?"

He pauses, holding the one blade between both his hands, and then his eyes flicker up at me. "Yes. How do you have it?" he asks. His eyes hold pain, and his jaw is tight.

"My mom gave it to me before I came to earth," I say. "Why?"

"No reason," he says.

"Seriously, please tell me."

"No. Forget I said anything." He starts backing up and turns on his heel.

The wind blows through my hair, returning the same familiar chill.

"Yes!" yells Elle. "She's got it." Elle stands watching Mira and Miles swinging their blades around at each other and doing spin moves. They practice their defensive skills. Miles swings at her for offensive, but she slips right past him. "You're getting it too, kind of," she says to Miles.

I pluck the rest of my blades from the board and sheath them. One of them slips through my fingers. I bend over quickly to pick it up, my hand brushes the snow. Another memory comes to me in a flash.

In a bent-over position, Max comes up beside me. He holds up a pale pink lotus flower. "For you," he says. "Would you like to go one last time before making a decision?"

I grab the book from the ground that I had dropped. It is gold and darkly leather bound. "Are you sure it's a good idea that we leave? My father, he'll never allow it. Will we leave Jeremy behind? He's important too. I know that you two have known each other for a very long time." I stand up and face him. I let him brush my long curls back and tuck the flower behind my ear.

I wear a white dress that ends at my knees, and my feet are bare.

Most days I have to wear dresses. It's practically all I own. Once a month I am allowed to wear pants, but I really don't mind. It's usually so hot; I don't mind wearing light dresses.

There is a beautiful garden around us; the pathway leading up to the palace is stone and cracked. My father was going to have it fixed, but I insisted that it added character and beauty, so he let it stay this way.

I hold the book in my hands and look at him. We have been talking about leaving Margaritan for a couple weeks now. I really do want to. I've seen the portal in the palace and have shown it to Max. Together we have seen the beauty of other places. He has his munera already, and so does Jeremy; they both received quite rare ones. Part of me wants to stay so I can get my munera too on my seventeenth birthday, but another part of me wants to leave so I can run away and be with Max. I know that my father will not allow it here because of what he is, a mixed blood and also a sorcerer, someone with mysteries for gifts.

"Hmm," says Max with a slight grin on his face. "He doesn't have to know, until we're gone. I think that he can move on. With his munera he can make any girl fall in love with him." He grabs one of my hands from my book. "Once more, can we look at it? You can decide whenever you're ready. I'm ready to leave at any time."

"All right," I agree, and we begin walking on the cracked stone path.

"I'm assuming you lost your shoes again," he says and grins at me. He has a look in his eyes that just makes me fall in love with him all over again.

"No I did not," I say, trying to put on a straight face. "We are playing hide and seek, and they're winning." I continually misplace them. Whenever they get uncomfortable, I take them off and put them in a place I usually think I'll remember, but then I just don't. I smile.

And then the memory fades into a blur of people running around, pain in my arms and legs and my brain hurting so badly, I scream in the memory. There is one other person being held in front of me. I can barely see his face; it fades faster and faster until I cannot see his face anymore.

I grasp the blade tightly in my hand and straighten. I didn't know how it would feel, getting detailed memories back. It feels almost as though what happened then is actually happening.

"Reena, you're up next," says Ruban, he strides toward me. "Sure you can throw blades, but can you actually fight with one?"

"Yes, I can," I whisper.

He stops in front of me. He wears a black hoodie and jeans and a dark toque hiding all of his hair. "What's up?" he asks. "It looks like you've seen a ghost."

"It's nothing," I start, but I see Ruban's eyebrows furrow. I continue to forget how much Ruban hates people lying to him. "I guess just remembering sucks," I spit out.

His face softens a little. "After-effects of cleaning up a distorter's mess?"

I nod.

"Hey, on the plus side, if you remember the distorter who did this to you, you can kick his ass after." He grins.

"Yeah," I say quietly. "Hey, please tell me something."

"What?" he says, sliding his fingers over the handle of his blade. The amethyst in the handle glints as he tilts it.

"Actually two things." I pause. He looks a little impatient, but he stays quiet. "One, please tell me they have the sheaths on." I point at Miles and Mira swinging their blades around. Elle and Isla are doing the same. Ace just mentors them. I don't know where Max has gone. Ruban chuckles for a moment and then turns to them.

"Yes they do. But when it comes to real battle, the sheaths are gone. What's the second thing?"

I look him in the eyes. They are a light brown. "How do you cope? You seem so strong, but I know there's more," I say.

"I've accepted what happened. I don't let anything weigh me down; there is no point. I just ignore what happened. It was years ago. The longer you linger in the past, the longer you'll be miserable," he says, straining himself. "For you, I recommend just taking everything one day at a time. Well, in our case, one hour at a time. There is no specific time we'll have to leave again."

"Thanks," I say, registering it.

"All right let's train. No more sad talk."

CHAPTER 17

"I SERIOUSLY WISH I KNEW WHAT THEY SHOT YOU WITH," SAYS Max. He stands beside the chair. Ruban impatiently sits by the dining table.

It has been several days since Max has returned my memories to me. I have slowly been getting used to using my munera around the cube. I guess it makes me stronger, practicing like this. More things continue to come back to me. Some things I'm not sure I even want to remember, like the times I've gotten into trouble, which is actually more times than I wish to count.

It has been extremely snowy and windy and the house feels cooler, even though the heaters are working.

"Can't you just cut the stupid thing out?" yells Ruban. The black mark under his skin has grown since it first appeared. "If you won't, I will."

Max studies it for a second. He looks like his mind is working in a million different ways. "Fine. Give me your blade. I'll try to dig it out, but honestly I don't know what it is. There are no distinct features to it." He pauses, and Ruban passes him his blade. "Oh, if you get mad at me later, just remember that I have six witnesses to say that I had your permission."

"Fine, just get it out," he says, annoyed. I can barely see even a second of fear in his eyes; it comes and goes in a matter of a millisecond.

"Mira, Miles, come with me," says Isla. Her face looks a little paler than usual as she walks by. Even though she won't admit to it, I can tell that blood kind of bothers her. When we were attacked that first time at the motel, Ace quickly came in the room to take her away from all the death.

"But I …" hesitates Miles. He looks disappointed and ready to argue.

"Go," says Ruban rather quietly. That settles it. Whatever Miles was going to say gets pushed back into his mouth, and he, Mira, and Isla walk toward the staircase, not looking back.

"Hold this to your arm for a bit," says Max, holding a folded towel filled with snow to Ruban's arm.

Elle stands by the sink. She strides over and grabs a dishrag from the drawer. She dampens it under the tap and folds it as she heads toward Ruban and Max. The first aid kit is opened, and some of its contents are spread around the table. "Bite this if it hurts too much," she says.

Max disinfects the blade with an antiseptic wipe. I feel my stomach turn. I look over at Ace. He leans against the back of the couch; he doesn't even say anything comforting to Ruban, knowing he would hate it. For the same reason, I keep my mouth shut.

Outside the wind howls like an angry beast. We haven't been able to train outside because of the weather; instead we've been indoors working on man-to-man combat, using our powers. We can all use our muneras by the cube now, some of us stronger than the others, especially Mira; she has been able to without any practice. I still don't understand how that works. How is she stronger than the rest of us?

"Ready?" asks Max. He flicks Ruban's arm. "Did you feel that?"

"Not really," says Ruban.

"Good." Max steadies Ruban's shoulder with one hand, and with the other he holds the tip of Ruban's blade inches away from his skin.

He nods his head once; his teeth are clenched on the rag in his mouth. With that Max pierces the skin with the blade. A thin steady stream of blood runs down his arm.

"Elle, go get a bowl," Max suggests. He wipes away some of the blood with a handful of gauze, but it continues to run in a steady stream onto the paper towels under the chair.

I can see a bead of sweat run down the side of Ruban's face. His eyes are closed.

I remember one time when I was a kid, I fell really hard on a bunch of sharp rocks and sliced my elbow. The healer had to clean it out and numbed it so they could get the rest of the debris out. I can imagine how Ruban feels, although they are both under very different circumstances that we had people digging into our arms.

Elle comes back around the counter with the bowl and sets it on the table. Max works silently with the blade, nudging the skin to the side, so he can get to the dark spot. It's deeper than I thought.

Ruban lets out a low, harsh breath; his jaw clenches and un-clenches on the rag. I can see more sweat build up near his fore-head, and a tear rolls down his cheek.

"Ace, go see if we have a bottle of strong liquor in the garage. I'm sure we have some," orders Max. He turns to Elle and says, "Go get more snow, so we can numb his arm again. I think the effect is wearing off."

Quickly they both leave the room, leaving only Ruban, me, and Max alone.

"Um …" I start to say and stand up from the couch.

"Reena, I need you here," says Max calmly, but urgently. I almost run to his side.

Ruban clenches his fists. He barely opens his eyes at me and then closes them again. "I need you to use your telekinesis to get this out."

"What?" I ask, almost stunned.

"Look. It's some kind of device, and it's not just under his skin like we thought. It's actually attached to his bone." Ruban winces. "I don't want this open longer than it needs to be. I don't want it to get infected."

I feel my insides turn. "And the blade can't get it off?" I ask, looking at the open gash leaking with blood running down his arm.

"No. The device, if anything touches it, retracts away," he says. "So if you can pull it out, without physically touching it, the sooner I can close up his arm."

"All right," I say. Max passes me one of the septic wipes, also wiping his own hands down with one. It doesn't do him any good, the blood just smears.

The door to the garage opens wide; quickly Ace comes in, with a dark brown glass bottle. He kicks the door closed, pops the cork on the bottle, and speedily comes to Ruban's side. He pushes the bottle close to Ruban's mouth. "Drink," he says. Ruban takes a huge gulp of the dark liquid inside. It looks a lot like the bottle that was being passed around at the bonfire. It feels like so long ago that I went to that. Ruban's face contorts as he swallows another gulp of the foul-smelling liquid. His face and hair are covered in sweat.

I lift my hands just above the gash and feel a cold gust of wind as Elle slams the door closed. I see the strange device attached to his bone, and I look at Max. He just nods his head once at me with kind and understanding eyes. I twist my fingers in a way that

I would if I was actually trying to grab hold of the object. I can almost feel it unfasten itself from the bone.

Suddenly something bashes into my ribs, just as I notice the device is nearly off. I curl inward from the blow. Ruban's good arm is suddenly yanked backward, away from me. Why did he hit? He grunts in agony and lets out a loud gasp that sounds almost like a sob. Tears run from his eyes as Ace and Max try to restrain him in his chair. His arm is a bloody mess, and the metal device protrudes halfway out of his arm. "Stop!" he cries. "Stop!" He takes a deep breath and sobs again. "Just stop."

I look at Max as he struggles to hold him down. "Get it out," he yells.

Elle tries to help, but he won't stop fighting.

I raise my hands again, and this time a little less carefully, I jerk them quickly. Ruban lets out a muffled scream. The device falls to the floor, bent, along with a heavy stream of blood.

Ruban continues to thrash under their weight. "I've had it!" shouts Ace. He lets go and punches him in the head. At that point he stops thrashing and goes limp. "Sorry buddy," he whispers, relaxing his shoulders a little.

"I guess that works," says Max, releasing his hold too. He quickly grabs a handful of gauze. "Now I've got to clean this mess up." Taking the gauze, he presses it onto Ruban's arm to slow down the bleeding.

He is silent as he works. "How come you couldn't just heal him, like you did for me, rather than digging into his arm?" I ask, a little upset.

Removing the gauze, he places both his hands on Ruban's bloody arm, one at his shoulder and the other at his wrist. I watch as the wound cleans itself and the skin stitches back together slowly. He releases Ruban's arm, letting it drop at the limp figure's side.

"There was nothing to heal. The device didn't even pierce the skin." He pauses and picks it up off the floor. "Look, we had to get it out and that was the only way," he says sternly and points to Ruban.

"Where are we putting him?" Ace asks, leaning against the counter. Ruban sits crumpled in the chair, and his eyes slowly start to blink. He is completely covered in sweat. His arm is covered in blood despite the fact his wound is closed and there is no trace of where the blood came from.

"Nowhere. He's good to go," says Max, irritated.

Ruban sits up in his chair and glances over at his arm. His face is red, and he places his hand on his head. "Ow."

"Oh, by the way, you're gonna have a headache for a while," says Ace, with no regret in his voice.

"You're an ass," Ruban says, with very little anger. He drops his hand to his lap, with Elle standing at his side. "What the hell is that thing?"

"Don't know," says Max, examining it. "Go shower or something. You smell bad."

"Fine," he says and stands to leave.

I can see the sweat on his chest start to dry, but he looks shiny all over, in every crease between his highly noticeable muscles.

"Even though you helped and all, it still doesn't mean I like you," Ruban says to me, meeting my eyes.

"That's fine, I don't expect you to," I say. "But let me know when you finally do."

He takes a step toward me. "Like that will ever happen," he says and turns in the direction of the hallway.

I feel my heart drop slightly; I wish I could actually understand why he doesn't like me so much. Right when I feel like I'm starting to make progress, he shuts that down and reminds me that he doesn't like me. I look at Ace, and he just shrugs his shoulders.

On the floor by the chair is a pool of blood and gauze. If a regular person were to walk into the house right now, they'd probably think that someone was murdered. Ruban probably would've died or came close to bleeding out if Max hadn't possessed the gift of a healer.

"Ignore him," says Ace. "He doesn't like a lot of people."

Elle starts wiping up the mess with a rag and the bowl, but it gets soaked at her first dab at erasing the puddle. "I think you might be close to his respect level," she says, as she looks up with a short grin.

"I hope so," I say. "Because we will need to have each other's backs if something goes wrong." I pause for a second and then change the subject. "That's not going to work." I nod toward her attempt at cleaning the mess.

I cross over to her and grab the other bowl from the table. I don't know what Max wants it for, but I'm gonna use it instead. He stands there quietly with Ace, examining the device.

I set the bowl down beside Elle and the mess.

"To be completely honest, however you plan on cleaning this, it probably won't surprise me at this point." Elle drops the rag into her bowl.

If the future wasn't such a tangled mess of "I don't know" I think we could actually be good friends. I already consider Isla, Miles, and Ace good friends. Elle is finally starting to soften toward Mira and me. Max is quite quiet. He hasn't spoken much to me, only when he's giving me fighting advice, even though I can already beat him every time when blades are involved. I think that ever since I mentioned seeing him in my memories, he might be trying to avoid thinking about it or anything that relates to me. I can see that it hurts him when the topic is brought up. I've been trying to avoid it, but I really want to know what happened.

"The great thing about telekinesis is that you don't have to touch stuff you don't want to but can get the work done anyways," I tell her. I tilt my hand at an angle above the bowl and the mess. The blood drains into the bowl in a steady stream, until it is all gone from the floor.

"I wish—" starts Elle sadly.

"Hey," says Max, cutting her off. "Do you remember the medallion you tore from the Onychinus's throat?"

I remember it. How could I not? It has an onyx stone clasped between silver threads connected into a chain. I took it just before we left the motel a little over a week ago. "Yeah, why?"

"I need it; can you get it for me, please?"

"Sure," I say, a little confused, and get to my feet.

Mira sits on our bed fiddling with her blade, while Isla sits behind her and weaves her liquid gold hair.

"Is it out?" asks Isla, her face slightly concerned, her eyebrows raised.

"Yeah. Now that I inflicted pain on him, he has a real reason not to like me," I try to joke, but I don't really feel it has much humor. I pick up my bag.

"Oh well," she says. "Hey. Does Max or anyone know what it is?"

"Not yet. Max wanted to see this medallion I found. I think he thinks they're connected or something," I say as I search for the chain. Instead I find the golden pearl sitting there. It is hard to understand what my father meant by "bearer of the golden pearl." Why am I the bearer? Why did I get it and not someone else? I wonder if someone else at the banquet had gone before me, would I have gotten it anyway? I wonder if I was specifically chosen. "Ha, I found it!" I say and close up my bag, hiding the pearl from my view.

"That's weird," she says. "All of them had those same medallions."

I nod and place the strap of my bag over my shoulder. "Yeah. I'm gonna go bring this to him," I say and hold up the silver chain with the pendent as dark as night. "Oh, by the way, Mira, your hair looks amazing."

She smiles and brushes her fingers over the braid Isla weaved behind her.

I walk out of the room and back down the stairs. The pendent feels warm in my hands.

The device is oddly shaped now that I actually look at it, probably because it never got the chance to reach its full size; we ripped it out before that could happen. I can't believe it was growing onto his bone, and it didn't even pierce through his skin getting there.

"Can I see that?" asks Ace. Not even waiting for an answer, he plucks the pendant from my cold fingers. "Cool … thief!" he says with a grin.

"I am not! They were dead; he technically didn't own it anymore."

"Whatever. Keep telling yourself that." He shrugs. "Thief!"

Just then the device in Max's hand starts buzzing, a really high squealing noise that pierces my eardrums.

"Oh, great," says Max, frowning. "Let me see that." He holds his hand out and Ace drops the necklace into it. The squealing continues, only much louder the closer it is to the device. "It's a tracker."

"What is it?" asks Elle, almost yelling.

"A tracker," Max repeats. "They know where we are."

"Are you sure of that? How long do you think?" Ace asks, standing beside me. He shuffles toward it.

Max presses the medallion to the mangled tracker, and almost immediately the squealing diminishes. "I think this whole time," he says.

"Well, why aren't they attacking?" I ask, feeling something

tighten in the pit of my stomach. Ace walks past me, leaving a chill that runs down my spine.

"Isla!" Ace calls from the base of the staircase. "Can you guys come downstairs?"

Max drops the medallion and tracker on the table. "Shit," he says and brushes his fingers through his already tousled hair. He always does that every time he's either frustrated or in the process of trying to figure something out … or both.

Miles is the first one down the stairs, holding his sheathed Amethystus blade, his face straight and serious. He's wearing a dark blue hooded sweater, making his dark hair stand out against his pale skin. Mira and Isla are second to follow, both of them, their hair wound in complicated-looking braids. They both wear slight grins, but they fade as soon as they notice the tension.

"What?" Isla asks.

"It's a tracker, like a GPS, although it was expanding," explains Max.

"So they—" interrupts Miles.

"They know where we are," finishes Max. He looks up when he notices Ruban walking down the hall, his hair slick and shiny with water, and he looks upset at the news.

I wonder if there is anything in my bag that could be of any importance. My father did leave some other stuff, but I haven't had any time to look at any of it. Now is the time. I walk over toward the table and take a seat just to Max's right. I can hear them all arguing, but I block them out. I unlatch my bag and then with one deep breath, I dump all of its contents out into the open. Everyone turns toward me.

"Max, I know you know what this is," I say and pick up the leather-bound book. It feels so delicate in my hands. He looks weary when I reach it out to him. "Can you look and see if there is anything we can use from the information?"

He slowly takes it from my hands; he looks at it like he's seeing a ghost. "Sure." It comes out almost as a whisper. The frustration is gone from his face, and it is replaced with awe.

"How is any of this junk going to make any difference? They know where we are. We are as good as dead," shouts Ruban.

"Look," I shout back. "To be honest I have no idea if any of it will help out at all. The truth is that I need to know what this junk is! I can't rely on the memories coming back to me; they come and leave just as fast. I don't understand them. So sorry if I have hope; I don't want to die!"

"Fine, look at it, but it's a waste of time." He frowns and a crease forms between his eyebrows. He brushes a hand through his hair, making drops of water fling in every direction. He slides a chair out of place across from me and sits. "Since there is nothing better to do, because of this shit weather, I'm gonna snoop." He picks up one of the pouches and starts looking inside.

"Whatever," I say as Elle slips into the chair beside him and Isla in the next, then Mira slowly comes by me.

Max stands still, and I watch as his fingers hesitantly undo the binding. His hand shakes as he flips to the very first page. I can see the remembrance in his eyes and they suddenly get glassy. He lifts them to me, making eye contact. I should look away, but I don't want to.

I know something—well, I think that I do. As much as I want it to be true, a part of me hates the idea, though it would make perfect sense. It would solve the complicated connection between us. Some of the words from my past echo in my head.

I think that I am *Lilyryn*.

CHAPTER 18

A GUST OF COLD AIR HUSHES THROUGH THE ROOM. I WAKE TO A chill and notice the window open. A small scattered layer of snow covers the floor between the bed and the window.

I slip out from underneath the covers and run to the window. It is almost frozen open. "Mira, can you help me close this?" I ask Mira and tug on the top of the window. I look over my shoulder. My heart drops when I see her lying on the floor barefoot, with her sketchpad. Her fingers are bloody and blistered. She is silent when she falls into her trances of drawing. I let go of the window. It stays open, and I drop to my knees by her side. "Mira," I whisper, pulling her into a sitting position, propping her back against the wall. "Mira!" I whisper louder, my heart plummeting.

Her skin is ice cold under my fingertips. The wind picks up and gusts snow into the room. I shiver. "Stupid thing!" I shout and wave my hand downward at it. It slides down fast, slamming shut.

I yank one of the spare blankets down from the bed and cover her with it. Her eyes are closed. She looks both tense and really pale, and her lips are slightly turning blue. She had to have been drawing, but why would she open the window? How could she have opened it? What could she have possibly been drawing at this late hour?

Snatching her sketchbook, my fingers scramble over the cover to open it.

"Don't," I hear Mira croak and see her scared eyes. She watches me and a tear rolls down her cheek.

The book is already open to the last page with charcoal. There is a storm and many pencil sketched people are treading in the snow, lost. They are not very clear, so I have no idea who these people are; I can only guess.

"Mira, who are these people?" I ask, my fingers gripping the sides of the book.

"It wasn't clear," she says, pointing at it, "obviously."

"Yeah, I can see that." I set it on the bed. "How about the window. Why did you open it?"

"I wanted to see if there was a possibility of it being us. The glass was frosted, and I wanted to see outside," she says. "Are you mad?"

I think about it for a few seconds and say, "No. Not in the least, not at you anyway. I just found you and as crazy as the situation is. I'm glad you're here."

"Me too," she says. "I'm glad I have a sister. I thought that all of you were dead, and then I see you in a vision. I thought that it was just teasing me, because all the professors told me that my family died in a plane crash, and that I was left with a babysitter that night. After that I was put into the system. The nuns at the academy took me in when I was small. They raised me, fed me, gave me clothes, and let me have a room of my very own on one of the upper floors where the rest of the girls dorm."

I sigh. I wonder where that story came from.

"So does this mean everyone else is alive too?" she asks, worry in her expression. I shiver again, not just because I'm cold but because I know where this conversation is going. Coral.

"Let's get on the bed, and I'll tell you about them."

"Okay," she says wearily.

I snatch the sketchbook and crawl back onto the side of the bed closer to the door. "All righty," I say and pull the quilt back onto my lap, tucking the book by my legs. "As far as I know five out of six are still alive."

"What? Who died?"

I run my fingers over the clasp of my necklace. I undo it and slip the chain from my neck. This is actually the first time I've taken it off; it makes me feel bare.

"This is Flora," I say, snapping the locket open to show her. She leans in and drinks up the photo with her eyes. "This is Coral, me, and that's mom and dad," I say, showing her all of us. It feels so strange actually telling someone the truth about my family—our family. When I lived in Chyraville with Clay and Haley, none of my friends were allowed to know the truth. It just feels strange finally talking about it. Sure I've told Max a little bit about my family, but it's just different with Mira because she is family. Family should know that one another exists. It breaks my heart to know that I never got to actually grow up with her, braid each other's hair, play tag around the palace, sing like fools together, annoy and pick fun at our older sisters. I never got to do any of that, and now that we finally know each other we're running for our lives and trying to come up with a plan to save our home. If I can even call Margaritan that anymore. A part of me still wonders what a home even is. I know what Ace told me, that a home is different for everyone, but really right now I'm not sure what mine is.

"So who's … gone?" she whispers, discontinuing that continually painful thought. I push it to the back of my mind and continue trying to lock it there. I don't like when I have to convince myself and come up with theories to make any of it seem fair.

I take a very deep breath and point to Coral. It hurts to see her in the photo and know that I won't get to see her smile ever again. It's bad enough I never even got to say good-bye to her before I was banished.

"The people we're running from, they killed her." It feels almost unreal. She's gone. Her hair is long and a bit darker than mine; her face is sharp and attentive but also fragile and beautiful, making her look mature and fair. She was engaged too. She was to be married in the early year coming up; she was so excited. Now though, she will never get to marry the man she loved or become the queen she was meant to be after she was married.

"She was so beautiful," says Mira, clear admiration all over her face.

"Yes, she was," I say. "I can't believe she's gone." A tear burns my cheek as it leaks from the corner of my eye. "Last time I saw her was on my birthday, months ago."

"Hey," she whispers, patting my arm. "At least you got to know her."

I nod. She stays quiet with her hand still gently resting on my arm. She's right—I already know my family, and the locket just treasures them closer to my heart. Unfortunately Mira never got the chance to know them. "Here." I hold out the necklace to her. "I want you to have it."

She looks up at me, her eyes glazing over. "I can't accept this. It's yours and it's special."

"Yes, it's very special—that is why I'm giving it to you. As a princess, you have to show respect and accept gifts given to you from your older sister." I wink at her.

She giggles at that and nods her head once, lifting her hand to accept the locket.

I feel my heart drop the moment I place the necklace in her delicate hands. "This means a lot to me, but because you mean more, it's yours," I tell her.

"Thank you," she says, brushing her fingers across the surface of the soft metal.

I think it might be tears clouding my vision, but it's not. It's the same feeling I had when I was at the hospital back in Chyraville.

Mira and the darkness of the room blurs. The last thing I see is Mira leaning over me, shaking my shoulders …

The fuzziness clears slowly into what looks like a prison.

"Sir, they're in the middle of a storm. It is way too blinding to go for them now," says a narrow built man. His hair is shortly cropped to his head, and it shines silver, but the build of his face is far too young for the aged color of his hair.

"Is it possible?" a familiar stern voice asks. It's the man who killed Coral. They stand beside a shiny metal desk right beside a door.

"Well, yes, but it'll be a lot harder to find them, and it works to their advantage." He pauses. "Sir, it is possible they can escape."

"Why would they escape?" yells the man. "We have a greater supply of manpower, and it would be an embarrassment to lose eight kids. It's bad enough they got away the first time!"

"Um," says the younger man and swallows.

"Give the order!" The leader stares down, angrily. "You better get it done properly or you're going to lose your rank. All that really needs to be done is," he lowers his voice, "bring me the girl with the pearl and Max and you have the order to kill the others. I have absolutely no need for those Amethystus junkies; they should have been dead with their planet years ago."

"But sir?"

"It's a simple enough job. Do not question me. I can strip you from your rank this very moment, and I know just how hard you worked for

it. Bring me the pearl, the girl, and the boy and kill the others. That's it!" Both of them leave after that, slamming the door shut behind them.

Something shiny catches my eye, and I walk toward the cells. My heart flutters when I see my father sitting in one cell a few rows in and Jeremy in the one beside him. I know this is another directive, and I think it's Jeremy who's been sending them. The cells are closed off by glass panels, separating them. There are quite a few of them, and they seem to all be occupied. Some prisoners look bored and just lean against the wall and others just look terrified.

I reach the cell my father sits in. He has a cot, a toilet that is covered on both sides, and a small table off to the side. His back is against the foot of the bed, and it looks like he's lost some weight and color to his skin.

I press my hand up against the glass, but I don't feel it; my hand just stops. I sigh and move to Jeremy's. He sits propped up on his cot, his back against the wall, and he stares at the glass in front of him. His eyes flicker toward mine, making contact. Can he actually see me? I wonder if he could see me with Max the first time I got a directive.

"They're coming," he whispers to me. He looks different from when I last saw him; he looks exhausted, with dark bruises under his eyes. He looks like he's lost some weight too. "Bring it to the piscinæ fati."

I nod and feel a tightening in my chest. I know what he means though he doesn't chance saying it out loud.

"Be careful," he whispers, a sense of concern and sadness in his voice.

A fist slams against the glass right beside my hand. I nearly jump out of my skin. I take a step back.

"What are you muttering about, boy?" he shouts.

"Nothing," Jeremy lies. The guard frowns; clearly he does not believe him. "Just recalling my last conversation with my girlfriend; funny how good comebacks only come to you after the argument is over." He carries on naturally, with a grin.

"Yeah," agrees the guard and chuckles. "So true. Anyway, you have to shut your mouth. Otherwise you're gonna get into some major trouble

with Commander Drusus." And with that, he moves on down the row of glass cells, pacing his footsteps evenly, his face plastered with a blank gaze.

Then the vision fades, and the last thing I see are Jeremy's eyes staring into mine as they blur into darkness.

My shirt sticks to me, and my heart is pounding. I know my father and Jeremy are all right, but by the sound of the wind howling outside, I remember *they're coming* and they're close.

Mira sits beside me shaking my shoulders and Max on my right, close to the door. I gasp for air, and my eyes ever so slowly begin to focus, drawing me back. Mira must have gotten Max at some point.

"Good," says Mira, dropping her hands from my shoulders. "You know? Directives kind of freak me out."

"What did you see?" Max asks a little forcefully. He leans closer to me, and I can smell his comforting scent of cologne and fresh air.

"They're coming, during a storm," I whisper. "Max, my father and Jeremy are both still alive, but they are locked up on Onychinus."

Max gets up and runs over to the window and looks past the frozen glass. "Crap!" he mutters. I know that it's already beginning to be a blizzard because the wind creaks the house in its gusts. "I'll be right back," he says and starts toward the open door.

"Mira, I have an idea," I say, sitting up straight.

"What is it?"

"I need you to make another golden pearl," I whisper, so only she can hear.

"What? How can I do that?" she asks a little frantically, her green eyes widening.

I know it's going to be hard to follow, but I have a plan. It's dangerous. I have faith that it's going to work. "Mira, you are the only one of us who can compress light together. I need you to make a copy of the pearl. From the journal, I read that if light is compressed hard enough, your magic will make it an actual solid object."

"But I've never done that before. I don't know if I can," she says.

"I need you to," I tell her.

She shuffles, slipping her legs underneath her. "What do you need it for?"

I don't want to tell her the truth, but in order to earn her trust and support, I need to. I look down at my hands in the blanket. "So we can trick them. I'll be honest with you; I know that some of us might get caught. We're gonna try our best to get the real pearl back to Margaritan. It's our only chance."

"Who's going to have the real one?"

"You will."

"What!" I can't even tell a specific emotion in her face. Horrified, frightened, maybe angry, I'm not sure. That's just it— she looks completely unsure, as I am.

"You're the only one who hasn't reached into the *piscinæ fati*. Max and I both already have. If we touch it again, we could get very ill and possibly even die. There is a strong chance that it won't happen to you. And if we don't get the pearl back, many people are going to die." My chest feels heavy, and I can already sense the lives lost. "Can I trust you?"

I know it's a lot to ask of a terrified eleven-year-old, but there is really no other option. She stares at the door behind me, wide open. Her hands tremble, and her face is pale. "All right," she whispers, her voice as small as a ghost's.

There is shuffling down the hall where Ruban and Ace's voices echo off the walls as they argue about something.

Max turns the corner into our room. His blue eyes are serious and focused, but they also look weary. "We have to get the pearl back to Margaritan."

"Yeah, we were just talking about that," I say, slipping out from under the covers. "The safest place is the *piscinæ fati*."

"I can't put it in there," he says.

"Neither can I," I say, "but Mira can." He raises an eyebrow and then looks over my shoulder, at Mira. "She is the only one of the three of us who can."

"Okay," he says quietly. "Oh, Ace and Ruban are working on destroying the tracker. Hopefully that should buy us some time."

I nod and reach for my bag under the bed, right where I'd left it last. My head still feels a little fuzzy from the directive, but I'm not going to let it mess with me.

"So, yeah, grab whatever you guys need and bring it down-stairs as soon as possible," he says and turns to leave. "Oh, and put something warm on."

He's almost through the door. "Max, there's something I need to tell you." One of the memories has returned to me, and it won't let me sleep until I tell somebody, mostly the somebody standing in front of me. The handsome somebody with the dark hair, the kindness he shows to everyone, and the crystal blue eyes that know what you're going to say before you say it, except what I'm about to say.

"What is it?" he asks, his hand resting against the door frame.

"Mira, can you try to do what I asked of you? I'll only be a moment." I gesture my hand toward the hallway and follow him out of the room, closing the door behind me. I can still hear people bustling downstairs, along with the echoes of their voices.

"So what is it you needed to tell me?" He stands only a few feet in front of me, and I can hear his breath quicken.

I lean up against the wall, and close my eyes for a brief moment. "Max, I'm really sorry." My voice shakes, though I really don't care at the moment.

"Why? You never did anything?"

"It's ..." I pause. "You were—right. I did go by a different name on Margaritan. My name isn't Arianna."

His eyebrows furrow, and I can't really tell his expression—it's somewhere between confused and bewildered. I don't know what's wrong with me. I can't place other people's emotions anymore, and it just confuses me when I try. "Then what is it?"

I take another shaky deep breath and look in his eyes; in very dim light they look almost gray rather than their natural crystal blue. "My name is Lilyryn."

He takes a step back. His eyebrows are raised, and he looks at me from head-to-toe, like he's suddenly seeing me for the first time. *"When the contact is made the connection will be granted, and when girl remembers so shall he."* The words echo in my head like it was a spell.

All of a sudden his face falls into a relieved smile, and his shoulders relax. He remembers; I see it on his face. "It's really you!" he says, almost stunned. "You this whole time?" His voice shakes and he walks toward me, wrapping his arms around me. His warmth radiates through my entire body.

I feel a longing in my heart; I've missed him so dearly, even though I had forgotten him, not at all by choice. We've finally found each other.

He pulls back a bit and presses his lips to my forehead. "How have I not known this whole time?" he whispers, his lips brushing against my ear.

Then all of a sudden a window shatters downstairs and Max pulls back, though his arms are still around me protectively. I shiver.

CHAPTER 19

"What the hell was that?" asks Max just as Miles comes bolting up the stairs.

His eyes drop when he sees Max's hands on my back, he doesn't look pleased. I remember that awkward conversation when he had told me about some girl that had broken Max's heart, and that he didn't want me messing with him. As it turns out the girl who broke his heart the first time, who got him banished, and who in the end got her erased from his memory—she was lied to repeatedly and also was banished by her own father because she was chosen as the bearer of the golden pearl and was declared a Sorceress; that girl was me—Lilyryn. Lilyryn, a powerful name. When my mind had been altered and I couldn't remember anything, even that, my own name, I would shudder at the stories of her—of me.

"Just a tree that fell," says Miles. "It broke the window. But um, Elle wants to get as far away from here as possible. So in my words translating what she said in a less vulgar way, 'Hurry up!'"

"Okay, will do," Max says, lowering his arms to his sides. "Just gotta round up some stuff and we'll be all set to go." He brushes a hand through his dark hair, and I can see the bulk of muscles on his arms through his dark long-sleeved T-shirt. His eyes flicker to mine for a brief second and then back on Miles.

Miles nods his head and turns to the door of his and Max's room. When he goes in, he doesn't even look back.

"He's acting stranger than usual," Max whispers close to my ear.

"Oh, that. It's because he told me not to mess with you, and then he comes upstairs and sees your arms around me. That might be it," I whisper back with a grin.

"Doesn't surprise me all that much." He kisses my forehead quickly. "What did you ask Mira to do?"

"I asked her to get our bags." The lie slips easily through my lips, except the only problem is that Max knows.

"All right," he says and puts on a straight face. "Go help her then, see you in a bit." Then he turns and disappears through the same door Miles disappeared in. He knows I'm lying, but really he doesn't need to know. Maybe it'll work; maybe it won't. Either way it doesn't matter. I close my eyes for a moment and then head into my own room.

It's cold. I can feel the goose bumps rising on my arms. "Mira, why did you open the ..." I start and then I actually see what she's doing and close my mouth. I kick the door shut and watch as snow blows in through the window and dances around the room. Mira stands at the foot of the bed. Her arms are opened wide. My journal is placed in front of her and opened. The snow gathers in a spinning form between both of her hands. The golden pearl sits beside the journal along with the locket I gave Mira. It needs a source of light, I remember, and something to make it gold.

Somehow Mira manages to lift the locket into the center of tightly clustered spinning snow. Tiny particles of gold disperse from their grasp onto each other into a jumbled gold and white pattern. She compresses her hands closer inward, shoving the particles together. I rub my arms, trying desperately to warm them, but it doesn't help. The harder she compresses the mixture, the more it glows. Finally when there is absolutely no space left between the particles, the gold sphere drops to the bed.

"It is finished," she says, allowing her arms to fall to her sides. With a quick flick of my wrist, the window falls shut.

Taking a few steps forward, I look down at the sphere and raise my eyebrows. They look identical. I pick them both up, one in each hand. The real pearl is warm and has a pulse, almost like a beating heart; the fake one is still rather cold, but it too has a rather pulse that beats almost simultaneously.

"How did you get this one to have a pulse?" I ask, holding up the fake one.

"I spoke to it," she says quietly. "It has a piece of a planet in it—the snow, it has memories of life—the photos from the locket. The gold of the locket gives it the resemblance of the real one. And it has light—from the moon, so more energy. With multiple types of energy combined, it does react." She looks down at the book lying open, black ink dancing across the pages. "I'm sorry about destroying the locket. I didn't want to, but it was the only way it would work."

"It's amazing," I whisper.

"It should last a few months, maybe two," she says. "Then it will begin to fall apart." Then she turns and picks up my duffel bag from behind her, and starts shoving stuff in.

"I'll tell you what; I'll try to make it up to you," I say. "I will find you the best locket on Margaritan, and it will be yours."

A slight smile inches its way on her face, but then it falls into a straight line. "I don't care to have another locket," she whispers. "I want a family, and if you risk your life and … and … not make it, then I will have lost the only family I know."

"Mira, you're not going to lose me. Believe me, you won't ever lose me. I will always be there for you." I step closer to her and give her a tight hug. "Mira." I hold out the real pearl. "You're in charge of this one—protect it." Her tiny hands close around it, and she puts it in her sweater pocket, zipping it up.

"I will." Her voice is quiet.

I nod my head once and pick up the journal.

It takes only a few short minutes to get everything from the room. I quickly slip into a good pair of dark skinnys and a sweat-shirt and throw my hair up into a ponytail.

Downstairs everyone is moving around quickly, collecting some of the food and the box of blades. Ruban comes in quickly through the front door, letting in another gust of snow and wind. I'm sick of the snow and the cold even though I've only lived in it for a few weeks! I feel bad for the people who've lived here longer. "What's left?" he asks.

"Just this," Isla says, pointing to the box of food and blades.

The window beside the counter has been boarded up with a sheet of wood; I'm assuming that it was found in the garage.

"Ready to go?" Max asks, coming up beside me.

I blink out of a haze. "What? Yeah."

"Good," he says and snatches the blade sticking out from my back pocket.

"Hey!" I start to protest.

He holds it up. "You know where to put this if you need to defend yourself," he says. "Do not hesitate. Drive it in the heart if you can." Then he places the blade back into my hand.

"Catch," says Elle smugly, and two coats come hurling at my face. I lift my arm up just in time to deflect them, and they fall to the floor. "Nice catch," she says, smirking.

My face gets warm, and I snatch them off the floor and pass Max his.

"Anyway, out," Elle says. "It's time to go." She starts toward the door; her hair is pulled up in several braids, they whip behind her, falling down the back of her dark blue jacket.

No one else is in the house. It looks just as deserted as it did when we first arrived, which is strange.

"Max," I whisper.

"Yeah."

"Whatever happens, get Mira and the pearl to the *piscinæ fati*. No one can get to it if it's there," I say.

"You're going to be there too," he says, starting to raise his voice.

"I hope so."

"No. You will be. You're not leaving my sight. Promise me you are not going to do anything stupid."

"I can't promise that," I whisper, my voice straining. "But I can promise you that my heart will always be yours."

"That's not good enough! This is not a good-bye! Promise me you're not going to do anything that will separate us, again." He pauses. "Two years was long enough. I just got you back." His voice cracks.

I can't promise that. As much as I want to, I can't. If we do get separated—which I'm sure we will—it might kill me, if something or someone doesn't kill me first.

"Promise?" he asks

I hesitate with my answer. "All right, I promise." Guilt suddenly washes over me, but I push it away. I'm not going to let that stand in my way. I'm going to follow my initial plan. I will be the distraction while the others follow Max to Margaritan.

"Good, thank you."

"We should probably go," I tell him. My eyes burn as I fight to restrain tears back.

"You're probably right."

The wind slaps me in the face the moment I step off the patio. The trees sway and the wind howls. I almost get blown over, but Max quickly swings his arm around me, steadying me. We run the rest of the way, linked to each other, toward the two cars parked and ready to go.

Max slips into the passenger seat and I in the seat just behind him.

Ace pops the vehicle into drive as soon as our doors close, and immediately we follow the others ahead of us.

"Ace, do you know where the portal is?" I ask.

His face is serious, narrow, and his eyebrows are knitted together. "Yes." As soon as we're on the main road, he continues. "It's up in the rocks by that lake in between Chyraville and your house."

"Okay, great. We just need to get the pearl to Margaritan and find a way to get those soldiers out," I say.

"Um ... not trying to be rude, but do you have any idea how to do that?" he asks. The vehicle sways a little in the wind, and the snow is hypnotizing against the windshield.

"There is something. I know it. Maybe my dad can stop it," I tell them. I look to Mira. "Mira, I'm going to need you to stay with Max no matter what, okay?"

"All right," she whispers, her hand resting against her pocket with the pearl inside it.

"He won't let anything bad happen to you," I tell her, knowing it to be the whole truth.

Max looks over his shoulder at Mira and nods. He pats her knee once. "Try to get some sleep. We'll wake you if anything changes."

She opens her mouth to protest, but I reach over and grab her hand. She closes her mouth. When Max pulls his arm back, she nods, closing her eyes and leans her head against the headrest.

The clock reads 2:17 a.m., but I'm not actually tired.

I wish I could see Max's face, and I wish I knew what he was thinking. He rarely ever complains. He doesn't say when he's tired, feeling ill, or afraid. He's always been like that; he's always hated pity.

When we were younger, his mother passed away, and he had no siblings or any other relatives. He never knew his father because of certain circumstances, so that was why he went to live with Jeremy and his family. Max's mom used to work with Jeremy's mother; they were explorers—that was their career. Jeremy's mom was married to a nobleman of the kingdom. Because of his position, the two boys were at the palace a lot of the time. *I now remember.* When we first met ... I was ten and they were both twelve. It wasn't at first school that we met; it was in my favorite garden with the chipped pathway. I was picking flowers to give to Coral. It was her birthday. Jeremy jumped out of the tree above me and Max right after him. They were polite when they introduced themselves and I remember the kindness in both of them, but they really had a mischievous side to them.

I remember the strength Max has always carried with him, though he never spoke about any of the things that troubled his heart. The garden became our official meeting place whenever we had spare time. When Max and Jeremy both turned seventeen, they were placed in training to become part of the palace guard. I got to see a lot more of them because they were both moved into the guard chambers in the lower levels of the palace. My father always wanted me to marry a prince, or if not a prince, then Jeremy. Since I first saw Max in the garden, I've been in love with him, but that could never be allowed.

I open my eyes feeling very groggy. I don't even remember drifting off, but now the sky is a dark gray rather than pitch black, making the snow appear not as bad as it had earlier. I glance at the clock on the dash; it says 4:31 a.m. I slept for two hours? Mira is still asleep. The only thing different is Max is in the driver's seat.

"Max," I whisper.

He glances over his shoulder quickly and then faces the road again. "What's up?"

"Um, I'm just curious why they haven't made their move yet," I say.

"Me too. I'm not sure what they're waiting for," he replies. "Oh, Ace wanted to have a look at your journal, so I took over driving. Did you find anything?" he asks Ace.

"How does the *piscinæ fati* work?"

"Well, that's a tricky one," I say. "It was a gift to the planet from our universe's great creator. Every planet he created, he gave a gift of some sort. There are no two planets that received the same gift."

"That's quite extraordinary; I really hope I get to see it."

Max gives him a pointed look. "You probably will."

"I'm also curious how there's so much widely ranged information in here."

I wrote it. I used to spend hours by the portal searching for more knowledge. I also spent a lot of time in the library, learning as much as I could about the universe and my home. I wrote down everything I believed was important and worth remembering.

Just up ahead is another town. It is brightly lit, and I remember passing it on the way to the house. The snow continues coming fast at the windshield in its hypnotic waves.

"Whoa! What's with that?" Ace squints through his window into the rearview mirror. At that moment our vehicle gets rammed, jerking us into the oncoming lane. An aching pain pierces my right side. Lucky for me my jacket is fairly thick. It absorbs most of the blast, but my side still takes quite the impact.

Almost immediately Max turns off the highway, speeding into the snow-blanketed town.

"Reena?" Mira whispers. "What's going on?" Her voice is thick with panic.

"Hey, Reena. I guess this is their move," says Max, clearly pissed off. His jaw is set as he jerks the wheel hard, turning the vehicle into a side street.

I turn my head around to look out the back window. There are a few dark vehicles following us, though they almost appear invisible because their lights are turned off. They look like the night is moving. The people from Onychinus live basically with natural lighting like this—dim and dark.

We steer another hard right down an alley. My insides shake as we go skidding onto another street, and I jump when the phone starts ringing.

"Elle?" Ace asks into the phone.

I barely make out her voice over the tiny muffled speaker. "Where are you guys? Are you all right?"

"We just got rear-ended. I think *they* caught up to us," he says. "Where are you guys?"

"Still on the highway. We couldn't see your lights anymore and got worried. Do you want us to turn back?" she asks.

Max quickly turns the wheel again. "No," he says through clenched teeth.

"Max says not to," he repeats into the phone. "It's safer to just stay on the road. Stick to the plan; we'll catch up to you." He turns the phone off and stuffs it into his pocket.

Max skids the vehicle down another alley across from a set of lights. My arm throbs when I lean over to Mira and whisper, "Stay with Max, no matter what."

She nods her head quickly in response, tears streaking her face. I know I promised Max, but I also know that if I want to save them ... I have to break that promise. Two dark vans come to a stop, blocking us in the alley.

"Hold on," Max says as his foot stomps onto the gas pedal. I brace myself and hold my breath as we pass through the tiny gap between the vans. There is a loud squeal of metal scraping against metal, just like fingernails on the chalkboard. I cringe just hearing it.

Another vehicle rams into my side as we break free of the other two. The speed of it causes us to roll. It happens so quickly I don't have time to feel the pain in my side.

"Shit!" Max hisses, pressing his hands to his temples. We hang upside down in the car. The only thing holding us in place are the seat belts. "Ace, can you turn us?"

"What?" I murmur. Blood rushes to my head, and I suddenly feel very nauseous. Then I remember. Ace's munera that Max gave him is invisibility. It works out perfectly. Luck is on our side.

"No, only two of you. I have only two hands, remember?" I guess luck is *not* on our side. He unbuckles himself and twists his body so he doesn't fall on his head. Max does the same. Mira and I look at each other and do what they just did. She has a red patch on her forehead, which I think will eventually turn into a bruise.

"Take Mira and Reena." Max spits out blood.

"No."

"Reena, don't be stupid. You're going with Ace," says Max stubbornly.

"Don't tell me what I will and will not do! I am sticking to the plan. So will you." I glare at him, and he becomes silent, a look of betrayal appears in his face. Sweat and blood run from his hairline.

"That's not part of the plan," he whispers.

"It was part of mine. Now go!" The sound of boots crunching snow is now very close and is threateningly near. "Max, the commander wants us both and the pearl. Let's only give him one. Take care of Mira and bring the pearl back. I have the copy," I whisper quickly and breathless. "Go!"

I look away from their faces as they back outside through the shattered window. Another shadow looms closer and closer.

CHAPTER 20

Ace, Mira, and Max are gone. I don't see them anymore. I don't see anything really. It's so dark. I slide through the two front seats right into the driver's spot to make it look like I am the only one who's here. Something's wrong with my right leg. I bend it, but something restricts the movement. I look down. There just above my knee is a rather large bulge. I glide my hand over it and let out a loud gasp. Something is sticking out of my leg. Warm black blood seeps through the fabric of my leggings.

I can't seem to stop my trembling hands. I know that I'm basically handing myself over, but I still don't want to go down without a fight. I pull out my blade with its pearls and its ornately carved metal handle. I rip the pearly sheath off. A cold sweat drenches my forehead, and my breathing is ragged. I don't even want to look at my leg. The fabric is the only thing keeping me from passing out.

I can no longer hear the crunching of the snow under their boots. My heart pounds so fast inside my chest I'm afraid it may break through.

The lack of sound doesn't affect me as much as the shower

of crystal remnants that come raining down. The driver's side window is now only a frame in a metal mess. I hold my arm in a tight L shape and wait for my offender.

The dark figure appears outside the window. He holds a rifle-like gun in his gloved hands. I cringe. He's barely out of my reach. I can't attack him. The gun goes off. The vehicle starts rocking, and a loud ringing pierces my ears. My leg pulses at every movement. My insides are turning, and I want to puke.

A different man rips the door away, and snow flurries rush in, biting my face and hands. My body feels too numb and tingly to move. I can't uncurl from my cramped position, so I press my back against the upside-down headrest.

"You have two choices," says a deep voice from outside. I shudder and wipe away the sweat from my forehead. "You can stay in the vehicle and refuse to come out, where we will be forced to remove you, or you can come out voluntarily and be unharmed. You have thirty seconds." I can crawl out and let them take me or I can wait in here stubbornly only for them to hurt me. My leg is already hurt. Why should I want to be hurt anymore? Or I could crawl out, but hide my blade and then attack—that won't work. I stuff the sheath back over the blade and shove it into my bag and quickly hang it across my body.

I gasp as I begin to move. My right leg bumps the steering wheel. I wish Max was here. He could fix me up. *You told him to go*, I tell myself. Why do I honestly have to be so stupid? Why? *Why?*

The ground is covered thickly in snow and sharp pieces of ice. I practically drag myself out of the car, and sweat drenches my forehead. A thousand knives all at once, the pain is so great, worse than when I had my concussion and was in the hospital for a week. The snow is so cold under my burning-up body, and I have difficulty maintaining steady breathing. I know that if I panic I'll bleed out faster or I'll give them the idea that I'm terrified of them. Either way, it won't help me.

The only light around is coming from the street light just up ahead. I pull myself up into an almost sitting position, and I look at the ground behind me. A trail of blood contrasts with the white of the snow. I almost gag. The cold stings my face, and I squint my eyes to see the figures surrounding me.

They all wear black military clothing, toques, and some kind of fabric that covers from the neck of their uniforms to the middle of their noses, leaving only a small portion of their faces visible and ghostly white. The name comes to me—scarf.

Several of them are holding guns. The man closest to me nods his head, and three others come to my side. "Search her," he says. One rips at my bag.

"Hey!" I shout.

"Only a precaution," says the man patiently. "You are Lilyryn, correct?" I nod once. A few months ago if someone were to call me by that name, I'd have denied knowing it.

One of the men takes my bag from me, pulling it over my head. My blade is in there! My heart nearly skips a beat. I am weaponless. I am wounded. I am in the center of a pit of vultures. The other man pats down my pockets to see if he can find anything, and the other two search through my bag. I hate them.

"You're not alone," another figure concludes. "Where are the others?"

"I am alone." I struggle with the words, the pain oozing in. That figure cocks his head to the side. I slide my left leg up to protect my right. Maybe if I keep talking it will distract his attention from my wound. "I left without them."

"You're lying to me."

"Seeing as I am the only one you're speaking to, that means there are no others. Why does it matter? I have what you want," I tell them, my voice shaking. I'm not lying; I *did* leave the crashed vehicle without them ... they left before I did. I hold out the copy of the pearl in my hand for them to see. The street lamp catches its smooth surface, lighting it up.

In the distance sirens begin to wail. Some of the people must have been woken up by the noise. Quite a few of the figures run to their vehicles and flick the lights on so it appears like they are normal people. The man makes eye contact with me. He comes forward with sure movements and snatches the pearl from my hand. Someone from behind me scoops me up into his arms. I cry out at the sudden movement of my leg. He shoves me into the back of the closest van and climbs in, closing the door.

I wonder how they're going to leave the place. I know the police will want to know what happened. I wonder if they will follow us. I hope not. I don't want these innocent people harmed by trying to intervene in a fight that isn't even theirs.

"Girl, you caused a lot of trouble," says the man. It's really dark in here too, but at least there's no wind. My head feels fuzzy. The man grabs my leg and examines it. I suck in a deep breath and choke down a sob.

"Don't touch me," I whisper. He slices through my pants halfway up my thigh. My back is pressed up against a wall beside a bench, and the man sits beside me. His scarf is pulled down away from his face. He is pale and has dark hair and eyes; he looks pretty young, maybe a few years older than Max. I push his hands away from me and glare at him, though my eyes are filled with tears.

"Look, I have to stop the bleeding," he says, his voice rather low. "I can't let you die."

"And why not? Huh? You guys are going to kill me anyway. Why fix this? It'll just finish the job sooner," I snap at him, but my voice shakes and I start to tremble. I really don't want to bleed out. That would be a horrible way to die.

He looks over his shoulder. There are two people in the front, but I can only see the sides of their heads because there is only a small square opening. He looks back at me as the vehicle hits a large bump. I hiss through my teeth and grab at my leg. "It's not only your life on the line," he says silently, checking over his shoulder again. Clearly he doesn't want the others to hear him. "We all have something to lose too. If you die or we don't bring back the pearl, the group of us who screwed up will be killed. I have a wife who's expecting anytime now, back home. I can't die. Who will take care of them if I die?" He looks me in the eyes. I can see the pain and worry in his. I never realized how cruel his job was. I thought that all people from Onychinus were harsh and cruel and only wanted power. They're not; they're just like the people from Earth and Margaritan. I *almost* feel guilty that it's not the real pearl that they have.

My whole body is trembling uncontrollably, but I manage to pull my hands away. I look at my leg. Most of the pant leg is torn away. He nods his head once, questioning if he can begin again. I nod back. He rips the rest of the bundled fabric away. I see the blood before I see what's sticking out of my leg. The blood-soaked bone pierces through the red skin just above my knee cap. I gag.

The man pushes a small-sized garbage can toward me. My head is in it before I know what I'm doing. My stomach wrenches, and everything I ate pours out into the can.

"What's going on back there?" asks one of the men from the front. The one in the passenger seat turns to look through the square opening.

"She saw her leg," says the kind one beside me. "It's really bad."

"Do you think she'll make the trip, or do you think we should stop at a hospital?"

"It's a few days before we make it to the portal," says the voice beside me. He puts his hand on my side. My stomach wrenches again, and my mouth tastes like acid. "I can try and push the bone back in the leg and cauterize it, but you'd better drive like a mad man or the only other option is to stop at one of the hospitals." My stomach quivers again, when he says to just push the bone back in and cauterize it. *Like touch my bone and burn my skin?* He presses his gloved hand above where the bone sticks out. The pain is so great I let out a shriek. "Let's get to the nearest hospital."

"Why did she have to get hurt?" the man in the passenger seat mutters.

There are several jackets hanging on small hooks, and under one of the benches are some boxes. The man beside me pulls out a box, opens it, and takes out a thin gray blanket. He stuffs the box back and begins unfolding it. Then he tosses it over me, hiding my hideous leg from view and tucks in the edges. "My name is Officer Theo Evans, but you can just call me Theo," he whispers. I nod once and wipe the sweat from my forehead.

Theo looks around the small space. "Where's the first aid box?"

"Under the bench there," says the man in the front. Theo scrambles for it and pulls out another small case. He pulls the blanket up, putting pressure on the broken bone in my leg. I gasp and then bite the inside of my cheeks. He wraps a strip of my destroyed pants around the top part of my thigh and slips some kind of rod through a knot and begins twisting it making the pressure much greater. Then he ties the rod in place. The blanket is pulled back into place, hiding the mess of my leg from me, and then he props my leg up on the bench.

"Why are you so kind to me, Theo?" I ask, breathless. "Besides the fact you cut … cut the circulation off … off in ma … my leg," I stutter.

He tilts his head rather confused, but then understands and answers. "I want to be a man my wife and child will be proud of." He pauses. "Besides, you have done *me* no wrong, only I'll have to be strict when the others are around, and for that I apologize ahead of time."

"'S fine, considering I kind of figured you'd-d be cruel in the … the beg … ginning," I mumble, but my voice is barely audible and my body won't stop shaking. At first it was numbness, then a tremble, and now I can't stop the shaking. My skin is cold even though I feel like there is a fire burning through me.

"Hurry," Theo shouts over me, "I think she's going into shock." His words are muffled though his face hovers above me.

I want Max," I mumble even more silently. It's almost as if no sound comes out of my mouth. The vehicle sways in the wind, and the sky gradually lightens.

I look over at the floor. There's blood, lots of it. Theo tucks the edges of the blanket under my legs. I almost don't feel it anymore. I think I'm ready to go home now. Wait, the pearl, I can't go home. Mira has it, and … Max? Max is with Mira and Ace; they're bringing the pearl back home, to Margaritan. "Stop thinking," I want to yell at myself.

It feels like an eternity goes by. I hear muffled voices, and the guy in the passenger seat has a phone of some sort pressed up against his ear. I blank out.

I can't even tell if my body's moving anymore. I don't feel it, but the memory of the van crashing into my side jumps into my thoughts and my heart shudders. I remember I closed my eyes just as it happened. I felt the pain of my bone breaking and pushing through my skin, and seeing Max's chest ram into the steering wheel. *I want Max.* I want my family, Maybell, Jeremy, Sandy. I want Clay, Haley; I even want Kelly, Nish, and Bre. I don't want Brad. Even though Ruban doesn't like me, I want him and Miles, Ace, Elle, Isla. I feel like my body is shutting down on me. I don't want to die. I want to *live.* I was chosen to be the bearer of the golden pearl; surely there was meant to be more for me, in this life. It can't be finished.

I wonder how everything would've turned out if I was never banished. Would I have been killed instead of Coral? Would my planet already be destroyed? I do know that if none of this ever happened I never would have met Mira or the others. I would never have remembered Max or the truth about my past. I never would have found real love or made good friends. Also then again, I wouldn't be dying now if none of this happened.

More voices surround me, and I'm lifted out of the van—at least I think I'm still in the van. I don't feel the pain anymore. I don't feel anything. A huge stack of material falls as I am moved. Did Theo put all those coats on top of me?

"She's barely conscious. Here, put her on the gurney," says a strange voice. I don't recognize it. "Good on you for thinking fast." I know Theo is beside me because he is the one who most wants me alive, so he can be back home with his family. The squeaking of the wheels is distracting. I notice it more than the people around me saying numbers and pressing an oxygen mask to my face. This is not the first time this has happened—me being pushed into the hospital on a gurney in a huge rush.

"Sir! Sir, you can't come in, it's an emergency surgery. You'll have to wait in the waiting room with everyone else," says a doctor angrily.

"Look, that girl is strictly under my protection. I have to keep close," Theo says. The wheels come to a stop, I think he grabbed on to it.

"Well, she's close to death, so I'd say you're doing a great job protecting her," the doctor yells sarcastically. "If you want you can watch from the observation room, but you are *not* coming in!"

Theo grunts, his hand lifts from the gurney, and the wheels start squeaking again. The last thing I see is him following until the swinging doors close, and then he looks through the rectangle glass windows and I meet his eyes.

I close my eyes and shut the world out.

CHAPTER 21

I DON'T KNOW HOW LONG IT IS BEEN SINCE I SAW THE ONYCHINUS man, Theo, standing behind the rectangle window in the swinging doors. I know I'm still alive because my body is sore all over.

My eyes blur when I open them. I blink to get rid of the fuzzy feeling. Around me are white walls and silver curtains hiding a thick plated-glass window. The floor is tiled and clean. There is a dresser in the corner and a mirror on the wall and a chair right beside it, and also a small bathroom close by. I lie on a bed that is very soft, and white blankets with silver embroidery cover me. Where am I? I look to the door; it is painted gray, contrasting with the walls. I wonder if it's locked.

I drag my upper body up, leaning on my forearms. My head feels weird, but I push myself up and lean my back against the headboard, which too, is gray. What happened to me while I was out? My lower body feels like a million pounds is tied to it. Oh no ... My leg? I rip the sheets back and see that it's still there. A wave of relief rushes through me. A cast covers my leg from my foot to my upper thigh ... that's why it's so heavy! I've never had a cast before. If Max had been there I wouldn't have needed one at all. I wonder where he is now. I hope he managed to get to the portal and back to Margaritan.

The sky is gray outside the thick glass. Do my powers work? I raise my right hand and angle it toward the window. I want to see if I can push the curtains aside. They barely move. I feel the energy flow, but a force pushes back on me. The curtains only slightly move but they fall back into place almost instantly. My heart rate quickens, and panic fills my body.

I look around. All along the ceiling is a type of metal that matches the same kind of metal that covered the cube we trained with. There is way too much. It would take months—that I don't have—in order for me to be able to use even one of my muneras in here. *Where* am I?

I hear a slight noise by the door, and I jerk my head that way. It creaks on its hinges as it opens. In walks a lean man dressed in dark cargo pants and a long-sleeved shirt rolled up to his elbows, and a vest. He too has a pale complexion, though his hair is a dark gray, contrasting with his skin tone. He stands in the open door and makes eye contact with me and starts to open his mouth.

The sudden realization hits me so hard, I gasp, and tears begin to form in my eyes. I really am on Onychinus. I am going to *die*. I pull my hands up to my face and cover my eyes.

His mouth shuts instantly. He holds up a bag on a hanger and walks over to the foot of the bed. "Apologies, miss, the commander requests your company. You are to change your clothes, and then someone else will arrive shortly to escort you." He sets the bag on top of the blankets. "If you require assistance, don't be afraid to ask. The commander cares about your condition." I know he's still there, but I don't really want to uncover my eyes.

"Isn't he going to kill me?" I whisper, pulling my hands away from my face.

The man looks slightly taken aback, but he calmly answers,

"As far as I am concerned, I have not heard any news of the sort. Even if I do hear such news, I'm not sure I'll be the one delivering it. I apologize again." He turns and walks out, closing the door behind him.

I don't want to go, but I look down at what I am wearing, a simple light cotton type of hospital gown. Why is it I have to wake up in another one of these? I have to quit getting injured.

I honestly don't understand why the commander wants me alive. What does he need me for, and why exactly is he making his servants be so … nice to me? Whatever, I don't want to upset them. Who knows what they'd do? I reach for the bag and pull it up onto my lap. I will only do what they want until I know the pearl is safe and I can actually walk. I'm gonna try and find the portal and my fellow citizens.

The bag unzips easily, and on the hanger is a deep green dress. I slip it off the hanger and rub my thumb across the surface; it is soft and slides easily between my fingers. Inside the bag is also a small pouch with silver-colored undergarments inside. I quickly slip into the clothes, which is surprisingly easy, despite my cast being so stiff. The dress falls down to my knees, and the sleeves are a light see-through green fabric that fall down to my elbows. I run my fingers through my hair, which shockingly isn't knotted and is actually quite soft.

I sit and lean against the headboard. I can't lift my leg very high off the bed, it's so heavy. I know they probably have better medical techniques. I bet they probably wouldn't have used such a heavy cast; this is Earth's form of casting.

A knock comes at the door, getting my attention. In walks a woman after a short moment. She wears a navy blue suit coat and skirt, and her hair is pulled back tightly away from her face. She holds a pair of crutches as she nears the bed. I think she knows I'm going to behave because I could use them as weapons. I take them from her and give a slight nod. If I were to see these last year I would never have understood what they were. It's been almost six months since my birthday. I remember being told that the first year after receiving our munera would be the hardest. I suppose for me and Max it really *is* not a lie. Banishment truly isn't easy to deal with. I hoist myself out of the bed and pull myself up with the crutches under my armpits.

"Follow me," she says and heads out of the room.

I almost trip on my way out. My cast—weighing me down—it takes some time to get the swinging motion proper.

"Keep up," she says, looking back at me. She is already half-way up the hall, which is long and narrow and the wall panels are silver. I quicken my pace.

I'm not sure why, but I want to smack her in the back of the head with the bottom of my crutch.

We turn down two more halls before we actually see another person. There are quite a few doors, but we don't go through any of them. I wonder which one the fake pearl is behind. It could be any of them. We turn down one more corner. This hallway is brightly lit. It has the same light fixtures, but there are windows running all along the right side. It's easy to tell that it is thick glass. I slow down to take everything in.

Outside is a light gray sky with three moons spread out evenly. There is a large ocean reaching across the surface below, and just beneath the window are large, sharp rocks poking up from the waves. I see some trees along the edges but mostly water. There are also ships further down. I wonder, if a person jumped, would he or she survive?

The lady stands at the end of the hall staring at me. I hurry to catch up to her.

"Listen, hold your tongue, no snide comments; the last one lost hers because she wouldn't stop arguing." She looks at me pointedly. "Also one more thing ... behave. Do you understand?"

"Yeah, got it."

"Good."

We leave the windowed hallway and enter a large room. The walls are painted a light color. I'm not exactly sure what color. It looks rather like metallic beige. The floor is shiny black marble accented with lighter colors. The furniture is quite unique. The sitting chairs have shiny silver darkened legs that are curved in strange angles, and the cushions are plush green. It's the same with the sofas. The feet are curved despite their short height, with matching cushions. Paintings hang on the walls. I hadn't noticed any movements. Then I see guards lined up along the walls. They all wear matching uniforms that consist of black pants and jackets with swords attached to their belts. Silver name tags are embedded on the front pockets of their jackets.

The lady stops at a door, holding it open for me. I walk past her into the room; it has shelves lining the walls. There are some kind of devices on the shelves; I kind of expected them to be books or something. There is a large desk in the middle with two big chairs in front of it.

"Commander will be here in a moment." All of a sudden a tall figure walks into the room through a door opposite from me.

"Glad to see you've come around," he says. His voice slightly reminds me of a rustier version of Max's. "Please have a seat." He gestures to the chairs.

Hate ripples up in my core. This man killed my sister, and he isn't aware that I know what he's done.

He nods to the lady, and she walks out, closing the door behind her. I'm afraid of what else this man is capable of. I have to be careful and play my cards right. I don't want them to realize just yet that they don't have the real pearl. I come in further, and he pulls out a chair for me, reaching for my crutches. I eye him wearily before I hand them over and take a seat in the chair. The cast restricts my every movement.

"Put your leg up too," he says, bringing around a stool. He lifts my foot so my leg rests upward. Surprisingly it takes away a numb, throbbing feeling I was unaware that was there.

I look up at him as he walks around the table to his chair. I want to say something, but I just keep my mouth shut.

"So you and your friends put up quite the fight when my men first came for you," he says. His eyes are deep, and it makes me rather uncomfortable to look at them. His pupils are large, so the irises are really thin. "I'm not surprised."

"Oh?"

"It would have seemed rather unnatural if you hadn't. However, when they did manage to capture you, you were alone and surrendered yourself. I understand that with your injury it was the smartest thing you could have done." His face seems to drop a little in curiosity. "But what I don't understand is why you were alone."

"I decided to go on my own; it wasn't safe for them to be with me." It is not a lie at all—well, maybe just holding a portion of the truth. I say it confidently, sitting up a little straighter in my chair.

"You do realize I've killed people before, correct?" he asks. I nod. "What I also can't seem to wrap my head around is why he didn't stay behind with you."

"I beg your pardon?" I whisper. I feel my heart skip a beat. Does he know?

"Most men have a tendency to stay with the women they love, to make sure no harm is done to them, and to protect them at any cost. I would have thought that my son would have grown to be a gentleman and try to protect the woman he loves. I'm already aware that he's quite strong, but I would have thought that he'd have a heart like his mother's." He says the last part with uncertainty.

Max? Is he …? "Your son?" I whisper.

"Max. Indeed, he is my son. Surely you've wondered why his father has never been around. Well, that's because your father never allowed me to come and see him, ever. I've tried reaching out, but it never seemed to work. I haven't seen his mother since the last time she came here for a mission."

"Max's mother passed away," I say quietly.

He looks taken aback. "How long?"

It takes me a moment before I can say anything. I'm still stunned that this murderer in front of me is Max's father.

"How long?" he demands.

"Seven, going on eight years," I stammer. I feel more uncomfortable sitting here now than I did when I first came in.

"Oh my." He looks down, his face sullen, and his hands are clasped together on top of the desk.

So, he feels remorse for Max's mother's death but not for the lives he's taken himself? It doesn't make any sense.

He shakes his head once and then changes the subject. "Anyway, you killed quite a few of my men, and I am not pleased with that. You are also holding back the truth from me." He sits up straighter in his chair and looks into my eyes with his dark ones. I do see somewhat of a resemblance. Max has his father's lean but muscular build, sharp jawline, and thick, dark hair. "I want you to tell me where Max and the others are. I have men searching everywhere for them, but I think it would be much faster if you were to just tell me where. I will give them all immunity if you tell me."

I hesitate; I don't trust him. I already heard him tell one of his men to kill them on the spot; all he needed was the pearl, Max and me. If I tell him, it will get them all killed except for

Max. "I'm currently unsure of their whereabouts," I say as calmly as I can.

His face turns slightly red, but he answers sedately, "As you are most likely aware, you are unable to use your munera here. Would you like to know why?" he asks rhetorically. "Because *veto iron* lines every room in this palace. You and everyone else we collect are vulnerable by this; you are weak as it is. I have experts who could have fixed your leg right up without the need of a cast of such bulk. I considered this, but I thought it would be better if you were unable to travel without the assistance of crutches. We injected you with pain medication, which will wear off in about three hours. So tell me where they are or you won't receive another dose."

"I don't know where they are," I reply, the words sticking in my mouth. I really don't know where they are, but I hope they made it to Margaritan.

"You're lying! Where are they?"

"I don't know."

He takes a deep breath and stands up. "I have been treating you surprisingly well. I've had my maids tend to your health while you were out. You've woken up in a comfortable chamber, and I haven't killed you. I think you should be grateful."

"I'm telling you the truth," I say, pulling my leg down from the stool. "You're not a king. How do you have maids and a palace?" I ask, changing the subject. I don't want to be here.

"I am a king!" he shouts. "Here commander and king mean the same thing. Max has royal blood flowing through his veins! That is one reason why I hate how your father treated him so wrongly." He wears an odd expression. "I was so thrilled when I finally buried my sword in his chest."

I gasp. He did what? My heart skips another beat, and my stomach drops. Why does this happen to me? Why does my family have to die? I wouldn't wish it on anyone else, but I certainly wish it didn't happen to me. For a while I hated my father. He humiliated and banished me. He banished my little sister when she was just a baby. He took the love of my life away and had a distorter make me forget who I was and the man I loved. He made it so the *real* me was gone. I hated him. But after everything that's happened these past months, I've ignored what he's done, because I found everything I needed. I don't want him dead; he can't be.

I want *this* man dead.

My face is soaked with tears before he begins speaking again. "Now more people you love will die if you don't speak up."

"I don't know where they are!" I scream at him. My heart throbs, and my body begins trembling again. *I actually don't know where they are.*

"Very well," he says. I can tell he's angry, but I know he can't harm me if he wants Max's approval. I know Max—he will never approve of him. He slams a button on his desk.

A moment after, the door opens, and in come two guards.

"Take her back to her chambers, and make sure she gets a dose of pain medication in seven hours rather than three."

I don't move from my chair, so the two guards come around and pick me up easily, and my body crumples in their arms.

The commander comes around his desk and says directly to me, "I have several Margaritan citizens in my keep. If we don't find *them* in the next few weeks, half of your citizens here are going to be killed."

I hold back my nasty comments because the lady from before said the last girl had her tongue ripped out.

The guards carry me back to my room using different hallways. We don't pass the hall with the windows again. I'm glad because the sky looks like it does on a wretched day on Margaritan.

I'm miserable enough, let alone having to see a dejected sky. They set me on the bed and leave the room, closing the door on their way out. I'm really tired, and I just want to go home. I'm still not sure where that is, but anywhere's better than here.

I want to see my father again. The last time I saw him was in the directive when Jeremy was telling me to leave. My head pounds. Only distorters can send directives. Jeremy was the only one who could see me and speak to me in the directive. Jeremy's a distorter. I try to link the pieces together, but the realization hurts. My father has always wanted me to marry Jeremy. Why? The memory flashes instantly in my head.

I'm screaming though my throat is hoarse, and I am struggling to get to him. He is only a few meters from me, and all I want is to reach out for him, but men with arms as strong as iron hold me back. Max's face is sweaty, and he has deep purple bags under his eyes. He wears a white V-neck T-shirt that is sweaty and stained with dirt. He is held back so tightly he can't even budge. My father is there. He is angry and yelling at the both of us. I see him now and I don't just feel upset about my father's death, but I feel angry now. Jeremy comes around a corner, and he looks distraught.

"You'll have anything you want if you do this job," my father tells him. "Swipe her memory." He looks directly at me with anger. "Him, swipe only the image of her. I want him to always remember a girl but never remember what she looks like; he will only remember if she does."

Jeremy looks absolutely shaken. His jaw clenches and unclenches. "This is wrong. I'm not sure I'm the one to do this."

I remember pushing so hard against the arms restraining me that I had bruises for two weeks afterward.

"Jeremy, if you do this you can marry her when she's old enough. She won't remember Max. She'll have a clean slate, and you can make her fall in love with you if you want."

Jeremy nods, raising his hands as he comes near me.

I'm so angry right now it feels like my brain is boiling. Jeremy wasn't just a distorter; he was *the* distorter who stripped my memories and my heart. I won't ever love him. I did a few months ago, but now I know that it was never real. I trusted him. Max trusted him. *Why?* I think if I ever see him in person again I'm going to punch him and not at all lightly.

My father's gone, so I don't know what to do about that. He wasn't all bad; it was only when I got older that he began to get worse. I wonder if it was the guilt or the stress.

I pull my face into a pillow and scream. I scream so hard that my throat feels raw, like it's bleeding. I don't want this room. I don't want to be comfortable. I want to let the pain rush in and take over. Instead of tugging at it and pushing it aside, maybe if I let it consume me I can finally let it all go. I want the pain to be gone; I want to be free of my inner ghosts.

I open my heart and let everything flow through it—everything. The pain, the loss, all my happy memories, the memories of who I actually was and the memories of when I wasn't myself. I let my childhood memories come in, the flowers, the dances, the cuts and bruises. I remember everything, even the things I've been holding back and trying to forget. I let everything come in. This is it. I take a step back and look at my life. I've had bad things happen to me, but I've also had so much good.

"I forgive you, my father," I whisper.

Just like that, all of it is gone. My mind is clear, but my heart still aches. I forgive everyone who's ever wronged me in any way. It feels incredible to just let it all go. Though when I come across Jeremy, I will still punch him, for Max. All I have left is to wait for the cast to come off in a few more weeks, and pray that Max, Mira, and the others are all right. I do, but I don't want them to come back for me. I can't have any of them die for me. I won't allow it.

CHAPTER 22

Mira said that the fake pearl will only last a few months—two—give or take. I think I've been here for a week maybe a week and a half. I should theoretically be out of the cast before the time is up. I haven't gotten any directives recently, and it's starting to bother me. I know that the commander/king, whatever he is, says that my father is dead, but if I got another directive I could be sure, though I still don't really want to see Jeremy right now.

A knock comes at the door; I turn to see who the visitor is. Theo stands at the door dressed in his mandatory uniform. I'm excited to see him; I don't remember having seen him since the hospital swinging doors back on Earth. I've been looking outside a lot lately, just standing by the window because I'm sick of sitting down. I need to move around and get some exercise. Otherwise my body won't work for me when I am out of the cast.

"Girl, are you feeling dead yet?" he jokingly asks.

"Yes," I say, turning back slightly to the window. It's quite dark out. Then again, it's always dark here.

"Ready to go for a walk?"

I turn back to face him. He holds up a set of crutches. "Please," I say. He walks into the room where I stand by the window, and he hands them to me. I know I shouldn't be standing as much as I have been, but I've been putting most of my weight on my left leg so there's less pain.

Theo has been assigned to be my main guard. The commander hasn't requested to see me recently, though he's made sure I can't wander from my room. Someone is *always* outside my door.

"How's your wife doing?" I ask quietly once we're halfway down the hall. He walks slower for me, though I have gotten quite a bit faster on crutches.

"She's doing well, but the doctors insist that she stay bedridden for a while, but our baby is incredible."

"What have you named him?" I ask quietly. I want to have at least one guard as a friend, and I'd like it to be Theo. He seems genuine.

"His name is Aukusti, which means 'great,'" he says proudly.

"I'm happy for you," I say, and I mean it.

My eyes are on the floor, but I can tell he looks at me and gives a small smile. The castle is very big, much like my own back on Margaritan, though I haven't found any doors leading outside yet. It makes me rather frustrated to be so helpless. I know that being here is a good enough distraction from them getting the real pearl. The commander still believes that he has the real one, but what I wonder is where he's holding the chests. I know that almost half of them are filled, and it bothers me. Maybe if I find that room I can take the jewels before I leave—if I can find the portal even.

"Are you sure you don't know where that boy is?" he asks quickly.

"I am sure," I mutter. "I haven't seen him since Earth. How am I supposed to know where he is?"

"You spoke to him about where to go, I'm certain."

"How? How can you be so certain?" My voice rises. I stop in the middle of the hallway; it is the one with the windows over-looking the ocean.

"Because, what kind of plan would that have been? Honestly? Why would you guys go separate ways without telling each other?" His voice is filled with agitation.

"I never said that we didn't talk about it."

"Tell me then, where did he go?" He is persistent. His body is turned toward me, and his eyes drill into my soul. I shudder, feeling a gust of cold air. I'm not sure what to do. My armpits hurt with bruises from the crutches, and I don't have a quick escape.

"I'm curious about something. Would you tell your captors your wife's location in order to save not only your own skin but a few of your fellow citizens, or would you give everything up in order to save her?" I yell at him. "If you truly love the person, what would you do?" I am almost in tears. "What would you do?" The pain medicine has almost completely worn off, and I am way overtired. It has been days since I slept properly. The commander has cut back my doses of pain medication, instead of getting them every ten hours, I get them once every two days. I can't seem to hold myself together very well anymore. When the pain comes back my emotions get thrown out of whack, and I can barely think clearly … like now.

"Don't bring my wife into this! It's different!"

"No it is not. It is a fair question. I want … no … I *need* an honest answer." My voice begins to shake, and I can't hold on any-more. The strong leg and the crutches holding me up are doing a lousy job. They want to let go of the weight. I begin to sway back and forth on the crutches.

"I'm not sure what I would do," he says. "But I do know that I wouldn't want my fellow citizens to die. It's a choice—save one life or save all but one. Besides, in your case, all you have to do is say where he went and no one is going to get hurt. Your people will be set free as soon as Max is acquired."

"I don't believe that," I say, feeling weaker and weaker each moment. "The commander murdered my father and sister; he's not going to just let everyone else go. He won't." I know how the commander works. He is furtive and unpredictable. I don't think that he would stay true to his word. With what happened to Amethystus, I think he will only do it again and again. He's going to kill everyone I love.

"I'll tell you what—I'll speak to the commander, and if he agrees, I can arrange for you to go down to the cells and see some of your people. You will only be allowed to speak to one of them, your choice."

"I want you to return me to my chambers," I say weakly. I don't want to argue anymore. It's not going to get me anywhere. My body is beginning to feel faint again. I have lost some weight within this past week and a half, so I'm not sure why it feels as though I weigh a million pounds.

He inhales deeply before he starts to say anything. The dull throbbing pain returns, making my stomach churn. "Very well." I honestly am not sure what he's thinking. I used to be very good at reading people and knowing what they were gonna say before they said it. Now I can barely read their thoughts while I try and hide from my own.

The walk back to my room is long and agonizing. I almost trip when my crutch bumps into the wall, but Theo's arm comes up and steadies me. "Watch your step," he mutters. I know that I've disappointed him. I want to be his friend, but I can't just tell him what he wants to know. It could get a lot of my people killed.

I let out a deep breath when we finally get to my door with its silver plated disc numbered 117. Theo unlocks the door from the outside and holds it open for me. I enter and quickly crawl on the bed and drag my plastered leg up with me. Both Theo and I look up when we hear tapping nearing the door.

A woman walks in with her heels tapping loudly on the floor. "Apologies, Officer Evans, Lilyryn's presence is requested in the mechanics corridor." I recognize her; she is the woman who brought me to the commander the first time he wanted to speak with me. I think she must be one of his top assistants.

"She's very pale," says Theo. "I think she may pass out just on the way down there."

"The commander said to just shoot her with a tiny dose of pain medication if she was like this. It'll last maybe an hour or two." The woman hands a covered syringe to Theo. I hate needles. I wish it could be pills or better yet, just get rid of the problem all together. A sharp pain pierces my side. I know that it's going to leave a bruise. It did the last time. "He also doesn't want her to know the way down there."

"Very well," says Theo. He sounds rather disgusted. The woman also hands him a piece of a dark fabric.

"Be down there in ten minutes." She leaves the room, her heels echoing down the hallway. What's waiting for me in the mechanics corridor?

"That leaves us two minutes before we need to actually go down there," Theo tells me. I don't say anything back. I just fold my hands together and tug at my sleeves. The commander had several dresses made and brought to me. I've really only been wearing the ones with sleeves though. I am not used to the constant chill; there is no sun here so it is quite cold. It was cold on Earth too, but at least there were times when it was actually warm.

"Why does the commander need me?" I ask. "I understand why he wants Max, but why does he need me? Theo?"

"Honestly I am not allowed to say. You should, however, bring that question to him though. Okay, we should start heading out," he says, folding the dark fabric. "Turn your head."

I turn my head toward the wall. Theo pats my hair down in the back and brings the fabric in front of my face, tying it tightly around my head. Theo hoists me up into his arms. My shoulder presses into his chest and my leg sticks straight out while my good one is bent comfortably.

It bothers me how comfortable everyone else is with saying my real name, and it bothers me to even know that it belongs to me. I like the name Max gave me, and it makes me sad that I won't hear him call me it again for a while. As much as I want him to come back for me, I don't want him to get hurt, and coming here will not make things any better. I remember Max used to sneak me out into the village and teach me a commoner's way of life. He taught me to play hopscotch and how to round up cattle on a farm just on the outskirts of town. He taught me how to skip stones on the glassy surface of the ocean on a clear night, which was when we had our first kiss. I miss him—not just because I haven't seen him since Earth but because we missed out on so much time together.

I barely notice when Theo begins speaking. My head is spinning. I want for Theo to be Max, and instead of him taking me to the mechanics corridor, I want him to be holding me close in the depths of space on our way home.

"Thank you, Officer Evans. You can just set her down there." It bothers me how similar the commander's voice and Max's are.

Theo lowers me onto a bench and takes the blindfold away from my face. It is suddenly very bright, and I have to squint my eyes in order to make the shapes out.

"That will be all for now," says the commander. Theo nods his head once and leaves the room. I almost want him to come back; I don't trust the commander, and I certainly don't want to be alone with him.

"So, Miss Lilyryn. Do you have anything you would like to share with me?"

I stay quiet. The room is large and full of tools, computers, and instruments of all sorts; I don't like the look of it.

"Look, I don't like to have to do this, but you leave me no choice." He whistles and waits a moment. My heart pounds. What is he doing?

In comes a soldier. He tightly grips the arm of a thin girl. Her blondish brown hair spills over her shoulders, making her look wild. She pushes back against the soldier and fights to pull her arm away. The soldier grips tighter onto her arm and hits her upside the head violently; she nearly falls to the floor. She catches her footing and then looks up at me with storm-gray eyes.

"*Sandy?*" I whisper. The commander grins and takes a step to the side while the soldier brings her in front of me.

"Ah! You know each other?"

I don't say anything. I just want to know why Sandy is here.

"My princess, why are you here? We thought you were dead," Sandy asks breathlessly. She looks dangerously pale and much skinnier than the last time I saw her. I can't seem to say anything. No words form in my mouth.

"Well, this is just perfect, Lilyryn. Tell me where Max is, and Sandy will live." The commander's words are careful and barbarous. Sandy's face falls. Permanent tears stain her cheeks and she shakes her head.

"You're a sick man." The words seethe through my teeth.

The commander slips something off the table nearest to him that glints gold in the light.

"Don't tell him, Princess. He's going to kill me no matter what." Sandy struggles to speak. I notice bruises on her neck that are darker, suggesting a recent endeavor. She was choked or beaten recently.

"Don't touch her," I say.

The commander holds my blade up in his hands. "Then talk. It's been two weeks and you still haven't given me any news." I thought I was only here a week, maybe a week and a half. *Two weeks?* "Talk."

"I'm not sure exactly." My heart pounds in my chest.

"Not good enough." The commander walks over to where Sandy kneels on the floor. He presses the blade against her neck.

"I can't ..." I stutter. "No ... Please ... don't."

It happens so fast. I gag. Sandy's body falls to the floor. Blood flows around her. A piercing scream interrupts the immediate silence; I realize it's my own.

"Get rid of the body," the commander says to the soldier. They exchange a nod. Then the commander comes up beside me. "Girl, shut your mouth." He brings the bloody blade close to my face. "You're selfish and arrogant. Max doesn't need a girl like you. He can do so much better." He presses the bloody blade against the side of my neck, digging in a bit when I shy away. He grabs a handful of my hair and pulls. "When I have everything I need, I will kill you, and your body will be sent through the portal. No one will remember you, and no one will care that you are gone. Do you understand me? No one will miss you!" he yells in my face. "Do you understand me?" I nod my head despite the blade pressed to my throat and the hand gripping my hair. "I will keep killing your friends until you simply tell me where Max has gone."

In come several soldiers and another prisoner. I recognize him instantly—Jeremy. "I know that you recognize this young man." The blade is pulled away from my neck, leaving behind a dull stinging.

"Arianna?" Jeremy asks when he sees me.

"That is *not* my name," I yell automatically. He *knows*.

"Ah! A feud I sense," says the commander. "What is it that you've done to make her hate you so much?"

Jeremy takes a deep breath as he is driven to his knees closer to me than where Sandy was. "I made her forget who Max was." His forehead is badly bruised and moves painfully as though he's been beaten.

"Oh, I like you. Maybe after I have some of the information I need, you can do that again," says the commander.

"Where is Max?" the commander asks again.

"Not here!" I yell.

"I know that!" he yells back. "Hold his hand down."

I hate Jeremy at the moment, but I hate the commander more and I don't want him to win. Jeremy struggles against the weight of the soldiers, but they manage to hold his hand down on the floor.

"Tell me now!"

"Lily, Max is tough. He'll be fine." Jeremy gives me a desperate look. "He loves you."

The commander bends down beside Jeremy, holding the still-bloody blade. "Where?" he yells again.

"Don't do this—" I start to say but am interrupted by another loud noise. Jeremy lets out a shriek and turns even paler.

"Tell me now or he loses more than just another finger," spits the commander.

"Fine, you want to know?" I shout. I hear in my head Theo's words from the first time I met him, *You're not the only one with something to lose.*

"Yes!"

"He's gone to Margaritan, happy? That's where he went, and he will not want to know that you of all people are his dad. Yes, people may not care or even remember me when I am dead, but at least I didn't massacre five planets and all of their inhabitants. I am not a mass serial killer!"

One of the soldiers grabs a device from nearby and presses the end of it to the bloody stub, where Jeremy's pinky used to be. He lets out another shriek as the soldier cauterizes it. I gag.

"Keep him alive, but go kill three of the others."

"What?" I yell, "I just told you what you wanted to know. I thought you would have already guessed. You can't kill anyone else! Please!"

"You're right, I had an idea where he went, but it's the fact that it took so many times to get you to finally tell the truth. You don't deserve to have your people live."

"*They* deserve to live, not me, all right? Just kill me instead and let them go," I beg. "They're innocent. Please don't touch them."

"I've already made up my mind," he says as they drag Jeremy out of the room. I make eye contact with him momentarily. His eyes are hurt, and his body sags in the arms of the soldiers.

I start to stand up, but the cast restricts my movement. "You son of a bit—" I begin to yell. Something is stabbed into my arm, ending only the beginning of my rant. Another syringe, and my body goes almost entirely numb. All I can do is sit still and look up at him.

CHAPTER 23

I CAN WALK, ALTHOUGH IT HURTS TO PUT TOO MUCH WEIGHT ON my right leg. The commander had my cast removed; he also had his doctors fix my leg so the bone is properly intact. He didn't want it healed completely though. He wants me to be less of a flight risk, and the only way that can happen is if I have difficulty moving. A lot of the muscle in my leg shrank, which bothers me. I was skinny enough, and now a long scar runs up my thigh. I don't know how long I've been out, maybe hours, maybe days.

I almost wish the commander would be satisfied in killing me and then just stop killing everyone else. I feel guilty that I let Max's location be known and that Sandy was slain and Jeremy lost his finger and three other people were killed just because the commander felt like it. He was right; I don't deserve Max and I certainly don't deserve to even be alive. I don't deserve anything I've ever been given.

I brush my fingers through my hair; it's almost down to my waist now. I slipped into a black dress with lace-sleeves this morning—at least I think it was this morning. I can't tell the difference here. I wonder where Mira is. I hope Max got her somewhere safe.

I honestly have no idea what I would do if the commander killed her; it's bad enough I couldn't stop Coral's death.

I know the window may keep most of the cold air out but not all of it; a slight chill radiates from the thick-plated glass. I have to massage my arms in order to keep the heat in them. The water is rough today, and the wind howls. A lot of people are out by the docks tying down the ropes from the ships and attaching lengths of chain to them. I think they are preparing for a storm.

A knock sounds at the door. Theo stands in the opening. "Hey girl, how are you feeling?"

I turn back to face the window. I want it to be a huge storm. "Does it matter?" I ask stubbornly. I'm miserable and I don't want to be bothered, but that doesn't matter to him.

"Sure it does."

"No, it doesn't. What do you want?" I snarl and balance most of my weight on my left leg.

"The commander requests your presence," he says quietly. "I haven't done anything to harm you, and I will not. Please don't take your anger out on me."

"Why does the commander need me now? Is he going to kill more of my people? If he is, I'd much rather stay here in this pathetic little room. What is it?"

Theo looks rather uncomfortable; I don't think any girl has ever yelled at him before. I don't usually like to yell, but I don't care anymore. These people hurt my loved ones, and I don't care if my words hurt them. The commander is going to kill me anyway; he doesn't want me to be with Max. He really only needs one thing from me, and I don't even know what that is.

"Max—he's here. He turned himself in."

"What!" I yell, facing him again. Max, he came back for me?

"Yes, girl, he must really love you."

I limp toward him and the door. I need to see him. "Was

there anyone else with him?" I wonder if Ruban or Ace came with him or maybe one of the girls Elle or Isla. I haven't seen them in weeks.

"No." He pauses. "The commander also requests that you look well. He does not want you to say anything about what has happened to Max. Otherwise three more of your citizens will be killed." A tall lady sneaks in behind him. "This is Tara. She will fix you up, and then we'll go see them."

Tara walks in and pushes the chair in front of the mirror. "Sit," she demands. As soon as I sit in it, she immediately starts to put makeup on me. I don't argue. I know that if I do it will only take longer before I can see Max.

It feels like forever, though it's only moments before she's finished. When I look in the mirror, I'm surprised. The bags under my eyes are hidden, and I look less pale. She puts a fresh bandage on my neck where the commander dug the blade in because the other one bled through. Also half of my hair is pulled up and new earrings are put in my ears. Makeup is also put on the top of my hand, covering up a bruise I never realized was there. I honestly don't care how I look; I just want to go see Max.

"Finished," says Tara, dumping a few things back into her bag. Besides the fact I lost weight, I look normal, like nothing ever happened.

"Great, thanks, Tara." Theo smiles at her.

I stand up and walk toward Theo again. I can finally go. Theo leads the way, but I have a harder time walking. I don't miss the crutches because they were giving me bruises under the armpits, but I do miss being able to move faster. Even though I look normal, I feel like crap; my body hurts and I ache to see him, but I can't seem to get there fast enough.

There are voices coming from down the hallway. They are all low, but I still hear them.

"Hold my arm," says Theo as we enter the corridor with the metallic beige walls and strange furniture.

"Why?"

"Just do it, okay?"

I roll my eyes and link my arm in his. It surprisingly minimizes the severity of my limp to merely a hobble. My heart pounds so hard in my chest when we walk through the door I want to cry. Max leans against one of the shelves lining the wall, talking to the commander, who leans against his desk. He wears dark jeans and a dark jacket.

"Reena? Oh my gosh, Reena." Before I know it, I'm right where I've only ever wanted to be—in Max's arms. I wince at the sudden movement.

"Are you real?" I whisper only to him.

"Yes! As real as your blessed beating heart," he whispers back. "I came as soon as I could."

I look over at the commander. He glares at me like Brad once did. I think that if I ever see him again, I will thank him. Without him I probably would have met Max in a totally different way. I would never have had the head injury that needed healing, and I would have never remembered who I was. I would thank him for going easy on me, unlike the man standing just a short distance away.

"Now you know she's well. I'm an honest man the majority of the time. As you can see, I have just proved that to you." The commander gestures with his hands. Max pulls away but links his arm around me, pressing me close. The heat that radiates from him warms me.

"What is it that you want?" Max interrupts.

"Be polite! I thought your mother would have raised you better," he snaps.

I feel Max's body stiffen next to mine. "What the hell do

you know about my mother?" I know the answer to that. I wish I didn't, but I do. What do I do? Should I save him from this, or should I just let things play out? If I pretend to pass out then that would prolong the news. I feel weak enough. It would be rather simple.

"A lot more than you would think," the commander says, grinning. "It's nice to finally meet you, my son."

Max is so still, I'm not sure he's even breathing. I look up at him, at his face. I can't tell if he's angry or disappointed yet, but I can definitely tell he's shocked. They have the same body type, but Max is a little taller and he has a tan. They both have similar facial features though. "You're *not* my father."

The commander's face turns hard, but he simply says, "Why else would I have gone through so much trouble trying to find *you?* I need her for certain reasons, but for what reason do you think I would request *your* company here?"

"To kill me, just like you have the last five races."

"No, I don't want to kill you, and besides, you're half Onychinus. Not any of those other races are half as brilliant as you. Margaritan is one of a few races I actually respect, so you're a good mix." I don't understand. If he respects Margaritan, why is he trying to destroy it?

As if reading my thoughts, Max says, "Why is it you try and annihilate them as well, if you respect them?"

"Not annihilate. Perhaps we can speak of this at a later hour?"

"Why not now?" Max demands.

"Because I have important business to attend to," the commander interrupts and straightens up taller. "I will meet the two of you for dinner this evening. My guards will bring you to your chambers." He looks directly at Max and then turns to me, saying, "You as well."

"I'm staying with her," Max demands stubbornly. I admire

his boldness. I'm so glad he stands beside me right now. If his arm weren't around my waist, I'm sure I would have fallen down.

"No, Miss Lilyryn is to join me for a stroll. She will be brought to you within the hour." The commander gives him a calm smile. I don't trust this nice act. I've seen his cruelty and have experienced it, I want him dead. I don't want to be with him alone again.

Max's fingers dig into my flesh, bruising my side. Max knows, too, it's not a good idea. If I rebel, he's going to punish more of my people. If I do as he requests, less of my people will be harmed. All in all, the commander plans on eliminating us, not Max, but me and the rest of Margaritan.

"Very well," I say in a faint voice. The words taste like ash in my mouth.

"I wish to come along," says Max.

"Max, you're going to your chambers, and Miss Lilyryn will be along shortly!" His words are loud and harsh and leave no room for question or even a snide comment. They are absolute.

Max's fingers dig deeper in my side. Does he think we will become attached the harder he presses? I shy away slightly, and Max looks at me, like actually looks at me. Hurt fills his eyes.

"Gentlemen?" the commander calls out, and in come three officers dressed in green and black uniforms, swords strapped to their hips. "Take him to his chambers and call a butler for refreshments." Max presses his lips to my forehead before the men lead him out of the room.

There is an awkward silence that lingers in the room. The commander looks beyond the door frame. When he's satisfied with what he sees, he gestures for me to walk with him. When I don't budge from the spot where Max left me, he raises his voice saying, "Come."

I straighten up and glare at him as I walk past. I can feel his icy gaze follow me. I have no idea what he's going to do now, but

I'm sure it's not good. Immediately the commander steps into pace beside me. "The task I need you to do is actually quite simple, and it won't take long," he says, though I don't feel any bit reassured. Once the commander is done with me, he's going to kill me, and I know Max won't react well to that.

CHAPTER 24

We turn down into a narrower hallway, leaving the central one, the one where we can be seen by all. Several guards follow us, probably to make sure I won't attack the commander. Even if I wanted to I couldn't because my leg still feels weird and I don't trust it to allow me a quick getaway.

I blank my mind and try to steady my heartbeat. I can do this; just think of Max, I can see him soon. He's made sure of my sister's safety—well, at least one of them. I hope my mother and Flora are still alive. If the commander killed them too, I don't know what I'd do.

We turn another corner, and the commander opens a door with a key card. It slides open, revealing a staircase. He holds a hand out, gesturing me to go down. Deep in the pit of my core I feel a sudden, overwhelming fear. Something down there is going to kill me. I take a few steps slowly, one at a time. I hear the commander following me a few steps behind. I reach the bottom, only to find another door. My hands have started trembling again, and this time I'm not sure I can make them stop. The commander unlocks this one as well; he puts his hand on my back, prodding me in.

I get the sudden whiff of metal and sterilization when I walk in. There are multiple tinted glass enclosures at the far end and shiny silver shelves lining the side walls. In the center of the room is a podium that stands level with my ribs.

"What are those?" I ask. The chests—from Mira's drawing about a month and a half ago—sit in front of each of the tinted enclosures. Five of them are closed shut with a dull light, indicating they're occupied. There are four empty ones that just sit open against their doors. The last one, the tenth, sits on the podium. In it rests the fake golden pearl.

I don't know how to make it slow down. My heart is going wild. This is how I'd imagine a heart attack would feel like. The commander stands at my side speaking, but honestly I have no idea what he's saying.

I want Max.

The bearers from the annihilated planets are still alive. They are all still here. All of the closed chests sitting in front of their tinted enclosures are connected with the beings inside. I can sense them.

Oh my God, what is he doing to them?

What is he going to do to me?

I automatically switch my brain back on. I have to actually listen to what he's saying if I want to know what's going on.

The commander stands tall with a solemn face as he speaks. His words are calm and assertive. The only thing going on in my mind right now is the thought of how much I want to kill him! This dictator kills people for sport and has five individuals—pretty much the last of their kind—locked up like animals.

My body is completely frozen, going against my absolute urge to lunge for him, to kill him with my bare hands, if I could.

The guards line themselves up around the room in their trained, creepy manner.

"Listen up." The commander snaps his fingers in front of my face, now making his words clear. "Put. Your. Hand. Here," he says, pretty much spelling it out. I've never felt such a strong hate build up in me before, especially one that I *can't* let loose. A tablet of some sort is connected to several wires that link to the base of the chest. It looks intense.

"What will happen if I do?" I ask.

"As the bearer of the life source of your planet, a large portion of that power was contributed to your build up, the ultimate energy actually surges in your veins. You will simply be transferring the energy back into the source. It will make you feel strange, but you will live."

"And what will happen if I don't?" I glare up at him. He wants to take away all of my energy, my munera, and when that's gone there will be nothing left of me.

The commander grabs my arm, squeezing his fingers deep into my skin. It hurts, but I only stare up at him. "You will do it or I will put you under and force it out of you, and then you will have to wait much longer to talk to Max and Jeremy may lose more than just a finger." Spit flies out of his mouth as he yells in my face. "You better do it because three more of your people are going to be killed if you don't."

I glare at him, yanking my arm out of his tight grip. I slam my hand onto the tablet sitting in front of me. I know the pearl is not the real one but it scares me, just the same; I'm afraid that I'm going to make it equally as powerful as the real one.

I feel something leave my core. It is a slow draining sensation. My knees start knocking against each other, and I'm afraid I'm going to collapse. I've always known, even before I was given the golden pearl, that I was powerful. When I turned seventeen I got a real taste of my ultimate energy for the first time, but now as it leaves my body, I feel like I've been struck, beaten, and buried.

The commander rips my hand away from the tablet. "That's enough for today," he says, catching me by the waist before I fall. "About three more rounds and you will be done." He holds me up and whispers in my ear, "You will never have to worry about your people ever again."

I squint my eyes at the pearl. Mira said it will only last for so long. What now? When it disappears will the energy also? I hope so, before he can use it.

I don't know how long I was attached to it, but I feel absolutely drained. I don't know if I even have my munera anymore. I need to tell Max what happened.

"Miss Lilyryn." The commander holds me upright by the shoulders now, facing him. "You will not tell him anything. If I even suspect you have, I will end another life. Do you understand me?"

I simply nod though my eyes fill with tears.

The commander says something else, and the next thing I notice is I'm in the arms of a guard with dark hair. A clean handkerchief is pressed into my hand, and I'm told to wipe my nose. When I do blood comes off. The guard carries me up the stairs. He turns several corners until we make it to my room, where Tara is waiting for me.

The guard sets me down on the bed. Though I know my body is light, I feel as though I weigh a million pounds.

"Thanks, Officer Berend, you can wait outside. I'll call if I need anything." The officer looks at me and nods his head once. Does he not also appreciate what the commander is doing, or does he only feel sorry for me?

"Miss? Can you slide into the chair, please?" Tara says quietly.

I move to the edge, but I can't seem to manage getting up

on my own. She hooks her arm in mine. Supporting most of my weight, she leads me into the chair.

"I know how much that boy loves you," she whispers "Please, try and push through, for him. I don't know what the commander did to you, but I know you're stronger than this."

Do the commander's people really not like him that much?

I manage a small smile for her, and her face seems to light up a bit. She immediately straightens my hair and brings out her makeup bag. She takes the crumpled, bloody handkerchief out of my hands, pulls out a clean one, and dampens it under the tap in the bathroom. I look in the mirror when she's done. My face looks normal again. There's no more blood under my nose, and the dark bags under my eyes are still hidden with the little bit of makeup.

"Here, take off your dress and put this one on," she says, pulling out another bag on a hanger. She slips the new dress out, lays it on the bed, and then helps me make the switch, frowning when she sees the new fingerprinted bruises on my arm.

The new dress is long-sleeved and navy blue. Most of the back is open, and it falls to the floor. She places small flats on the floor.

I stand in front of the mirror looking like myself but feeling like I have weights in my body.

CHAPTER 25

OFFICER BEREND LEADS ME FROM THE ROOM, BRINGING ME TO Max.

I am so ready to see him.

His room is so far away from mine. I think the commander did that on purpose. He said I would be delivered within the hour. It doesn't feel like it's been an hour, but a lot longer.

Officer Berend knocks on the door, and on the other side Max rushes to open it. The look on his face is overwhelming. It fills me with so many emotions. Mostly I'm happy to see him, but the rest of me is filled with dread. The officer leaves, stopping across the hall, standing still.

I want to leap in his arms, but I end up standing in place crying.

"Oh, Reena," he whispers. He looks behind me at the officer and pulls me into his room, closing the door. His room is quite different from mine. He wraps his arms around me so tightly I feel warm for the first time in weeks,

"I'm so sorry," I say in a quiet sob. "Did everyone get out okay?"

"Yes, yes they did. We had to fight our way through, but the others are all right." As if knowing my next question he says, "Mira is safe too. She's with your mother, sister, and Maybell." I breathe out a sigh of relief.

"And …?"

He presses his lips next to my ear. "The pearl too."

I bury my head in his chest, and with that, he gently rubs my back with his hand. I can't believe it, the last time we saw each other I yelled at him to leave me behind, and I betrayed him. Now we stand in this quiet, foreign room, hugging it out.

"Max, I love you," I whisper, "and I'm very sorry."

"I know. I know why you did it. It's okay," he says, hushing me. I can't seem to stop sobbing. There's so much I need to tell him that the commander told me not to. If I do tell him then there goes another life. "Reena, you have absolutely no idea how much I love you."

I feel my knees almost give out, but Max's strong arms catch me, holding me up. He slips an arm under my knees and carries me to his bed. When he sets me down, I feel the same heaviness as before; I've lost too much energy today.

"What the hell did he do to you?" Max's face suddenly goes hard, and it scares me a little.

I shake my head, the tears streaming down my face. "Reena, you have to tell me what happened."

"I can't. He's gonna kill more of my people," I sob.

"Not if you tell me." His face is urgent and pained, and his dress shirt is wrinkled from my hug. "Reena, you've been here for a long time. Don't you want to go home? I can't return justice if I don't know what's happened."

I shake my head again. I don't care that Tara's makeup is probably running down my face right now. "Reena, just tell me."

He cups my face in his hands and then brushes a stray strand of hair out of my eyes.

"No …"

"Reena, please?" His face is serious.

"Fine, but I don't know how much time we have," I say, choking back the tears.

I tell him everything, the fact that he has the bearers from the other planets caged up downstairs and he's stripping them entirely of the energy they possess, down to the cellular level. That he started the process with me, not knowing he doesn't have the real pearl. I tell him what the commander said he did with my father, that he killed him. I explain how he killed Sandy trying to figure out where Max was and how he cut off Jeremy's finger. I tell him that the maids and officers—some of them—are actually nice, like Theo and Tara. Max listens even more intently when I tell him about breaking my leg in the crash. He thought that I stayed behind to protect them. That was mostly true, but it was also because I knew I would only slow them down because of my leg.

"You're my tough cookie," he whispers, a smile playing at his lips.

"I wish I could have warned you that he was your father though," I say at last.

Max's body goes rigid, and he just stares at the wall behind my head. "It's fine. A real father is someone who is there for his kid. That man was never there."

I move over so I'm sitting beside him, my legs hanging over the side of the bed beside his. I grab hold of his hands resting on his lap. We sit in silence for a few moments. "You should have seen your mother's face when I brought Mira to her," he whispers. "She instantly recognized her. It's the first time I remember seeing your mother so happy."

I smile to myself. She deserves this; she fell into a depressed state after Mira was sent away. I too don't ever remember seeing her extremely happy. I can only imagine. But now with Dad gone, how long will her happiness last? She's lost so much … we all have … *I* … have.

"She's a good kid," he says with admiration in his words. "She's brave, smart, beautiful, just like her incredible older sister. I managed to get your family into a safe house with the others. They are far away from the palace. I told them that we will come back for them when this is all over." I hold his hand in both of mine, and I lift it to my lips, planting a kiss on it.

"Thank you." I want to say more, but there are very few words that come to my mind. I feel like I haven't done anything significant for him compared to the amount of things he's done for me.

He leans over and kisses my head. "Anything for you, my love." I get the same fluttery feeling as I got nearly three years ago. The time has just flown by, and now I love Max even more as the days pass by. He's my first and only love.

A knock comes at the door, making us both jump. Max gently pulls his hand away from mine and walks over to open the door. I stand.

Officer Berend is on the other side of the door. They pass muffled words, but in the end Max accepts and comes to meet me.

"It's time," he whispers. "I promise we're going to find a way to get our people out soon."

CHAPTER 26

THE DINING HALL IS LARGE, WITH A LONG, SPRAWLED-OUT TABLE in the center of the room, and off to the side is a smaller sized circular one, set for three. It is even more decorative here than in the other rooms.

A handful of guards are lined up around the room, and Officer Berend leads us to the smaller table. "The commander will be along shortly," he says and then turns to leave the room.

Max pulls one of the chairs out for me and pushes it forward. Once I'm sitting, he takes his seat beside me.

"I wonder what he's going to say," I whisper, playing with the folds of the lengthy tablecloth. Then from where the officer just exited the commander strolls in wearing a crisp dark suit and tie with a flower of some sort in his jacket pocket.

"Guess we'll find out," Max mutters.

"It's a curious thing. On many occasions an individual will often wonder why it is that secrets are held at bay," the commander says with sure strides. "I'm certain Miss Lilyryn has updated you entirely about her stay here." His face is straight, and his eyes are boring into me.

"That is true. Thank you for taking care of her and making her feel comfortable here," says Max confidently. He's lying. He knows that the commander will go to great measures to destroy me if he knew the truth ... then again maybe he wanted me to tell Max everything in the first place? I sit up a little straighter in my chair when he slides into his own.

"It was my pleasure," says the commander, gesturing to the servers standing in the entrance of what I believe is the kitchen. "So, I'm not sure if you were aware, but we have an extremely advanced tech unit who have already discovered several ways to manipulate the portal. An example being, we can travel places much faster than the natural way." The commander unfolds his napkin across his lap while the servers set out plates in front of each of us. It looks like your regular garden salad. However, some of the vegetables I can't distinguish exactly what they are.

"Thank you," he says as they walk away.

"What do we care?" Max asks, picking at the strange salad with his fork.

"That we have much greater technology. We are highly more advanced than so many of the other races out there. We can create and destroy much more efficiently in comparison to everyone else." The commander raises his voice. "It would be quite beneficial if you, my son, were to stay here with my people. You can have a life like you've only ever imagined but with so much more to offer. You wouldn't ever have to worry about people betraying you or banishing you to another planet ever again. You can live the life your birth rights have deemed possible."

"What do you mean by birth rights?" Max asks.

"Royal birth rights," says the commander. "I'm a king. I prefer the title of commander. It creates a greater sense of fear and respect. You, my boy, are a prince."

Max looks completely mortified. With how people from my

planet treated him growing up, I'm sure he'd never expected that he was a prince.

When I was young, my father used to tell me that he preferred that I married a prince or the exception, a man being a noble. I wonder if he knew what Max was—that his father was actually a king. If he did know that Max was a prince then why was he so angry that we were dating?

The salad tastes sweet and bitter at the same time, and some of the berries in mine taste quite strange, kind of like cranberries from earth. I chew, trying to clear my mind to think of anything else. My dad did a lot of cruel things, but the cruelest thing was separating Max and me. I wonder if he was still alive, would he approve of us falling in love with each other all over again?

"Giving you this piece of information, I'm willing to make a proposition."

Max's face falls back into an emotionless mask. His jaw tightens, and his foot finds mine beneath the table and rests it beside mine. He nods his head once, and the commander proceeds. I can only imagine how he's feeling. I remember the moment I had all my memories returned to me. I learned so much about myself that I had lost. Now the answer's to Max's past are finally coming into focus. I used to ask him what he imagined his father was like, what he would tell me was quite different from the man who sits just across the table.

"You can choose to become the crown prince here and possess an immense power others can only dream of." At the moment I think of the five bearers downstairs being drained of every bit of power deep within their cells; that's going to be me. "Although if you rebelled against me that would mean some major consequences. Honestly, I'm not someone who will be played."

I can see Max's jaw clench tighter, and I'm sure he wants to get up and storm out of the room. He struggles to hold his composure. "That sounds like a moderately fair offer, for me," he says. "However, not for everyone else." He takes a short breath before he speaks again. "This girl here is not just someone who can be messed around with. You haven't mentioned any benefit for her."

"I kind of figured you'd say that," says the commander with a suppressed smile.

I hate when people talk about me like I'm not even present. But mostly I just want to slap the commander across the face and dig my blade deep in his chest and watch the life leave his eyes and the grin fall from his lips.

"You can marry her," says the commander. He's saying this, though I know that even if he allowed us to be married, he wouldn't allow me to live much longer. Max's posture goes rigid again. He knows it too.

"I don't need your permission," says Max. "I've loved this girl since we were children. It was always my intentions to marry her." My heart leaps. "Your permission means nothing to me."

The commander's face drops, and a hint of anger fills his eyes. He likes to have a control over everyone, but the thing is, he doesn't have anything that we want. He only has his threats that keep us from moving forward.

Our mostly untouched salads are taken away by servers— whom I never even noticed appear behind us. A new dish is placed in front of us. It looks like a roast of some sort, mashed potatoes, what appears to be white carrots, and there is some kind of cherry-colored sauce over the potatoes and meat. It smells very good. My stomach rumbles a little. I haven't actually eaten much of anything they've given me.

I notice the commander and Max just looking at each other, neither saying anything, but both look disappointed. I need to eat. I take one of the main course forks and a knife and begin to cut some of the roast. I have no idea when the next time I'm going to get food again, so I take a bite. The heat and flavor explodes in my mouth, and I take another bite, already taming the wild beast in my empty stomach.

"I'll give you until morning to make your decision," says the commander through clenched teeth.

"Very well," says Max. I know how the gears in his head are working. I know what he wants to do, and it's not possible.

His voice is low and dark. "The only alternative there is, is *death*."

This time I see him coming. A servant comes from the side. "Apologies, sir?"

"What is it?"

The servant leans down and whispers something in his ear. The commander's eyebrows furrow, and he stands abruptly. He makes eye contact with Max and says, "Make the right decision. I know you're smart. Someone will come for you later. Excuse me." He glares at me when Max looks away and then he hurries from the room.

"I wonder what that was all about," I whisper.

"I uh ... have no idea," says Max.

"He looked kind of pissed off when the servant came to him," I whisper.

Max stares blankly at the red liquid in his glass. There are dark circles under his eyes, and he looks pale. I reach across the table and touch his cold hand. At that, he looks up, his eyes meeting mine. "I'm certain the others knows you've told me everything," he whispers. "We have to be careful with what we say. Otherwise everything will go downhill. I'm sure he has ears all over the place. When we walked out of my room, I saw a small microphone just above the door."

"Oh my, he's an intense stalker in my opinion."

"Yeah, no doubt." Max chuckles. Then he takes both my hands in his and looks at me deeply. "Reena, I'm going to get us out of here. Do you trust me?"

It takes me a moment to get a hold on my words because I'm distracted by the intensity in his face. "Always."

A smile glints in his eyes, though he restrains having one on his mouth so no one else in the room will notice its presence. Then he lets go of one of my hands and whispers, "Eat. You don't look well."

We finish our dinner in hushed conversation. My stomach is full shortly after beginning. "Max, there is no way Ruban, Elle, Ace, and Isla are able to sit still and do nothing. Where are they actually?"

This time a small smile plays at his lips. "Isla, Elle and Miles *did* stay back to protect your family," he says so quietly it's hard for me to hear. He looks at me, and it's almost as if his words are just in my head and not spoken out. *"They came to help."*

"How did you do that? I can't use my munera here."

"I'll explain later."

We both go silent when we see Officer Berend enter the room and stride toward us. He stops right behind the commander's empty chair. "The commander implores that the both of you are to join him on a stroll in the gardens this evening."

"But there is to be a storm," I say.

"He's aware of that. That is why it won't be for long. A maid and butler have both brought down outer wear for you. I'm to take you to them."

My stomach drops. What does he want now?

Max stands up first and nods once. Than both the officer and Max look at me. I don't want to be anywhere near the commander. I take a large gulp of the dark-colored wine from the glass in front of me. It tastes bitter and tangy. I take a deep breath and then push my chair back. "Very well."

We follow him down the hall, taking a left turn, my hand in Max's, reaching what I believe is the main entrance. It seems almost like old times, the two us walking together, most often toward trouble.

A young lady and man both in palace uniforms stand waiting, holding our outerwear. They both have neutral expressions. I slip into a dark shawl and Max into an overcoat.

"Come along," says Officer Berend, motioning for the guards to open the doors. The cold hits me immediately, chilling me to the bone, and the wind whips my hair across my face.

Thunder cackles in the atmosphere and the wind howls, blowing the trees around angrily. I hold the shawl closer to my body as we walk along a concrete walking path. There is very little color pigment in the plants, the grass and leaves are all dark, almost a black-green, and the sky is disappearing behind black storm clouds. How they can live in near complete darkness is beyond me. It is insane how the commander needs to show us something so badly in such crappy weather.

Officer Berend doesn't appear all that impressed by the wind, nor does he seem all that affected by the chill. "Just a little further."

Max wraps his arm around my shoulders, holding me close and protecting me from the wind. I hold my shawl with one hand and place my arm around his waist.

It begins to spit tiny raindrops here and there. Our skin feels frigid. I hold onto him tighter, not wanting to ever let go. We walk as a group across a fairly high wooden bridge. Down below the water in the river is murky white and flowing quite fast. Small fish swim, leaping over the waves. They are bright red and black, and they stand out like a sore thumb in the white vastness. It's strange everything is so dark, and yet the water here is white.

"Don't fall in or you'll never come back out," says Officer Berend, slightly ahead of us.

"Why's that?" I ask.

"Acid water, and those aren't ordinary fish. The fish will clean your bones in less than ten minutes; the acid will paralyze you and then you're screwed."

I feel the sudden urge to pull a little further away from the edge. The wind begins to pick up and sends more water droplets into our faces. As soon as we're off the bridge, we make a turn and walk through the trees toward some kind of building. He opens the door quickly and follows us in.

It is very bright; the walls are all silver and metallic light fixtures hang from the ceiling.

"You're late," says the commander, taking long strides in our direction.

"Apologies sir," says the officer, bowing his head.

"All right. Well, follow me," he says. "You need to see something."

He begins walking toward the smaller glass-like wall across from us. There are so many tools and machines around it looks like a tornado flew through here. The wall moves without countenance. It looks much like the portal on Margaritan. "There are two different kinds of individuals in this universe—the ones who want power and the ones who have it. I have that power."

"What is this?" asks Max as we come to a stop about ten feet away.

"This is my portal, my access to every galaxy. She's almost ready to use. It won't be long before our design is perfect. I have the power to go anywhere I please and acquire whatever I want." The commander speaks proudly, brushing his hand across the slow-moving surface.

There are several tiny colored wires connected to a tablet built beside the wall; a dark sapphire, citrine, amethyst, a rhodolite, and the pure colorlessness of spinel and also one as dark as an onyx stone. The commander is using the energy from the bearers' home life sources to create his own portal. This is unnatural.

"Why do you need this, if there is a perfectly good one already?" asks Max. I'm not sure if he noticed the jewel-toned wires that are powering it. If I were close enough, I would just rip them out. The poor souls downstairs should not have to go through this.

"Because this, my dear boy, won't allow just anyone to come through it. Only those with Onychinus blood can enter and exit. There is no greater piece of perfection than this," says the commander. "One day you can have everything you've ever wanted."

"I already have everything I need," replies Max.

"Need and want are two completely different things. You've lived a poor life because of that girl's father. I tried to come back for you and your mother; I was planning on bringing you here so you could live the life you were meant to. I built this palace twenty years ago, just so I could have complete access to the natural portal. My first was about two hundred miles away, and now it holds a small portion of my military. Now you have the opportunity to live a life of greatness."

"I am aware of that." Max hesitates. He lets his arm slide from my shoulders to around my waist. He stands up straighter and with a confident voice says, "I'll keep all of this in mind. As you have said, I have until tomorrow to make my decision."

For just a moment I'm afraid of what he's going to choose, but I know that he is a good man and he will not abandon innocence. He won't say yes to this destruction. He can't. Would he?

"Very good," he says. "I'm sure you will choose wisely."

"I apologize, sir, the storm is to begin shortly, and it is unwise to stay another moment," interrupts Officer Berend, stepping away from a table full of tools. The commander looks rather annoyed, though he takes his advice without objection.

The storm is now overhead, and the wind and rain shake

us viciously. On Margaritan our rain storms were warm—long and heavy, but they were warm. The raindrops here send cold spikes deep into my skin. Max, while trying to protect me with his overcoat, also manages to keep me walking upright. I see Officer Berend several yards ahead of us, though I don't see the commander anywhere.

The trees dance like silhouettes among the darkness. Their branches sway in the rhythm of the whistling and the river with water of white and inhabitants the color of blood thrash about with joy. A moment like this comes around so rarely you nearly always miss it.

We stumble together up the steps, but I trip on the hem of my gown and fall hard, scraping my hands on my way down. The thunder clashes angrily in the sky, and light flashes with a mocking smile. "Reena!" Max gasps and picks me up at the waist. Slinging me over his shoulder, he takes the last of the stairs by twos.

Officer Berend is already inside taking off his soaked overcoat; he looks at us oddly when Max sets me back down. I'm entirely drenched through even though Max was trying to keep the rain from getting to me. I let the waterlogged shawl fall to the floor with a gross sloshing noise as it makes impact. Max slips out of his as well and picks mine up off the floor and hands it to the maid, who scurries by collecting them. It's the same maid who brought them to us earlier. She doesn't make eye contact. She simply does her job and leaves the room as quickly as she can. I wonder where the butler went.

"It certainly is a faster method," says the commander, strolling about the room. What the heck?

"Does that portal actually work?" asks Max, suppressing his mortified expression.

"Very much so. Once I have all of the *resources* I need, there won't be a realm I cannot have access to." A shiver works its way throughout my body, not only from the commander's words, but also from the icy gown clinging to my every curve and the bareness of my back. The lights from the ceiling begin to flicker as we hear another loud clap of thunder. I've never seen a storm as intense as this one before. The ones on Margaritan and Earth have a greater sense of domestication. They are less angry. "It is quite a late hour. Perhaps it's time to turn in?"

"Sir, if you want me to make a fair decision, I request that my room be next to Miss Lilyryn's this evening. I'd prefer a lesser distance," insists Max.

The commander tries to mask his emotions, though it is quite simple to see the pure disgust in his face. "Very well," he says through clenched teeth. "Officer Berend, can you take them to her room and the one next to it for him?"

"Yes sir."

"Thank you."

He watches as we pass by him. I don't know what it is about him that seems so odd. It seems as though he thrives on attention, and it's not the good kind; he'll do anything to hold people's interest. He wants Max to respect him, but I don't think he realizes that Margaritan will always be his home and no amount of bribing can change his heart. I'm afraid of what he's going to do when he doesn't get his way. I wonder how many people he's going to kill.

I CAN'T BEAR MY OWN WEIGHT ANYMORE. WITH THE COMmander draining my energy this afternoon and walking on my leg that has very little muscle in the freezing icy rain, I nearly collapse gasping for breath. Max is the only thing partially keeping me up.

"Reena! What's wrong?" he asks, letting me settle on the floor. Even Officer Berend stops and turns around. My head is pounding, and I can't stop shivering. He settles his hand on my open back, sending a flicker of warmth through me. I just shake my head.

"We should take her back to her room," says Officer Berend, coming to my other side. He presses the back of his hand to my forehead. "She's burning up."

Max scoops me up into his arms, holding me close to his chest. His heat pours through the cold wet fabric of his shirt. He stands the same as the officer, slightly panicked. "Lead the way."

Max can use his munera here, though I don't want him to; the commander can't know. It's our only chance at getting out of here. I can't think. The pain in my head is so great, and I can't stop the shivering.

They hurry me back to my room. Somewhere along the way I hear the officer asking someone to fetch the doctor. Without turning the light on, Max settles me down on the bed just as I begin to cough. My stomach muscles and lungs ache as I gasp for air and cough out fluid. "What's wrong with her?" asks Max, an edge in his voice.

"I have no idea," says the officer, pacing back and forth. "The doctor should be here shortly."

"Hang in there, Reena," he says, patting me on the back.

A tall, slim man comes into the room, quickly followed by a maid. The maid flicks on the lights. "What's happened?" He steps in beside me. His hair is white like his skin, and his eyes are dark and attentive. He holds a dark bag.

"She just collapsed coughing, and she has a high fever," says Officer Berend.

The doctor takes some kind of thermometer and glides it across my forehead. "Oh dear," he says.

I have no idea what it says, but I'm sure it's not good. My lungs fill with fluid, and I begin coughing again. He passes me a handkerchief. I take it, covering my mouth, as my body lurches forward with each cough. Max's hand stays pressed to my back the entire time. It feels slightly comforting. When I pull the handkerchief back, it's covered in light colored fluid. The doctor takes another device that is connected to a tablet and pricks my finger with the sharp needle end. He types in several things, his long narrow fingers moving across the pad really fast.

"She has hypo-amonia," he says at last. He turns quickly to the maid. "Run down to the hospital wing and go into the medicine cabinet and grab the bottle that says 'hypo-amonia' on it." He turns back to us. "Hypo-amonia is when you're extremely cold and your lungs fill with fumes that the river releases during a rainstorm. This affects those whose immune systems are weak."

The maid nods and leaves the room quickly. Max stands and starts talking to the doctor. I start coughing again, so I only make out small parts of what they are saying. "It's not usually this bad at first," and "she must have acquired it a few days ago." "It's a fairly easy fix as long as it's caught early." The maid rushes back into the room and hands a small bottle with literally only one word on it. "Miss," he says, coming back to my side. "You're going to have to try your best to breathe this in and hold your breath." He latches on a lid that allows for its contents to be misted. After I finish coughing, I nod. "Breathe as much as you can in and hold your breath for at least twenty seconds, okay?" I nod again, praying I won't cough again.

He sprays the medicine in front of me, and I inhale a large bit of it. It smells like mint. It's difficult to hold my breath. It burns its way through my lungs, and I start to feel another cough coming. I hold it back until my eyes start to water, and then I cough again, but this time there is no liquid.

"It'll take just a short moment for the rest of it to kick in," he says.

"Thank you," I whisper, not feeling the fluid in my lungs anymore. The pain in my head begins to slowly fade.

"I'll send Tara to come tend to you. I recommend warm clothes and lots of rest. Also, wait awhile before you go outside again; once you've had hypo-amonia it's quite common to get it again." He puts his stuff back into his bag and begins to leave. "Have a good evening, gentlemen and miss."

Officer Berend follows the doctor out of the room to talk to him.

Max wraps me in a hug. "You never used to get sick this often. Why now?" he asks rhetorically. "Tell me what else is hurt," he whispers silently in my ear.

"My leg," I whisper back. He puts his hand on my weaker leg, and I can feel his energy flow into the tissues of my muscles. I don't have to see my leg to know that it is healed. It makes me feel very relieved.

"Tonight is our last night," he whispers into my ear again. "We will be home by tomorrow. I promise." My heart stings when he says *promise.* There is no way to know for certain. He can't promise me something like this.

I want him to be confident, and the only way for that to happen is for him to know that I trust him, so I whisper two gentle words: "I know."

He presses his lips to mine, absorbing me in a kiss. I feel safe in this most unsafe moment. I don't understand why, but I somehow know that everything is going to work out. *"Ace and Ruban have found the others and will release them soon,"* he whispers in my head. I smile as he kisses me. Now I'm sure everything will work out.

It's been about two hours since Max was asked to leave the

room so that I could rest, and it's been about an hour since Tara left. My fever has left almost entirely thanks to Max and the doctor. I let my body rest and slowly drift off. I haven't been asleep for any more than half an hour before several people come into my room and grab me out of my bed.

CHAPTER 27

MY HEART THUMPS ANGRILY AGAINST MY CHEST AS I DEMAND them to release me. I kick and scratch as I try to pry myself out of their restraining arms. They drag me down a set of halls I don't exactly recognize, though I'm certain I remember where they lead to. The thunder still screams outside, and the lights indoors gradually flicker in protest. I have to get out of here. One of the officers opens a door with his key card, revealing the same set of stairs the commander brought me down earlier.

"No!" I scream, "Let me go!"

I'm dragged down the steps with brutal force, their hands bruising my arms and pulling my hair that falls down the back of my nightgown. I want Max. I scratch one of the men across the face, leaving a trail of blood across his cheek, and I kick another in the shins. One of them greets my aggression with a fist to my abdomen, and their fingers dig deeper into my skin as I cringe.

When we reach the bottom of the steps, they push me ahead of them, through the already open door. The instant smell of sterilization and metal hits me, and the light blinds me. The commander paces around the room angrily. His eyes are dark pits, and his usually pale skin is red.

"What the hell did you do to it!"

"Excuse me?" I ask as the officer pushes me forward.

"The pearl did not look like this several hours ago! Isn't this the real one?" he snarls, closing in on me. I feel his anger radiating toward me. "Tell me!" he yells in my face.

I pull back, but the officers hold me in place. I glance around him to have a look at the pearl. It floats slightly above its cushion. The casing is cracked, and smaller pieces break off, like snow melting. This pearl was made with the wind, the moonlight, the snow of earth, the gold of Margaritan, and the magic of a child more powerful than I. I am the bearer, but I know now that my only job was to get the pearl to Mira. She's the one of worth.

I don't see Theo or Officer Berend around anywhere. Do they know what the commander was planning to do?

"You're right." I stand up as straight as I can muster, my head barely level with his chin. "This is not the real one." I glare at him.

A pain very acute and abrupt swishes across my face. He's slapped me. My cheek burns and tingles sharply. I don't reach up to rub the feeling back into my face, and I refuse to let a tear slide down my cheek. I just hold my glare. "Your molecular buildup will certainly restore this one's strength! Gentlemen." All of a sudden the officers grip me tighter and practically yank me toward the podium. The commander grabs at my hand and presses it with great force onto the tablet, his large hand crushing mine beneath his. I can't move it away.

My body lurches forward as all of my fight begins to drain. Where's Max? The officers release me and take a step back, but the commander still holds me down. He's going to kill me. I can't let him. This man has taken so much from me; he's not going to take my life too. With my hand on the tablet, I imagine using my telekinesis to steal all of the power within the false pearl. I can see how greatly the tablet is trying to work opposite of me, but with every bit of remaining strength that I have, I pull as hard as I can. He won't take me away from my family, away from Max or Mira. *Fight! Fight! Fight! Hold on, you can't let go!* I hear in my head. I close my eyes tightly and use all of my might to collect my energy back. *Do it for those you love!* I feel the cold screen of the tablet crack beneath my hand. This has to work! Above me someone lets out a loud shriek, and the hand covering mine is no longer there.

I open my eyes. The skin on my hand is almost glowing, though my palm is bleeding from the broken glass of the tablet. The pearl is gone entirely, and I feel all of my energy returning. Max stands—dressed in his usual jeans and dark shirt—with a sword pointed at the commander's throat. All of the soldiers lie on the floor dead, and the commander's hand is bleeding profusely; it looks as though shrapnel has gone through it. I think the remains of the pearl went through his hand to get to mine. I stand up to my full height and glance down at the bodies. My stomach churns; there is so much blood.

"Nice to see you again, Reena," says a familiar voice. I turn around and see Ace wiping his sword clean. His face is clean-shaven, much like all of the guards here, and he wears one of the officer uniforms. He wears a smirk and nods at me once as he pushes one of the bodies to the side. I wonder how he's managed so easily to look like an Onychinus man. His hair is slicked back, so the purple tinge is almost nonexistent, and his eyes look like dark pits. Is he wearing contacts?

I smile at him. I want to say something to him, but I am at a loss for words.

"Son, you have no idea what you are doing," says the commander anxiously as Max presses the tip of his sword into his neck.

"One, you are not my father, and two, I know exactly what the hell I am doing," Max seethes through his teeth. "We're putting this to an end!"

Ruban comes up behind the commander, grabbing both of his wrists, and with great force he securely latches both of his hands together with several cable ties. The commander wrestles against Ruban's weight. He snarls angrily, "There is so much I could have given you, but you choose this path? Betray your own father!"

"That's exactly what I'm doing," says Max, the tip of his sword against his father's throat as Ruban pushes him to his knees. He looks up at me and Ace. "Collect the gems and free the bearers."

The commander looks absolutely mortified. "You can't do this!" he shouts.

I run my fingers across a Latin tablet on the wall. I press one button, and all of the tinted enclosures become clear. The chests sitting in front of the enclosures are hooked up with tiny wires similar to the ones we saw hooked up to the portal the commander was building. The individuals all look completely different, yet they all have deathly pale skin and some sit, practically hugging the floor, shielding their eyes from the light.

Ace opens the chest nearest to me. Inside it a natural clean-cut Rhodolite jewel hovers slightly above its cushion. The girl in the enclosure looks like death is in her midst. She is thin with dark reddish-pink hair. At a quick glance her irises are the same color as the jewel in the chest, but her pupils are tiny trying to adjust to the light. All five of the captives wear the same black long-sleeved tops and dark green pants and black shoes. I hit another button on the tablet, and all of the doors slide open. *Are you here to save us?* says a small voice in the back of my head. I don't know where the voice came from, but I see a small boy; he looks maybe ten years old, and his skin is as dark as night. His eyes are sapphire blue—the same as the stone in the chest in front of him. I look behind me, and Max simply nods at the boy.

"There is no way you can release them and expect them to survive!" the commander shouts. All of the bearers seem to scoot further back in their enclosures at the sound of his cruel voice, except for one. How many years have they been tortured?

The eldest of the captives appears to be about twenty years old and has golden hair and bronze-gold eyes—the bearer of Citrino. He looks peeved, and his sleeves are rolled up to his elbows, revealing years of scarring. "Just kill the man already," he snarls in an unfamiliar, thick accent. "If you won't I will."

The commander growls angrily and backs up in one swift motion, knocking Ruban off his feet. He leaps backward over his bound wrists, so his hands are now in front of him. Ruban stumbles forward, wrapping his outstretched arms around the commander's legs, tripping him.

"Get up, quickly," I say to the other bearers. The man of Citrino quickly picks up his chest that sits on the floor in front of him. It looks as though he hasn't held the thing in years, and to finally be able to hold something that belongs to him—to his people—is a glorious moment. Ace quickly steps into the Rhodolite girl's enclosure and helps her to her feet. She's very unsteady and clings onto him like her life depends on it. I run over to the enclosure with the little boy, pick up his chest, and hand it to him. Ace grabs the hovering Rhodolite from her chest, and all of a sudden she drops to the floor.

"Valencia!" shouts the man of Citrino. Holding his chest tightly under one arm, he runs to her side. The girl lies on the floor; she's not breathing, and a trickle of blood runs from her nose. I think she's dead. I don't know what happened. Was it because Ace grabbed the Rhodolite that she fell down dead?

Max and Ruban wrestle with the commander, trying to keep him still, but he manages to get past them and bangs his fists into a red panel on the wall. A siren wails upstairs.

The man who ran to *Valencia's* side stands up quickly and presses his chest into my arms with great force. "Hold this," he says. He gets around me quickly, taking the empty chest from the podium, and swings, bashing it into the commander's skull. "You did this, you son of a bitch!" The commander stumbles as Max and Ruban try to restrain him. The man of Citrino begins hitting him harder and harder, with so much rage the storm outside looks tame.

I hear voices and yelling coming from upstairs, and I just want to get out of here. I look to the little boy. "Do you know if there is any other exits besides that one?" I point to the door leading to the stairs.

"Uh," says the boy, struggling to hold up the chest that bears his precious sapphire. "I don't know." He looks down and begins to cry.

"No, no, sweetie, don't cry," says a thin girl who looks much like Isla. She rushes to his side and embraces him with the arm not holding her chest. "We're going to get out of here."

The last, the boy from Spinel, has white hair and blue eyes covered in a wash of thick black eyelashes. He looks to be about my age. He clutches his chest in his arms and looks directly at me. "Thirty-six years I've been here. It's this way." He gestures with his free arm. He has a similar build to the man with the golden hair—thin but muscular. "Eh, Auriel, enough waling on the man. I want to leave," he yells over all the noise, stopping the younger man from swinging the chest down once more. The commander's face is bloody and bruised. He looks scared and half unconscious, but he has enough strength to kick Auriel in the shins, causing him to stumble backward.

Max finds his sword again, but this time with all of his strength he sends the blade through the commander's heart. The commander gasps, and bubbles of blood spurt from his lips. I hear the sound of boots thundering down the stairs. I barely notice Ace as he manages to press the Rhodolite jewel into my hand and bounds over several of the dead bodies to slam the door shut. "Lead the way," I tell the boy from Spinel. Max looks uncomfortable with his actions but relieved with the result.

"What the heck, Clement?" Auriel yells in his thick accent. *"I voluit perficere eum!" I wanted to finish him.*

"Let's just go before it's too late," he says calmly, his white hair falling in his eyes. He is much wiser than he looks. His body and face are young, but his eyes seem … ancient. "Here, let me take that." He takes the Rhodolite gem from my hand and opens his chest, placing it next to his own. They hover side by side.

The officers begin pounding on the door, trying to bust it open; Ace has pulled down the barricade latches, so they can't open it with a simple key card.

"I don't know exactly where it leads to, but the commander always disappeared through this door after he finished our treatments. He wouldn't come back for hours, sometimes even days," says Clement. "When he would come back, it was always through that door." He points to the door getting pounded in.

Auriel comes to me and takes his chest from my hands. Clement quickly leads the way through a slightly concealed door just off to the side, leading to another. "We're not going to just leave Valencia here, are we?" asks the little boy.

"Sweetie," says the girl from Amethystus, "we don't have any other choice. There's no time."

He begins to sob, and Ruban just picks him up. "Time to go, bud." We race up the stairs and emerge through the door at the top.

We're in the commander's office. I feel very uncomfortable. I'm barefoot and I wear only my nightdress, whereas everyone else is fully clothed.

"Hey, Ace," says Max, following up behind me. "Can I borrow your jacket?"

Ruban sets the boy down, and Ace slips out of his officer jacket. "Here you go," he says, handing it to Max.

"Thanks man," he says and passes it to me. I slip the jacket on but it is so big, the bottom of it reaches down to my knees, and it weighs a ton.

"Thanks," I say, tying the rope tight around my waist. I hear voices hollering downstairs. I think they managed to get through the door. When they find out that the commander is dead, they won't stop searching for us. There's only a small handful of people here that I have met who hate the commander.

"Okay," says Max quickly. "Ace, do you remember where the portal is?"

"Yeah." He looks up quickly.

"I want you to take the bearers to Margaritan, and when you get there, get them to the safe house, okay? And don't come back for us."

"You sure you don't want help down here?" he asks.

"Yeah, I'm sure. Just get them to safety. They've been here long enough."

Ruban claps a hand on Ace's shoulder. "See you back on Margaritan, man."

"All right." Ace hesitates. "Be safe and make it back." He gives us a nod of respect and then leaves the room with the beautifully strange looking Bearers.

"Ruban. When you were with Ace, did you find the prison corridor?"

"Yes," he says quickly.

"Awesome, can you take us there?" asks Max as a loud noise comes from down the stairs. I run over to the door, pushing it till I hear it click shut, and press a button on the tablet attached to the door that says "seal."

CHAPTER 28

WE TURN DOWN INTO THE PRISON CORRIDOR. WE DON'T COME across too many officers through these halls; I think they are all still searching for us several hallways down. Whenever we do come across one, either Max or Ruban takes care of it.

It's the same corridor I saw in the directive Jeremy dragged me into last. The glass cells are mostly empty. There are about thirty cells, but maybe only nine are in use. Where did all of my people go? Was it because of me that the commander killed them all?

Ruban bashes his fist into the tablet on the wall, and all of the doors slide open. The prisoners step out of their stalls anxiously. They look beat up pretty bad and very thin. "Ready to go home?" I ask, and they rush forward toward me.

"Your Highness, we thought you were dead," some of them gasp.

"Not a chance," I say calmly. "Let's get you home." Then I see Jeremy. I step around my people who reach out for me, toward him. His hand is wrapped up in a bloody piece of cloth. He looks fairly strong despite malnourishment, injuries, and sleep deprivation.

"Lilyryn?" he asks.

I get close enough to make it look like I'm going to hug him, but instead I punch him in the stomach… hard. I know I shouldn't have, but it's something I've needed to do for a while now. "That's for erasing memories and lying to me for the past few years," I whisper harshly at him.

"I deserve that," he says.

"Oh, you deserve more than that," says Max.

"It's so good to see you again, Max, and I know, you can kill me later. Lily?" Jeremy says in a raspy voice, "Your dad."

"He's dead. I know, the commander has already told me," I growl.

"No, he's not dead, but he is hurt pretty bad." He starts walking further down the aisle. In the corner of one of the glass cells, my dad sits on his bed, with a homemade sling strapped across his chest. I can see a blood-soaked bandage underneath his shirt. His beard has grown in, and he looks weak. I have never seen him like this before.

"Dad?" I ask. "Oh no, Dad?"

"My dear, go without me," he says in a quiet voice. All of the years he coddled me and took care of me, and then he betrayed me not once, but twice. If I had no heart I would just agree with him and walk out of the room without him, but because he gave me more years of love than he did lies, I will not.

"We are not leaving without you," I say firmly.

Max steps around me and presses his hand on my father's shoulder. He heals him. He heals the man who has taken almost everything from him, and he does it without hesitation. "You should be well enough to travel the short distance, with a bit of assistance. Now do as the lady says," Max says through gritted teeth, taking a step away.

"Max?" my dad asks.

"In the flesh."

"I'm so sorry," says my father. "I thought I was doing the—" He gets cut off when we hear a call in the doorway.

"Doesn't matter now. Listen to your daughter for once," says Max, practically dragging him to his feet.

I turn toward where the voice came from in the doorway and see Ruban wiping blood off his sword. "There are more coming," he says sternly. "It might be best if this reunion could take place later."

"Yes," I agree, nodding my head.

Max helps my father stumble through the aisle, toward the door, and Jeremy helps some of the others who are injured. I quickly make my way around my people toward Ruban. He offers me the sword out of the dead guard's waistband, but when I try to lift it, it weighs my arm down. "Jeremy," I call. "Take this one." I pass him the sword, and Ruban slips one of his amethyst blades out from the inner pocket of his uniform. Like Ace, Ruban also looks much like an Onychinus officer. I wonder if it's a spell or contacts that make his eyes look so dark. Since his hair is entirely slicked back, it's nearly impossible to see his natural purple-tinted strands.

"Be careful," Ruban says as he presses it into my hands. "I want us to all make it out of here." I think I may have finally earned his respect. I give a small smile and nod once.

We all know where we're going without actually having to say it out loud. I just follow alongside Ruban toward the portal. I haven't seen the portal here because when I first arrived I was unconscious, so I just let Ruban lead the way. I look back and see Max with his arm around my father's shoulders. He doesn't like my father, but he's helping him because of me. They exchange several words, though I can't hear what they're saying.

We struggle to bring all of the prisoners through the halls. I know they're trying to be silent, but it's not working too well. We get them nearly to where Ruban says the portal is, and then it hits me. "Max!" I yell, stopping in my tracks, Ruban and the others continue on, but I wait up for Max and my dad. "The commander's portal. We have to destroy it!" I gasp.

The sudden realization hits him too. It's one thing to destroy the real one, but if we destroy just the one then there will be no way to destroy the commander's. There is no way of knowing what can happen with the commander's invented portal. It must be destroyed.

"Dad, go back to Margaritan with the others," I tell my father, grabbing his hands. "We have business to finish here."

"No! I am not leaving without you." His words echo mine from earlier, and I almost hate him for it.

"Uh, fine," I grumble because I know he's equally as stubborn as me. "Stay with Ruban and Jeremy by the portal. Make sure it's clear when we get there." I quickly kiss him on the cheek and shove him toward the rest of our citizens. One of them hooks his arm through my father's and leads him along with the group. I don't even look back at them as Max and I run the opposite way. If we're lucky, no one will be out in the storm.

Max gets to the entrance door first, and it takes the both of us to push it open against the wind. Where are all of the officers? It seems as though we haven't run into as many as I thought we would have. Max just killed their king and now they are nowhere to be seen? It doesn't make any sense.

The wind whips through my hair, and the icy rain soaks into the officer's jacket that hangs off me. Max grasps my hand tightly in his, and together we make a run for it. The rough cement scratches my bare feet. I push myself harder to keep up with Max, but my feet start to throb from numbness. It takes a lot of effort to see through the sheets of rain, and even more of an effort to find the bridge. The water swirls about beneath the bridge, and some of the acidic whiteness splashes up higher than the boards. The deadly red and black fish swim to the peak of the waves almost level with my feet.

"We're going to make a break for it. Okay?" yells Max, but his words are slightly muffled by the noise

I nod.

"Don't slip!" he yells as he holds onto my hand even more tightly. He looks down at my feet. "Oh shit!"

"What?" I ask.

"You don't have shoes!" There's a look of fear on his face. "You can't come with me."

"Why not?" I yell angrily, glaring at him.

"The water is acidic. I don't want you touching it."

"You're not going to stop me," I say to him. It would be stupid if he went by himself. What if all the officers are waiting there for us? I'm not letting him do this alone. "We're finishing this together."

"Fine, just promise me you'll be careful."

"I will." I let go of his hand and race straight for the bridge so he can't change his mind at the last second. It is really slippery, and the boards creak under my feet. My nightdress clings to my legs with each step I take. I hear Max step into pace beside me and hooks his arm through mine, hanging on tightly.

"Don't ever do that again," he says harshly as we continue further.

As the waves continue to swirl, the starving fish climb higher to reach us. A huge gust of wind forces the river to hurl up a large quantity of its murky water toward us. There's maybe a few more meters of bridge ahead of us before we reach firm ground. White water sprays upward as the wave clashes down, and Max switches places so I am on his left. Several droplets find my bare skin and burn. I hear Max grunt, and I am certain he just saved me from the worst part of it.

"Just a little ways further," I gasp as we struggle to find our way back to the path. My legs burn. I can't imagine how Max is feeling.

The thunder is so loud and the sky so dark it is nearly impossible to remember what light is like. Just a little ways and we will be there. I shiver as the icy rain's freezing fingers stroke my spine and send a chill through my entire body. Something is very wrong.

There is a faint light just above where the door is located in the building. Leaves fling from their spots on the trees as the wind bullies them into cowardice. I follow Max into the building, feeling sudden warmth, away from the hateful weather.

I look up, and there is a sword pressed to my neck. Something inside my stomach drops, and I feel sick. There are maybe thirty officers standing about the room, all of them with their swords drawn and I don't exactly understand their expressions. Maybe it's because of their eyes?

Besides Max there is only one other person in this room I care about; Theo, he doesn't exactly look surprised, though he doesn't seem too pleased either. If anything I think he's afraid.

I will distract them. You destroy that thing, I hear Max's words clearly, almost as if they were actually said out loud. He gives my hand a gentle squeeze and then drives his sword into the man who holds his to my neck. I slide the amethyst blade out and slice at everyone who is near me. I have to get across the room. The wall spins in patterns… I have to destroy it. I get by several of the officers who make a break for it. I don't think Max will have any chance if I don't get this done quickly. I dive around another two soldiers; they both miss me. I'm not sure what Max is doing, but it's working. No one has touched me yet.

I reach for the tablet on the wall; it's connected to several of the jewel-colored wires. I rip them out one by one. Sparks spurt out, but I just ignore them and yank the wires from the panel. I want to go home, and I don't want anyone from here to ever be able to get to my home, *ever* again.

"Reena!" Max yells. I crush a few more of the wires with the weight of a broken hammer.

I turn around quickly and watch as a sword comes down toward me. I hold my own blade out to protect myself. Theo stands before me. "I can't let you do this," he says. His voice shakes.

"Theo," I say. "You know that I wouldn't be doing this if I had another choice."

"I know," he says gruffly, "but if the commander knows that I haven't fulfilled my duty, my family will be no greater than a memory."

"Come with us then," I insist, breathless, pushing with my blade against the weight of his sword.

"I can't," he says with fear. "He'll know."

"The commander is dead," I grunt, pushing harder against his weight.

"He can't be." Genuine confusion is plastered entirely across Theo's face. Doesn't he know that we killed the commander?

"Max's sword went through him," I yell, struggling to keep the sword from coming any closer.

"That doesn't mean anything," he mutters loudly and incoherently. It's like his mind is in another dimension, and he doesn't realize what he's doing or even what he's saying. All of a sudden Theo falls slack and tumbles on top of me.

"Oh no," I gasp, frantically crawling out from underneath him and try to roll him onto his back.

Another officer looms over me with Theo's blood on his sword. "A weak officer," he grumbles, raising his sword toward me. I kick him in the shins, swinging my body to the side, and cut open his

Achilles tendon with my blade. He collapses, and I dive on top of him and dig my blade into the side of his neck.

"Theo!" I whisper and turn back toward the figure whose chest is rising and falling in an uneven gasping pattern.

Theo mutters something about the commander but I can't make it out and then he says. "I have ... wife of pure beauty and son ... son of ... of ... greatness." Then he mutters something about a new world and then his chest falls still and his mouth slack. He's gone. He wouldn't have killed me—I know he wouldn't have. His family now consists of a widow and a fatherless child.

I take a few shaky breaths before I can finish what I started. I have Theo's blood on my stolen jacket, and it feels like I have a rock in the pit of my stomach. There is so much noise around me I can barely concentrate. I take the handle end of my amethyst blade and crush the wires against the floor, watching the color drain from their cores. This has to work! I get to my feet and stab my blade as hard as I can through the tablet on the wall, making it shatter and spark. I pick up the sword with Theo's blood on it and begin to swing it at the wall, scratching at it and trying to crack its surface.

"Reena?" Max says, coming up behind me. I turn to face him, tears running down my face and anger darkening my color. "Let's just burn it."

I want so badly for Theo to still be alive right now that I just nod and agree with Max. I don't see any other officer around; they all lay in different angles and in different spots about the room. What did he do?

"I don't want to leave his body in here if we do that," I tell Max, gesturing down to one of the few *kind* Onychinus I've met.

"All right," says Max. He helps me bring Theo's body a short distance from the outside of the building. I wait with Theo in the cold while Max lights the flame indoors. I make sure Theo's eyes are closed, and I find a mostly intact flower nearby and gently place it underneath his hands. He deserved more. He deserved to live in a world greater than this—in a world that would've allowed him to live in peace and raise his son without fear.

I'm pretty certain the rain will put out the flames once the roof falls through. We just need to get rid of the portal; we don't need to get rid of the whole building. I barely notice Max's figure slip through the door. It is only when the tiny light above the door catches his slick hair that I notice him. I hold my breath, and the only thing I can focus on are his eyes, the blue that carry the courage within me.

He comes to me, breathing heavily. "It's done."

I give Theo's hand a gentle squeeze and get to my feet. The fabric of my nightdress hangs heavily with water, and I nearly trip over it. Max catches me by the elbow. I don't know where I put Ruban's blade, but I want it back. I must have left it by the portal. Then I see it in Max's other hand. He bends over and cuts through the material just above my knees. "Thank you," I say, though I can't hear myself through the thunder. He kisses my forehead and then takes my hand with his empty one.

The muck squishes between my toes, and I am even more afraid of the bridge now than I was earlier. I've seen how easy it is for a soul to leave a person's eyes. One slip here and those blank eyes will be mine. I'm more afraid for Max though. I don't want him to protect me in a way that will risk his own life. We get to the base of the bridge, and Max squeezes my hand tightly and says firmly, "Together."

It is so dark, it's difficult to see the end. Each step we take, we're closer to getting home. I'm certainly not happy, but I am very apprehensive. The little red fish continue to swim to the peaks of the waves, and the wind just blows them back down again. They remind me of puppets with the river as their master, much like the commander and his control over his people. It almost sickens me. Maybe we did these people a favor? I hope so.

We get misted with the acidic water just as we step off the bridge, and I feel it burn several spots on my cheek and side of my neck. Max hisses, but I don't know where he got hit. I squeeze his hand tighter, and I almost get blown over as we reach the steps of the palace.

It takes nearly all of our effort to crack the door open. I have to use all of my weight to pull it against the wind. "Get in," yells Max. I quickly step in and push from the inside just enough for him to maneuver through. He kisses me quickly, just as the door slams shut. The lights flicker above us. "I love you," he whispers in my hair and then turns away quickly, sliding his arm around my waist. He leads us quickly through the hallways. I wonder who's left guarding the natural portal; I fear someone may have been lost if a fight came about. The hallways look even drearier than they did before. Maybe it's because of the storm or maybe it's because we killed their master and this isn't a home to anyone anymore.

I see Ruban first—his tall, firm structure with his hair now tousled. Then I hear Jeremy's voice, and I see my father a little off to the side holding onto a sword. "Oh, my dear girl," gasps my father. He lets go of his sword and runs to me, wrapping his arms around my shoulders. He and Max pass a look to each other, almost of understanding?

"Did everyone get through safely?" I ask.

"Yes, they did, and I am so glad you're all right," he says, hugging me like if it's the last time he'll ever see me. I look down at the floor and realize that there is blood everywhere, and I gasp. At least fifteen or sixteen corpses lie strewn in the corner of the room. The guys must have dragged them away. I nearly gag. Several voices echo further down the hall; they're coming straight for us.

"All right, let's shut this baby down," says Ruban, kicking something across the room.

"How?" I whisper.

My dad lets me go and stares blankly behind me, at the moving shape. It's much different from the one on Margaritan yet strangely similar. "I'm going to shut it down," he says quietly.

"How?" I ask louder.

"It doesn't matter, as long as it gets done," he says, snapping back to reality.

The voices are getting closer. My heart throbs. What is he going to do?

"Guys, go on through. We'll meet you back on Margaritan," Max says in a low, restrained voice. Jeremy looks distraught, and Ruban looks surprisingly uneasy. What's happening? Does Max know what he's going to do?

"Dad?"

The voices are getting closer.

"Sweetheart, it is time for you to go fulfill your destiny on Margaritan. I have done everything I could have to be a good king. I say this as your father—go live your life and take care of our family. Flora never intended on becoming queen, so the throne is left to you. I am proud to call you my daughter, though I am ashamed of how I betrayed you."

The voices are almost at the corner.

"I love you. Please just remember that," he says and quickly kisses me on the cheek.

I feel an arm wrap around my waist and pick me up off the ground. I'm pretty sure a scream comes through my lips and I fight against Max, who hauls me away. I cry and watch in horror as Max leaps with me over his shoulder through the portal. The last thing I see is my dad reaching to the top of the portal, his feet spread, each of his extremities connecting the four corners. With all his might he crouches, the officers running toward him. A bright light.

Nothingness.

CHAPTER 29

I HATE HIM.

I hate them all.

I cling to Max, even though I can't exactly see him. We're a light ray. I'm glad I'm not alone. I love Max ... but I hate him too right now.

I will never see my dad again, and I hate him for it. Why did he have to leave me? I actually understand why; I just don't want to believe it.

It was his way of trying to right all of the wrong that he has done. I hear Max's voice in my head.

It's not comforting. Was *that* what they were talking about earlier? I feel a sudden heat on my forehead and hear him whisper, *Sleep.*

I'M SO ANGRY WHEN I WAKE UP. I'M NOT SURE HOW TO RESPOND to lying in my own bed.

It feels almost like I'm in a dream, but not the happy kind. The sun shines through my window, lighting up the room. It's so bright it hurts my eyes. I haven't seen it in months. I'm still wearing the same torn, filthy nightdress and stolen officer's jacket. I feel no pain though. I reach up and touch my cheek and slide my fingers down to the side of my neck. The acidic burns are gone. My feet are dirty, but they aren't cut up anymore.

I get to my feet and run across my room toward the door. I need to find the others. I rip off the lousy jacket and toss it on the floor, feeling suddenly a lot lighter. I turn the handle of my door and push hard against it, but it doesn't budge.

"No!" I yell. I test the door again even more anxiously, tears forming in my eyes when I can't make it move. Whoever locked me in here, *I am going to kill*!

I quickly move on. Sobbing I run to one of the chairs in the corner of my room and grab my light wrap. Pulling it over my shoulders I move on to the window. The last time I jumped out of this window was actually my last morning on Margaritan. I unhinge the clasp, open the window, and crawl out onto the ledge. The light is even brighter out in the open, and I feel like vomiting because of it. Now or never. I push off the ledge. I land on my feet but crumple to my knees. It will never get any easier. The courtyard is destroyed, and it sickens me to see it this way. My trees stand the same though; still tall, thick, and beautiful.

I look to my left and see a thin but muscular man with dark hair. He's handsome. The man leads several individuals out into the field, and he speaks to them with control. They nod to him with respect and go about as he requests. It is Max, and he looks at them with pride as they begin to clean up the courtyard. They must have similar gifts to Clay, who could control the elements. I miss him, and Haley.

Max looks out toward the palace, and somehow his eyes find me. I suddenly feel very self-conscious. I didn't even bother to look in the mirror before I jumped from my window. He begins walking toward me shaking his head, wearing almost a grin but not quite. Whatever. I walk to meet up with him.

"Good morning, sleeping beauty," he says.

I raise an eyebrow, and then his mouth spreads into a grin. "Why did you put me out?" I ask. "And lock my door?"

His smile fades, and he becomes serious. "I didn't want you to see anymore death, and to put you to sleep and lock you up was the easiest way to ensure that."

I nod and look down at my bare feet in the dirt. "Will you at least tell me what happened?"

"I'm not sure—"

"Tell me," I interrupt.

Max looks slightly taken aback at my sudden return of anger. "Very well," he says blankly. "As soon as we got here, most of the fight had already occurred. The prisoners we freed had gone through the palace in search for the Onychinus and … took care of business. They had gone down to the basement prison and freed our own soldiers. A large portion of the Onychinus were already dead when we got here. I brought you to your old room and locked the door so no one would get to you and so you wouldn't suddenly wake up when it wasn't safe."

"Oh."

"Yeah," agrees Max. "Had I remembered that blasted window and how you like to jump out of it, I would have sealed that as well."

I grin. "So what are they all doing?" I nod toward the gardeners.

"I was hoping the place would be cleaned up a bit before you woke up and before we brought your family home."

"I love you," I whisper and wrap my arms around him; he leans down and presses his lips to mine. I feel at home again. For several months I couldn't remember what a home was. Ace tried to explain it to me and it almost made sense, but now, this moment makes sense.

Max pulls back and says with a smile, "I love you too. Well, my dear, are you ready to bring your family home?"

I smile back at him in response, and he steers me toward the door leading back into the castle.

"You have to make me only one deal, promise?" asks Max.

"What's that?"

"Clean up before we go?"

"Yes," I say, feeling grimy next to him. He wears a clean pair of dress pants, shiny shoes, and a light blue dress shirt. "Um, how long have I been out?"

"Only a day and a half."

"What!" I almost yell, stopping dead in my tracks. "How!"

"That's a story for later," he says, "and yeah, you've been asleep for a little while." He brings me through the patio doors and leads me toward the hall that goes to my room. Surprisingly a lot of the maids and butlers are out and about cleaning up the place. It seems as though they all greatly respect Max, but no one can respect him more than I.

"My dad?" I ask, coming to tears with simply the memory.

"We spoke of what he was going to do, I'll admit that," says Max. He doesn't seem too pleased with himself. "He told me one thing that I will never forget: 'Be the sort of man who'll look out for the interest of the greater good and protect those you love, even if it causes hatred, even if not short-term.'"

"That does sound like something he would say," I whisper.

It doesn't take too long before we get to my room and Max slips a key out from his pocket and unlocks the door. "I'll see you soon," he says and kisses the top of my head before he disappears down the hallway again.

I close the door behind me, stepping further into my room.

I want to cry for everything I lost, but I also want to celebrate because we've destroyed the main threat to every planet across the universe.

I shower as quickly as I can and use a huge pick comb to untangle my hair. I end up choosing a light pink chiffon dress from my closet; it falls just above my knees and has thin straps. My wet hair curls naturally down my back, and I find a good pair of heeled sandals.

I don't know where I'm supposed to meet Max, but I know exactly where I need to be. I leave my room and walk by all of the maids and butlers scurrying up and down the halls. I get a lot of bows and curtsies along the way, and I smile at them. I realize only now how much I actually did miss them all. I feel guilty that I know only a handful of their names, but I'm going to make a point of remembering as many as I can from now on.

I finally find my way to the ballroom. The piscinæ fati stands powerfully at the other end of the room. I'm drawn to it. I need to see for myself that the pearl is back where it belongs. I make my way through the huge room. The last time I was here was on my seventeenth birthday, and that was the day that my life forever changed. I creep my way up the steps toward the great force field. I somehow know that I won't get hurt touching it; before I thought it was possible, but now it just feels different. Inside I see several different bright colors. I reach my hand in and pull out the golden pearl. It's beautiful, and it's mine. It feels alive in my hand, and for that I have never been more grateful for anything in my life. Every several hundred years Margaritan will give an individual its life source, to protect itself. It seems as though none of us have failed yet, and I am hoping that none of us ever will. This is my home, and I refuse to allow anyone else to try and take it from me. I put the pearl back. The other colors are actually from the other life sources.

"I kinda thought I'd find you here," calls a voice I'd recognize anywhere. I turn around. Max walks down the aisle toward me.

"I just needed to see for myself," I tell him.

"I know," he says sympathetically.

"Um, where are the other bearers?"

"I sent them to see a healer," he says. "They weren't doing so well, and we figured the safest place to put their stones was with ours."

"It was a smart idea," I tell him and glide my palm across the smooth surface of the force field. Max doesn't dare touch it. "Why didn't you tell me his plan?" I whisper, somewhat irritated.

"There was no time." He chooses his words with care. "I couldn't have. He made me promise him some things, and I couldn't go against his final wishes because he was going to do it no matter what I said."

It's hard for me to accept what has happened, and there's this aching pain in my chest that feels almost unbearable. I can no longer count how many people I've lost on one hand. So many people I care about have passed on. Tears pool in my eyes, and the next thing I know I am in Max's arms. He envelops me in a hug. Max is my anchor, my home, my love, and the one I want to spend the rest of my life with. If it weren't for him I would have died long ago.

"Let's go get your family," Max whispers in my hair. I nod in agreement, but the tears still fall from my eyes.

Everyone is working very hard to clean the place up before we bring my family back. I wonder where Max actually brought them. He said it was secluded and that they would be safe, but where is that?

The palace already is beginning to feel a little bit more homey, and it makes me rather glad. I'm not sure what the commander had his soldiers doing here, but they did mess up the place. They must have been looking for something because there is no reason for everything to be torn up like this.

"You've never been to my home before," Max tells me. I look at him a little in shock because for the years I have known him, I haven't actually seen his first home, where he was raised with his mother. "Do you want to walk or take a carriage? It's several miles," he asks, looking down at my heels.

"We can be back faster if we take the carriage," I suggest. It turns out Max already had some of my stablemen hook up a few horses to a carriage because they wait for us in front of the stables. It seems as though it has been forever since I've been down these roads.

THE WARM WIND BLOWS THROUGH MY HAIR, AND THE BRIGHT sun kisses my skin. I love the heat. I love snow too, but I much prefer the warmth. I miss Coral. The warmth reminds me of her, the simplistic, beautiful things that made her stand out from everyone else. She had a good heart. She would have made an incredible queen.

Max and I sit in silence as our driver takes us down the bumpy road. We sit hip to hip with his arm around me, and I am grateful. I know he's lost in thought, but I am glad he simply holds onto me. I have no idea how long, besides when he delivered my family here, how long it's been since he came here last. I want to ask him. I fear it may be a touchy subject, but he always does find a way to answer my questions … even if it pains him to tell me.

"Excuse me, sir?" I ask the driver.

The thin man with all his hair tucked under his cap turns to face me and brings the carriage to a slower pace. He seems a little on edge even though the danger is mostly gone. He has a kind face, though, with wrinkles by his eyes from years of squinting in the light. I wonder how old he is. "Yes, Your Highness?" he asks with a low note in his voice.

"If you don't mind, I'd like to walk the last few miles," I say kindly.

"Very well, miss," he says as I slip out from under Max's arm. He brings us to a stop, and Max gets out of the carriage and takes my hand to help me down.

"Sir, my apologies, but may I ask your name?"

"Tanner Gray," he says with a bow of his head.

"Mr. Gray, do you know the rest of the way?" I ask him.

"I do, quite well," he replies.

"Will you be able to drive on ahead and meet us there, please?" I ask, brushing some of the dust from my dress.

"I can do that," he says and starts to leave.

"And can you tell them we'll be along shortly?"

"Yes, Your Highness. Take care, all right?" he says with a kind smile and turns back to the road.

"Didn't feel like riding the bumps anymore, eh?" asks Max with a grin.

"No," I say, returning the grin. "That and I wanted to ask you something." I grab onto his hand and press my lips to it.

"What's that?"

"Can we start walking first?" I ask.

"Yes of course," he says, and we start walking along the tree line. The leaves hang heavily from their branches, and vines loop around the thick bases of their trunks. Max lets go of my hand and slips his arm around my waist, and I slip mine around his. We walk about a hundred yards in silence, absorbing every second of the peace. No one can come after us now. We don't have to live in fear anymore, but I still feel rather weary. "What is it that you wanted to ask me?"

"How long has it been?"

"How long has *what* been?" he asks.

"Since you've been home?" He seems slightly taken aback by my question, like he expected something else.

He kisses my forehead before he decides to respond back. "Three years … almost four years ago." That damn number! It seems like everything exciting, important, and crappy all happened three years ago. I'm starting to hate that number.

"How long before you were banished?" I ask.

"Honestly?"

"Yes."

"I had just returned the day before I was banished," he says. Remembering it like it was just recently, he brushes his hand through his hair and takes a deep breath. My heart drops. "Before that I hadn't been home in about six years, because I was living with Jeremy's family."

I'm silent for a short moment, but then I find my words. It is a pointless question, but it eats away at me. "Why?"

He sighs and then comes to a stop, slowing me down with him. "I was hoping to not bring it up for a few weeks until everything was settled and almost back to normal," he says.

"Please tell me," I ask.

He looks at me deeply, something in his eyes I have never seen before. He looks hopeful and fearful at the same time, like what he says next will change everything forever. There are smile lines around his lips. His eyebrows are slightly raised upward, and the light shines from the side, making his eyes so blue I have difficulty remembering to breathe. He lets go of me and slips his hand into his pocket and pulls out a small box. "I had gone back for this," he says and reveals a tiny hand-carved box. My heart leaps. What is this? I feel my face get warm when he looks at me.

"It's bad timing, and if you aren't ready, I completely understand. I will give you as much time as you need." His face is optimistic. He leads me closer to the tree line and lets me sit on a fallen tree, and he gets down on one knee. "My dearest, you have gone through so much these last few years, especially these past months." He opens the box, and inside sits the most beautiful ring I have ever seen. It is gold and handcrafted with the most intricate details. "You are the most important person in my existence, and I know I can't give you everything, but the one thing I can promise is to cherish and love you forever. I've lost you before. I've walked on a foreign planet, completely lost with nothing but a painful emptiness in my heart, which haunted me until that day by the lake when I was filled with a painful hope. I've nearly lost you several times since, and I can't bear to ever lose you again. Reena, my life and my love, will you do me the honor of becoming my wife?" His eyes are so hopeful, and I believe every word. He's had this ring for almost four years, and he was willing to wait for me until I was of age.

My heart is beating so fast I'm sure I will pass out. I feel a few tears escape the corners of my eyes. Max's face falls, and he closes the carved box. He wraps me in a hug.

"You can have as much time as you need." He sighs into my hair. "I know you're hurting, and if you choose not to be with me, that's all right. I just want you to be happy." Several tears escape his eyes too. I feel like I've just broken his heart.

"That's not it at all." I sob and take a deep breath.

He pulls back a bit and starts to say something, but I press my fingers to his lips. "To marry you is all I've ever wanted. Your love is my universe," I whisper. "You are my home."

"So?" he asks through glassy eyes.

"I will."

I've never seen someone's face light up as bright as the sun before. He reopens the box and slides the ring from its silky cushion as I hold out my hand. The ring fits perfectly. He slides his fingers down my cheeks, wiping away the tears, and then he brushes my curls away from my face and presses his lips gently to mine. I am completely overwhelmed with happiness. I feel almost guilty. I've lost so many people I love, and now I am very happy because I just promised the one I love that he will never lose me. I'm so engulfed with warmth that I feel like I could walk on the clouds. My heart beats so fast, and the tears just slide from both our eyes. I've never been this happy before, and I want to stay this way forever. Max is the first to pull back, and I miss him when he leaves.

"You mean everything to me," he whispers against my lips and kisses me gently again. Neither of us really wants to go anywhere, but we do.

The rest of the walk is in pure happiness.

CHAPTER 30

THE HOUSE IS VERY SIMPLE, AND THERE ARE VINES HANGING everywhere. Green engulfs the place, and there are rough stone tiles layering most of the ground. Mr. Gray, our driver, helps my family pack up some of their belongings. When I see my mother wearing a pair of overalls with dirt on her face and gardening gloves, I smile. She's never had the munera for it. She has just always loved to do it. When she sees me coming, her eyes become glassy. She gasps and runs for me. I meet her halfway, letting go of Max. She wraps me in the biggest hug she has ever given me and rocks me back and forth.

"Oh, Lilyryn, I have missed you so much!" she cries, kissing me on the cheek. Her warmth envelopes me even more than the warmth I was already feeling.

Mira peeks outside of the house, and then she comes running for us. "Reena!" she shouts. She almost knocks me and our mother over from her hug. I wonder where Flora is. Mira backs away and gives a huge hug to Max too. "I missed you guys so much. Don't ever do that again!"

I see Maybell. She stands still and starts crying on the spot, unable to move forward. My mom backs away and nods for me to go on. I take careful, steady steps toward Maybell and hug her tightly; she sobs in my shoulder. "I thought you were dead," she mumbles through her tears.

"I wouldn't die without saying good-bye." I wink at her when I pull away. "He proposed," I whisper to her. She looks past me at Max, who is speaking to my mother.

"Oh, my dear girl, I am so happy for you," she says. With tears streaking her face, she wraps me in another hug.

"Thank you," I say. "Um, where's Flora?"

"She's gone to visit the grave," she says sympathetically. She is aware that I know Coral has been killed; Mira must have told them.

"May I go too?" I ask. She wears pain in her eyes like it's natural.

THEY BURIED CORAL'S BODY IN THE ROYAL BURIAL GROUNDS. I'M surprised they even managed to do that. I request for a proper headstone to be made and placed on her grave. All that's there is a stone with her name marked on it with blood and the date of her birth and death. I have a difficult time saying good-bye. Max stands at my side. Mira, Maybell, my mother, and Flora all stand around her grave as well. I've cried nearly all the liquid in my eyes away. The pain is there, but I can't show any of it. We don't even have a body to put in my dad's grave. I've asked for a headstone to be made for him as well to be placed next to Corals.

A priest comes and does a proper service for us, and we've decided to bury a few of my dad's things for a little bit of closure. Both of them died heroes.

"Lilyryn." Flora comes next to me after the service. "Dad told you that you are going to be queen here, right?"

"Yes," I say.

"Good, because I can't," she sobs. "Too much has happened, and I need to leave. I am so sorry."

"It's all right," I tell her, pulling her thin frame into a hug. "We'll always be here when you visit, but you are going to stay and be my bridesmaid though," I whisper.

Her face lights up a little. "Of course, as long as you'll be mine?"

"What?" I exclaim.

She nods her head. "I'm engaged to the prince in our neighboring country. I'll be the queen there."

I nod. "Yes I will. I'm happy for you."

CHAPTER 31

TOMORROW IS THE BIG DAY.

Since my father has passed away, I am to inherit the throne as soon as possible. It was decided when Max and I were married, the coronation would be that same day. I am so nervous I have difficulty eating anything. It was my decision to choose what Max was going to become, either the crown prince or the king, because of my inheritance. I've chosen him to be the king. He will have slightly more power than I, but we think alike so we plan on being partners through everything.

"I want to come with you guys," Mira nags for the hundredth time. She's been living in the castle for about a week now, and she's already adapted easily. The staff adore her, and her coronation is on the same day as Max and I's. She's going to make a great princess. She too is my other bridesmaid. Max and I are heading to Earth to go give out a few invites for tomorrow.

"Mira, you can't come with us," I tell her again. "Max and I are going to go give out a few invites, that's it, nothing all that exciting."

"But why?"

"Sweetie, your dress needs to be altered. You're coming with us," says Flora, joining us in the doorway of the ballroom. Elle and Isla are next to her; they all wear simple, light summer dresses. I've chosen the four of them to be my bridesmaids, and they all have their dress fittings this morning. I really just want it to be Max and me going, no one else.

"I'll tell you what—we'll have a small party tonight when we get back," I tell her. Her face lights up a little bit. "You can be in charge of planning my bachelorette party." She considers this as I wink at the girls behind her and they just smile.

"All right," she says excitedly.

"Okay. Well, we have to go before it gets too late," I tell her.

Butlers and maids are everywhere. The piscinæ fati is at the end of the room, and all of the pews face it, just like every celebration. Both our wedding and our coronation will take place in this room, and then the reception will be in the bigger ballroom next room over. Flowers are everywhere, and all of the bouquets consist of white, gold, pink, and green. Everything is coming together. I let my mom and Maybell be in charge of a lot of the decorating, but I did pick all of the colors. I give them all hugs before I turn to leave. Max stands leaning against our red cushioned sofa. A grin plays at his lips.

"What?" I ask.

"I thought you didn't want a bachelorette party?"

"I didn't," I say. "That was the only way I could convince Mira not to come with us."

"She's quite easy to please," he says, still grinning.

"I'm kinda glad." I smile. "Are the guys throwing you a bachelor party when we get back?"

"Honestly I have no idea. Ruban seems to think I want one, so who knows what he plans to do?"

"I hope they do throw you one, 'cause if I have to go to one, so should you," I tell him and hook my arm through his. "Shall we?"

"Yes, we should be on our way."

I feel very uncomfortable being near a portal again. The image of my dad dying just keeps playing over and over in my head. I feel like I'm going to be sick. I've been having nightmares lately, and I haven't been able to stop them. There's nothing I can do. I was tempted to ask Jeremy if he could remove some of those memories just so the dreams would go away, but I need to know what happened. The commander's face haunts me every evening, sometimes even during the day in the moments where shadows seem to linger.

Max holds out his arm for me to take again as we stand in front of our portal. I take it, and he whispers into my hair, "Don't be afraid, I've got you." I smile at him even though I am completely terrified.

I barely notice the trip pass by. Hanging onto Max makes me forget everything, and I'm glad. We get through the barrier on Earth again just as easily as last time, but this is the first time I come here and actually make it through their portal. The first time I fell through the sky ... that wasn't supposed to happen.

I'm so glad when I can actually see Max again. His face becomes clear, his eyes become bluer, and his hand becomes warmer. Max earlier had agreed that we could go looking for Clay and Haley. I need to know if they're still alive. I barely got to say good-bye to them when I had the chance. Then when Mira drew that freaky picture indicating that the Onychinus had gone to their home, I panicked. I thought they were going to be killed as well.

We climb down the hill of rocks very carefully. There is no more snow here, the ground is defrosted for the most part, and tiny green leaves begin to peek their way out of their branches. I knew it was going to be much chillier here then on Margaritan, so I wore pants and a long-sleeved shirt, but I still wish I had something warmer. It's only a few miles before we will reach their farmhouse. If we start walking now we should get there in about a half an hour.

"I miss the heat already," says Max.

I grin at him. "Wussy." I wink, but then when I shiver, he just starts laughing. He rubs some heat into my arms, and I stand up on my tiptoes to give him a quick kiss.

"You're one to talk."

"I thought you looked pretty hot," I say, grinning again, except this time I feel my face get warmer. I like this. I like that we can be together without having anyone after us. I really hope that we actually find Clay and Haley. I want them at our wedding.

"Thank you. I know I am." He chuckles and wiggles his eyebrows at me, making me giggle.

We walk along the side of the road admiring the pine trees and baby leaves sprouting on the trees. The birds sing happily, giving me a little bit of hope.

"Here we are," whispers Max. We stop at the end of the driveway; I barely recognize the house. There are scorched burn marks on the entire one side of the building, and it looks broken down … but in renovation? Plastic seals off several holes in the wall, and there is a loud banging noise going on indoors. Clay's truck is still parked in front of the house in its usual place.

"What time is it, do you know?" I ask.

"I think the middle of the afternoon."

"Thank you for doing this for me," I say.

"Anything for my bride." He winks at me and leads me by the arm, down the driveway.

I shudder when we finally approach the door. I've wanted to

check on them for months, and now that I actually can … I don't know what I'm going to say to them. Max puts his hand against my lower back and uses his other hand to knock on the door.

The banging inside stops. There is a pause, and then it starts up again. Maybe he didn't hear us? I lift my balled-up hand and knock on the door as loudly as I can. The banging stops, and we hear the thumping of boots coming toward the entrance.

He looks thin and pale, but when he sees us it looks like a boulder was just lifted from his shoulders. "Oh my," he gasps, and his hands begin to shake uncontrollably. He lifts them to his face. "My dear ones," he gasps again. I reach out for his hands, but he just pulls us both into a hug.

"Clay, we thought you were dead," I whisper.

"What!" he yells in my ear and takes a step back. "Why did you think I was dead? Haley and I were extremely concerned about the two of you and the others you went with. You should have kept in touch!"

"We kinda got held up." It looks like he's going to try to interrupt, but I continue quickly, "We survived. I think that's all that matters … right?"

"Yes." He sighs and reaches for another hug. I give him one and kiss him on the cheek.

"Is Haley teaching today?" I ask.

"She doesn't have a class at this time, but she is at the school," he says. "Do you guys want to make a trip to town? I'm certain she'd appreciate it." He is still shaking, and I feel really sad for him. We kind of put him through hell these last few months just because we didn't update him. "I need to find my keys first. Come on in."

We both follow him inside. The inside looks to be all under renovation. "What happened here?" Max asks, though I think we both already know the answer.

"Uh, when the two of you left, we decided to pack up for a month and go elsewhere. When we got back, the house was nearly destroyed. We've been working on it very hard ever since."

"That was Onychinus," says Max.

"I kind of figured that much," Clay says, finding his keys under a newspaper on the kitchen counter. "I'm so glad we left when you guys did."

"Me too," I tell him. "I really missed you guys. I don't know what I would do if you guys were killed."

He nods his head once. "Um, you guys look cold. Do you want jackets?"

"Please," we say at the same moment. The corner of Clay's mouth turns up in a grin. He goes to the coat closet just off to the side and pulls out two, one of his own and one of Haley's. Max gets a blue lumberjack one, and I get a fitted black one.

"All righty, let's go," he says, command starting his truck.

On the way to town we explain to him almost everything that happened … leaving out a few near-death experiences; he doesn't need to know those. It takes pretty much the entire drive to cover the basics, and Max does most of the talking, which makes me so glad.

We pull up to the school, and I remember my first day like it was just yesterday. I was so nervous, and now I feel like I can conquer anything.

When we go in, I ask the office if they could call down three people for us. They remember me from before, so they don't even hesitate. It is now that I start to feel nervous again. We have to wait before we see the three of them coming down the stairs. My heart leaps, and I get really excited. Max lets go of my hand, and I race for them. I wrap my arms around them all.

"Arianna you're back?" they exclaim.

"I've actually been going by Reena lately, but yes, I'm back."

I smile at them. Haley looks the most excited. Nisha and Kelly look excited as well, and it makes me happy.

"Where the hell have you been?" Haley asks sternly.

"That's a long story," I tell her. "This is very sudden, but Max and I have something to tell you guys."

I back away and Max comes to my side, slipping his hand into mine again. We haven't told Clay about the wedding yet either. We were waiting till we could have all of them together.

"Nish, Kelly, this is Max," I tell them. "He's my fiancé." Their mouths drop slightly, and I feel like I have to explain.

"What?" asks Kelly.

"Can we go outside? I don't want to talk here," I say.

When we get outside, I tell them because they were my first real friends on Earth I wanted them to come. I explain how seventeen is actually "of age" on Margaritan and that I'm going to become queen tomorrow. "Let me show you my world, even just for a day."

I'm not too sure they believe me, but it doesn't exactly bother me. I don't expect them to understand right away.

"We'll be there," says Clay, and Haley seems so excited because this is her first time actually being able to come to Margaritan.

"If you guys don't want to come, I completely understand. I was just kind of hoping you could be there for us." I take them slightly aside as Max talks to Clay. "My bachelorette party is tonight. And also you'll get to meet really hot guys at the reception."

"All right I'm in," says Kelly, grinning, and Nish nods her head in agreement. "What do you want us to bring?"

"Nothing. Just tell your parents you're going away for two nights; we'll provide clothing and rooms."

"This is literally super exciting," Kelly gasps, and she's unable to stay still.

"Can we see the ring?" asks Nish.

"Yes, absolutely," I say and hold out my left hand. The gold catches the lighting perfectly, causing Nish and Kelly to gawk at it.

"Where the heck did he get something like that!" Nish restrains herself from yelling, but I see Max turn in the corner of my eye. He winks at me. I feel myself turn slightly pink.

"He's a special one, that's how he got it." I smile to myself. "Anyway, if you want to come, meet us at the lake on the way to my old place in about twenty minutes."

"Okay we'll see you soon then," says Kelly, squeezing me in a hug. "I'm so happy for you," she whispers in my ear, and Nish gives me a hug as well. Then they disappear into the school. I feel like they are still slightly skeptical, but oh well, I'm all right with that. I think they will understand better once they see what I mean.

"This is very sudden," says Haley. "Are you sure about this? Marriage is for life."

I nod my head and open my mouth to talk, but I'm not sure I can find the right words. "Max has always been the one for me, since we were children. I've always known," I assure her, but she looks doubtful. "We are young, I know, but my country needs a leader, and I need a husband to stand by my side. I can't do this alone."

"All right," she says, her hands on my shoulders. "As long as you are happy."

"I am," I tell her and feel a real smile creep onto my face. I am happy, the happiest I have been in months … years even.

"I'm glad," she says and looks genuine. "But if the big day is tomorrow, we should probably get you back home. You need your beauty sleep."

MAX, CLAY, AND I ARE THE FIRST ONES AT THE LAKE, AND THEN two other vehicles pull up a few minutes apart.

"So why exactly are we here?" asks Nish, slinging her purse over her shoulder. "I thought we were going to your planet."

"We are," says Max, stepping closer to me. "First you must promise never to show this to anyone."

"What's *this*?" asks Kelly.

"The portal. The less people who know about it the better. It is for everyone's safety that you do not come through it without one of us, ever."

"All right," she says, looking slightly afraid.

We climb up the rough rocks and slip through a thin crevice that is mostly concealed from the naked eye. The portal spins along the stone wall, and I am excited to be going back home. "Hold onto each other," I tell them. "This will feel weird, but make sure you don't let go."

Max takes my hand, and I take Haley's. She takes Clay's, and then Kelly and Nish link on at the end of the line. We step through.

I wish I could see their expressions. I feel so nervous when we pass by Onychinus. I don't know what it is, but something feels *wrong*. The five deceased planets cast a shadow of emptiness within the fullness of space.

Margaritan. It may seem absolutely biased, but I believe it is the most beautiful planet in our universe.

"Finally!" shouts Mira. She wears a light green breezy dress that sways when she stands from her chair. "It took you guys long enough."

"We came back as quickly as we could," I tell her, feeling somewhat annoyed. The eerie feeling Onychinus has left on me doesn't pass very quickly; it haunts me and chills me even in this heat.

"That was incredible." Kelly and Nish are so excited it rubs off on me, and some of my fears pass away a little.

"How did we not know that was there all that time?" Nish exclaims, her face red with joy.

"Guys, this is my little sister, Mira," I introduce them. I try and catch them all up as quickly as I can. Clay and Haley are absolutely thrilled with finally being able to meet Mira.

I feel so distracted. I just want to be with Max right now. They talk as a group, and Mira easily entertains them. I look up at Max and grab onto his arm. I want to leave. I think he understands the silent plea in my eyes. "Apologies, but we have some place we need to be. I'll send several maids and butlers here shortly to attend to your needs, provide proper attire, and assign you rooms," says Max. I'm so glad he's going to be my husband.

"But—" starts Mira.

"Please excuse us," I whisper. She shuts up. "I'm so glad you all were able to come. It means the world."

I hear them talking in a rather confused tone as we leave the room. Max says a few words to the two soldiers in the hallway, but I can't concentrate. I slip out of Haley's jacket and place it on one of the empty chairs. Max takes off his too, leaving it beside mine. He puts his hand on my lower back and leads me down the hallway. I don't exactly pay attention to where he's taking me until he's opening my bedroom door.

"Take a deep breath," he tells me, ushering me to sit on the edge of my bed.

I heave in gulps of air, unable to get enough. The tears fall from my eyes when I have difficulty getting enough oxygen. He runs to my bathroom and brings out a glass of cold water. My nerves have been at such a high level these past few days, and everything seems to be putting me on edge. "How are you, my love?" Max asks me with such concern I feel guilty for having outbursts like this.

I just shake my head and try to tame my breathing.

"Talk to me," he says, squatting on the ground in front of me. He sets the glass of water on the floor beside him.

"I don't know how I can do this," I sob.

"You're not having doubts about getting married, are you?" he asks, looking concerned.

"No, I have no doubts when it comes to marrying you," I tell him with my shaky voice.

"Then what is it?"

"I don't know if I can be a queen. It was never my given birthright."

"It seems as though Margaritan has always intended great things for you," says Max. He pauses. "You can do this. You pretty much saved everyone on this planet. You deserve to be a ruler."

"Thank you," I whisper.

"I will never leave you. You won't have to worry about doing any of this on your own," he says. "I love you."

I place my hands on the sides of his handsome face and gently slide my thumbs against his cheekbones. He lifts his face close to mine, and his lips brush mine. "I love you." I breathe the words through his lips.

The light in the room is already beginning to fade, but it plays tricks with the colors of my room.

"I should let you get ready for your party this evening," Max says, quietly pulling away. I don't want him to leave.

"I'm not sure why I agreed to this." I chuckle to hide my anxiety.

"Because you wanted to please the ones you love, like always, that's why," he concludes, getting to his feet. We both ended up sitting side-by-side on the floor, and I really don't want to move now. "You will be a great queen."

I smile at him as he helps me up. "You are a worthy man," I tell him, "and you have no idea how excited I am to call you my husband and my king."

His eyes light up, warming my heart. He kisses me gently on the cheek

"Have a good evening, Miss Lilyryn Garcia." He winks at me as he walks toward my door. "I'll see you at the altar."

"Thank you, my love. I'll see you tomorrow. Have a good evening."

He smiles and leaves the room.

I quickly slip into a dress and a nice pair of shoes and splash water on my face. I fix my curls as I leave the room and quickly walk down the hall toward Mira's room. Time for my bachelorette party. I wonder what the guys are doing for Max's this evening.

I'm met by a loud applause of women in her room and greeted with grins. What do they have planned?

CHAPTER 32

TODAY IS THE DAY.

Maybell comes into my room and helps me into my gown. It is tight at the top and is buttoned entirely down my back. It has no straps and poofs slightly at my hips and continues to flare out down to the floor. The bodice is beaded and elegant. My hair is pinned up, but a few ringlets fall out, framing my face, and I wear simple makeup, which mostly just brightens my eyes.

My bridesmaids are supposed to be here any moment. I can't stop pacing. I've always wanted my father to walk me down the aisle and give me away, but that won't happen. I keep wishing he'll sneak in here and have his words melt from his mouth in awe. I keep hoping that he's going to show up at the last moment. I found out last night that my father had actually given Max permission to marry me back when we were on Onychinus. My heart throbs.

"Absolutely beautiful," says Maybell, and she places the gold crown with pearls on my head. "You're going to make our country proud."

I hug her. I am speechless, and I am close to being in shock.

"Knock, knock," says a voice at the door. Mira comes into the room, and the other girls follow her. I'm surprised I was even able to convince Isla and Elle to wear the gold dresses. They are strapless and a pale gold chiffon style that falls just above the knees. Flora loved the idea.

"Hello," says Maybell. "Oh, you all look so lovely."

"Reena," gasps Elle. "You're stunning."

I feel my cheeks get warm. I know that I can do this.

"Thank you," I whisper.

Mira wraps me in a hug. "I'm so happy for you!"

I smile ... I can do this.

Another knock comes at the door. This time Maybell answers it. Two soldiers stand in the doorway, and they exchange a few words.

"All set?" she asks, coming up behind us, leaving the soldiers in the hallway. She adjusts the veil on my head, pulling it so it covers my face.

THE WALK TO THE CEREMONY FEELS LIKE AN ETERNITY. I CAN do this.

I hear the voices before I see who they are coming from. The pews are entirely filled, and I struggle to slow my breathing. I need Max. I need to just see him.

I can do this.

All these people here—they are here for me and Max.

We are steered to the back of the room ... same as on my birthday. The aisle is long. Please don't fall.

I can't see him.

My bridesmaids line up with Max's groomsmen. Ace gives me a thumbs-up, and Ruban winks at me. I feel myself blush, though I know they can't tell because my face is hidden behind my veil. I have finally earned Ruban's respect, and I am glad. It gives me a little bit of hope; maybe we can be friends now.

I hold my bouquet tightly with clammy hands. I barely notice when the music starts, but I certainly notice when the couple ahead of me become more distant down the aisle. I have to move now. My brain clicks back on when Clay's arm slides into mine.

"You look lovely," he whispers. "My brother would be proud to know how great his daughter has become."

"Thank you for doing this for me," I whisper back.

"I wouldn't miss it for the world," he says. "Shall we?"

I nod, and he guides me down the aisle. I still can't see Max. Then we pass by this one lady's tall hat, and I see him. He stands at the end waiting for me. The world seems to go in slow motion, and my heart beats just a little faster. I focus on his face, those kind eyes, that dorky grin, and his love that is reserved just for me.

Clay leads me up the steps closer to Max. He stops just before the last step and gives me a hug. Taking my cold, clammy hand in his, he puts it into Max's.

There is a sudden warmth that envelopes me when Max holds my hand. He leads me up the last step so we can stand together next to the priest. My veil isn't supposed to be lifted until just before we kiss, but Max is too impatient. His fingers caress my cheeks, and he lifts the veil away from my face. I feel my face get warmer when I notice his eyes gazing deeply into mine.

The ceremony continues on. After the traditional blessings come the vows.

"Do you, Max Nathaniel Drusus Alvarez, take Lilyryn May Marie Garcia to be your faithfully wedded wife, to care for in sickness and in health and to have and to hold until death do you part?" asks the priest.

"I do," says Max, confidently grinning at me.

"And do you, Lilyryn May Marie Garcia, take Max Nathaniel

Drusus Alvarez to be your faithfully wedded husband, to care for in sickness and in health and to have and to hold until death do you part?" he asks me.

"I do," I say, speaking with my heart.

"I now pronounce you man and wife. You may now kiss the bride," he announces.

Max engulfs me in a warm kiss, and I am distracted from the noisy applause around me. I am home.

The wedding ceremony is over within about twenty minutes. I dread the coronation, which will take longer. The piscinæ fati is only meters away, and it finishes the look of the room. I feel its power; our crowns are to be blessed within the water. Max gives my hand a gentle squeeze.

It is because of him the coronation surprisingly goes by faster than I thought it would. It is late afternoon when the crowns are placed on our heads. My gold pearl tiara is replaced with a more elegant and appropriate one. I have never had more attention given to me in one day before, even when I was announced a sorceress.

I am so grateful when we are finally finished. There are so many people my head pounds. The ones most important to me all stood with us during the wedding, and the other few sat in the first row. I'm so happy that Clay was able to walk me down the aisle. I think I would have been heartbroken if he had said no. All slowly make their way into the ballroom, the next room over.

"How are you?" Max whispers against my ear.

"A little overwhelmed," I admit.

I see understanding in his eyes. "Same here." We stand beside the piscinæ fati, and even though I wear high heels, I still stand on my tippy toes to kiss him. He pulls back slightly and says just a millimeter away from my lips, "You are the most beautiful woman I have ever seen. I am the luckiest man alive to be able to call you my wife."

"Max, to be able to call you my husband is truly the greatest honor, far, far greater than receiving the life source of this planet."

"I love you," we whisper in the same moment.

There is barely anyone else left in the room. They all have moved over to the next. He kisses me again on the cheek, and then we walk hand in hand into the other room.

I feel so much calmer now that Max is by my side and is my husband. But I still feel slightly antsy. I was right about Kelly and Nish meeting lots of guys. They flirt excitedly and seem quite happy with their surroundings. Mira dances with Miles on the dance floor; they were paired up for the march down the aisle. Pretty much all the pairs of our bridesmaids and groomsman dance together, even Clay and Haley.

"My dear wife, may I have this dance?" asks Max, holding his hand out for me. I take it.

He takes me to the center of the dance floor. He places his hand on my side, and he holds my other hand and glides me around the dance floor to the gentle music. I feel like there is no one else in the room with how comfortable I feel with him. I smile, allowing myself to be overwhelmed with happiness.

"On a scale of one to ten, how would you rate today?" whispers Max, bowing me into a dip.

"Scale would be broken," I whisper back, watching happiness fill his eyes.

"Really?" he asks.

"Absolutely."

"I'm glad." His smile reaches his eyes.

"Oh, I forgot—I have a wedding present for you." He spins me around, and my dress sways around both of our legs.

"There is nothing that I want," he says. "I have everything I need."

"So I take it you don't want your old blades back?" I ask him.

"What?" he exclaims. "You found them?"

"Yes, they were in my father's office. If you want, we can go and get them," I say as the song comes to a stop. "Maybe get away from staring people?" I whisper.

"I really like that idea."

We leave the ballroom, and even though it is quite crowded, we are still noticed by some guests, trying to escape.

The hallway isn't dark at all, and I am glad. Soldiers line both sides of the walls, and I am glad they're here.

"So I found them just behind that book—" I open the door and start to say, but that's when I see the slim dark figure.

He sits in my father's big desk. His feet are up on the desk, and he picks at his cuticles with the tip of a very familiar gold-handled blade. My heart stops beating, and I freeze. Max does the same. "You weren't kidding when you said you were going to marry her, no matter what I said?" says a voice like Max's.

"We thought you were dead," I say in shock.

"I will never die," says the commander. There are no indications that we killed him before. So this is what Theo was so confused about before he died. He was trying to warn us! The commander wears a grin as he looks us over. Every ounce of happiness I had drains, and fear tingles in my every cell. I grasp Max's hand tightly.

ACKNOWLEDGEMENTS

I'd like to thank God for giving me the courage and creativity to follow my dreams.

My grade one teacher; Florrie Reid for teaching me how to read novels and being the inspiration behind my love for literature.

My loving mother, who usually hates reading but read 'The Golden Pearl' several times, giving me wonderful advice, supporting and believing in me all the way through this journey.

Giselle Pereira, with her huge heart and great passion who helped improve my characters.

My siblings Savannah, Darwin and Mikaylee who listened to my rambles of ideas for hours and hours and gave their own ideas.

Bill Lazenby, who is brilliant with punctuation and grammar, who spent endless hours going through every sentence multiple times, making every page better.

Rylan Burak, my high school pal, who read 'The Golden Pearl' in its early stages and gave me some input to help improve a few of the scenes.

Christine Kent, one of my high school English teachers, for her strong advice in making my novel better and reading it even when it was simply one of the earlier drafts.

Special thanks to my editing team at Archway Publishing who used their incredible skills, to make my novel the best it could possibly be. Also to my consultant Kayla, who helped me make all of this possible.

Printed in the United States
By Bookmasters